Readers love the Changing Moon
series SUI LYNN

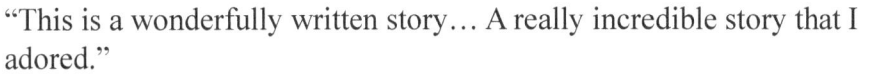

The Pauper Prince

"This is a wonderfully written story… A really incredible story that I adored."

—MM Good Book Reviews

"A mesmerizing, expertly crafted tale of love, redemption, and mystery unfolds. *The Pauper Prince* takes readers on an incredible journey"

—Joyfully Reviewed

A Royal Bind

"…the author has created a world with such interesting main characters… and fantastic secondary characters…"

—Gay List Book Reviews

By SUI LYNN

Blue Rose

CHANGING MOON
The Pauper Prince
A Royal Bind
Blood Ties

ELEMENTS OF LOVE
Adel's Purr
Nico's Fire
Elements of Love - Books 1 & 2 (Print Only)

Published by DREAMSPINNER PRESS
www.dreamspinnerpress.com

ELEMENTS OF LOVE
BOOKS 1 & 2

SUI LYNN

Published by
DREAMSPINNER PRESS

5032 Capital Circle SW, Suite 2, PMB# 279, Tallahassee, FL 32305-7886 USA
www.dreamspinnerpress.com

Elements of Love - Books 1 & 2
© 2015 Sui Lynn.

Cover Art
© 2015 L.C. Chase.
http://www.lcchase.com
Cover content is for illustrative purposes only and any person depicted on the cover is a model.

ISBN: 978-1-63476-700-2
Library of Congress Control Number: 2015950139
Second Edition November 2015
First Edition of Adel's Purr published by Silver Publishing, 2011.
First Edition of Nico's Fire published by Silver Publishing, May 2012.

Printed in the United States of America
∞
This paper meets the requirements of
ANSI/NISO Z39.48-1992 (Permanence of Paper).

ADEL'S PURR

To all of you who can look at a rock and
have the imagination to see it breathe…
To all of you who can see that breathing rock and
imagine it has emotions…
To all of you who want a rock of your own…
Thank you!

Chapter 1

GARGOYLE LORE

As written by the scribes and entombed in the Church Archives:

Gargoyles

Physical Attributes:

1. Carved from a single piece of natural stone. Cannot be made of stone composite, or molded. Their original form is carved.
2. Their spirit is called to life by an Earth Elemental they call their Maker.
3. They become living stone: stone by day and living, breathing flesh and blood by night.

May 14, 2215—Just before sunset

THE MODERN-DAY equivalent of a hermit, Evan Halvard lived by himself on a couple of acres of forested land in the mountains, far enough away from civilization that people couldn't bother him. He liked to tell his friends he lived close enough to town to do business easily, yet far enough up in the mountains that people had to be determined in order to find him. The arrangement served him well, keeping most of the unwanted interruptions away and giving him a modicum of privacy.

Spring felt cool this year, but as Evan stood in his garden, tilling the soil, nature spoke to him of green and growing things. Winter's last bite of the season had come and gone. The tender seeds he planted would flourish. Most people would find the soil cold and painful, but Evan loved the feeling of the earth beneath his feet and between his toes. He'd often told his father if he stood barefoot in the soil, the ground would speak to him, but no matter how many times Evan's father had humored him, Evan seemed to be the only one who heard the earth whispering.

He stood and rested an arm on his hoe, smiling to himself as he reached into his back pocket and pulled out a large leather hair tie. He pulled back his unruly dark brown dreadlocks and tied them out of the way at the back of his neck. He pulled off his T-shirt and wiped it across his face and chest, absorbing the sheen of sweat forming on his light mocha skin. Evan worked as a stonemason and was accustomed to physical labor: repairing walls, laying brick, and pretty much anything that dealt with rock. Standing in the last rays of the setting sun—bent over a hoe, prepping the soil for seeds—didn't count as work but was a labor of love.

Evan thought of how his father, Peter Stein, would've scolded him for doing what Peter would have considered women's work. To his father, men were hunters and women were supposed to tend to the plants. But Evan couldn't help his love of nature. He loved caring for green things almost as much as he loved his stonework. Spring, his favorite time of year, spoke of awakenings, beginnings, and plantings. It was the personification of life. Since he had no intention of ever marrying a woman—he'd discovered long ago he was not attracted to females—he had to do his own planting to supplement his meals. He preferred to be as self-sufficient as possible.

Besides, women were few and far between, and fertile females were even less available, as they were monopolized by the Church's breeding program. Children were raised by their fathers, or in fosterling homes if the father was incapable of caring for his offspring. The condition in these homes meant little to the Church as long as the population increased. Men whose seed was genetically predisposed toward female children were paid well for their sperm donations, as the female population of the Earth was very small. Only one child in every four children born was female. The hardest part was that one out of every four females born was infertile, and others often had a hard time carrying their pregnancies to full term. It was an ever-declining cycle that the Church was attempting to fight at every turn to prevent humanity's extinction.

Some believed the human race was in the autumn of its existence. It had had a great and glorious run and now fought a losing battle to hold on to its continuance, like a tree in fall trying to hold on to its leaves against the ever-persistent draw of gravity. A battle the tree couldn't win. Those people believed humanity would pass into the annals of the extinct, like the dinosaur, and just as inevitably.

Evan didn't believe that. Mankind might be in the midst of a population decline and trying to resurrect itself from a destruction the likes of which nature could not have created, but Evan hoped it was not the end. Maybe this season of mankind wasn't fall, but winter, and soon it would be the spring and a new beginning. He certainly hoped so.

If the death of millions of people in the great war—two-thirds of the world's population—couldn't be considered the autumn of mankind and the horrible years after the beginning of winter, Evan didn't know what could. In most of the places around the world, they were still rediscovering old technologies and relearning how to use them, all under the careful supervision of the Church, which determined what technologies were safe to relearn and which had led to the evil downfall. All part of the perpetual winter of mankind—a winter Evan wanted to see come to an end.

He loved spring. The green things around him were connections to the earth, and they gave him a sense of peace and security he felt from nothing else. The earth's awakening, as the frost of winter receded and things came back from that deathlike sleep, gave new life to Evan as well.

Evan watched the sun drop below the pine-covered horizon of his home in the Black Hills of South Dakota. The last rays of direct sunlight disappeared into dusk, signaling the beginning of night and the time when his closest friend awoke.

He felt the familiar tingle at his throat and reached up to stroke the stone necklace, caressing warm scales instead of rock. A tiny, rumbling purr began against his collarbone. "Evening, Cela." Evan felt the little dragon unwrap himself from around his neck, stretch, and coo merrily.

As Evan stretched work-stiffened muscles, his awareness of the tiny points of consciousness that belonged to the minds of his other awakening friends grew. They were gargoyles, similar in some ways to Cela. He could feel their approach as they made their way from various daytime perches to venture into the night.

He always knew when he was in the presence of gargoyles, even during the daytime. He could easily distinguish between living stone and statues. He'd been fifteen and an apprentice to his father the first time it happened: he'd discovered Cela. Well, he hadn't really *discovered* Cela; he had awoken the dragon. He'd unknowingly called to the gargoyle's sleeping soul, bequeathed to the statue by the artist who'd sculpted the dragon with loving care. And so Evan had given the statue life, awakening the gargoyle as living stone.

Ten years earlier at a cemetery jobsite

"Hey, Dad, what's that?" Evan asked.

"What's what?" Peter asked, looking at his son, then following his gaze. "Oh, you mean the dragon statue. That's a gargoyle, a guardian, and a pretty small one at that. They used to adorn many structures. Our ancestors believed they'd guard our souls from the evil in the night. You don't see them much anymore. The hunters from the Abbey, under orders from the Bishop's Service and their deputies, have smashed most of them. I guess it's so small they must've overlooked that one." Peter looked at the little gargoyle.

"What a beautiful dragon."

"Yeah, and dangerous, just like their mythical counterparts. Just having statues that look like gargoyles on our property could bring the Inquisition to our door. They believe gargoyles depict mankind's violent nature and are proof of his inherent evil. They believe they represent evil or, in the worst cases, are personifications of the Devil."

"But, Dad, how can anything so beautiful be evil?" Evan asked.

"Sorry, son, I never did understand their logic. I just know not to question the Church. Few survive the Inquisition, and those who do are never the same. Come on. Let's get to work."

Peter and Evan went back to working on the crumbling stonework walls, repairing the damage done by time and nature.

"Dad?"

"What?"

"What are gargoyles like?"

Peter smiled at his son. Evan had always been inquisitive, and a little thing like the Church disliking something was incentive for him to ask questions. "Well, let me see. My father used to tell tales of gargoyles from before the war. Before modernization, gargoyles were the nighttime protectors of the people. They kept people safe from evil."

"Really? Were they super strong and super fast?" Evan asked.

Peter chuckled. "Not that I remember him ever saying. They could fly, though. They could sleep for years in hibernation and then, when called at night, would awaken and protect the people."

"Are they born?"

"No. Gargoyles are carved by artisans, like all statues. But there are special people in the world who have extraordinary powers. They are known as Elementals. Only a specific type of person can call the spirit to life and change a carved statue into living stone. Only a specific Elemental, an Earth Elemental, can make a statue into a gargoyle."

"That's so cool! Do you know any Elementals?"

"Maybe…. Hand me the mortar." Peter held out his left hand so Evan could pass him the bucket. "Get the supports ready."

"Okay. Can they be killed?"

"Can who be killed?" Peter asked, studying the rock wall before him as he plastered cracks in the mortar.

Evan shored up the broken wall, getting it ready for repair. "Gargoyles."

"They are immortal, but they can be killed. If the stone form is broken, then they can never awaken again. That's how the Church eliminated most of them: destroying them while they were vulnerable and unable to defend themselves. They can also be killed when they are flesh and blood, at night." Peter moved to where Evan had finished bracing the wall and had begun adding new rocks, placing them and then mortaring them into position. "Good… good. Keep at it. I'm going around to work on the other side."

"So they don't run around as hard rock, but they move at night?"

"Not from what your grandfather said. They turn to regular flesh and blood at night. They hunt and eat, just like any other beast, although he did say some of the older ones could talk. But I've never seen any larger than the little dragon you found earlier." Peter stood and stretched. As father and son completed their work, the sun set over the horizon, leaving everything bathed in the half-shadow world of twilight. "Come on, Evan. Let's get home before it gets too dark." Peter patted Evan on the shoulder and grinned. "Your mom will have dinner ready and waiting for us."

"Okay, sounds good," Evan replied, a little distracted. "Dad, can I go check out the dragon statue? It'd be a real shame if something so small and fragile got damaged." Evan frowned, thinking in horror of someone intentionally smashing the little statue.

"Sure, go on. No one's around, and I don't think anyone here'll report you for being interested in a gargoyle. Just keep the thing to yourself. I don't want to know what you do with it. I'm going to the truck. I know nothing." Peter smiled warmly.

"Thanks, Dad." Evan took off at a run to find the little gargoyle statue before his father changed his mind. He found the mausoleum easily; there was only the one crypt in the small cemetery. He looked up to where the gargoyle should've been perched, but the spot was now empty. No dragon roosted over the door.

"I could've sworn—" Evan mumbled to himself, looking around to see if he'd somehow gotten the location wrong. No, the gargoyle had to be here. Evan walked around the perimeter of the structure, looking for the little statue.

What could've happened to it? He and his dad were the only ones in the cemetery.

Then he caught sight of a reddish glimmer high up in a nearby tree. Evan frowned and looked a bit closer. The glimmer blinked and the red glow flashed. "It's okay, I won't hurt you. You can't stay here. You're not safe." Evan spoke softly, trying to coax the little creature from the tree. "Come on, little one. Dad's waiting for us." He extended his hands to the small gargoyle. "My name's Evan Halvard. Dad says my name means 'rock defender' in the old language. I won't hurt you." Evan crooned and babbled, remembering being told animals didn't understand what you said, but your tone of voice could either soothe or incite them. He had no idea if the same applied to creatures of living stone.

Evan heard a couple of cheeps and whistles, which sounded vaguely birdlike, and the little gargoyle appeared, hanging on the central bark of the tree. "There you are! Aren't you cute? Come down. We have to go home. You can't stay here. There's no one to protect you."

He watched patiently as the small gargoyle crept slowly closer. It had four legs, tiny wings, a little spade tail, and sharp-looking little teeth and claws. *How cute!* It had shiny red scales that glinted in the light of the moon, not at all like its dirty-brown appearance when Evan had first seen it perched on the mausoleum. Now its eyes glowed bright red, like rubies on fire.

"Please, we don't have a lot of time, little friend," Evan said urgently, trying to coax the dragon. Hesitantly at first, the creature crept down the tree toward him. Evan wrapped his arm with his jacket, fearful of the damage those sharp talons could do, and offered it as a perch. "Here you go."

The small creature jumped from the tree and landed on Evan's arm with ease. It chirped and whistled, tipping its head to look at Evan with its fire-filled eyes. Evan scratched under its chin and above its eye ridges. The dragon purred. It ran the length of Evan's arm and ducked under his long brown dreadlocks, curling his tail around Evan's neck. In his peripheral vision, Evan nervously eyed the gargoyle's talons. One misplaced talon could slice open his throat like butter. Yet the small beast moved with care and placed its claws gently, seeming to realize the harm they could inflict. It clung to Evan's T-shirt, blanketed by his hair, apparently content to curl against Evan's warm skin.

"Well, I guess that's as good a place as any." Evan petted the dragon while he headed for the truck and his father.

"Did you find it?" asked his father, staring directly at the little dragon curled around his son's neck.

"Nope, no statues."

Peter laughed. "By the way, cool necklace."

"Thanks. I think so too."

The little dragon didn't move or make a peep as he peered from beneath Evan's hair.

"Just don't let your mother see it."

Present day

EVAN LISTENED to Cela, his little dragon gargoyle, croon and sing into the night as the others came running to gather about his feet. Evan found harmony and a gentle peace in the nature surrounding him. These were his friends, the ones he had been waiting to awaken throughout the day. The ones who gave his life meaning. The ones he risked his life for in an effort to keep their species from being exterminated. When they joined him, his loneliness faded, and until the rising sun, he would not be alone.

The path of Evan's life had been decided that day, ten years ago, with the rescue of his closest friend. And Cela had remained with him every day since. His life, set in stone like the rocks he worked with, had turned against the authorities and a belief system he couldn't support. He would be a criminal in the eyes of the Church if they knew about him. Evan Halvard had become a rescuer of living stone, or as his father had explained in one of his many lessons, gargoyles.

Before his death, Peter—who had adopted Evan as his own son when he'd been orphaned by the death of his biological father, Dustin—encouraged Evan to follow his heart. He and Dustin were half brothers, born of the same mother, Patience, in the Church's breeding program. Even though they had different fathers, they had grown up together in a fosterling home. They were very close and had similar beliefs and eventually were recruited into the same resistance movement. When Dustin was killed, Peter had chosen to raise Evan as he hoped his brother would've wanted, educating him but allowing him to make his own choices. Yet Peter resolutely refused to assist Evan in anything remotely like what he and Dustin had been involved in, saying the Church had cured him of his rebellious tendencies long ago when the movement was quashed.

The brands on Peter's arms attested to his punishment at the hands of the Inquisition—punishment that had resulted in Dustin's death when his wounds had become septic while serving his sentence in the reform camps. The brands appeared as two crosses on Peter's forearms, seared far into the flesh, almost to the bone. The muscles had healed around the burns, leaving him with much less strength in his arms than he'd had in his youth. Yet he'd survived and excelled at his work.

Upon his death, he'd bequeathed Evan a lodge in a remote part of the forest, away from prying eyes. It had become a sanctuary for Evan and his gargoyles.

Evan remembered the first time he'd entered the cabin, the day he'd buried his father. He had been struck by the state of it. His father obviously hadn't been there for many years, as nothing had disturbed the thick layer of dust that covered everything like a shroud. On the kitchen table sat a cracked, leather-bound book: a diary. Evan ran a hand over the cover, revealing an embossed name: Elizabeth Peterson. She was Patience's mother, and therefore both of his fathers' grandmother. Peter must've meant for him to have it.

Cela had taken great joy in showing Evan what his father had begun for him. Evan had found the trapdoor in no time, hidden in the kitchen under a dirty but colorful maze-print rug. The door opened to a dark staircase. After grabbing a flashlight, Evan had proceeded down the stairs into a labyrinth of tunnels. Cela had led Evan through a confusion of turns, guiding him to one of the many exits emerging from a combination of both mine shafts and natural caves beneath the cabin. Evan had retraced his steps back to the area under the small house. As he looked around, he found a large side cave with a couple of secondary caves attached and had decided this would be a great place to live. The major gift of living in the caves would be privacy, a commodity nobody took for granted when the Vatican's Bishop's Service could search your home for any reason—and frequently did. The cabin above would be a stage, always appropriately set for potential Bishop's Service visits. Down here, with some modifications, he could relax and have his real home with his gargoyles—a truly private place of his own, safe from the Church's investigations.

And soon, he'd begun filling those caves with family. Four winged, dragon-style gargoyles—one midnight blue, one forest green, one ruby red, and the last golden brown—soon joined Evan. Their clear jewel-tone eyes matched the shine of their scales, while the golden-brown dragon had solid golden eyes. The musketeers, as he called them, were each a bit larger than Cela, making them closer to the size of full-grown house cats. If allowed, this quartet would croon into the night, singing to the stars. They were never far from one another and seemed to carry an "all for one and one for all" attitude. So Evan named them d'Artagnan, Porthos, Athos, and Aramis after his favorite childhood story, *The Three Musketeers*. His father had recited the story verbatim each time Evan had asked it of him.

Evan squatted down, leaning heavily on his hoe as his musketeers appeared out of the night, flying low over the ground in a lazy fashion. The quartet was followed by a larger pair of Chinese lion-dog gargoyles Evan had rescued from a temple in New York City and named Yin and Yang. Regardless of the season, his friends always greeted him with enthusiasm when they awoke. It had become a ritual he thoroughly enjoyed.

"Hello, my friends. Be careful. It's a new moon and a dark night." Evan reached out to give each of the musketeers a scratch from their ears down their necks and to stroke between their wings. Then he treated the lion-dogs to a similar attention, ruffling their ears and massaging over their shoulders, ending in a rub on the top of their protruding muzzles, the spot they seemed to enjoy having petted the most. Yin and Yang's appreciation could be felt as well as heard, their purr-like growls rumbling deep in their chests, reverberating through their bodies.

Evan stood and watched as each of the dragons ran in a different direction, while the lion-dogs trotted straight down the driveway of the cabin to stand guard at the entrance. He watched until his friends disappeared into the darkness of the night. He trusted they would be careful. They were gargoyles, guardians and eaters of evil. They would not be happy as his pets. As his father had explained long ago, gargoyles were created to protect the living through the night, to keep evil at bay, to keep it from accosting souls. So his friends guarded him and their sanctuary.

Evan sighed with contentment and went into the cabin to find dinner and prepare for his trip the next day. He'd received a request to check out an old mausoleum in a dilapidated cemetery. Some long-forgotten documents made mention of a gargoyle being placed in the tomb of a cardinal who'd dedicated his life to helping troubled teens. Often these documents were wrong, the stonework long destroyed or moved to a new location, but he'd gladly check it out on the off chance they proved correct.

EVAN PULLED his battered pickup truck in to the cemetery at sunrise and reached for his work orders. He'd fabricated them to appear as if he'd been contracted to do some repairs on the O'Brian family tomb. That way, he'd have a valid reason to be on the grounds.

He looked up in time to notice the black Lincoln Town Car with the red-and-blue light bar mounted on top and the insignia of the Bishop's Service emblazoned on the side. It was parked next to a run-down mausoleum. The name over the door had long since deteriorated. Father Michael, the diocesan head of security at the Bishop's Service, and his deputies were pulling out a large stone statue, trying to work together to get it out of the dilapidated gothic stone structure. They had bound and covered the statue with a black plastic tarp.

Evan cringed as the statue's head missed the top of the seven-foot door by mere inches. This piece stood much taller than the ones Father Michael usually went after, well over six feet. From what Evan could see of the exposed stone at the base, the sculpture, done in a pristine white marble, appeared flawless. Pure-white marble was rare, especially in large quantities, and he could find many uses for it in his line of work, but this was no ordinary stone. The very ground around him whispered, telling him this was a gargoyle, not marble statuary. He assumed Father Michael would have his deputies destroy it as an abomination in the eyes of the Church. A gargoyle this large and ancient—a wonder worth sacrificing everything to protect—made him shiver despite the sunlight. *I don't have a choice*, he thought, self-consciously stroking the sleeping Cela on his neck. He had to rescue this marvelous creature.

"Father Michael, how nice to see you. How are you doing these days?" Evan plastered a wide, friendly grin on his face and swallowed the bile that threatened to choke him. He willed himself not to be sick as the older man turned upon hearing his name.

Shrewd black eyes examined Evan carefully as if searching him for an underlying reason for being in the cemetery before leisurely stripping the clothing from his body in his own mind. Father Michael *wanted* him, and Evan knew it, regardless of the fact that the priest always played at being a pure man of the cloth. His barely concealed and hardly controlled lust repelled Evan. And worse, Father Michael's role in the Bishop's Service meant he was a constant threat to Evan and his friends. Besides his downright hideous appearance, Father Michael gave off a vile, evil vibe that made Evan feel soiled just by being in the man's presence.

"Well, if it isn't Evan Halvard! Why are you here, boy?" Father Michael stood six foot four inches tall and skeletally thin. His too-large black robes hung loosely on his body, emphasizing his emaciated appearance. He wore a silver cross, which appeared more daggerlike than religious icon, on a heavy silver chain around his neck. What little hair he had wisped about him, thin and white, showing the scalp beneath. If this were anyone other than Father Michael, Evan would've thought him near death. What creeped him out the most were Father Michael's eyes—always staring, as if he were trying to see into Evan's soul. It made his skin crawl. He watched Father Michael lick his lips with just the tip of his tongue, as if he were seducing Evan. He always felt surprised when he saw Father Michael's tongue wasn't forked.

"I've a commission in this cemetery. The O'Brian family has asked me to repair their family monument. The stone wall is crumbling, and I've agreed to do the work for them in exchange for some scrap slate they had lying around after a kitchen remodel." He smiled widely because every word was a lie, but if he was asked to produce a work order, he had phony papers in his glove box. Father Michael rarely went that far in his interrogations. Usually with a bit of a smile or the sway of his hips, Evan would have Father Michael panting after him like a wanton. If he were more substantial, instead of a walking skeleton, Evan would fear the day Father Michael made a move on him physically. As it stood, he'd have to have help before he'd be able to force Evan to do much of anything. It was the unrequited lust in his eyes that made Evan nervous. A desperate man was a dangerous man.

"I see. Well, then, you had better get busy."

"You aren't looking very well, Father. Are you ill? You need to eat more." Evan's voice dripped with concern.

"I'm fine," Father Michael snapped. "My constitution is very strong, and God looks out for his faithful." As he spoke, a snide smile curved the corners of his mouth. He took a step closer, reaching out toward Evan with his right hand before he snatched it back and folded his hands firmly in front of him.

"Please, come out to the cabin sometime. I'll make you a stew from wild venison and the spring potatoes from my garden. It's sure to put some meat on those bones. You know we can't have a prominent member of the clergy and an officer of the Bishop's Service fall ill." Evan spoke with innocence and false concern, frowning slightly as if Father Michael's health truly troubled him.

"We shall see. I haven't been to your cabin in some time. Maybe a visit is in order, but I couldn't accept such hospitality. A conflict of interest, regardless of how fond I am of you."

"Fine. Of course, Father. I wouldn't want anyone questioning your integrity because of me. Will you have any spare marble from the statuary?" Evan inquired carefully. "What I can see of the stone looks like pure-white marble. Once ground, it would make a marvelous composite countertop, or floor, even. I wouldn't have to treat the stone before being able to use it."

"No, this isn't marble, Evan. The Church has no use for regular stone. You understand, don't you, Evan?" Father Michael came over and rested a hand on his shoulder, as if Evan were a young child needing guidance. Father Michael's gaze drilled into Evan and made him feel even more uncomfortable. Then he put his arm around Evan's waist, drawing him just that much closer. He grazed his hand across Evan's buttocks before he pressed his palm into the small of Evan's back, guiding him away from the statue. Evan struggled to keep from cringing away from Father Michael's touch, and put a shocked and slightly horrified look on his face.

"Oh!" Evan exclaimed and crossed himself as if to ward off an evil.

Father Michael smiled and patted Evan's shoulder, ruffling his hair as he would a small child.

Evan blinked innocently and glanced back at the covered statue, shuddering, watching carefully to make sure Father Michael got the whole show. "Will you be removing and destroying it today?" Evan crossed his fingers and schooled his expression to keep the hope in his heart from betraying him.

He thought of a prayer his dad had taught him early on in his training. *Father of the Heaven and the Earth, awaken this Guardian. Awaken his spirit of love and protection. Fill him with your love so he can fulfill his duty and honor your will. Guardian, awaken!* Evan chanted in his thoughts, directing his feelings of love and protection toward the gargoyle, praying the call would awaken him even if the words weren't spoken aloud. Evan couldn't work openly against Father Michael without forfeiting his life. He brought himself back to the conversation, trying to refocus.

"...too large to dispose of here, and we don't have a way to transport something this size today. The truck from the abbey will be arriving in the morning to take it for proper disposal. You've nothing to fear. I've placed holy wards around the area, and we've tied the creature down. When I leave this evening, the monks will stand guard to protect us from this vile monster," Father Michael said confidently.

"Okay, you know best, but be careful, Father. I'd be very sad if anything happened to you." Evan frowned, and then, with a gentle sway of his hips, he stepped away from the priest, heading in the direction of the mausoleum. "I need to get to work. I want to leave this area as soon as possible and be out of your way."

"Good boy. Go with God, Evan." Father Michael looked reluctant to let Evan leave. He heard him take couple of steps as if to follow Evan, before his shuffling gait stopped.

Evan continued to move away, fully aware that he'd be carefully watched until he left the area. It was a sick relationship, but one with its advantages as his stalker could be manipulated to a certain degree. The pitfalls being Father Michael was always watching him.

His plan was simple: the musketeers would distract the monks while he and Cela rescued the gargoyle and brought it to the cabin. Of course, it was simple in thought only. The execution would take a lot more work. He'd been preparing for a job like this for some time. He sneaked a surreptitious peek over his left shoulder. The statue remained still and unmoving.

Evan worked happily on the mausoleum; the physical labor allowed him time to figure out his plan, while surveying the area the gargoyle was being kept in. He felt certain that in a few hours he'd be able to prove his name and make his father proud.

Chapter 2

GARGOYLE LORE

As written by the scribes and entombed in the Church Archives:

4. They are protectors. Guardians. Intensely loyal and devoted to their human charges.

HAVING RENTED a room nearby, Evan sat in the hotel parking lot in the large semitruck he used when working commissions. The trailer contained a small mobile workshop and plenty of space to haul wood, cement slabs, or any other rock he needed. It also served as an excellent way to move whatever living stone gargoyles he rescued among his supplies without raising suspicions.

His mind was running amok with nervous energy as he went over his plan again. He needed everything to go off flawlessly, but his little band of gargoyle warriors had never before attempted a rescue where the gargoyle was quite this large. He'd picked up the musketeers, and they slept in stone hibernation on the floor of the cab, a tarp covering them. He desperately needed to calm down, so he sat in the dimming light of the afternoon sun. He listened to music on his iPod with his eyes closed, trying to envision their successful rescue and maybe catch a nap.

A rap on his window brought him around. Father Michael stood outside the cab, appearing rather unhappy, as always.

Evan grinned in welcome but trembled nervously inside. His gargoyle friends were much too close to Father Michael for comfort. One wrong move and Father Michael would search his truck and find his friends. In preparation for the rescue, he'd even unwound Cela from around his neck and put him under the tarp with the musketeers.

He opened the door and climbed out of the cab, leaving the door open, feigning innocence and a forthrightness he was far from feeling. He'd become good at lies but worried about the day he'd be caught in them. With his friends barely hidden from sight, he feared today would be that day. "Father! Twice in one day! What a nice surprise. How can I help you?" Evan put every ounce of virtue into his golden brown eyes, for he knew they attracted Father Michael like a moth to a flame. He needed Father Michael to focus on him and not the truck.

"What are you doing here, Evan? I thought you were returning home," Father Michael inquired sternly.

"Oh, I did. I needed to get the big truck. I'm heading to La Cruz in the morning. They're dismantling an estate, and I purchased two stone fireplaces, including the marble mantel, which I need to pick up. The truck I drove earlier couldn't carry the load I'm expecting." Evan put his hands on his hips and tipped his head to one side. "I decided to stay here at the hotel for the night. You know, halfway between here and there. Then I'll be able to be home by tomorrow evening." Evan had learned if he gave Father Michael a long-winded story up front and went on a bit, Father Michael would get bored with his animated babbling and not question him further.

"I see." Father Michael's tone already belied boredom with Evan's story. "Then why didn't you bring this truck this morning and save yourself the trip back?"

"Well, I didn't actually win the bid on the stone till this afternoon. I don't like driving this truck because it's much harder on gas, so I drove the other one in case I didn't win." Evan batted his eyes and grabbed one of his dreadlocks, twisting it while feigning deep thought.

"Ah, well, you need to be careful, my boy. An innocent young man such as yourself is easily taken advantage of by the unscrupulous." Father Michael reached forward and set a hand on Evan's neck. "By the way, this is the first time I've ever seen you without your… necklace. Where is it?"

"There is no air-conditioning in this old truck, and I got hot in the stuffy cab. I took it off. Here, just a second." Evan climbed back into the truck. Wrapped around the gearshift was a replica of Cela he'd made long ago. He watched nervously as Father Michael took the necklace, gazing skeptically at the inert stone and leather. "Dad crafted that necklace ages ago. I'm nowhere near as skilled an artist as he was."

"Is this really the same necklace?" Father Michael's voice dripped with suspicion as he rolled the pieces about in his hand.

"None other. Dad gave it to me when I completed my training as a stonemason. My mom always said it was my dad's best work." Evan took the necklace from Father Michael and secured the clasp behind his neck. The leather and stones fell easily into place, becoming a perfect reproduction of the dragon that usually lay around Evan's neck.

"What curious craftsmanship," Father Michael said, a touch of awe in his voice as he reached out with his long bony fingers and stroked the necklace, as well as the skin of Evan's throat.

Evan struggled to contain his revulsion, and to keep from pulling away from Father Michael's caress. "My dad was a true artisan with stone. He could make such wonderful things. I'm afraid I've never had his skill." Evan sighed greatly, staring at the ground. "I miss him." He didn't have to fake or hide his longing. He truly missed his dad.

"I'm sure you do, my son, but your father is with the ancestors in Heaven, his soul absolved of his youthful rebellion. Fear not. He watches over you from God's side. I'm sure he's proud of the good man you're becoming." Father Michael's teeth shone in a predatory smile, doing nothing to reassure or console Evan.

"Thank you, Father. I'm sure you're right. Well, I'm going to listen to my music a little longer, then go into my room. I debated whether I should stay or continue driving through the night, but I don't care for travel after dark. So many vile things in the night, you know. Besides, Mom would be upset. She's always worrying."

Father Michael ate up his innocent act as if his soul hungered to corrupt and devour him. "Please be careful driving. I'd ask that you wait till dawn, but I know you are too stubborn to listen to my opinion. If you are here, make sure you are in your room before the sun goes down. It isn't safe to be out after dark these days, with the devil beast we found in the cemetery, and there might be more. We haven't checked the entire cemetery yet," Father Michael purred, still stroking Evan's throat.

Evan leaned into his touch slightly before flashing him a winning smile and turning to the cab of the truck, barely controlling his disgust. "I will, Father. Good night." He climbed back into his truck and closed the door. He smiled and put his earphones back on, resting his head against the headrest.

Watching Father Michael through the slits in his barely open eyes, he saw him eye the empty bed of the truck suspiciously as he walked back to his waiting car. Evan watched him drive off with a grateful sigh and a prayer of thanks to the powers for watching over him, and for protecting both him and the gargoyles from the vile man.

NIGHT HAD fallen. Evan stretched in the cab of the truck. He'd driven to the edge of the cemetery and turned off the engine, keeping to the shadows. "Okay, my friends, we have a new brother or sister to rescue." The musketeers sat on the back gate of the truck, looking intently at Evan. "Aramis, d'Artagnan, find the cameras and cut their circuits, then help distract the monks. Athos, Porthos, I need you to get the monks to chase you and draw them away from us, without leading them toward the cabin. All you need to do is keep them busy while Cela and I do the rest. I'll blow the whistle when we're finished. Then you lose the monks and come home."

An ultrasonic dog whistle hung from a cord around Evan's neck. The musketeers would hear when he blew it, even if they were a mile or more away. They'd know their task was complete and withdraw to safety. Evan stroked each of the little dragons affectionately. They rubbed against his hands and purred, licking at his fingers. Then Evan watched as they took to the air, their dark forms vanishing into the night. He marveled at the strength and craftiness of his musketeers. They were mischievous, but at times like this, their cunning came in handy.

"Hey, did you see that?" the guard on the left whispered as he stared out into the shroud of darkness beyond their camp in the cemetery. The large overhead lights kept the encroaching night at bay, but made it even harder for them to see into the distance.

"What are they?" asked another as he raised a baseball bat to his shoulder.

"They're gargoyles! Get them!" screamed their leader as he led the charge into the night.

Yells of alarm from the monks let Evan know his musketeers were hard at work. With Cela curled around his neck, Evan took off at a sprint for the chained gargoyle.

It began to struggle, pulling against the bindings that kept it captive.

"Easy, brother, we're here to free you. Please don't fight me. I need to work these bindings free." He rested a hand on the black plastic tarp, crooning softly so only the gargoyle could hear, trying to soothe it, hoping to ease some of the fear and distrust the creature must be feeling from having awoken to find itself bound.

Evan carefully looked over the chains, which had been attached to stakes and pounded into the ground. "Cela, bite here," Evan directed the little dragon, whose armored teeth broke the metal chains with ease. With a last snap of Cela's teeth against the final chain, the captive gargoyle roared, sending the tarp and chains flying to the ground.

Evan stood motionless, stunned by the sight of the most awe inspiring creature he'd ever seen. The guardian was nude and most definitely male, with sharp, defined angular features. His eyes were wide and sapphire blue, with long lashes. He had high cheekbones and a straight, Roman nose. If Evan hadn't seen the white marble legs and freed him from the bindings, he would've sworn the gargoyle could only be something far more angelic.

His skin looked porcelain white and silky smooth, with darker blue, tigerlike stripes decorating his back and flowing down along his arms and legs. There was a decidedly feline cast to his large almond-shaped eyes. His pupils were ever-so-slightly elliptical. A cascade of long blue-black hair flowed down between his large, white, outstretched, bat-like wings. His muscular shoulders and chest were broad and deep, with defined abdominal muscles narrowing to his hips. His arms and legs were long, and his hands were large, with deadly-looking talons that seemed to clench spasmodically, retracting and extending like a cat's protractile claws. Muscular legs extended to feet with the same retractable claws, flexing, slipping from their sheaths into the earth as he displayed his agitation.

The gargoyle eyed Evan suspiciously, giving a deep, continuous warning growl that kept Evan in his place. He crouched defensively before Evan, wings raised, ready to attack, claws bared. He was clearly dangerous and without a doubt deadly. He could and would inflict harm or kill if threatened.

"Easy, brother. We're not here to hurt you." Evan held up his hands in defense. Cela leaped to his arm, crooning in distress, chirping and fluttering his wings in agitation at the gargoyle's aggressive stance toward Evan.

"It's okay, Cela. Our brother is frightened and has every right to be. Be calm, little one." He gently reached over and scratched under Cela's chin to soothe the dragon.

Cela, once reassured, ran up his arm and curled around his throat, purring contentedly.

"Please, brother, we don't have much time and we've a ways to travel. I mean you no harm," Evan said to the large gargoyle, who obviously didn't trust him. "We need to hurry. The musketeers can only hold off the monks so long before the lazy bastards'll give up chasing them and return here to check on you."

The gargoyle stood erect, folded his wings flat against his back until they all but disappeared, and retracted his claws. He seemed to relax a bit, to realize Evan wanted to help him.

Evan approached and grasped the gargoyle's wrist lightly but firmly. "Come on. We have to go." He took off, running toward his truck. He grabbed the whistle around his neck and blew two sharp tones, then opened the passenger door of the cab. He guided the gargoyle inside, mindful of the tail so he didn't slam it in the door.

The gargoyle watched nervously as Evan climbed into the driver's seat.

"Okay, be calm now. The engine is very noisy and I'm not sure how long you've slept. Do you know what cars and trucks are?" Evan asked cautiously, watching the gargoyle as he turned over the key.

The roar of the engine shocked the gargoyle, his eyes large as he stared at the front of the truck.

As the engine groaned, Evan put a sympathetic hand on the gargoyle's arm. "I'm sorry. I don't have time to explain the truck. We've got to get out of here before we're seen." Evan threw the truck into gear and stepped on the gas. The truck lurched forward onto the road. Once on the highway, Evan turned on the headlights and eased out onto the old, rutted, winding road, going as fast as he dared. They really weren't far from the cabin—just a couple of hours' slow travel down the remains of an aged highway and they'd be safe.

"I promise, the truck is just a machine. It won't hurt you. It's just noisy." Evan tried to sound reassuring, but the road didn't allow him to give much more than an occasional glance at his companion. These roads saw little traffic and had never been repaired, at least as far as Evan knew. There were stretches that were in good condition and others where nature, if left unchecked, would soon make the road impassable.

"I know it has to be unsettling if you've never ridden in a truck before, but this really is the fastest way to put some distance between you and those monks. Just try to relax and we'll be there soon." He was rambling. He just didn't know what to say to an ancient creature who had just awoken and now sat in his truck, especially when that being could easily kill if he panicked. Sighing, he stared out the windshield at the night, and, deciding it was wiser to let the gargoyle get accustomed to things on his own, he concentrated on the road.

As the silence lengthened and the purr of the engine continued to drone on, the distinct popping sound of claws being pulled from vinyl drew Evan's gaze from the road. Evan laughed as his companion rubbed at the holes he'd left in the seat. "Looks like I'm going to have to get out the repair kit after we get home. I can't have Father Michael seeing those."

Cela sat on Evan's shoulder and began to croon, singing happily, as he often did when everything was going well. Evan stroked Cela's jaw, and the little dragon quieted down. Cela eyed the large gargoyle curiously, tipping his head first to the right and then left as he examined him. Before Evan could stop him, he scampered along Evan's shoulder to the back of the bench seat and across the top, where he stood and examined the gargoyle's hands, which were larger than Cela's whole body.

"He is but a babe. Nevertheless, he trusts you as though you were his mother." The gargoyle spoke softly, gently. He reached out a single claw and rubbed the underside of Cela's jaw, just as Evan had.

"You speak!" Evan said, shocked. "I didn't know you could talk. None of the others speak."

"Most of our kind cannot, but we do understand everything you say, just like this little one who serves you. Who are you? Are you the Maker?" the gargoyle asked as Cela scurried up his arm and rubbed himself in the long blue-black hair, singing softly on his shoulder.

"My name is Evan Halvard. I'm not the *Maker*, I don't think. I'm not exactly sure what you mean. What's your name? How long have you been asleep?" Evan asked as he glanced from the road to his large companion.

The gargoyle looked away from Evan and out the window into the enveloping darkness. He looked as if he could see beyond the headlights, beyond the night itself, instead of the encroaching pine forest that threatened to overtake the narrow and partially overgrown road. "I have no name. I have been hibernating since His Holiness Pope John Paul V became the vicar."

"Have you always been here—I mean, guarding in that cemetery?"

"No. Many years ago I was assigned to guard the mausoleum where you awakened me."

"How old are you?" Evan's curiosity was getting the best of him. The gargoyle was *talking*, and Evan had nothing but endless questions he wanted to ask.

"The passage of time means little to stone. I am not sure of my exact age. I awaken generally once a century from hibernation to hunt, seek the Maker or a mate. I have seen machines like this truck, but I have never been in one." The gargoyle eyed the dashboard with curiosity.

"My father used to tell me stories about gargoyles like you, but I've never seen one."

"I have not seen another like myself for a very long time. The last time I awoke, I found the night sky empty of my kind. Even though I called for my brothers and sisters and searched, it was in vain." He turned to stare at Evan. "I returned to my den to sleep. Then you woke me. I felt you call to God. I heard your heart call to me, but then you were gone. I knew others had arrived while I slept, but they were unusually hostile. I have never before been restrained. As a guardian, I have never had enemies amongst the humans, yet I awoke in chains, unable to free myself."

"I worried you might not hear me. I couldn't say the words aloud. Father Michael's a dangerous man and would've stopped me and probably killed me, if he'd known. I'm glad you heard me and knew I wasn't going to hurt you."

"I felt your return. I tried to free myself. But I do not understand. Humans have never been our enemies… well, at least not most of them. Those obeying the lure of evil are our enemies, but even those humans have never dared to attack a gargoyle—asleep or otherwise." He growled in frustration.

Evan turned off the main highway onto the dirt road that led to the cabin. "Things have changed a great deal over the past century. There was a war, and many people were killed by biological weapons. Many turned to the Church for absolution, begging forgiveness for creating the lethal weapons that nearly destroyed humanity, and for comfort for the loss of loved ones and innocents killed by our ignorance."

"Mankind has ever struggled amongst itself. Man strikes out at all he does not understand, feels is abhorrent, different, or unnatural. He is a beast whose mind I have never understood."

Evan sighed, nodding. "The Church took over, and although they mandate love and forgiveness, they preach that, because of original sin, humanity is inherently violent. The Church claims they have a divine obligation to God to keep humanity's soul as pure as possible. They dole out extreme punishments for anything they view as sinful. They have humanity cowering on its knees and are unopposed."

"But why would they do this?"

"Since man was made in God's image, the Church teaches us that by limiting mankind's exposure to sin, his natural 'godlike' humanity will emerge and sin will cease, returning us all to God's perfect state, closer to his original design, as Adam was in the garden of Eden before the fall from grace." Evan spoke the words by rote, as he'd been taught as a child.

"This course will only turn them into the violent oppressors they are trying to save humanity from."

"Logically, yes. But they deny that conclusion. So they mandate anything depicting sin in any form must be destroyed." Evan scanned the tree line in the darkness, watching for animals as he proceeded as quickly as he could manage down the road.

"If all is destroyed, then how do the children learn right from wrong? One cannot learn one without knowledge of the other."

"Right is glorified. Wrong is harshly punished and hidden from sight as if it doesn't exist. First, they expunged all violence from history, rewriting it to reflect only the goodness and peacefulness of humanity. A strange, utopian golden age of growth and godliness became our past."

"So nothing of the truth remains?"

Evan shook his head. "All reference to actual history is gone, including those depicted in the arts and literature. Wars no longer exist and are not taught in the schools. Even the word has been stricken from our vocabulary. But some brave tales of the past are still told as bedtime stories to children in the quiet of night and around campfires, along with ghost stories."

"None have tried to prevent this atrocity?"

"There are a few like myself who attempt to protect pieces of human history from the Church. An underground, if you will. We are anonymous, even to one another, to protect ourselves if we're discovered. I can contact them if I need help."

"Why you?"

"Because I've always been drawn to gargoyles, and I've skills with stone that my father taught me, which come in handy as a cover. We each have our areas of specialty. One of them sent me a message about the cemetery you were sleeping in. I was trying to check it out, but the Church discovered you were there, and I had to work quickly or you would've been destroyed."

EVAN SIGHED and pulled up to an iron gate that blocked the road and extended into a fence that continued in both directions. He noticed Aramis and Athos inside the gate, awaiting their arrival. There were days he envied their ability to fly, although today was not one of those days; he'd enjoyed his drive with the ancient gargoyle. He pressed a button on the visor of the truck, and the gate unlocked and slid open. He pulled through the gate and pressed the button again, reversing the gate's direction. Of course, the gate only served as a deterrent for the general public. Officers of the Church, like Father Michael, had frequencies to all the automated systems and could get inside. Even so, Evan's security system would be alerted and he'd know someone was approaching his home.

The gate stood a full two miles from the cabin. Evan had installed a detector on a hill in the cabin's direct line of sight. It would give him about a five-minute warning before company came up his road and within sight of his sanctuary.

Evan watched with amusement as the gargoyle stared out at the sparsely forested land they drove through. The roadside was dotted with statues: angels and animals in various poses appeared along their route. There were also fountains, chairs, benches, barbeque pits, planters, and various other items in many different colors and textures, all made of composite stone. He watched with interest and curiosity as they passed by.

When they neared the cabin, Evan pulled the truck directly in to the workshop. The large doors closed behind them. He got out of the truck and opened the door for the gargoyle. "Cela, open the door for the others. They might as well come and meet our new friend." Evan stroked the head of the little dragon, who then launched himself into the air and flew off. He quickly returned and perched, not on Evan's shoulder, but on the large gargoyle's, chirping and crooning happily.

"He is quite friendly, is he not?" The gargoyle purred back and rubbed Cela carefully between the wings with a finger, showing no sign of his retractable claws.

"Yes. I've never seen him snap at anyone, unless he's hunting, of course." Evan chuckled.

Yin and Yang bounded into the garage and rubbed up against Evan, purring happily.

"Easy, guys. You'll knock me off my feet." Evan knelt down to greet them, encircling their necks with an arm around each of them. "Are you being good? Guarding the house?" They both licked at his face, knocking him off his feet as he'd warned they would in their enthusiasm to greet him. Evan shook with peals of belly laughter as he struggled upright, scratched behind their ears, and tried to push them off him.

The large gargoyle watched as the menagerie increased once the musketeers made their entrance, all purring and rubbing against Evan, vying for his attention.

"You did very well. I'm so glad you were careful. Did you have fun? I bet you did." Evan stroked each one, giving them all attention and scratching their favorite itchy places. He laughed, almost landing on his rear a second time thanks to their enthusiasm. Finally, with everyone greeted and thanked, he stood without fear of being returned abruptly to the ground.

"This is my family. The Chinese lion-dogs are Yin and Yang. The four dragons are the musketeers: d'Artagnan, Athos, Porthos, and Aramis. And you've met Cela. Welcome." Evan smiled as the gargoyle sat on the ground to greet them.

Yin and Yang licked the visitor's face as the musketeers rubbed against his thighs.

"Thank you for your… welcome."

"So what's your story? On the drive home, you said you weren't always in that mausoleum. Where were you born or created?"

"I have avoided humans for the most part. My Maker did not keep me around very long after I came to be. I was commissioned for duty at a large sanctuary for many centuries, standing guard at night with many brothers and sisters like myself." The large gargoyle got a distant look in his eyes for a moment before he refocused on Evan. "After that, I went to the new world and again did my duty, standing guard, this time for a much smaller sanctuary, until such time as one of the great fathers passed away." The gargoyle buried his hands in Yang's thick coat, scratching as grunts of pleasure came from the lion-dog. "They gave me the honor of watching over his body as the guardian of his resting place. This duty freed me to hibernate as I pleased. I did not realize at first how much time was passing."

"Didn't you get lonely?"

"Not at first, but eventually I began searching for my own kind. I thought as there was no Maker living in the New World to create us, it was natural there were fewer of us here. These young ones are the only others I have come across in many decades." The gargoyle reached for Yin and rubbed his own face against the lion-dog, purring his excitement and happiness as if he were about to cry. "I feared myself to be the last of my kind. I am pleased to see I am not. I will no longer sleep alone."

"You're not alone." Evan put a hand on his arm and smiled down into his face. "Come on. Let me show you around our home. This is the garage for the trucks, and in the back is my workshop."

"You said you work with stone?"

"Yes, I'm a stonemason. I grind up stone and re-form it to make flooring and walls. I do some composite sculpture, which you saw out in the garden along the driveway. There isn't much call for sculpture, as the Church has pretty much banned most forms of artistic expression. They only sanction certain designs." Evan walked from the garage toward the cabin.

"What of the religious icons? Not all of them are benevolent. The Lord's sacrifice is hardly nonviolent."

"The Lord's sacrifice for our sins is hidden to all but the most devout monks, as even violence depicted in the Bible is forbidden to be read by the public. The Church even has specially trained monks hunting for depictions of such violence, including specific statues: those of living stone." Evan frowned.

"Why would the Church hunt us? We have always been their guardians." Confusion filled the gargoyle's voice.

"They hunt gargoyles and destroy them regardless of your centuries of service. They've named your kind as depictions of evil in sculpture and, therefore, demonic. They've become so obsessed with their laws, they're now fanatical and controlling. All we can do is try to save as much of human history and living stone as possible and hope our work carries through to the next generation so they can learn from our mistakes."

"Then my being here—all of us being here—is dangerous for you."

"Yes, I'm a criminal of sorts," Evan said, smiling mischievously before he became serious again. "But I can't abide those who'd distort history, believing that by doing so they can prevent violence. I believe ignorance begets fear of the unknown, and mankind inevitably seems to hate and destroy what he fears and doesn't understand." He sighed sadly. Then, giving himself a shake, he smiled up at his new gargoyle friend. "I'm glad you are here."

"I will do everything in my power to make sure my presence does not bring you harm."

"Come. I want to show you the cabin and the sanctuary." Evan took the large gargoyle's wrist and led him out into the night. There were no lights on in the cabin, but the surrounding meadow blazed with fireflies. Looking at the horizon across the meadow, it appeared as though the stars had come down out of the sky to dance.

"Beautiful." The gargoyle stopped and stared out across the meadow.

"You most certainly are," Evan whispered to himself. His gaze was on the slightly glowing gargoyle, who stood beside him. The gargoyle eyed him curiously, and Evan hummed to himself, shaking his head as he led the way to the side door of the cabin.

"The main floor up here I don't really use. It's more for show for the Bishop's Service and Father Michael in particular. I use the kitchen from time to time when I'm working in the shop. Sorry about the mess, but I keep it looking 'lived in' on purpose. I'm a hard-working manual laborer, after all, and a bachelor too. A certain level of messiness, I've discovered, is expected. Otherwise Father Michael gets suspicious."

The gargoyle looked around. He curled his nose up at the piles of dirty clothes that lay on the bedroom floor and the stack of unwashed dishes in the kitchen sink.

Evan chuckled at his reaction. "If the place is too clean, they start poking into my personal life, asking if I have a girlfriend or if I'm seeing anyone. If I name anyone I'm interested in, then the Church goes after them. I've learned to keep to myself and stay out of personal relationships. Father Michael seems to prefer me to be uninvolved, and I need to keep him happy and unsuspecting. Our real home is below."

Yin and Yang grabbed a corner of the rug in the center of the kitchen floor and carefully drew it back to reveal a large trapdoor. Evan pulled on the release, and the door dropped slightly and slid silently under the floor to reveal a well-lit stairway. Yin and Yang were the first down the stairs, followed by two of the musketeers, the other two having disappeared outside, probably to stand guard at the entrance. It was still a couple of hours until dawn.

Evan walked down the stairs, and the gargoyle followed. There was a small room at the base of the stairs, like a foyer. Evan slipped off his shoes and led the way down a hallway and through a doorway on the right into a large living room. Spotlessly clean and tastefully decorated, this was Evan's home. Large rugs covered the bedrock floor, while bookcases covered the walls. A television with a full surround-sound system sat at one side.

"I don't know if you read, but you're welcome to whatever interests you. You can watch TV or you can listen to the stereo. I have CDs of most any type of music. I'll teach you how to use the electronics." Evan looked around. "My bedroom and office are in the next room, as well as the master bathroom." He led the way in, and to his frustration, he found Yin and Yang on the bed, playing and growling at each other. "Get down, you two. How many times do I have to tell you? Don't play on the bed," Evan scolded the two lion-dogs, who looked at him and panted, tongues lolling out the sides of their mouths, trying to entice him to join in their play. Evan got down on his knees and wrapped his arms first around Yang, with the blue-green eyes, and then Yin, with the golden eyes, hugging them both and rubbing his face against theirs. "Not tonight, boys. Go on now. The sun will be rising soon. Go find your roosts." He lovingly scratched each of the lion-dogs, who then took off at a run from the bedroom toward the living room.

The large gargoyle watched them go. He looked around the room at the deep blue velvet-draped bed with the matching blue plush carpet in front of it and the complex electronics equipment on the desk. Images on several computer monitors flashed through a sequence of different locations, one after the other. The gargoyle watched the scenes with increasing curiosity. He seemed to recognize the front of the cabin, as well as the gate they'd passed through on the way. "That is outside, here?" the gargoyle asked, pointing at the monitors.

"Those are live pictures of the area around the outside of the cabin and the gated entrance to the driveway. I can see who's here or who's coming to the house before they arrive." Evan smiled at the gargoyle's awed confusion.

"Powerful magic," the gargoyle growled in suspicion.

"Not magic. This is machinery and electronics. I'll teach you. There's nothing mystical or magical about it. Just science and technology." Evan smiled warmly as he pointed at the screen. "See? There's Aramis and Athos over there. They're heading for the south entrance to the mineshafts. They like to sleep in the southern end of the labyrinth of tunnels. You're welcome to go find yourself a spot if you like, or you're welcome to stay here. I don't mind. Whatever will make you the most comfortable."

"If you do not mind, I have been alone for a very long time. I would really like to be close to you. I am not ready to sleep alone again." The gargoyle spoke softly with his head down, as if embarrassed by his request.

"You're more than welcome to stay. Make yourself comfortable. I'll be working on my computer for most of the day and watching for Father Michael's imminent arrival. He will undoubtedly be coming by to check to see if I'm here."

"He will be searching for me."

"Don't worry, he won't find you. He comes pretty much weekly and has no idea there's anything down here. These mountains are full of iron ore, and the mineral interferes with his electronic equipment. They're unable to get a scan of the mountain and have no idea the mines and caves running for miles beneath the cabin even exist. Besides, I've also got a couple of electronic items that mess with their scanners. I believe he thinks to catch me off guard and push his weight around." Evan smiled, looking at the gargoyle, who appeared to be debating something with himself.

"Um… where do you want me to go?" the gargoyle nervously asked, rocking a bit from foot to foot, watching Evan.

"It doesn't matter." Evan walked over and sat on the edge of the plush blue rug. "Sit down. Make yourself comfortable." He patted the rug for the gargoyle to join him. "If you like, I'll sit with you till you sleep."

The gargoyle sat on the carpet, ran a hand across the pile of the rug, then lay next to Evan. The gargoyle rubbed his face against the plush pile of the carpet and seemed to delight in its fuzzy texture.

Evan lay down, stretching out alongside the creature and pillowing his head on his arm.

"I have never lain in such a luxurious place." The gargoyle purred contentedly, rolling onto his side and curling slightly until he faced Evan, blinking sleepily.

Evan reached out and ran his fingers through the gargoyle's silky hair. The strands flowed like gossamer through his fingers, soft and thick. He tucked them behind the large pointed ears. The gargoyle's sapphire eyes closed as he relaxed into sleep and dawn arose. To Evan's amazement, the hair he stroked didn't turn to stone as he had expected, but remained pliant and silken under his fingers. He continued to stroke the blue-black hair, feeling his own contentment rise at being in his presence.

Evan felt the adrenaline leaving his system as exhaustion settled in. With a regretful sigh, he got up and went to his computer to make sure the entrance gate and the cabin doors were closed and locked, including the trapdoor. He checked the monitors that showed the inside of the cabin, making certain the rug was in place in the room upstairs. Cords attached to the trapdoor had pulled the rug into place, just as always. With everything secure, Evan headed for a shower to wash away the dirt and grime of the day. When he emerged from the bathroom, he gazed again at the gargoyle on the rug by his bed.

"I'm going to have to come up with a name for you. I can't go about calling you 'hey you,' now, can I? This may require some thought. You deserve a very special name."

As exhaustion took over, Evan yawned and stumbled to his bed, climbed beneath the blankets, closed his eyes, and drifted off to sleep.

ARAMIS AND Athos had chosen to check the perimeter of Evan's property.

"*The Maker sleeps,*" Athos hissed, his thoughts joining those of his brothers as they ran along the fence that separated their territory from that of their neighbor's property.

"*Yes, we must keep him safe,*" Aramis replied silently.

"*We are not alone.*" Athos moved slowly and carefully, with determination in the direction of the presence.

"*Where does it hide? We must find it.*" Aramis followed at his brother's heels as they drew near.

The evil drew the gargoyles like a fish to a cat. They hungered for it, and when they destroyed it, they would draw sustenance from the energy essence of the evil. The reason gargoyles existed, their calling and duty, was to protect all from the creatures of evil. They protected the souls of the good from the evils of Hell and dark magic; they were the guardians. To hunt evil down, to eat it, and prevent it from touching the pure soul of their friend and master, Evan, would be their great pleasure.

"*It was here, but it fades away,*" Aramis growled at his brother.

"*We are not allowed beyond. It will be back. We will wait for it to return.*" Athos shook his body. Waves of frustration at their disrupted hunt irritated the gargoyle.

"*Dawn comes. We must sleep.*" Aramis turned and looked over his shoulder at his brother, who gave a last warning snarl in the direction of the fleeing evil. Together, Aramis and Athos ran for the caves, launched themselves into the sky, and flew as quickly as they could to their secluded perches deep in the rock caves before sunrise.

Chapter 3

FROM THE diary of Elizabeth Peterson: November 17, 2110

> My Dearest Nicolas,
> It's my thirty-second birthday, the third since you've been gone. The priest came today to tell me that you were believed to have been killed in the first wave on the battlefield. I don't know if it's true or not, but I know if you weren't dead, you would have returned to me by now. They can't even tell me where you are buried, although I suppose one mass grave marked "The Loved and the Lost" is much like another. I went with the priests and placed flowers at the mass grave in town. It was cathartic. Even though I know you aren't there, I found some peace.
> Things are changing, my love. I never thought I'd see the day the governments fell; it happened so quickly. There are so few of us left alive after the biological weapons were released. Now there is so much pain, suffering, and overwhelming sadness. I don't believe there is a person alive who hasn't been touched by the death of numerous friends and family. I miss you, my love.
> Elizabeth

EVAN AWOKE to the sound of incessant beeping a couple of hours after he'd lain down. His mind fuzzy from lack of sleep, he struggled to remember what the beeping meant. Finally consciousness broke through, and coherent thought reasoned the alarm was his perimeter alert. *Damn the man to Hell. Father Michael just had to show up. Why can't the man leave me the fuck alone?* Evan groused to himself.

He sighed as he got up, grabbing a dirty shirt and jeans from the hamper. Dirty clothes gave him the appearance of a morning filled with hard work instead of trying to get some much-needed sleep. He got dressed and hit a couple of buttons on the computer, which activated the automatic starters, turning on the grinding machinery in the shop. They would be running and noisy by the time Father Michael pulled in to the yard.

Evan went out to the living room and then down a different hallway that led him to one of the other access points; this one took him to the hidden entrance in his workshop. He trotted up the stairs and through the trapdoor, which opened into the office of his masonry shop and the garage for his trucks.

The spring-loaded door slammed shut when he let go, and he slid the dirty rug back into place. He grabbed his work goggles, headphones, and heavy gloves. He slid the goggles over his eyes, and after turning on the music to protect his ears from the noise of the heavy machinery, he took his place in front of the grinder. He slipped his hands into the gloves, tossed a couple of large chunks of marble into the hopper, and focused on his work, feeding the machine as he waited.

Evan heard the beep from his computer inside his headphones, letting him know the shop door had been opened. Father Michael must be standing behind him, probably staring at him, so he made a show of dancing to his music as he worked. He almost jumped out of his skin when Father Michael finally gave up on hollering his name and tapped him on the shoulder to get his attention. He hit a button on the machine to turn it off, waiting for the grinder to wind down. "Father, you scared me. I didn't hear you come in."

"Boy, you need to be more careful. I'd hate to see you get hurt with all this big machinery," Father Michael admonished.

Evan always let Father Michael surprise him because he seemed to take pleasure in feeling superior to those around him. That made him easier to deal with. "Sorry, Father. How about we go into the cabin for a cup of coffee?" He smiled and motioned to the door.

"That's a good idea. I've something I wish to discuss with you." Father Michael smiled and let Evan lead the way to the cabin.

"Have a seat, Father, and I'll bring the coffee." Evan moved into the kitchen and stuck a couple of coffee mugs with water into the microwave. He never bothered to brew coffee for Father Michael. Instant coffee was more than good enough. He didn't want to give the man any reason to feel comfortable or encourage him to stay longer. Besides, Evan wanted decaf so he could go back to sleep once Father Michael left.

When the microwave dinged, Evan stirred in the coffee crystals and carried the mugs out to the father, who sat on the sofa, glaring around the cluttered cabin. "Sorry, Father. You know I only do instant around here." Evan handed the hot mug to Father Michael, who accepted it, closing his long, heavily jointed fingers around the handle of the cup.

Father Michael gave Evan a conciliatory smile at his attempted hospitality before he placed the cup on a coaster on the coffee table between the sofa where he sat and a nearby armchair where Evan had settled himself. "I'm surprised to find you home, Evan. Weren't you going to check out some estate sale or something?" Father Michael seemed irritated at finding Evan home, but at the same time, pleased to see him.

"I did, but the stone wasn't what I expected, so I came straight home. I remembered you saying not to be out if I didn't have to, so I figured the safest place would be at home, working. You're looking tired, Father. Are you eating properly? You look like you've lost weight." Evan answered Father Michael's question and oozed concern for the vile man. *The things I do to keep him from suspecting me.*

"We had a bit of a problem last night. A very large evil escaped us. I worried about you. I actually hoped you weren't home. Sometimes, my boy, I think your being out here all by yourself isn't wise." Father Michael sighed, as if Evan's safety were a constant burden for him.

"Surely the evil wouldn't make it all the way up here. The cemetery I left you at yesterday is a couple hours' travel from here." Evan sipped at the instant coffee he'd made and tried not to grimace at the taste.

"Two hours if you follow that rutted, curving road they call a highway to get back into these woods, yes. But take out the switchbacks, the rotten road, and if you were able to make any kind of speed at all… well, as the bird or evil flies, you are much closer than it seems. It's dangerous, Evan. Such exposure can be deadly."

"Now, Father, you know my work is difficult and loud. Can you imagine the problems I'd face running the grinder in town, with neighbors all around? Besides, I've always implemented the security measures you've recommended to me. Don't worry. I'm perfectly safe."

"I know you try to be safe," Father Michael argued.

"I'm not a child, after all, and you come to check up on me…. My mom calls daily. I'm hardly out of touch."

"I'm fully aware that you're not a child anymore, Evan, but—"

"I'm not here very often, you know. I'm on the road a lot, looking for raw materials. I stay in town with Mom on occasion, when she isn't entertaining one of her husbands." Evan smiled softly at Father Michael. "But I thank you for your concern. It warms my heart to know you think of me."

"I guess the incident last night has me upset. I'm being overprotective. At least do me a favor and stay indoors at night. I don't want you wandering around in your garden, gazing at the statues in the moonlight or whatever you do to inspire yourself. Safety has to be your first consideration until the beast is located and destroyed. Leave your lights on and don't take any chances. If you see anything out of the ordinary, please call me." Father Michael pushed back his untouched mug of coffee on the table and stood abruptly.

"I will, Father." Evan smiled, slowly closing his eyes and nodding coyly with a slight turn of his head to the side. He rose with the father to walk him out to his car.

"Please, my boy. I really do worry about you." Father Michael patted Evan on the back, between his shoulder blades. Evan fought to keep from cringing from his skeletal touch as Father Michael slowly slid his hand down his back to brush against his ass before reaching for the car door.

"Really, Father, I'm more worried about you. You need to eat something. A strong gust of wind could carry you away," Evan fussed as Father Michael smiled while he slid into the driver's seat. Evan closed the car door and tried to believe the smile was intended to be friendly, but to him, it more closely resembled a sneer. The lasciviousness reflected in Father Michael's eyes never let a truly friendly smile reach them. Evan shivered involuntarily as he waved at the car pulling away.

Good riddance. He sighed, ran a hand up and over his hair, and pulled at it in frustration. The shows he put on for Father Michael were exhausting. Sometimes he wondered if it wouldn't be safer to leave the area than continue to live in the shadow of Father Michael's evil. Maybe he'd have been wiser to leave the country in the guise of attending school to free himself from Father Michael. Evan considered the option again, but then shook his head. No, he needed to stay. *Better the devil you know than the one you don't.* Besides, travel with his friends, especially his newest friend, would be inconvenient at best and a true nightmare if they were discovered. No, he wouldn't be able to leave and still protect his family.

As he thought of the beautiful gargoyle in his bedroom, asleep on the rug, he smiled. He wouldn't awaken till sundown, and thanks to Father Michael, with the adrenaline in his system, Evan couldn't sleep just yet. He dumped the two mugs of instant coffee into the sink and rinsed them. He wouldn't drink instant swill when he had an espresso machine in the basement.

Evan's feet seemed to have a mind of their own and soon carried him to his bedroom. He gazed at the beauty curled up on the rug. The gargoyle lay exactly where Evan had left him. He was stunning... and very well endowed, Evan noticed, not for the first time. He began to wonder what those large hands would feel like against his skin.

He gave himself a shake. He shouldn't be thinking of—desiring—his charge. He had a duty to protect the gargoyles, not think about fucking one. Although the gargoyle's beauty outshone any other, he was still a creature. Granted, he was an amazingly intelligent and well-spoken one. But Evan should be his caretaker, not be thinking of how many different ways the gargoyle could take care of him.

He must be getting horny. Evan hadn't been with anyone regularly since he and his last boyfriend, Jonathan, had broken up. Heck, he hadn't even gone into town for a quick fuck in ages. Sighing, Evan considered making just such a trip this week to take the edge off his libido. He just hated the fallout because Father Michael always found out about his indiscretions. Inevitably someone loyal to Father Michael would see him and report his whereabouts. There were people willing to turn in others to protect themselves or win his favor, afraid for their families and loved ones. Nobody had a private life. Everyone lived under the Church's watchful eyes because anyone could be watching. Anyone could be an informant. Once Evan was discovered, Father Michael would lecture him for days about the immorality and sin of lying with another man. It wasn't as if Evan needed another reason to despise him; Father Michael's hypocritical attitude was reason enough.

That did it. Thoughts of Father Michael cooled his out-of-control libido instantly, better than ice water.

Evan walked over to his computer. He needed to come up with a name for the gargoyle. He sat down and did a search for male names meaning "rock." Of course, the list that followed included his own name, his father's name, Peter, and Cela, his little rock, as well as others. He wanted something unique yet appropriate, like the gargoyle himself. Finally he came across Adelstan, from Old English, which meant "noble stone." It was an old name and unique in the modern world, but "noble stone" did fit the beautiful gargoyle well. So Adelstan it would be—Adel, for short. Evan smiled to himself as he returned the computer to sleep mode. The adrenaline from earlier was finally beginning to wear off. He felt fatigue seeping into his veins as he yawned and stretched.

He stood and walked to the gargoyle, smiling down at him. He looked so peaceful, curled up, unmoving perfection in stone. His body appeared to be white stone with dark gray tiger stripes that looked like natural lines in the white marble. Though it made Evan want to laugh at his own silliness, he took the blanket from his bed and covered the sleeping gargoyle, who had no need of additional warmth as a statue. However, it would hide the stunning body that threatened to keep him awake all day.

He tried to deny the urge to curl up with him, just for a nap. No one would be any the wiser. He'd be awake long before the gargoyle, of course. The temptation proved too great. Evan's mindless body decided for him. He grabbed his pillow from the bed and curled up under the blanket on the blue rug with the pillow lying against the gargoyle's forearm.

Stretched out across the rug, Evan gave in to sleep. He sighed as fatigue and exhaustion won out over his body, and he thought of Adel. Yes, the perfect name for his beautiful gargoyle. Noble Stone.

SEVERAL HOURS later, the sound of Cela hissing and scolding brought Evan around to consciousness. He felt so warm and comfortable, he just wanted Cela to shut up so he could go back to sleep. As he began to wake, he realized he was on the floor and not in bed. He knew there had to be a reason for that but couldn't remember what.

"No, little one, let him sleep," a soft, deep voice whispered.

Evan liked the voice, but the continued screeching and squawking told him Cela wouldn't stop. Cela demanded he wake and address the issue. Still, Evan's sleep-clouded mind tried to ignore the dragon, instead latching on to that voice. It refused to let him slip back into the netherworld of sleep.

He felt so warm and comfortable, he sighed and let his eyes stay shut, basking in the coziness that surrounded him. He felt as well as heard a chuckle nearby that thrummed with vibration about him. He felt the reverberations within his own chest, as if he were purring.

A large hand gently brushed his hair from his face. "You cannot fool me, Evan. I know you are awake." The voice was commanding yet gentle in its insistence.

Evan took a deep breath and sighed. The comforting scents of earth and spring rain, mixed with a masculine musk, surrounded him in the warmth of the blanket. "Let me sleep. Just a little bit longer, please," Evan mumbled, snuggling farther into the rug. His body in its semiconscious state instinctively sought the warmth he felt along his back. The bass tones laughed quietly again, and something heavy came across his body, pulling him in closer. Evan sighed in contentment as feelings of safety washed over him. He hadn't felt this protected or comforted since he was a small child being held by his mother.

The cheeping and squawking continued, and as Cela's anger increased, his hissing grew louder.

"Cela, please! Knock it off. Father Michael's been here and gone already. He won't be back for a while. Let me be already," Evan grumbled.

Cela cheeped once, then began to cry piteously, as if he were being tortured.

"Ugh! Fine!" Evan grumbled and opened his eyes to see Cela glaring at him unhappily. "What?" He looked at Cela, who just stared back at him, then pointedly looked at something over his shoulder. Evan sat up a bit higher and turned to look, sitting up the rest of the way abruptly. "Oh! I'm so sorry!" he stuttered, embarrassed. "I thought I'd wake before you." He always had awoken before Cela, always before sunset, and had been sure it would be no different now. He had always been a restless sleeper and rarely felt secure enough, even in his sanctuary, to sleep soundly or for more than a couple of hours at a time.

"It is all right. For some reason Cela's upset you chose to curl up at my side. I know you had promised to stay close, but it did surprise me as well to find you… this close." The gargoyle raised an eyebrow, and a half smile touched his lips, showing just the slightest flash of the deadly fangs they covered. "Surprised, but happy you are not afraid of me. Sleep if you wish. The sun has barely gone down. The night is young. I will keep watch while you sleep. You are safe." The gargoyle reached out and stroked Evan's cheek gently. He encircled Evan in his arms and drew him back down into the blanket, gently guiding his head back to the pillow.

Evan gazed into those blue eyes and found he couldn't resist. His mind was already shutting down, going back to sleep. Evan closed his eyes.

He felt the familiar warmth from before swathed around him as the gargoyle curled his body around him. The gargoyle's gentle purring sang him to sleep, surer than any mother's lullaby. As the lull of sleep shrouded his mind and relaxed his body, he felt safe, securely snuggled against the warmth of the strong body wrapped around him. Completely content, Evan sighed, his mind numb to any danger this creature could pose to him.

"You are a Maker, my little Evan. I can feel the power deep inside you. I will be here to protect you. I will never leave your side," the gargoyle's deep voice rumbled softly in his ear.

"Adelstan," Evan whispered, half-asleep. "Adel…." He frowned, trying to draw himself back to full consciousness again.

"Shhh… it is all right, little Maker," the gargoyle whispered, stroking Evan's hair, like a parent consoling a child.

Evan took hold of Adel's hand and clutched it tightly to his chest. "Your name is Adel. My Adelstan…." Evan exhaled the words so softly, he wasn't sure he'd spoken at all or if this was just a dream and the hand he clutched merely his pillow.

"Thank you, Evan. I am honored." Adel laid his head down behind Evan's.

Cela seemed to have calmed down. *At least he's stopped screeching*, Evan thought as he drifted toward sleep, unconcerned where the little dragon had gone.

"Such a trusting, silly child," Adel purred. "You fearlessly curl up with a monster and sleep, lost in the dreams of such innocence. You are so like little Cela. You do not even know your own abilities. Hush, child. I *will* watch over you, while you learn who you are."

ARAMIS AND Athos ran out into the night, with d'Artagnan and Porthos on their heels. They headed for the spot where they'd discovered the evil scent the previous night. The scent remained, although it had grown faint. After getting a good whiff, the musketeers set out on patrol, each heading in a separate direction, taking a different section of the property, running up and down along the fence. They would defend their home and welcomed the challenge posed by any approaching corruption. The existence of evil gave them their reason to live, and they relished the chance to defend what they loved. Knowing that the wicked sought a way past them made their hunt all the more exciting.

Chapter 4

GARGOYLE LORE

As written by the scribes and entombed in the Church Archives:
Hibernation:

1. Gargoyles put themselves into hibernation and sleep as stone for centuries if they feel they are unwanted or not needed and can awaken whenever they choose or when called.
2. Usually only an unmated gargoyle will hibernate.
3. Birth of an Elemental/Maker will awaken small/young gargoyles who will then seek out the Maker to guard him/her.
4. Elementals/Makers can call a larger/older gargoyle from hibernation into service to protect him/her.

SEVERAL HOURS later, Evan finally awoke feeling very rested. He couldn't remember ever having slept as soundly. He still felt as warm and safe as he had earlier. The feeling was addictive, and one he hoped he would never lose.

"Are you really awake this time?" asked Adelstan, his voice filled with amusement.

"Oh!" Evan sat up suddenly, staring wide-eyed at the gargoyle. "I'm so sorry."

"It is all right. I really did not mind. I enjoyed watching you sleep. You are very expressive. I could almost imagine your dreams. You talk in your sleep too." Adel chuckled and sat up, leaning into Evan and nuzzling his neck, then sat back against the bed.

"Well, um… thank you, I guess. I don't know about dreams. I don't remember them. I must've really needed the rest. I don't normally… I mean, I guess it's been awhile since I've felt secure enough to really let my guard down." Evan stood, realizing he wore the same dirty jeans and T-shirt he'd donned for Father Michael's visit. He glanced at the clock to see he'd slept through the afternoon and most of the night. Dawn was but a couple of hours away. "Ugh, I need a shower." Evan heard the soft growling of a stomach. It didn't belong to him but to Adel. "Are you hungry? I'm starved. Let's go find something to eat. The shower can wait." Evan led the way out of the bedroom to the living room and then into the kitchen. He turned on the coffeemaker and dug through the refrigerator.

Adel stood back a bit as Evan pulled out eggs, steaks, frozen hash browns, and green peppers and onions from the vegetable crisper. He stared as Evan turned on the stove, added butter to one pan and oil to another, and began to brown the hash browns, then cut up the green peppers and onions and added them to the pan with a heavy dose of garlic and black pepper. The steaks he put under the broiler after he had seasoned them.

Evan turned to the coffeemaker, and although it hissed and bubbled merrily, he impatiently tapped his fingers on the countertop as he waited for it to finish perking before he poured two mugs and replaced the carafe. "Here, sit down." Evan pulled out a stool at the breakfast bar and guided Adel to sit. He placed one of the mugs in front of Adel, then picked up his own mug and sipped the hot brew. He watched as Adel sniffed the coffee, eyeing the strong, dark brew skeptically. "It's called coffee. Kind of an acquired taste. It's strong and a bit bitter. You may not like it. The first cup of the day, I usually drink black, like this, but I tend to add milk and sugar to the next cups."

Adel carefully picked up the cup and took a hesitant sip as Evan turned back to the stove, flipped the steaks on the broiler, then broke the eggs into the remaining pan and scrambled them. He loosened the potatoes and turned them so they could brown on the other side.

"I think I prefer tea," said the deep voice behind him, followed by the sound of the cup being pushed away. "It smells good, but the flavor is very bitter."

Evan smiled, took the milk out of the refrigerator, and grabbed the sugar bowl. He added the milk and sugar to the cup, then put the cup back in front of Adel. "Try it now. This is how I usually drink it. The flavor is much less bitter and much smoother." Evan turned back to his stove and filled two plates. He turned back to see Adel sip at the coffee a second time. His eyes lit with surprise at the difference in taste. "Good?" Evan placed a plate and silverware in front of Adel.

"Yes, much better." Adel looked at the steaming plate of food placed before him. "I do not know what to do. I have not dined with humans often. We do not hunt often, but when we do, we do not generally cook the meat."

Adel frowned and looked at the utensils, then at how Evan held the fork and knife in his hands.

Evan slowly demonstrated their use so Adel could watch how he manipulated the utensils. He made no comment as Adel struggled to coordinate them in his large hands while also trying to keep his claws retracted and out of the way. "I'm sorry if this isn't something you would normally eat. I know Cela likes coffee and will eat some things, but he and the others take care of themselves, hunting wild game in the woods. If this fare isn't palatable, don't worry about hurting my feelings. Feel free to hunt for yourself. I want you to feel comfortable here." Evan smiled.

He enjoyed watching Adel's discovery of cooked food. Adel sniffed the aroma, then mimicked how Evan scooped up some of the scrambled eggs for a bite. The surprise on Adel's face made Evan laugh as Adel dug in to the meal heartily. It wasn't long before Adel belched resoundingly. He'd eaten his entire portion and cleaned up everything in the pans before Evan pushed back his own plate, his hunger satisfied. Adel eyed the eggs and hash browns Evan hadn't finished. With a smile, Evan pushed his dish toward Adel, who ate those leftovers as well.

"That was quite exceptional. Thank you." Adel's eyes were almost half-closed with pleasure. Even though he stood on the far side of the counter, Evan could feel Adel's rumble of contentment.

"I'm glad you enjoyed it." Evan led the way back into his bedroom to check the monitors.

"You were going to explain your magic." Adel stared at the computer screens as Evan took a seat at the desk and moved the mouse.

The monitors came to life, showing various locations around the property. He did a sensor check. All the cameras were functioning properly, showing the various gargoyles in different locations. Each of the musketeers patrolled a different part of the property. Yin and Yang stood guard on the main road to the house, in the bushes, well out of sight of anyone who might approach.

Evan turned and eyed Adel, contemplating where to begin. "It's called a computer. It's a machine whose main function is to store and compile information, as well as send information across great distances. Another function is to transfer pictures from cameras such as the ones out by the entrances, or out by the fences where the musketeers are, and outside the gate, alerting me when someone is coming up the road. The computer can also control the entrances and the trapdoors coming into the mines, which lead to these living quarters."

Evan pointed to a screen with a bird's-eye view of the property. "There are several entrances, all sizes, all hidden. Some are so small only Cela and the musketeers can use them. Others are large enough I can drive the truck through them if I need to. The main entrances all have cameras, which are monitored by the computer. If the entrance is too small for a person to get into, I don't have a camera monitoring it." Evan turned and looked at Adel, frowning at his own confusing explanations.

"Honestly, I do not understand what you are trying to tell me, but I can see the result. If you say it is not dark magic, then I will believe you. I do not sense the use of magic anywhere in your home, so I have no reason to doubt you. Do you believe in magic at all? Or are all the mysteries of the world solved for you?" Adel asked, a sad look in his eyes.

"Well, let's just say I don't disbelieve. The logical part of me says we only call things magic when we don't understand them properly. Then the unexplained or unexplainable becomes magic. I know I have abilities which I don't understand. Are these abilities magic? I do believe in the power of the spirit. I don't believe life is simply a series of chemical reactions and all of a sudden we have sentience, which is simply advanced self-awareness." Evan smiled at the irony. Here he sat discussing the merits of science versus spirituality with the most magical and undeniably the most unexplainable creature he had ever met. "I guess I am willing to be open-minded."

Adel sat on the blue rug, leaned back against the bed, and motioned for Evan to join him. "I am glad to hear you say that. I thought perhaps all the wonders of your world had been explained. Conceivably, life may no longer hold any mystery for you, and you would not be able to believe in the possibility of what I am about to tell you." Adel seemed to relax a bit as Evan settled on the rug, leaning against the wall to face Adel.

Cela floated down from the bedpost nearby to land on Adel's shoulder. He rubbed his face against Adel's, who snorted in amusement and scratched under Cela's chin.

"The spirit is the stuff of stars. It creates life. Everyone can control the spirit to a certain extent, but some special individuals have more ability than others. Evan, you are one of those individuals with this special gift." Adel spoke calmly and watched Evan frown with confusion.

"I don't understand." Evan drew his knees to his chest defensively.

"You are a *Maker*, Evan. With your spirit, you have the power to mold and create our kind. You speak directly to the rocks of the Earth herself, and they bend themselves to your will. The Earth Mother gives you her strength and power. This spirit is why Cela lives today. You gave him life, even though you may not have intended to do so. Your interest in him awoke the spirit within the stone. When you noticed him and wanted to see him, he obliged and came at your call." Adel grinned as Cela crooned and cheeped contentedly.

"How? I didn't even touch Cela. In fact, I had to coax him out of a tree after the sun had set."

"With one as small and young as Cela, your undivided attention was enough to awaken him. He has a beautiful spirit and is very protective of you. He would defend you at all costs, even against one much more powerful than himself, like me." Adel chuckled and gazed at Cela affectionately. "Makers of each of the elements are born into this world periodically. But only a Maker whose spirit is of the earth can create my kind. The Earth Maker is one of the rarest to be born."

"How can you possibly know these things?"

"Only your arrival saved my life. The humans moving me would not have been enough to draw me out of hibernation. I would have slept through my own destruction and never awoken again. But because you came, the proximity of your spirit pulled me from my hibernation to find you. You called to me." Adel smiled and leaned forward. He gently stroked Evan's cheek with the knuckles of his hand. "Another reason is this: the first time I went to sleep here, you stroked my hair until I turned to stone, but my hair remained silken in your hands instead of turning to stone like the rest of me. Only in your hands, in the hands of an Earth Maker, can any part of me be prevented from turning to stone after sunrise. Only an Earth Maker can awaken us when we should be asleep or put us to sleep when we should be awake."

Adel looked at little Cela, who'd caught Evan's eye as he considered what Adel had told him. He pictured the dragon curling up on his hand and going to sleep. Cela crooned sleepily and launched himself from Adel's shoulder. He glided with open wings into Evan's hands, curled up, and turned immediately to stone.

Evan's jaw dropped open as he looked from little Cela's sleeping stone form, which remained strangely pliable in his hands, his coloring the dull red-brown of leather, to the brilliant white and blue-black Adel, who sat across from him. "Why?" Evan trembled and stroked Cela, afraid the little dragon wouldn't revive. Cela had only ever changed with the sunrise or sunset before.

"He felt your desire for him to sleep. Even your powers are trying to awaken you to their existence. The position of the sun will never bother you again. In your presence, if you will it, we can observe the beauty of the sun in the sky. The use of these powers will be very exhausting for you, as each change draws on you and your energies to make the change in us. Telling Cela to sleep a little before sunrise would take very little energy from you. Bidding one of us to be awake at midday, when we are normally in our stone sleeping form, would be a very different matter. I would not suggest you try anything that drastic."

"I-I don't know what to say. I've never dreamed—"

Adel sighed regretfully. "The dawn approaches and I need to rest. Will you remain with me for a while?" He lay down on the blue rug as he had the previous dawn and stretched out, pillowing his head on his arm.

Evan got to his feet and covered Adel with the blanket from earlier, and Adel chuckled.

"You realize I am stone and can hardly get cold."

"I know. Go to sleep. I'll stay here." Evan smiled, amazed at his desire, his almost compulsive need, to take care of Adel. He sat back down on the rug beside Adel's head, stroking his hair as he had the day before. He watched as, before his eyes, Adel turned to a smooth, milky-white marble, all except his hair, which Evan stroked between his fingers.

Evan sat stunned, amazed by everything he'd learned, in complete awe of Adel—he was made of pale white stone, yet Evan was able to run his fingers through the silken black strands of his hair. He glanced over to the computer monitors to see the sun had risen. Evan smiled, and turned to look down on Adel. He gently ran a fingertip over his closed eyes. The silky smooth, flawless surface of the rock met his touch but radiated heat, like the stone of a fireplace hearth. Even in sleep, Adel was warm and solid, his life force thrumming beneath Evan's fingertips.

"I wish I could understand. I really don't know what to think of all this, Adel. Why can I do this? What does it mean to be a Maker?" Evan sighed, holding the silken hair in his hands. Trembling, he brought the hair to his nose and inhaled the rich, loamy scent that saturated it: freshly turned earth mixed with the air after a spring rain. Evan shook his head in confusion and frustration. "Sleep well, my friend. I'm going to take a shower, and then I'll be back."

D'ARTAGNAN RAN along the eastern fence line. His brothers were in their sectors, patrolling the dark property. He'd made this same pass about ten times this evening, both from the ground and from the air, watching for the evil that had approached their perimeter the night before. He'd eaten when he and Aramis had met at the corner of their adjoining areas and the two of them had flushed a rabbit. They'd hungrily devoured it, bones and all, leaving nothing for the scavengers.

The trees were thick here, leaving little room to maneuver. This would be a bad place to be cornered. At the same time, because of the dense cover, this would be a good place for a visitor to try to cross into their territory. Both Aramis and d'Artagnan were aware of this, carefully scanning the perimeter, seeking the evil that threatened their home.

Nothing hid the smell of evil from a gargoyle, and d'Artagnan recognized it immediately. It permeated the forest.

"Brothers, our prey awaits us here!" D'Artagnan sent a silent call. Evil hid beyond their borders. Apparently, it would attempt to come through at this location. D'Artagnan walked along the outer edge of the dense thicket. All he had to do was make his presence known and keep the evil away from his home till his brothers arrived. Then, together, as they'd planned, they would devour the evil threat.

Aramis was the first to arrive. He stood beside d'Artagnan, his lips pulled back over his teeth as he searched for unfamiliar scents in the air. He hunched his back, stretched his wings, and hissed, shaking his head from side to side. Next to arrive was Athos. With Porthos right behind him, he burst through the undergrowth.

The musketeers approached the coppice at the same time, surrounded the evil within, and pounced like a cat on a field mouse in tall grass. They flushed out two small demons. Even though they were small, they were slightly larger than the gargoyles and heavier. Their red leathery skin was stretched tight over gaunt bones. They snarled at the gargoyles, flashing grisly, sharp-pointed teeth. The demons struck out at the musketeers, and their black claws and horns glinted in the moonlight.

They attacked. Screams and growls filled the night air as claws scraped against scales and punctured leather. The demons were outmatched, as they fought independently to save their own skins while the gargoyles worked together, having the advantage of numbers. The musketeers had the demons ripped to shreds in no time and devoured the essence of the evil that had sustained them. They feasted, literally consuming the evil, leaving nothing behind to let the master of such low-rank demons know what had happened to his minions. They simply ceased to exist.

Chapter 5

FROM THE diary of Elizabeth Peterson: March 3, 2115

> *My Dearest Nicolas,*
> *Yesterday my son was born. I named him Nicolas*
> *Halvard, after you. I didn't think you'd mind. I'm one of very*
> *few females who survived the Great Death, and the Church*
> *has mandated that each female of reproductive age has a*
> *duty to her people to carry one child per year to repopulate*
> *mankind. There is no one in my life, no one in my heart*
> *besides you, and there never will be, so I allowed myself to*
> *be artificially inseminated.*
>
> *It is amazing, really. Because there are so few females,*
> *the Church has relaxed its stance on same-sex unions and is*
> *encouraging priests to marry, all while tightening its hold*
> *on the roles of females. The only way I can live outside of*
> *marriage is to join a convent, which I've done. I could never*
> *marry another after you, my love.*
>
> *The Church has stepped up and replaced the*
> *governments around the world. The priests have been there,*
> *comforting and helping out everywhere they can, so it just*
> *seemed natural when they started implementing laws and*
> *enforcing them. The world has become a very quiet place, my*
> *love. I'm sure that the hard times are far from over.*
>
> *I miss you, my love.*
> *Elizabeth*

EVAN TOOK a shower and changed his clothes. Then he grabbed a pair of clean jeans and a T-shirt from his dresser and put them on. He checked on Adel, who slept in the same position he'd been in before, of course. Stone didn't move. Evan had placed Cela's sleeping stone form on Adel's hip when he left to shower. Now he picked the little stone dragon back up and wrapped him around his throat. Cela would sleep the day away as his stone necklace.

Thinking about it, after everything Adel had told him, it did seem odd that Cela's solid stone form remained pliant in his hands, when to others like his father, Cela was just rock when he slept, immovable. It had remained a conundrum for years to Evan, and he had given up on figuring it out. But now he understood his power as a Maker was what made the stone of Cela's body malleable in his hands.

He looked down upon the large sleeping gargoyle and stroked his cheek. Adel's stone form had cooled to the touch, the heat now gone, melted into the stone of the floor, leaving no hint that life remained in the stone. Evan sighed, left the bedroom, and walked down the hall and up the stairs to his workshop.

Evan put on his apron, protective goggles, headphones, and gloves, and started up the grinder. He worked for a couple of hours, throwing chunks of old marble into the jaws, which—when the processing was complete—would turn the stone to dust. He would mix the stone dust with other components to make a marble composite he could mold and cut into slabs for a countertop or flooring. The customer for this particular job lived a several-hour drive away, but because of the complexity of installing the marble composite, Evan would make the trip to the West Coast and do the installation as well.

Customers who came to him for their stone needs were aware there were very few people who still worked with stone and knew they'd have a hefty bill at the end. The customer always paid for his trip and lodging. He always asked for half up front and the other half once delivery and the install work were complete. Even though these jobs required a long trip, there'd be time to stop at several quarries on the way to search for raw materials. None of the mines were in operation, but there could be some stone around that he might be able to scavenge. Raw materials were hard to come by since the Church had banned all forms of sculpture not commissioned or approved by them. Pursuing the sacrilegious could get you killed in an Inquisition.

After a couple of hours of mindless drudgery, Evan gave up. His heart and mind weren't in his work, and he couldn't seem to make himself stay there when Adel slept below. The beautiful gargoyle seemed to draw his soul, calling to him even while he slept. Evan had so many questions that only Adel could answer. But that wasn't what drew him to Adel's side. Wonder, amazement—those were the surface feelings Evan felt, along with an undeniable need to be ever nearer. He sighed and turned off the rock crusher. He walked outside and noticed the sun was high in the sky. It was almost noon.

Evan returned below, walked into the bedroom, and sat at Adel's head. At his touch, Adel's hair became like gossamer, and Evan found comfort and reassurance in the act of drawing his fingers through the strands. He couldn't deny his attraction to Adel.

From what he could tell, there were some significant flaws in what he'd always been taught about living stone. The way the Church described it, living stone was a type of stone like marble or quartz. But looking at his friends, he decided living stone was a state of being made of stone and simultaneously having life. Were that true, he could awaken any stone statue to life, not just those made of a specific type of stone. If he truly commanded this power, the Church would kill him if he were to be discovered. In the eyes of the Church, no one could bring life to this world but God. Yet Adel claimed Evan had brought Cela to life. He could call the spirit of life to the stone and awaken it.

Sitting there staring at Adel, he felt strange. He took Cela from around his neck and set him on the bed behind them. He rested his head on his hand and stared blankly at Adel's sleeping form. Adel lay so still, and yet Evan could feel the vibrations of life in him. Evan trembled. He suddenly felt so alone. He reached out and stroked Adel's cheek and strong brow, his heavy forehead. If he intended to continue down this path, gathering sleeping and hibernating living-stone gargoyles like Adel, Yin and Yang, the musketeers, and his Cela, he'd need help, a protector. He felt so insignificant and powerless next to the enormity of the Church.

As he gazed at Adel, his fears receded a bit. His soul began to calm. Beautiful, strong Adel. Evan had no doubt that when awake, Adel could and would protect him. Adel made him feel safe. He was enormously powerful, with sharp claws and phenomenal strength that could be deadly. Evan laid his head on the stone shoulder and continued to gaze into Adel's face as he stroked his cheek. The stone beneath his fingers began to warm, began to feel soft to the touch, very unlike stone. Adel seemed to breathe under Evan's hand.

If he could only be with me all the time. With him at my side, I'd be safe, Evan thought, but there was a definite problem inherent in having Adel by his side. Adel couldn't walk in the daylight, and although he'd said Evan had power over his form, Evan wondered if he had enough power to draw Adel into the light, as he did the hair under his fingers.

Adel's face and eyes were captivating, strong, and masculine. If Adel were human, he'd be the center of attention. Evan smiled at the thought of women fawning over Adel, and him being oblivious to their efforts.

Evan stroked a finger down Adel's cheek and jaw, before glancing over his shoulder at his wings. Adel's wings were large and leathery, like a bat's, with claws at three of the five points, and they were folded so tightly against his back, that they practically disappeared. With some careful tailoring, Evan could provide modern clothing for him, and as long as they stuck with long sleeves and long pants, the tiger stripes would be covered. He would always appear pale but not so much as to be unreal— just exotic. Evan sighed, closing his eyes, and his consciousness drifted as sleep overtook him and he lost his awareness of his surroundings to the welcoming emptiness.

Evan dreamed of feeling Adel's warmth draped securely over him. His unconscious mind told him of the impossibility, but he couldn't argue as he felt himself being gently pulled into Adel's chest by strong arms. Adel's wings wrapped about them both, and a deep, resonant purr of contentment vibrated against his back. Adel slept as stone, and stone couldn't purr, yet Evan's body told his mind he felt it.

"*Sleep, little Maker, my Evan,*" came the deep voice of Adel, more feeling than sound.

Evan's dreams centered on Adel. As his body gave in to exhaustion and he curled to spoon into Adel's chest, a final thought struck him: *If only I could see my beautiful Adel, dazzling and awake with the light of the sun glowing all around him, then I wouldn't have to be alone.*

Evan sighed blissfully into oblivion. Here he could rest, with Adel's purr removing all his worries and concerns.

THE SUN sank below the horizon, and the musketeers were on the prowl. They had been on alert since the invasion by the two demons. Yin and Yang were now on guard duty. They'd taken up positions in the bushes alongside the gates to the road, leaving the musketeers more time to watch the property boundaries. They were not going to let anything in.

"*I went to see our master. Adel stands watch over him. He still sleeps,*" Yin thought to his brother Yang, sending him a vision of Evan wrapped in blankets on his bed in Adel's arms.

"*He cannot go on sleeping. His kind do not hibernate as we do,*" Yang answered.

"*Adel says his powers are new and a bit unpredictable because he does not understand them. Adel believes he will awaken soon, that his moments of partial wakefulness are becoming more frequent.*" Yin's thoughts were colored with concern.

"*Adel sees to his care. He makes sure the Maker has water and assists him to the bathroom when Evan becomes partially lucid with need. Adel will do everything he can to take care of Evan. We must do everything we can to keep them both safe so Adel can care for Evan.*" Yang's determination and loyalty were evident.

"*It is just that it has been so long. He should not be asleep for days, and it has been five.*" Yin paced back and forth along a few feet of the fence in the darkness, his frustration getting the better of him.

"*Trust in our brother. He will take care of Evan.*"

Chapter 6

FROM THE diary of Elizabeth Peterson: September 23, 2115

> *My Dearest Nicolas,*
>
> *Nico is growing so quickly. He's going to be a strong, beautiful boy. He is the light of my life. The convent has set up a school and day care, as there are quite a few children being born. The Church has mandated that in order to preserve mankind's peaceful nature, all evidence of our violence is to be eliminated. Nobody is really sure what this mandate means for us yet.*
>
> *There are rumors that the dead cities, Salt Lake City being one, are on fire. I guess it was bound to happen eventually. Without anyone there to put the fires out, I'm guessing the entire city will burn until nature is able to take care of itself. It is odd. The number of burnings does seem to be increasing. Even here, the city library burned to the ground, the old capital building and law library, the museum and art gallery... all gone. So much knowledge and history gone up in flames. I guess it is a blessing nobody was hurt or lost their homes in the fires, but nobody lives there anymore. People don't have time for reading or the arts these days anyway. We are much more concerned with survival.*
>
> *I miss you, my love.*
>
> *Elizabeth*

EVAN DIDN'T know how long he slept, but his body demanded attention even through the listless exhaustion that claimed him. He needed to get to the bathroom, and he felt starved. Not to mention the fact that his body ached like he'd been in a bar fight. He still couldn't seem to open his eyes. They refused to obey him, even though his body screamed for him to wake up. Reaching consciousness seemed a struggle he wasn't sure he could surmount. Like walking through sucking mud, the exhaustion strove to keep him under, and he had to force himself to the forefront of his mind. He awoke slowly, realizing he lay in bed with Adel spooned against him. But Evan knew he'd fallen asleep on the floor.

"Oh, my little Maker, what did you do? I did not teach you about your power so you would go experimenting on your own. I told you that there are always consequences to you when you use your power. You were not prepared for this." Adel gently caressed Evan's face. "I know you are waking up, my little Maker. You really do need to be more careful. Your powers are dangerous to play with. You could have killed yourself for naught," Adel scolded as he continued to stroke Evan's face gently.

"Didn't do anything," Evan mumbled in a dry, scratchy voice. He struggled to wake up completely. Keeping his eyes still tightly closed, he was pleased to realize Adel was snuggled up against him.

"You really think not. I see. I wonder what you'll say when you open your eyes. My stupid, beautiful, foolish little Maker. Why, Evan? Why would you attempt to draw me into the daylight? Did you even consider how I would feel if you had died while I slept because of such a foolish endeavor?" Adel's voice seemed full of concern and frustration, but Evan couldn't remember what he'd done.

"Didn't make any changes. Just want to stay with you, always." Evan sighed, and Adel pulled him tighter into his arms, possessively.

"Come now, Evan. Time to wake up. I am hungry, so you must be hungry. Humans eat much more often than my kind, and you have been asleep for a week." Adel growled, and Evan felt sharp teeth nip at his ear, pinching the tender skin on the cartilage at the edge.

"A *week*!" Evan squeaked. He sat up suddenly, his eyes now wide open. He immediately regretted the action, as his head felt like it would explode and darkness spread across his vision with sparks of incandescent light. He trembled and his world spun dizzily, his eyes rolling back up into his head as he struggled to stay conscious.

"Oh no, you will not fall back into sleep." Adel snarled and held him in place, steadying his body, preventing him from falling back onto the bed.

Evan breathed deeply, focusing on gaining control of his wildly spinning world.

"Slowly, little Maker. Your body is not used to being unconscious for so long." Adel rubbed gently at Evan's back as he held him upright.

"I'm okay, I think. Did you say a week? I've been asleep for a week?" Evan blinked furiously, attempting to dissipate the darkness and focus on his surroundings. "Ah, damn! How many times has Father Michael been here, then? I bet he's been through every inch of the property by now, looking for me. Okay, I have got to go to the bathroom or this is not going to be a dry bed much longer." Evan weakly pushed at Adel's arm across his chest and scooted to the edge of the bed. Taking a deep breath, he forced himself to his feet. With gratitude, he realized things weren't swirling erratically about. He took a step forward and would've fallen if Adel hadn't caught him.

"Let me help you," Adel said softly, holding Evan steady, keeping him from hitting the floor. "I've done it often as you attempted to leave my side while asleep. The first time you got up, I thought you were awake, but when you didn't speak, I realized you were not truly conscious."

"I've never walked in my sleep before. I really need to get to the bathroom. I need to relieve myself, and I'm so thirsty." Evan's voice sounded gravelly, harsh from disuse.

Adel swept Evan off his feet and carried him into the bathroom with quick, sure strides.

Evan glanced at the computer monitors and did a double take, noticing the waning light of late afternoon. "Adel?" he whispered.

"Yes." Adel chuckled as Evan stared.

"What time is it? What happened?" Evan asked, putting a hand to Adel's face, completely confused.

Adel set him gently on his feet, steadying him before releasing him. "It is evening, about an hour before sunset."

"Bef—before sunset!" Evan gasped and Adel chuckled.

"Will you be all right alone? I've assisted you with this before, but you were not… yourself."

"Ah, yes." Evan flushed red with embarrassment.

Adel moved to stand right outside the bathroom. "You, my little Maker, happened to me. The last time we spoke, I told you not to experiment with your power because large changes could be dangerous for you. It seems you either refused my advice as insignificant or cared little for my opinion and worries over your welfare. Ultimately, you played with your powers and your extended sleep was the result," Adel scolded.

Evan stood leaning against the open doorframe and looked closely at Adel. Physically he didn't appear any different, but that he stood clearly awake while the sun still shone in the evening sky was change enough, and evidently it had forced Evan to sleep for a week. "I didn't mean to, Adel. I—"

"I do not know how to cook, but I will go and find you something to eat." Adel left the bathroom.

Evan watched him go. Obviously what he'd done had really pissed Adel off. Evan trembled and sat down heavily on the commode. He'd wanted Adel to be able to be with him everywhere and anytime. Was that so bad? Was it selfish to want to keep Adel with him always? Yes, obviously it was. He hadn't even asked Adel. He hadn't intended to change him. He'd assumed it would take more than just thinking about it, but evidently that wasn't the case.

When Adel returned to the bathroom, Evan stood in the shower, letting the hot water wash over his body, awakening his sleeping mind and muscles. Evan trembled, his knees buckling, refusing to hold him upright, his hands sliding on the wet tile as he fell.

Adel's strong arms slid under his and caught him before he hit the shower floor. "Do not push yourself so. You are too weak." Adel braced Evan, and Evan leaned back heavily into Adel's embrace, soaking him in the process.

"I just needed to take a shower. I feel awful and I stink," Evan complained as Adel helped him wash his body and hair.

Adel sat Evan back on the commode with a towel so he could dry himself off, and then grabbed a towel for himself. Then Adel carried Evan back into the bedroom. Under Evan's direction, Adel grabbed shorts, underwear, and a T-shirt for him from the dresser, and Evan dressed. By the time he finished the simple chore, exhaustion threatened to put him back to sleep.

"I remembered how to make coffee. It is brewing and should be done by now." Adel picked him up, carried him out to the kitchen, and sat him in a chair.

"All I want to do is sleep. Can't I sleep for just a little while? You can wake me after a nap." Evan laid his head on his arms on the counter, unable to do more.

Adel took an apple from a nearby bowl and placed it in Evan's hand. "Eat that and tell me what to do. You really need to eat something more than fruit, and I have limited knowledge about human food." Adel awaited Evan's directions impatiently.

Evan reluctantly bit into the apple. It seemed too much work until the juices from the fruit hit his taste buds and filled his mouth. He devoured the apple voraciously as he directed Adel to take steaks from the freezer and thaw them in the microwave, then to take potatoes from the bin.

"Adel, what exactly did I do? I mean, all I remember was sitting on the rug next to you."

"You tried to go against the natural order of my kind. Just as it is normal for you to breathe air and not water, my species must remain stone in the daytime and flesh and blood at night. You attempted to circumvent the constant my species lives by. While it is within your power to do so, it takes incredible amounts of energy to compel that change." Adel sighed, but he cleaned the potatoes and pierced the skin, setting them aside as they waited for the steaks to finish thawing.

"How could I have attempted to do anything? I don't remember anything but going to sleep?"

The microwave dinged and Adel took the thawed steaks out and put the potatoes in the microwave to bake. "You must have done, said, or thought about something before you went to sleep."

"I just thought it would be nice if you could be with me always, day or night. That it'd be your choice when you slept and turned to stone, not the determination of whether the sun was in the sky or not. I'm sorry, Adel. I didn't mean to do anything. I didn't know that just thinking about something could start something like this. It just kind of happened."

"Your goals are admirable, Maker, but dangerous. You are very lucky. Your own self-preservation must have kicked in, because you have drained yourself in the effort to change me. From what I have experienced, you have gained me about an hour after dawn that I am able to be awake, and an hour before sunset."

"Two hours, and I slept for a week." Evan sat, dumbfounded at the revelation.

Adel poured the coffee and added milk and sugar to the brew before handing the cup to Evan. "What should I do next?"

"Put the steaks under the broiler," Evan instructed. "Did Father Michael visit while I slept?" He shook his head with disbelief at how long he'd been out.

"Yes. I watched him on the computer. He looked around the yard and shop a lot and forced his way into the house, but he did not disturb anything. After hollering and cursing a great deal, he left. I am quite sure he will return."

"Father Michael is nothing but trouble. You need to be very careful when he's around. He's very bad news." Evan sighed. Exhaustion threatened to overtake him again as he rested his elbows on the counter and propped his head on his hands.

Adel turned and looked at Evan, frowning slightly. "Bad news? I would not expect that his visit would be good news to you."

Evan chuckled. "No, I mean that he's a bad man and he'll try and hurt and destroy you, should he realize you aren't human. You need to be careful around him. We need to think about getting you some clothes, see if something of mine might fit you."

"Why should I wear clothes?" Adel frowned in apparent disgust.

"Because people wear clothes, and with clothes on, you will look human. It's just a precaution." *A shame to cover him up, but I can't take the chance that he could be seen if someone were to breach my security early in the morning and Adel was outside.* Evan didn't give voice to his concerns.

"Clothes…. I suppose I could get used to wearing such things as long as they do not restrict my movement. I cannot properly protect you if I am unable to get free of the bindings you wrap me in."

Adel took the steaks out of the broiler and potatoes from the microwave, then dished up plates for both of them. The smell of hot food before him roused Evan. He dug in hungrily and succeeded in wolfing down about half the steak and a good portion of his potato before his stomach refused to hold any more. He felt bloated, having overindulged, but at the same time, he felt sated and he belched loudly. He covered his face with his hands, giggling absurdly as his mind began to shut down, exhaustion from his ordeal overriding his senses and making him feel slightly light-headed. Evan gazed in admiration at Adel, feeling so positive nothing could ruin his sense of euphoria.

"Adel, did I really do this to you just by touching you and imagining you with me all the time? How can I control something like this, if I can make changes without realizing I'm doing anything?" Evan shook his head in awe.

"Yes, you wrought the change. With your control over stone, when we sleep, your will becomes reality. Your desires change us into whatever you want and need. Those changes take energy to create. Your power draws on your energy to accomplish them. The larger the changes, the more energy required to accomplish them," Adel said between mouthfuls.

Evan enjoyed watching Adel eat. He truly enjoyed the food, devouring his steak and potatoes. "You can have what's left of mine if you want." He pushed his plate toward Adel, who snatched what remained of the steak and then the leftover potatoes. "Are you still hungry?" Evan asked.

"Well, I could eat more. But you're full, and I should not eat all your food." Adel hung his head a bit sheepishly. "It is kind that you are sharing your food at all. You do not have to, you know. I am capable of getting my own meat."

"I don't mind. It's nice to share a meal. How about this? Take whatever you want. I'm assuming you mostly eat meat." Evan smiled as Adel nodded slowly. "Then however many steaks you want. Prepare them, cook them under the broiler, and enjoy them. Later, you can hunt and bring the carcass into the shop. We'll prepare the meat together and freeze the extra. We'll have enough to satisfy us both." Evan smiled as Adel turned to the freezer and grabbed a couple more packages of steaks, unwrapped them, and placed them directly under the broiler.

Adel's pleasure in the smell of the searing meat that filled the kitchen was obvious from the smile on his face. Evan smiled as well, knowing that with the steaks going straight from the freezer to the broiler, the centers would probably be cold and rare when the outsides were done, but he suspected Adel would enjoy the meat that way. Adel pulled the barely browned meat from the broiler and ate his fill. The leftovers from the small feast he'd prepared went into the refrigerator for later.

BY THE time Adel finished eating, Evan had dozed off, his head pillowed on his arms on the counter. A gentle snore escaped his lips when he exhaled. Cela had flown in and sat on the counter, looking at Evan with his head tipped to the side, then whistled up at Adel.

"Our Maker has exhausted himself, but he should be all right come morning, Cela." Adel picked Evan up and carried him back to the bed he'd been sleeping in for the past week. "It is amazing what he wrought, but a miracle he did not kill himself in the process." Adel gazed at Cela, who chattered and whistled in response. "No, I am not surprised. If the Church is so zealous, they are destroying our kind without considering the consequences. I am sure they would destroy him as well if they were to discover him." Adel took hold of the blanket and covered Evan. "I have often awoken from hibernation on my own. I've been called to awaken by a Maker very rarely. In all that time, I have never felt a Maker as powerful as you, not in my entire existence."

As Adel moved off the bed, Evan squirmed in his sleep, restless without Adel's touch. "Adel... don't? Adel... where?" Evan mumbled, frowning until Adel lay down at his side.

"Shhh. I am here. I guess I am not going hunting tonight, my young Maker." Adel lay next to Evan, who immediately slipped into a deeper sleep. Adel stroked the hair away from Evan's face, and Evan snuggled closer. With a conciliatory sigh at the thought of his missed hunting, Adel pulled Evan against him.

It was no hardship to spend time curled next to Evan, and the deep resonance of a contented purr vibrated through Adel's chest. Evan's closeness drew such warm feelings from the depths of his being, the likes of which Adel hadn't experienced in a very long time—centuries, in fact. He felt protective and possessive of Evan. Having him snuggled against his stomach, wrapped in his arms, gave rise to passions previously unknown to him. Adel nuzzled Evan's hair as he would a mate.

Yes, he could accept Evan. Adel closed his eyes and drank in Evan's scent, imprinting it into his memory. *Yes, mate.* His Maker belonged to him: scent never lied. He'd tried to deny the bond he felt growing, but now Evan was exhibiting signs of the bond as well. Evan didn't like it when he was left alone to sleep and seemed to like touching Adel, who sighed softly.

I will be gentle with you, my fragile little mate.

"*OUR MAKER is sleeping*," hissed Aramis as he stared out into the night, seeking their enemy.

"*Adel says he made changes and didn't prepare for the energy drain.*" D'Artagnan's eyes sparkled reflectively in the darkness as he stepped up beside Aramis, rubbing his body against his brother in greeting.

"*The Maker doesn't understand what he is or what he can do.*" Porthos landed silently alongside his brothers, tucking his wings along his body.

"*Adel says he is vulnerable right now, and we are needed. We have to guard and protect him.*" Athos strutted out from the underbrush and nuzzled Porthos before moving to greet Aramis and d'Artagnan in the same fashion.

"*The evil comes nightly, drawn by the power of the Maker. The more power he exhibits, the more the evil will be drawn to him. During the day, the light keeps the evil in the shadows.*" D'Artagnan snarled.

"*At night we hunt. We fight. We feed.*" Aramis hissed, excitement coloring his declaration as the brothers ran through the clearing and took flight out into the night, seeking out their encroaching prey.

The musketeers ranged around the edge of the property while Yin and Yang stood guard at the doors. When the alarm sounded, the lion-dogs would guard the house and the dragons would dispatch the evil demons. They were still lucky. The evil spawn that came nightly remained small, low-level demons, not one of the larger monsters that lurked in the depths of Hell. The wielder of evil who attempted to hurt Evan must have sensed the power of the Maker radiating from him but underestimated the protection that surrounded him.

Once the evil realized the spawn he sent out had continued to fail, larger demons would come. Until then, the gargoyles absorbed the evil, destroying and using its energy to grow and strengthen themselves. Still, the spawn didn't have all that much power, as they were meant to only last one night and fade with the dawn. These little scouts were just cannon fodder to the evil who sought to harm Evan. And so, not a single one of these pesky, malicious fiends would return to its master to report on their whereabouts or the strength of their Maker. Evan's charges would not fail him.

Chapter 7

GARGOYLE LORE

As written by the scribes and entombed in the Church Archives:

Mating:

1. Gargoyles live a long, immortal life and strive to find a mate to share their immortality. Gargoyles know their fated mates often on first sight or by scent.
2. Gargoyles' devotion to the safety of their mate is overwhelming. A gargoyle who loses a mate will perish of a broken heart, often going into hibernation and never reawakening.

EVAN WOKE feeling better than he had in a long time. As he opened his eyes, he felt fully rested and relaxed. He sighed contentedly, relishing the presence of a solid rock form fitted along his back. Adel felt hot, like the granite used to ring a campfire when it retained the warmth of the flames. Adel's form must be retaining the heat of his body from when he'd been awake. Evan had discovered that sleeping next to Adel was better than sleeping with an electric blanket. His temperature when he was flesh and blood ran warmer than Evan's by a few degrees. Being wrapped in Adel's arms and engulfed by that heat felt wonderful. Evan knew Adel had lain with him through the night, and a glance at the clock proved he'd been there for most of the day as well.

Thoughts of Adel's hot body soon had Evan's semihard erection throbbing with his heartbeat. He could just imagine Adel wrapping one hand around his shaft while he cupped Evan's ass with the other. A shiver of excitement passed through his body. He bit down on his bottom lip, trying to stifle the moan as he took his cock in hand and thumped the head sharply, trying to get himself under control.

Evan hissed as the sharp pain helped to deflate his hard-on. He was not going to jack off in bed with Adel's stone body curled around him. He just didn't feel right about it. No matter how good it was being curled against Adel, masturbating while the rock-hard body at his back couldn't participate in the fun just seemed wrong.

Evan got to his feet, stretching and yawning as he went to the bathroom. He had a couple of hours until Adel awoke. He wanted to shower, maybe jack off, and then make a meal for the two of them. He was starved. If Adel had been lying by his side the entire time, then he had to be just as hungry.

Evan let hot water run down his body. It felt wonderful. He could just imagine Adel following the trails of water with his hands. The image had him leaning heavily against the shower wall; he ran one hand over his chest and flicked a nipple while he fisted the cap of his cock with his other hand.

"Adel," Evan mumbled as he stroked his erection from the base to the top, giving it a twist and then running a fingernail against the slit. He squeezed his rod tight, groaning with pleasure. He imagined Adel pressed against his back. Evan panted as he leaned his forehead against the tiled wall. He was so close. He spread his legs and ran a hand over his ass until he pressed his fingers against his hole, and a wanton moan escaped his lips. A couple of tight, hard pulls in time with the fingers sunk into his ass, and Evan screamed his release, shooting a stream of white against the shower wall that mixed with the water and disappeared down the drain. Evan trembled and let the water run over him as he pulled himself together. He finished washing quickly, before he ran out of hot water.

Evan had to admit the shower left him feeling much more like himself. He truly felt good when he returned to his bedroom to dress. Adel lay still as stone in his bed. Never had the phrase "slept like a rock" been more appropriate. Evan checked: the stone had cooled to the touch.

Adel's flawless resplendence amazed Evan. He continued to be stunned by it daily. Adel was, without a doubt, the most glorious creature Evan had ever seen. He was more—more male, more sexy, more magnificent—just *more*. Lying in his bed, Adel's sleeping form resembled a statue of perfection personified. He appeared as a man, draped in his wings, his claws retracted and all but invisible. He was more perfect than Michelangelo's *David*. Adel simply captured Evan's heart.

Evan had come to realize he cared very deeply for Adel, and those feelings were growing steadily. It wasn't just that Adel would protect him, because he felt just as protective of Adel. He seemed incalculably wise but incredibly innocent and pure at the same time, a steady force to be relied upon. His strength was not just physical, but of character and honor, all of which called to Evan. He caressed the stone and impulsively leaned down and kissed Adel's cheek.

Then he turned to his dresser and dug through it, looking for something that might fit Adel. He pulled out a black, long-sleeved T-shirt, then went in search of the jeans his mother had sent him last year. They'd been much too big for him, but should fit Adel well enough. He laid the clothes at the end of the bed and gazed down at Adel. "The clothes are for you," Evan said as he moved back to Adel's side. "Sleep well." He ran his hand over the cool, carved hair, which instantly became soft and silken at his touch. He smiled, petting the black gossamer strands, and chuckled to himself, amazed at this simple proof of his power over this living stone.

He sighed, giving himself a shake. This was bad. He'd have to be so careful. He knew without a doubt that falling for Adel would be very painful and no doubt unrequited.

Evan went to his kitchen, pulled two chickens from the freezer, and thawed them in the microwave. He cleaned potatoes, carrots, and celery. Then he placed the chickens into a large roaster and scattered the vegetables around them. He added spices and broth before putting the glass cover on the roaster and hefting it into the oven. In a couple of hours, once Adel awoke, a meal would be waiting for him. By then the kitchen would be filled with the warm, wonderful scent of the roasting chickens.

Evan smiled and went up to the main house. The afternoon sunlight felt good against his skin. He went out to the backyard and his vegetable garden, which desperately needed a good weeding and watering. He gathered the hoe and garden hose he'd need from the garden shed. He went back out to the garden and earnestly hoed the weeds threatening his tender young plants. His country life had few benefits, but his garden qualified as a perk. He had a way with plants; they seemed to thrive under his care. He would often gather the seeds in the fall, on his many trips about the country, and dry them for planting in the spring. The results were often promising. Fresh vegetables, which were expensive and sometimes difficult to get, added much-needed nutrients to his diet. After the war, food, water, and fuel had been hard to come by until the Church took control of the government, but even now, the more self-sufficient you were, the better.

He worked in the garden for about an hour. If Adel was right, he should be awakening soon, as there was about an hour or so before the sun would set, leaving his little valley in the half-light of the evening twilight.

Evan decided to start putting away his tools and to return below. He wanted to be there when Adel awoke.

He jumped slightly, feeling the remote in his jeans pocket vibrate. Someone had passed through his gate and was coming up the drive. Evan continued to work, pretending to be unaware. He pulled weeds from around the cucumbers, carefully looking over the blossoms that would sprout vegetables before long, tenderly caring for the resilient plants.

A car from the Bishop's Service parked in his driveway, and Evan stood. He recognized the car and knew Father Michael had come to pay him a visit. *Oh goody*, Evan thought sarcastically. He plastered a welcoming smile on his face, even though all he wanted to do was get this man away from Adel. Father Michael made his skin crawl.

Father Michael got out of the car, his usual black robes billowing around him, and strode up the drive and across the yard toward the garden and Evan.

Evan's smile stayed serenely plastered across his face, and he walked toward Father Michael, meeting him partway between the garden and the cabin. "Father! So good to see you. How have you been? I've missed you." Evan braced himself against his repulsion. He embraced Father Michael warmly and felt those skeletally thin arms wrap about him. He imagined being embraced by Death would feel similar to being hugged by Father Michael. He couldn't imagine how he remained alive, but the father seemed even skinnier than before. It felt like he was literally bones covered by skin.

"Evan. Where have you been? I've been so worried about you." Father Michael's sickly sweet voice turned Evan's stomach almost as much as having his hand caress his hair.

"My mother called. She's been feeling ill, so I went to see her and some of my cousins. It's a very long way, and a cousin from up north picked me up on his way home. He brought me back yesterday," Evan lied. He'd been lying to Father Michael for quite a few years now, and knew just how to bat his eyes and smile to keep the man off balance and unsuspecting.

"You really should let me know when you're going to be gone. With you living all by yourself out here, I feared something had happened to you when I couldn't find you and the vehicles were in the shop. We haven't captured the creature that broke free from us. You really had me worried. I felt sure something awful had happened," Father Michael whined.

Evan felt a tingling sensation at the base of his spine. It spread throughout his body, and he realized he'd just felt Adel awaken. Father Michael still held him, and somehow Evan knew Adel wouldn't be happy about Father Michael touching him. Evan moved away from him, heading in the direction of the cabin and Adel. He could feel Adel coming, and his body responded by moving toward Adel and away from Father Michael.

"Really, Father, you worry too much. I'm perfectly safe here. There's nothing in these woods that would harm me." Evan smiled as Adel came walking out of the cabin, having retracted his wings completely and tucked them beneath the loose, long-sleeved T-shirt. The jeans Evan had left him had been baggy on him, but on Adel they were very tight fitting, and the transformation from gargoyle to human was practically flawless. Adel had his arm outstretched, beckoning to Evan. It filled Evan's heart with desire, and he wanted to squeal with delight and run into Adel's waiting, protective arms. But he knew he couldn't reveal his feelings to Father Michael. The priest would undoubtedly use them to manipulate Evan if he knew.

"Ah, Father, I've someone I want you to meet. This is Adelstan Noble. Adel, this is Father Michael of the Bishop's Service. He's the Church constable in this diocese." Evan took Adel's hand and found himself pulled snugly, possessively, against the gargoyle's side. A shiver went through Evan's body at the solid mass of muscle that pressed against him.

Adel frowned slightly at Evan and then looked at Father Michael, who glared menacingly at Adel.

Evan could feel the rumbling of a growl deep in Adel's chest. As the two stared each other down, Evan felt like a human chew toy being possessively claimed by two alpha males, but he only wanted—only belonged—to Adel.

"Father," Adel said, holding out his hand in greeting, and Evan sighed, relieved to see his claws sheathed, but he could just see the point of a fang peeking out.

"Mr. Noble," Father Michael hissed, taking Adel's hand and wincing slightly at the strength in Adel's grip.

Evan watched Adel smile a bit vindictively as he realized how much stronger he was than Father Michael.

"You need not worry about Evan being alone any longer. I will be here for him from now on. I will keep him safe." Though Adel smiled, his voice was just this side of a warning snarl.

"I see. And just *who* are you?" Father Michael pressed. Clearly he felt Evan belonged to him and he wanted Adel gone, quickly.

"Adel is family. My cousin. My aunt and mother didn't like me living here alone either, and since there's more than enough work, I've taken Adel on as my apprentice." Evan tried not to grin too widely; there was no way for Father Michael to object to family moving in with him.

"He's your cousin." Father Michael frowned, watching Adel stand between him and Evan, having pulled Evan behind him slightly.

"Yes. Adel and I used to play together as children. He's been looking for work, and when I found out he had an interest in stonework, I asked him to join me. I'm really glad too. I like having family around. I won't be alone anymore." Evan struggled to keep from laughing at the anger and frustration on Father Michael's face. Adel's presence effectively put a stop to his nefarious sexual advances.

"It is good to have family around. So where will you be living, Adel? In town?" Father Michael asked, unable to keep the hope from his voice.

"I will live here... with Evan, of course. This place is plenty large enough for the both of us." Adel looked at Evan and winked. He understood the game Father Michael was playing. The father couldn't confront him directly because Adel claimed to be family, but as an agent of the Church and a member of the Bishop's Service, he could make some inquiries and press them for private details of their living arrangement.

"Father, Adel was going to join me in the garden. We have a little time left today before the daylight leaves us entirely, and the weeds have overrun the plants. There is plenty of work to do. I'm sure I could find a hoe for you as well, if you care to join us." Evan looked back toward the garden, knowing full well Father Michael would be too busy. In all the years Evan had known him, Father Michael had never once done any physical labor, much less broken a sweat. "You've always said to never put off until tomorrow what can be accomplished today with God's grace."

"No, Evan, I've no time today. I was just concerned for your welfare and wanted to check up on you. Now that I know you're well, I must get back to work. I'll stop by another time."

"I'm sorry for worrying you, Father. I'm sure it's a relief to know I'm no longer living alone." Evan poked at him, knowing he played with fire. It was a dangerous game, but he couldn't stop himself.

The priest held a great deal of power in the Bishop's Service, and if he were to discover who or what Adel was, they would come after him while he slept and would not stop hunting him until both Adel and himself were dead. Adel might be incredibly strong when awake, but he was just flesh and blood. He could die just as much as any other living being. Immortality was no guarantee of a long life. But for the moment, Father Michael's anger prevented him from seeing what was in front of him.

"You be safe, Evan. Adel," Father Michael said. Then, frowning, he headed back to his car.

Evan felt the tingle at the base of his spine alerting him to the awakening of the rest of his family as the last rays of the sun disappeared over the horizon and twilight reigned.

"I will make sure of that," Adel stated coolly, causing Father Michael to pause and look back briefly, then get into his car and drive away.

There was still enough light to work by, so Evan and Adel turned to the garden and weeded until the remote in Evan's pocket buzzed. The gate had opened once again. Adel stood when Yang appeared. The lion-dog barked and seemed to stare at Adel momentarily, then disappeared again into the twilight.

"Yang says Father Michael parked up on top of the hill and watched us for a while, but has left the property," Adel said.

"You can talk to them?"

"Mainly to Cela, Yin, and Yang. Our conversations are passed mind to mind, more so than with sounds, although sometimes sounds do express urgency or aggression along with the thoughts." Adel smiled as Cela landed on Evan's shoulder and curled himself around Evan's neck. "The musketeers are different, though. I know they talk to one another, but I can barely understand them, and I do not believe it is because of their age. They are older than they appear." Adel moved to Evan and enfolded him protectively into his arms. "I believe the four may have come from one stone carving. They are actually more like four parts of one whole being, and as such, function with a more hive-like mind. They understand me and all of us clearly enough, but I am not able to communicate as they do. I mainly receive emotions more than actual words from them." Adel reached out and gently stroked Cela's head.

"Wow, I never would have thought that. I figured they couldn't have been much older than Cela, as they aren't much bigger than he is." Evan rested his head back against Adel's chest.

"I envy you, little brother," Adel said softly.

Cela crooned, pushing into Adel's touch, then nuzzled Evan before unwrapping himself and leaping into the night sky.

"Where is he going?" Evan watched with rapt attention as Adel stripped the baggy T-shirt off over his head. He stretched the bat-like wings, which had been practically invisible, fully displaying them for Evan. Ligaments and tendons snapped as the finely boned, highly muscular structures—vaguely resembling enormous hands—opened, each finger making up a bone in the wing skeleton supports, with black membranes extending between them.

Adel dropped the T-shirt in the grass. "He is going hunting and giving us some privacy." Adel picked Evan up, cradling him in his arms, and launched himself into the sky.

"Hey!" Evan squeaked, startled, as he clung to Adel's neck.

Adel chuckled and pulled him closer to his chest. His enormous wings beat out a steady, strong rhythm, soaring over the trees and carrying them into the night. "I would never drop you. You are safe," Adel rumbled with amusement.

"I know. You just surprised me." Evan flushed with embarrassment.

"I was very upset and more than a little annoyed when I awoke and you were not at my side. You have been so weak, I worried something might have happened to you. Then I felt your presence out here and I saw him on the computer screen. He held you as if you belonged to him. I became quite angry."

"I'm sorry, Adel. I don't like it when he touches me, but I have to keep him happy. He's a very dangerous man."

"No one should touch you except me. You're mine, little Maker," Adel snarled, and Evan felt him tremble. Adel's wave of protectiveness and possessiveness passed through his own body.

"I'm so sorry. I felt you awaken. I felt a tingling go through my body and knew you were waking up early. I sensed you weren't happy, and that you were coming." Evan rested his head against Adel's chest as he landed lightly on the top of a grassy hill overlooking the homestead. They had a beautiful, unobstructed view of the star-filled night sky. "I'm so glad you were here."

"Evan, my little Maker, you are not understanding what I am trying to tell you." Adel sat in the soft grass and pulled Evan onto his lap, draping his arms around him. His large wings surrounded them both, keeping out the chill of the night like a cloak.

"I understand, Adel. You worry about me and care for me. I'm a Maker and you've been looking for a Maker, so you're protective of me. I'm very grateful and happy you are." Evan put a hand on one of the strong arms wrapped around him as he struggled to control his emotions. His feelings for Adel were becoming stronger with each bit of care and protectiveness Adel showed him.

"Yes, that may be part of it, but not all. My kind live a very long time, and we come in a variety of shapes, types of beings, and genders. We search for our mate all of our lives, and then, once found, never leave their side."

"And you want to search for your mate now?" Evan hated the idea that Adel might want someone else, that he might want to leave. There was no denying that he wanted Adel and that he didn't care Adel was a gargoyle. He wanted this beautiful being to belong to him. He wanted so badly to touch, stroke, lick, and taste every inch of Adel's beautiful white skin, to feel his strong muscles move beneath him, to enjoy the body of the one who made him feel so safe and protected. If only Adel could really care about him for himself, and not just as a Maker. He would gladly lose his heart to him and be happy with whatever he could give him in return.

"We search for and protect the Makers because they have the power of creation, and our mate may be born at their hands." Adel purred softly and pulled Evan closer to him, snuggling Evan into his chest.

"You want me to try to create a mate for you," Evan said, a heavy sadness landing on his heart. His body betrayed his emotions, trembling as he fought the depression threatening to overwhelm him. He needed to get ahold of himself, to get away from Adel, but Adel refused to let him budge.

"No, I do not need you to create a mate for me, my little Maker." Adel rubbed his face against Evan's hair. "I heard you speak to me before I awoke… felt your kiss when you got up this morning. Before… I did not know your feelings or my own, so I held back. I have felt very possessive of you from the very beginning. Now I am sure. I know why. You are my mate, Evan, and my little Maker. I will be with you for the rest of our lives. For me, there is no other but you—if you will have me?" Adel rained kisses on Evan's hair.

"I'm your mate? But I'm a man. I'm not a gargoyle. And I'm… male," Evan stammered, incredulous, as he tightly gripped the arms that held him.

His heartbeat picked up and pounded as Adel declared himself. Evan feared Adel might be mistaken in what he said, but prayed he wasn't and hoped Adel truly wanted him.

"It does not matter. My kind can hardly say we are all one type of being. Often we are a chimera of creatures and genders. Our hearts know our chosen, our mate, from the moment we are born. You are mine. I cannot bear to have you away from me. The only time I am at peace is when you are safely in my arms." Adel's rumbling continued to get stronger as he kissed Evan's neck and nibbled his ear. "It doesn't matter that you are a man. You are mine."

Evan felt the vibration throughout Adel's body, and it sent shivers of joy through him. Each touch and caress seemed connected directly to his engorging cock. "Adel, I don't know what…." Evan groaned as Adel grazed the skin of his neck with his teeth and began to explore Evan's body with his hands.

"Evan, we mate for life. I want to… I need to mark you, love you… make you mine. You will be mine for all of our lives, and I will be yours. Will you let me claim you, Evan?" Adel's breath, a hot whisper filled with need and desire, caressed Evan's ear.

Evan had never thought—never dreamed—his love would be returned, that Adel would want him, care about him. He couldn't understand how this beautiful, majestic creature could find him desirable in comparison to his own perfection. But in that moment, Evan didn't care. His feelings for Adel were overwhelming. He prayed Adel was right. He couldn't believe Adel would want him, but he wasn't about to turn him away.

"Adel, from the moment I first saw you, I thought you were magnificent. I wanted to protect you. I've always wanted you to be mine, Adel." Evan reached up and laid a hand on Adel's jawline.

Adel loosened his hold slightly so Evan could turn around in his grasp. Evan knelt in the grass between Adel's legs and wrapped his arms around Adel's elegant neck, knotting his fingers in Adel's hair. Adel grasped Evan and pulled him against his chest so tightly, Evan almost had to struggle for breath. Adel seemed to want to absorb Evan, draw him into his own body, make the two of them one. He stared into Evan's eyes, and Evan's heart stopped. In this moment, for him, there was only Adel. Adel lowered his head to Evan's. Their lips met in an infinitely gentle caress.

The soft, silken touch sent heat flooding through Evan's body, centering on his groin. The tender, light-as-air touch slowly increased in pressure as Adel nibbled at Evan's lips, sending sensations coursing through his body. Evan panted as they broke apart, his desire increasing with each glide of Adel's hands across his skin. Evan arched his body into Adel's, needing to be closer.

"Evan," Adel whispered, stroking his back. The tips of his razor-sharp claws grazed lightly over Evan's skin, sending shockwaves of pleasure through his body. Adel's denim-encased rod pressed against his thigh, while his own rock-hard erection tightened uncomfortably against the restriction of his zipper. Waves of heat and need washed over them, radiating out from Adel and enveloping Evan in a cocoon of desire.

"Evan, I need you. I want you. Will you give yourself to me?" Adel's voice trembled, becoming gravelly with desire as he pulled at Evan's cotton T-shirt.

"I'm yours, Adel," Evan whispered as he felt the T-shirt shred beneath Adel's claws, followed by his jeans and the jeans Adel had worn. The soft silk of Adel's skin caressed Evan's body, sending ticklish sensations washing over him as he stretched his body out against Adel's, their hard cocks pressed between them. As Evan moved to reach for Adel, his cock was caressed by the thick white peach-fuzz fur covering Adel's tight abdominal muscles. Evan gasped at the feeling of the silky fur stroking his cock.

"Evan, my heart—" Adel moaned. He latched on to Evan's open, gasping mouth and sank his tongue deeply inside. His hot breath filled Evan's mouth as he invaded Evan with his tongue. The intense heat and need scattered Evan's thoughts and stoked the flames of his desire. Their tongues met, caressing, tasting. Adel drew Evan's tongue back into the inferno of heat within Adel's mouth, where he held it and sucked it with great care. Adel greedily explored Evan's body, stroking his skin. Sharp claws glided lightly across his shoulders and chest. Adel brushed against Evan's nipples, causing him to groan with pleasure in a voice Evan barely recognized as his own. Adel groaned his pleasure in response.

Forcing his gaze to follow Adel's fingers across his skin, Evan saw the thin red lines left by Adel's claws. They barely qualified as scratches, but the idea of being marked by Adel sent Evan's desire skyrocketing so quickly, he almost lost control.

Adel circled Evan's reddening areolae and flicked the hardening nipples.

Evan gasped at the sensations flowing through his body. His engorged cock throbbed with each beat of his heart and a bead of precome seeped from the tip.

Adel pushed Evan to the grass, kissing him deeply. "Lie still for me, my heart." Adel growled and moved slowly down over Evan's body until he hovered over Evan's feet. Adel drew his lips back, exposing his fangs, and his claws retracted from razor-sharp pinpoints to slightly shorter talons extending from his hands and feet, tearing at the ground as he rocked back and forth, from side to side. His wings raised over him, extended fully over his back, revealing Adel in all his glory.

Evan suspected he should be terrified of the sight before him, but he sensed the importance of this display of primal alpha male magnificence. He watched in awe as Adel displayed his strength and ability to defend his mate, to protect him, and his obvious willingness to fight for him. The wild power of Adel overwhelmed him. Any vestiges of fear of the more feral side of Adel had long ago fallen away, if ever they had existed. Adel personified a force of nature, an untamed beauty. He was as solid as the earth, and yet just as volatile and wild, and he wanted Evan. Evan's heart couldn't contain the simple joy of just knowing Adel wanted him.

Adel lingered at Evan's feet, wings now tucked tightly against his back, claws retracted to mere pinpricks of their deadly potential. Staring intently at Evan, he licked, nibbled, and stroked every inch of Evan's skin, his teeth and claws caressing it, leaving him panting breathlessly and wanting more. Adel moved slowly from Evan's feet, from his calves to his thighs, first up one leg, then back down to ease up the other side, until he lingered over Evan's groin. He avoided Evan's steel-hard cock, not touching his erection, but paused, breathing hard and inhaling deeply, lips drawn back even farther from his fangs. Adel pushed his face into the tight curls of Evan's pubic hair, and Evan gasped and groaned. Adel laved his ball sac, and first one ball, then the other, was warmed by Adel's breath before being suckled.

"Mine…. Evan. You are so beautiful." Adel hissed, then licked his way up Evan's body, outlining each muscle on his abs with his tongue before dipping into his belly button. Evan's skin shone with the combination of sweat and saliva in the growing moonlight of the clear night sky, as Adel continued to claim his body. "You taste so good. *You* are mine."

"Adel, Oh God! Ah… mnn—" Evan screamed as Adel latched on to a nipple, drawing it forward while he teased the nub with his tongue. Evan cried out, arching his back toward Adel, bucking his hips up against Adel's stomach. His needy, outstretched member left a damp trail of precome.

Adel growled as Evan laced his fingers in his hair, clenching his hands and tugging as he whimpered with need. "Evan," Adel rumbled as he tasted every inch of skin on Evan's body and then returned to the curve of his neck, suckling along his collarbone.

Evan arched back, his head tipping instinctively to the side to bare his neck submissively to Adel, who kissed the exposed jugular before nibbling on his ear. "Adel… so hot… I need you. I c-can't take much more," Evan stuttered as he dug his fingernails deeply into Adel's shoulders. The ache in his groin became unbearable. He needed to have Adel inside him, to feel the hot rod that was Adel brand him from the inside as his tongue had on the outside.

Adel snarled softly as he turned Evan onto his stomach and drew his hips into the air. With his claws retracted, Adel ran his fingers down Evan's spine, outlining his backbone, ending at the top of the valley between Evan's ass cheeks. Adel followed the separation down to Evan's hole. He trailed his fingers farther, caressing the skin between Evan's sphincter and balls. Adel spread Evan's cheeks and kissed his hole, darting his tongue around the edge of the clenched muscle in ever-widening circles. He left a sloppy, wet trail across Evan's skin, only to repeat the circles, moving back in toward Evan's waiting ass. As the muscles relaxed, Adel dove his tongue into Evan and then retreated, coaxing him farther open, pushing saliva into Evan with each thrust of his tongue. Adel set a slow rhythm as he fucked Evan with his long, firm tongue, sucking gently as he felt Evan quiver beneath him.

Saliva ran from his entrance, down across his skin, to drip from his balls. "Adel, please!" Evan begged, reaching for his own painfully hard cock, needing release.

Adel knocked his hand away, replacing it with the tips of Adel's claws, grazing lightly along the shaft, touching but not touching. Evan screamed as the air-light touch was replaced by Adel locking his hand tightly around the base of his cock, preventing him from coming, while he slid a finger past Evan's clenching sphincter into his depths. Adel stroked the sides of Evan's walls, working the muscles, massaging, spreading him until he could sink in two fingers, and then three. He drew Evan open with each stroke, seeking out and finding Evan's prostate.

Evan arched his back and screamed his pleasure. A continuous, mindless rant of begging and moans poured from between his lips, encouraging Adel as he pleaded for more. The heady scent of cut grass and fresh earth surrounded them as Evan keened, rocking his head from side to side, fisting his hands in the grass, ripping out clumps as his desire overwhelmed him and he sought release. Evan panted, lost in the sensation of Adel stroking his body. He couldn't get enough; delicious as they felt, the hot fingers stroking him weren't enough to satisfy his needs. "More! Adel—" Evan moaned.

Adel answered his pleas with a rumble combined with a chuffing sound Evan could only associate with amusement. Adel sank his fingers again and again into Evan's depths, each time unerringly stroking the little gland, until, in his need, Evan wantonly thrust his hips against Adel's fingers.

"My heart—" Adel took hold of Evan's hips.

Evan felt Adel rise over his back, heard him spit repeatedly, and then the blunt head of Adel's cock rubbed against his opening. Evan reached back to caress Adel's engorged member and began to panic. Adel was huge, much larger than Evan remembered him being from the cemetery. Adel was more than he had ever taken. "Adel, I can't! It won't—" Evan pleaded, his body trembling.

"Shhh…. My heart…. My love. You can. You are made for me. The only one for me. I know you can." Adel held perfectly still, and Evan's panic subsided. Adel rained kisses and little nips across his shoulders and neck.

Evan relaxed and eased back until Adel's large mushroom head breached the ring of muscle guarding his opening. Evan whimpered, enjoying the burn and stretch of his body as it accommodated Adel's massive cock. The overwhelming heat of Adel's rod made him pant. Sweat poured from his body. Never before had sex been like this. Never before had making love been like this.

Adel rocked gently, easing forward inch by inch as Evan moaned with need.

Waves of emotions inundated Evan: lust, possessiveness, protectiveness, and overwhelming love engulfed him in a cocoon of fervor that mixed with his own. Evan felt a bond with Adel forming in his mind. It was loose at first—cords of Adel's feelings wrapping around him in ever-expanding rings, flowing into him and back out, carrying his love back to Adel. The intensity and tightness of the bands increased with every touch, every sigh, every whispered word between them, binding them one to the other—heart to heart, body to body, soul to soul—until they were not two but one.

Adel pushed into Evan until he'd sunk completely into Evan's depths, sheathed in Evan's tight embrace. Adel's molten-hot rod filled him. Adel laid his chest along Evan's back, mewling and licking the nape of Evan's neck. Adel shifted his hips from side to side, eliciting groans of pleasure from Evan. Adel drew back and began to pound into Evan, slowly at first, then with increasing speed. Adel pumped Evan's cock in rhythm to his thrusts.

Evan responded to Adel's fervor with a feral abandon of his own as he thrust his hips back to meet Adel's forward motion, grinding Adel's cock into his sweet spot and shooting ecstasy through his body. "Adel, I can't…. Ah!" Evan gasped and arched his back with release, covering Adel's hand with his seed. His muscles clamped down hard on Adel.

With a roar, Adel filled Evan with his hot essence and dropped with Evan as he collapsed onto the grass. Adel gently withdrew from Evan's body, swept him into his arms and onto his chest, and wrapped his wings around them both, as whirling stars and darkness stole over Evan's vision and drew him into blissful unconsciousness.

EVAN AWOKE with the contented sound of Adel's purr reverberating through his body. He lay warmly encased in Adel's wings with his head pillowed on Adel's shoulder. Stars sparkled above in the cool night, but cocooned in the heat of Adel's body and love, he only knew bliss. Adel gazed down at him, a mixture of fear, love, and contentment shining on his beautiful face.

Evan smiled and put a hand on Adel's cheek, caressing him gently. Exhausted and sore, he knew he wouldn't be standing on his own for a while. His body still trembled from the exertion, and a numbness had spread through his lower back and hips from the pounding he'd taken. The feeling extended down his legs, which felt about as stable as cooked noodles. He would be sore for days, and he couldn't be happier; he felt totally loved.

"My Adel. My beautiful Adel." Evan's voice came out softer than a sigh. His eyes drifted closed, as there was no place safer than in Adel's arms.

"My heart," Adel crooned, and then he lifted Evan into his arms. He leaped into the air, and with a flap of his wings, they were airborne, flying over the forest and floating on the air currents. They glided down into the front yard of the cabin, and Adel carried Evan in, then through the trapdoor and into his bedroom. With infinite gentleness, Adel laid Evan between the sheets, went to the bathroom, then returned with a warm washcloth and cleaned his mate. When Adel tossed the washcloth back into the bathroom, it made a soggy splat as it landed in the sink. He climbed between the sheets, spooned up against Evan, and pulled him snugly into his arms.

Chapter 8

GARGOYLE LORE

As written by the scribes and entombed in the Church Archives:

Hunting:

1. Gargoyles can smell evil, and when they are flesh, they will defend a territory from evil. If they discover evil, they will hunt and kill to protect their charges, consuming the evil in its entirety.

EVAN DIDN'T know what woke him. In fact, he wasn't sure where he was for a minute before he realized Adel had tucked him into bed. He turned, hearing a whimpering at his ear and the incessant beeping of an alarm. The smell of his roasted chicken wafted through the house, tantalizing his taste buds and drawing a growl of hunger from his stomach.

Evan opened his eyes to see that Cela sat at his shoulder, crying nervously. "Cela, what's wrong?" Evan asked, sitting up and hissing as the stiffness in his muscles reminded him of his earlier activities with Adel. The ceaseless beeping of the oven timer combined with Adel's furious growling continued to get louder. Evan figured he'd better get to the kitchen just as the loud, obnoxious sound of crunching metal and the sudden silence of the timer became a death toll for his oven.

Oh, shit. He tried to get out of bed, only to find his legs were still like rubber bands and refused to support him. Tingling pins and needles ran up and down his legs; they had gone to sleep and refused to do Evan's bidding. He tripped over his numb feet and crumpled to the floor with a thump.

Adel instantly appeared at his side, swept him into his arms, and pulled him against his chest. "Evan." Adel sighed. All the aggression Evan had heard earlier coming from the kitchen was gone, and Adel cradled Evan against his chest.

"What's wrong, Adel? I heard the oven timer going off, then a loud crushing sound. Is the chicken done?" Evan asked.

Adel hung his head sheepishly, but still nuzzled Evan's hair. "I did not wish to awaken you, but I could not make the beeping stop. Cela did not know how to stop it either. I thought I had hurt you… I just wanted to give you some time to heal, but the infernal thing would not stop beeping."

"You didn't hurt me, my love."

"I had to make it stop." Adel whined and rubbed his face against Evan's hair. "I am sorry, I fear I have broken your… oven."

"Well, if you did, then you'll have to help me replace it."

"Are you sure I did not injure you? You passed out. I thought I had… I would never intentionally harm you.…"

"I'm fine. You exhausted me, and I feel wonderful. I think I passed out because I'm still not quite a hundred percent, even after sleeping for a week. Help me get to the kitchen. I need to see how broken the oven is." Evan laughed as Adel huffed, but he grabbed a blanket from the bed, wrapped Evan up, and carried him out to the breakfast bar. Adel kissed him gently, then set him carefully on the stool, and Evan groaned slightly. When Adel moved and Evan saw the stove, he burst into a torrent of hard guffaws.

The white appliance had a large fist-shaped dent where the timer should've been.

"Well, I think the stove can be saved. I just need to replace the control panel."

Cela sat on the counter, jeering and hissing at Adel, obviously scolding him. He had absolutely no fear of Adel, regardless of how much he snarled back at him.

Evan put a hand on Cela. "Enough, Cela. Adel feels bad and apologized. Leave off already."

Cela hissed once more for good measure, then jumped to Evan's shoulder and curled up around Evan's neck and appeared to go to sleep.

Adel growled, but Evan instructed him how to open the oven and remove the roaster with their chicken dinner. When the timer had rung, the oven had automatically turned off. The roaster was covered, which kept the meal hot.

Evan burst into laughter as Adel attempted to open the oven door, only to have it fall into his hand, the hinges snapped.

"I am terribly sorry, my heart," Adel mumbled contritely.

Evan couldn't bring himself to scold Adel. Seeing him be so sweet and apologetic was worth a little appliance repair. How Adel could appear both majestic and cute at the same time was a true mystery for the ages, but somehow his Adel managed it.

"Come here, Adel." Evan motioned Adel to his side.

Adel hissed at Cela, who unwound from Evan's throat and jumped onto the counter.

"It's okay, Adel, but next time, if you don't know what to do, wake me up." Adel's head still hung, so Evan draped his arms around Adel's neck and drew him down to kiss him soundly. He snuggled against Adel's chest, sighing as Adel wrapped both arms and wings around him. Evan stared up into the beautiful eyes of his beloved and smiled.

Adel drew back and nuzzled Evan's neck, licking everywhere Cela had lain, removing the scent of the little dragon. "My heart," Adel purred when only his own scent and that of his mate remained.

"Are you hungry?" Evan reached up and stroked Adel's cheek. He heard the telltale grumblings of Adel's stomach and smiled knowingly up at him. "'Cause I'm starved."

Adel got the plates, and Evan dished himself up a helping of the potatoes and carrots and cut away a couple of pieces of the chicken. Adel pulled the other bird from the roaster and devoured it with relish.

Evan smiled, watching Adel enjoy himself. He could watch Adel eat any time. The satisfaction he took from food was unlike anything he'd ever seen. He didn't just eat like people would, barely acknowledging the contents of their plates before rushing off to other tasks. Adel enjoyed eating and did so with the enthusiasm of a child with a sweet tooth tasting chocolate for the first time. His expression of complete approval as he sank his teeth into the tender meat of the chicken made Evan's heart soar.

When they were finished with the meal, Evan instructed Adel how to load the dishwasher and put the leftovers into containers and then into the refrigerator. With the cleanup complete, Adel and Evan wandered back to their bedroom so Evan could begin working on Adel's family file. Evan needed to ask one of his computer contacts to add the file to the Church's archive. The file wouldn't hold up long under direct scrutiny or comparison to the master file in Rome, but if Father Michael was inclined to dig, he'd find corroboration of Adel's existence and he might not go any further.

It didn't take Evan long to create the file, but encrypting it and sending it to his friend took a bit more doing. The man he needed to contact had access to Church records and family files, but the risk of getting caught modifying any part of the Church's archive could easily get you killed. His contact would either accept the job and make the changes to the family records, or refuse. No questions would be asked.

Of all the things he'd asked of this contact, he'd never trusted him with something as important as this. He'd asked for files to be modified before, just never his own family's records, but he reassured himself that the contact wouldn't know how personal the request really was. Adel's life was of the utmost importance, and if Father Michael suspected the depth of his feelings for Adel, he'd try to pull Adel in for an interrogation. Adel would never survive an inquisitor's scrutiny no matter how much they practiced, and Evan wouldn't be able to rescue him. If he were captured, once sunrise came, Adel would reveal himself by turning to stone, and they'd destroy him.

JudassaninC, as he was known by the underground, was a calculated risk. Evan had sent him information and had received information in turn regarding Father Michael's nefarious deeds and conduct. Hopefully JudassaninC would help, not betray him. Adel's life depended on it.

Evan prepared and sent the file with a message to his contact:

> *JudassaninC*
> *sending attached encrypted file code (baby takes a walk)*
> *high priority // need identity cover // please add to family file*
> *must keep new friend from suspicious FM in BS*
> *hope for the future*
> *Stone*

Exhaustion began to claim him. Evan had been working on the file for quite a while. They didn't have long before Adel would become stone, shortly after dawn. All Evan wanted was to curl up with Adel and sleep. He also wanted to make love to Adel, to do so slowly and gently, but with their time limited, and as he was still aching from their previous lovemaking, they'd make do with snuggling until morning.

Evan turned around to see Adel sitting against the headboard, watching Evan work with a blissful smile on his beautiful face. "Have I told you lately how much I'm falling for you?" Evan grinned and climbed into bed alongside Adel, resting his head against Adel's chest as Adel caressed his back.

"I think I might recall you mentioning something, a while back," Adel teased as he reached out and carefully unwrapped Cela from around Evan's throat and placed him on the pillow beside them. "Evan, I do not wish to be difficult, but please, my heart, do not allow Cela to curl around your neck anymore. I know you have a special relationship with him, but it sets my teeth on edge to smell another on you so intimately." The sheepish look on Adel's face as he admitted his jealousy was endearing. "Logically, I know he is too young and small to be your mate, but his scent is still masculine, and to see him resting there makes me crazy. I do not want to hurt him or you if you try to protect him for something I consciously understand is innocent. My instincts scream and make me see red at any male scent other than my own on your body." Adel grumbled as he rambled on, all the while glaring at the little dragon who watched curiously from his pillow.

"Look, I love Cela. I found him first, and he has been with me throughout the years while I learned about gargoyles. He'll always be my friend... my family." Evan watched as Adel tensed. "But I can do that for you."

"I know he's your friend and I'm glad. I like him too, but I can't... please, Evan—" Adel tried to explain.

"I understand, Adel. I want the two of you to get along. If you don't want him with me, then will you allow him to be with you? It'd ease my mind knowing he's safe with you," Evan said, stroking Adel's arms. "I think of Cela, the musketeers, Yin, and Yang as my family, my children. I love them all and I'd protect them with my life."

"You are a Maker, Evan. Of course you want to protect us," Adel said. "So if you are the parent and I am your mate, does that mean I am also a parent to these wild ones?" Adel chuckled.

"In our special family... yes, I guess so. If you want to be. But they're my responsibility, not yours." Evan smiled, his eyes drifting closed as he drifted off to sleep.

"Yes, as Maker you are parent to us all, but lover and mate only to me." Adel purred, the deep resonance a lullaby to Evan as he sank further into sleep. He listened to Adel's promises, which Evan couldn't seem to get enough of. "Mine... my heart."

Chapter 9

Gargoyle Lore

As written by the scribes and entombed in the Church Archives:
Hunting:

1. Gargoyles, when flesh, will hunt and eat as any living being; they need sustenance for the flesh to remain strong and vibrant.
2. A starved gargoyle will go into hibernation until it can hunt freely.
3. Gargoyles are carnivores. Although they can eat some vegetables, they do not need them as part of a healthy diet.
4. Gargoyles can consume either cooked or raw meat.

As he awoke, Evan realized his internal clock seemed to want to run on Adel's time. Daytime seemed to be losing its hold on him and as each day passed, he had begun to spend more of it asleep with Adel and awake with him at night. The digital numbers he read from the nightstand said it was well into the afternoon. He sighed contentedly and snuggled against Adel's stone chest, again amazed at how stone could stay so warm. Evan smiled as he reached behind him and stroked Adel's arm. It was a bittersweet feeling to awaken before his magnificent mate: sweet because he knew he was loved and always would be; bitter because Adel was not free to awaken whenever he wished, and Evan would have to be patient until then.

"I love you. I wish I could free you to choose being awake or stone."

Evan sighed. Although Adel did wake before sundown and seemed to awaken a little earlier every day, he was nowhere near able to choose when he wanted to sleep. Evan didn't know if he had the power to free Adel completely from the night, but he hoped to find out soon. He just didn't want to try until he learned more about his abilities. Adel's warnings about how the power needed to make a transformation could drain him, and his recent weeklong siesta, had given him cause to be more cautious.

"I know, I know. I can hear you lecturing me and you aren't even awake. No, I won't try anything." Evan rolled over and ran a finger along

Adel's face. "If you can't tell me, love, then we are just going to have to start experimenting so I can learn how to control the power. I can't risk something happening by accident, like… I don't know. Maybe levitating a stone and hitting Father Michael in the head with it the next time he pisses me off." Evan snickered, picturing the stunned, angry look on Father Michael's face as he tried to find out who'd thrown the stone when only Evan stood there. It would be, of course, a quick way to be sent to the Inquisition and killed.

Evan got out of bed and headed for the bathroom and a shower. Father Michael's visits had become more regular since he'd learned of Adel's existence. Father Michael used every word spoken by Adel as an excuse to question him, to exercise his suspicions. The fact that there was nothing negative for Father Michael to find when he researched the Church databases for Adelstan Noble didn't seem to matter.

Evan put on clean clothes and walked upstairs just as his perimeter alarm went off. *God, not again! He was just here yesterday. Why can't that man just leave us alone? Get a goddamn hobby already! I'd even be happy to mail him some personal vibrating toys if he'd just leave me the hell alone!* Evan shivered with disgust as he filled the sink with water and soap to make it look like he was doing dishes.

A knock at the door brought Evan out of his grumbling, and after placing a smile on his face, Evan opened the door and turned on the charm. "Father, what a lovely surprise. Twice in as many days. To what do I owe this wonderful visit this beautiful afternoon?" It was getting exhausting doing this day after day. When would the man get over it?

"Good afternoon, Evan. Where's your houseguest today?" Father Michael sneered, although it might have been meant as a smile. Evan was never sure. Father Michael placed a hand on Evan's shoulder as he entered the house and looked around, evidently for Adel.

"I believe he's out hunting. I told him to see if he could bag a turkey. I make a really great roast turkey, and then there are always leftovers for sandwiches. Why, did you need to speak to him? I'm sure I can call his cell and see if he can make his way back here to talk. Shouldn't take him longer than an hour or two." Evan judged that sundown was about three hours away, meaning Adel would awaken in about an hour and a half.

"No. I was just curious, as I didn't see him around. I don't get to talk to you alone much anymore. He always seems to show up just as we get started."

"Ah. Well, he does live here now. I'm so glad too. We've been able to increase production, so I've been able to take more orders. Business is good."

"I'm glad as well. But are you sure you're comfortable with him here with you, Evan? I don't much care for him. I know he is family to you, but I don't like the way he is always touching you. He isn't behaving inappropriately, is he? You know you can tell me if he is. You can confide in me." Father Michael took hold of Evan's arm and squeezed almost to the point of pain. Evan wondered if there would be a bruise. Adel would be pissed if there was.

"Of course not. Adel would never do anything like that. We've been friends for years, and yes, he is protective of me, but I'm just as protective of him. He is family, after all. I love him like a brother." Evan wanted to taunt Father Michael more, but thought better of it when the grip on his arm became punishingly tight and he was given a bit of a push away, as the father grabbed the doorknob and pulled open the door to leave.

"Well, as long as you are all right. I guess there is nothing for me to be concerned about. But please, my boy, if he ever does anything suspicious, let me know. I really don't like his presence in this house." Father Michael folded his hands in front of him as he motioned for Evan to precede him outside. He draped an arm about Evan's shoulders. "You have my number if you find yourself in need. Please do not hesitate to call me if you need my... assistance."

Evan opened the car door for him, and Father Michael got behind the wheel. "I will, Father. You'll be the first person I call if I have problems. You know I look to you as I would my own father," Evan said, trying not to grit his teeth at the lie.

"Fine. Fine. I'll check in on you another day. I'm sorry I don't have a lot of time today." Father Michael closed the door and, with a wave, drove off in a cloud of dust.

Evan's frustration increased with the visit. He went down to the sanctuary to lie in bed with Adel. "Father Michael was just here. The man is a complete asshole. He was trying to get me to tell him that you are abusing me. I can't believe his audacity. The sheer hypocrisy of the man," Evan mumbled. He knew Adel heard him as he always did, whether stone or flesh and blood.

A surge of electricity in the air tingled over Evan's skin, and Adel awoke and wrapped Evan into his arms. "I am sorry, my heart. I wish he would leave you alone, but I suspect he has no intention of ever leaving you be. Even if I was not here, annoying him, he would still be harassing you. That man wants you, and if he ever gives in to his desires, he will blame you and have you killed as a temptation to a pure man." Adel hissed as he held Evan against him.

"I know. You're right. If he comes after me, it would end up with me being held by the Inquisition, and then I'd disappear or be given a death sentence and formally killed."

"I will not let that happen. None of us will, my heart." Adel leaned down and kissed Evan, outlining Evan's lips with his tongue before slipping in between them. He devoured Evan's mouth until Evan couldn't think of anything but Adel.

EVAN SAT down heavily at his computer. He glanced at his security monitors; it was early afternoon and Adel would sleep for a while longer. He needed to check in with the underground and see if there were any developments. Every contact had a specialty. Being a stonemason, his specialty was sculpture. Over the years he'd been able to save a few pieces from destruction by the Church in addition to the gargoyles he'd rescued.

As he'd begun sleeping more and more during the day and indulging himself in Adel's company and love at night, he'd become distracted, but he still had a job to do. Checking over his contacts, he found he'd received a call for assistance that morning. The request had come through a contact from the monks who'd given him Yin and Yang, and meant there was a very real threat to a gargoyle's life:

> *Stone*
> *Hot Commodity*
> *Direct through China, granite with unique qualities*
> *Necessary to relocate before destruction*
> *San Francisco ASAP*
> *JudassaninC*

Evan would need to get busy. He went upstairs, wrote a note, and stuck the paper to the front door for Father Michael:

Father Michael,
I don't want you to worry, so I'm leaving you this
note. Adel and I have gone to visit my aunt and let her
know how things are going. We're then going on to pick up
some granite from a sale in California. We'll be gone for
several weeks before coming back from this venture.
Evan and Adel

Evan laughed as he read the note. Father Michael would probably be upset because he'd included Adel in the note, but at least he should stay away after he read it. His aunt had gone to visit her brother and would be out of town in case Father Michael went looking for them, and it would be the perfect excuse later for their change of plans. He hurried to the shop for the truck and hid the vehicle in the woods. Once Adel awoke later that afternoon, they could hit the road with no one the wiser.

Evan packed a light bag and placed Cela around Adel's neck. The stone body moved readily in Evan's hands as if the little gargoyle were awake.

"Since you prefer that Cela not curl around my neck, beloved, he'll need to be around yours. We may need him when we get to California." Evan kissed Adel's cheek, then patted Cela's head.

He went back into the tunnels and found the sleeping places of Yin and Yang. "Sleep well, my friends. Guard our home and keep each other safe." He ran a hand over each of their stone heads and sought out the musketeers. "Stay out of trouble, you guys. With luck, you'll have a new brother or sister gargoyle when we return from California." Evan touched each of the four, then returned to his bedroom.

With his preparations to leave completed, he climbed back into bed with Adel, relaxing against the cool stone, knowing Adel would awaken soon. Evan closed his eyes and imagined Father Michael's reaction to his note. The familiar car pulling into the yard. Father Michael walking to the door and finding the note. The resulting tantrum and yelling in a most unholy manner. Father Michael storming about the yard, searching the shop and garage, before returning to his car and driving off in a snit.

EVAN GLANCED over, checking Adel's appearance. He'd chosen clothes he thought would best hide the slight bulge on Adel's back. Evan could feel Adel's heart racing and realized that he looked far calmer than he felt. "Okay, remember they're going to ask us questions and look at the papers. Just stay calm and answer as quickly and concisely as possible." Evan pulled in to the checkpoint and glanced one last time at Adel.

"I understand. It will be fine, my heart."

Their papers had to be approved to move from one diocese into the next, and this was the first checkpoint. They'd see if the paperwork Evan's contact had provided them would work.

Evan nervously crossed his fingers and rolled down his window. "Good evening." He grinned at the Bishop's Service officer who approached the truck.

"Yes, good evening. Where are you going?" the officer asked, taking the papers Evan handed him.

"California. For business," Evan said.

"Uh-huh. And when will you be returning?"

"In a few days. We should have a full load then, hopefully."

"Oh, of what?" The officer shuffled Evan's papers and looked at Adel's.

"Granite."

"Rocks?"

"Yes, I make countertops and flooring," Evan said, knowing his occupation was stated on the paperwork.

"Uh-huh. Okay, you're clear. Travel safely." The officer handed their paperwork back and pressed a button to open the gate and allow them to pass.

Once they were a mile down the road, Evan started to tremble, pulled over, and turned off the engine.

Adel unbuckled his seat belt and pulled Evan into his arms. "Shhh, beloved. We are fine. The papers worked, and we are safe."

"I know. I just hate that one wrong move could mean your life, our lives."

Adel chuckled. "Not at a place like this. Yes, it might be a complication, and you might lose the truck. I would just knock the humans unconscious and take you and fly away. They cannot stop me when I am awake. I would only be vulnerable to them when asleep."

"Well, I won't be going through any checkpoints while you sleep. Since the papers work, it will be easier to keep you safe without taking the chance of them seeing your stone form." Evan knotted his fingers into Adel's hair and pulled him down for a kiss, still trying to reassure himself that they'd made it through the checkpoint.

Adel stroked his back and held him tight against his chest until his heart rate evened out.

Vaguely, as his heartbeat steadied, he began to hear a soft, incessant chirp. "Cela!" he squeaked as Adel opened the glove box, allowing a rather pissed-off dragon out. "Sorry, but you had to stay out of sight for the checkpoint."

Cela squawked and hissed at them indignantly as he hopped up onto the dashboard instead of taking his usual place on Adel's shoulder or around his neck.

"Easy, little brother. It was necessary and all is well now." Adel reached over and scratched Cela below the chin until the little dragon began to purr. Having evidently forgiven them, he leaped from the dashboard to the back of the seat to nuzzle into Adel's hair.

Evan leaned up and kissed Adel one last time before moving back behind the wheel and starting the truck.

Just as dawn topped the horizon, Evan pulled in to their hotel and got them checked in. Evan always stayed at cheap hotels, because the cheaper the hotel, the fewer questions were asked. They made it to the room with but a few moments to spare for Adel to strip and lie down on the bed before he turned to stone. Evan made sure the door was locked and the curtains were closed tightly as Adel's sweatshirt and jeans had hit the floor. It had only taken a moment, but it was long enough that when he turned around, Adel lay, a beautiful statue curled on the bed. Evan covered him with blankets from the extra bed to keep him from sight. He didn't care to explain the statue in his bed to a passing maid.

Evan picked up the clothing and sat it on the extra bed before sitting down at the table. He set up his laptop and logged in to the hotel wireless network. He sent his contact an encoded message:

JudassaninC
seeking Opportunity in CA
send loc
Stone

Evan closed the computer, then took off his clothing and laid it neatly next to Adel's before climbing into bed with him. He sighed with contentment as he snuggled up against Adel's chest. The warmth coming from Adel's stone form flowed into his travel-weary arms and legs, lulling Evan into a semiconscious state before true sleep came.

The drive across the country had been exhausting. There hadn't been any villages or even towns between Evan's home in the Black Hills of South Dakota and San Francisco, just one ghost town after another. The worst had been driving through the decaying buildings of Salt Lake City, Utah. The dead city, once alive and full of people, was now an enormous sprawling ruin, deafening in its silence. It gave Evan chills and left him cold, with goose bumps covering his skin. Nature had reclaimed much of the suburban sprawl, destroying the streets and sidewalks. Eventually all the buildings and manmade structures would fall and be absorbed by the trees and wildlife in the area, reclaiming from man what had originally belonged to the wild.

Despite the devastation they'd driven through and the unknown dangers they would face, here with Adel, Evan felt relaxed. Maybe safe, even. He closed his eyes and snuggled against Adel. Sinking into oblivion, he could feel Adel's deep purr lulling him to sleep.

A soft smile graced Evan's sleeping face. He loved his magnificent gargoyle and would for the rest of his life.

Chapter 10

My Dearest Nicolas,

I'm so very tired. I know this little one I carry is important to the world, yet my own exhaustion and despondency can't be good for her or him. This will be the tenth child I've borne for the good of the world. I feel like I've made my contribution to mankind and now I just seek rest. My broken heart is weary and aches to be with you.

The Church has regulated the police force, which I think is a good thing. It will be overseen by priests, with deputies who are members of the congregation. They have named it the Bishop's Service. Your cousin, Daniel Jamison, has joined. He's a good choice. He's grown into a proper young man and has a strong moral character. He comes to visit me on occasion. He and his wife are looking after Nico, who is twelve years old now. I lost track of the other children after they were born—the Church put them into various family homes to be raised.

One of the fathers has taken an interest in me and has asked me to marry him after the child I currently carry is born. I have been putting him off, as I don't truly believe I'll survive this birth. I'm trying to just stay out of his way as much as possible. He's a power-hungry, vile little man. I have to wonder how he became a man of the cloth.

This body is tired and weak. I hope to see you soon, beloved.

I love you.
Elizabeth

EVAN AWOKE with a start. His unfamiliar surroundings unsettled him and he tried to remember where he was. The room had a dusty, ill-used smell, and the bed was obviously not his. The late-afternoon sun peeked through a crack in the dirty curtains of the small motel room, but the purr against his back sent a thrill through his body. Adel held him tightly against his chest. Evan relaxed as he remembered the drive and realized where they were. He sighed and snuggled back into Adel's warm embrace. They must have slept most of the day away.

"My heart," Adel whispered, gently stroking Evan's hair and pulling him even tighter against his chest.

Evan could feel Adel's arousal, hard and thick against his back. His own excitement quickly caught up. He smiled and reached behind himself to palm Adel's hardening cock. Adel breathed against his neck and caressed his ear with his tongue, which sent a wave of shivers running through Evan's body. He suspected Adel's fingertips had a direct line to his cock, because every touch and caress made it stand up and take notice.

"Adel, lover," Evan whispered. He turned over in his arms until they were chest to chest, reached out for Adel, and wrapped his arms around Adel's neck.

Adel chuckled softly as he caressed Evan's lips with his and slipped his tongue between to plunder his mouth. Then he moved his hand across Evan's back, sliding it across his skin to cup his ass. Adel purred his approval as Evan lifted his leg to rest it on Adel's thigh. Sliding his fingers over the curving line of Evan's ass to find his entrance, Adel stroked the muscles, massaging them, waiting for the wanton groan of lust.

Evan moaned and leaned his head forward against Adel's chest, reaching between them to press their erections together. He moved slowly in long, gentle motions, stroking from the top. He ran a finger along the slit in the dark purple head, then around to the underside of the mushroom-shaped glans and down the veined length to the base and back up again. Adel's cock, larger and longer than his, would have given him second thoughts if he hadn't already had it buried deep inside. Even so, the size still gave him pause. He pictured Adel's beautiful cock and the feeling of them joined, his balls rubbing against his asscheeks, and groaned in pleasure at the thought.

"Adel, we need the lube," Evan whispered breathlessly, latching on to one of Adel's nipples and lavishing circles around the stiffening peak. He started to push back slightly against Adel's chest, and then gasped as cool liquid trickled onto his hole from Adel's fingers.

Adel nuzzled his neck. "Already in hand, my heart."

Evan heard the snap of the lid on the bottle behind him. He gently bit down on Adel's nipple, tugging the hard nub toward him while glancing up at Adel's face. He smiled to see Adel's half-closed eyes, his lips pulled back from his teeth in a decidedly feline grin. Adel's purring changed to a full-throated growl, filling their hotel room with the sound of his pleasure as Evan increased the speed of his stroke on their erections.

Evan gasped as Adel slipped one finger, followed almost immediately by a second, into his depths. He struggled to keep from coming when Adel found and stroked his prostate. Adel hissed and bit Evan gently on top of his ear. Evan's breath came in gasping, ragged pants. His strokes on their erections became more erratic with his increasing need.

"Evan. Turn over, my heart. I need you," Adel hissed between gritted teeth.

Evan looked up at Adel, mindless, his eyes half-closed. Adel chuckled, his voice a harsh growl as he gripped Evan's hips and flipped him onto his hands and knees. Evan squealed in surprise as Adel moved behind him, drew his hips into the air until he was on his knees, and then gently pushed them apart before placing a hand between Evan's shoulder blades and pressing his shoulders down.

"Adel!" Evan cried out as the head of Adel's cock penetrated his sphincter. He saw an explosion of stars behind his closed eyelids, and his cock dripped precome as Adel's deep thrust caressed his prostate.

Adel sheathed himself in Evan's tight grip, stretching him to a point that was almost beyond his tolerance, but it burned so good. He reached around Evan, took his cock in hand, picked up the wet that leaked from the slit, brought it to his lips, and sucked the nectar from his fingers.

Looking back, Evan watched Adel and shuddered. The sight of Adel's tongue sent a thrill through his body. Adel shifted his weight from side to side, wiggling within Evan's tight grip, each movement sending waves of pleasure through Evan's body. "Please, Adel," Evan called, pushing his hips back farther into Adel's. "Fuck me now." Evan grasped at the sheets, clenching and unclenching his fingers in an effort to stave off his climax, to prolong the pleasure.

Adel pulled back and then thrust forward, slowly, carefully, into Evan. Each stroke elicited passion-filled gasps, which changed to whimpers as Adel's hot prick stroked against his prostate.

"You feel so tight, my heart. You like my cock in your ass?" Adel hissed. "Does it feel good?"

"Yes. God, yes! Adel!" Evan panted as Adel gripped Evan's hips and pounded rapidly into him. Evan reached between his legs and took his hard cock in hand, stroking himself in time with Adel's canting hips.

Unable to hold back any longer, Adel set a frantic pace, slamming into Evan. Adel slightly sank his claws into Evan's hips as he lay along Evan's back. A tiny rivulet of blood trickled from each piercing pinprick.

Evan threw back his head and his hips, moaning as he covered Adel's hands with his, lacing their fingers, smearing the blood.

Adel nipped at the taut muscles at the back of Evan's neck, moving between the shoulder blades and below his ear. Adel's strokes grew wild and uncontrolled as he tasted Evan's flesh and dragged his razor-sharp canines across the surface of Evan's skin, leaving shallow, bruising bites welling with blood that Adel greedily lapped and sucked. "Evan, come for me, my heart. I want to feel how much you want me," Adel crooned into Evan's ear.

Evan panted, his hands fisted with Adel's, locked on his hips. He arched his back, pressing into Adel. The stinging bite of Adel's claws as they sank into his hips was a burning pleasure he'd never known before. "Adel!" Evan's head flew back as Adel bit into the tender, abused flesh on his neck, then immediately laved the wound, drawing part of Evan into himself. The combination of pain and pleasure sent Evan over the edge into his orgasm.

Adel roared Evan's name as he thrust one last time, finding his release as Evan's muscles contracted, gripping and milking Adel's cock. Evan collapsed into a bliss-filled orgasmic release, with semen covering his belly.

EVAN AWOKE for the second time to the sound of Adel's distressed whimpering as he swept his tongue over the bite mark on his shoulder, and Evan couldn't stop the contented smile that washed over his face. He snuggled into Adel's warm, strong chest as Adel wrapped muscular arms around him, anchoring him securely. There was no greater paradise than this moment in his lover's arms. He could happily stay here for eternity.

"Lover, are you okay?" Evan asked sleepily.

"My heart," Adel whimpered, his concern palpable.

"My love, you are amazing." Evan turned his face to Adel's chest and rubbed his cheek against his strong muscles, sinking deeper into Adel's embrace. Adel smelled so rich, like the earth after a spring rain. Evan loved Adel's scent, so wild and masculine. He'd never get enough.

"I hurt you. I am so sorry," Adel whined. "I lost control. I never meant to hurt you."

"You didn't hurt me, love. I feel wonderful." Evan rolled over, wincing a bit, and then he giggled at the soreness in his rear. Walking would be a bit uncomfortable later, Evan thought. He looked deeply into Adel's eyes. "You could never hurt me. That was truly fantastic." Evan blushed as he remembered how completely Adel had loved him. He tenderly cupped Adel's face, caressing his cheek with a finger, trying to express his love to his beautiful Adel, and noticed his hand had blood on it from the claw piercings on his hips.

"But you were bleeding. My claws, and my teeth…."

Evan took Adel's hands and brought them to his lips, seeing the touch of red that tipped each of Adel's claws. He smiled and kissed them, then rubbed his face into Adel's large, strong hands. "My love, when my nails dig into your shoulders and I leave marks in your skin, am I hurting you? Even if your shoulders bleed?" Evan looked up to meet Adel's sad eyes.

"Of course not. Little scratches like these do not bother one such as me. Besides, they will be completely gone after I sleep. You know any minor injury I suffer will be gone once I awaken, as if it never happened." Adel scoffed at the idea Evan could physically hurt him.

"I may take a little longer to heal completely, but these small wounds don't hurt enough for me to regret them. They show me how much you want and love me. I like that they're going to stick around for a while. They remind me of your love." Evan smiled and snuggled into Adel's embrace. "I love you so much, Adel."

"My heart," Adel purred, rubbing his face into Evan's hair. A smile graced his face as he looked down upon Evan.

The computer pinged, alerting them of an incoming message. Evan grimaced in frustration. Groaning slightly, he climbed out of bed, grabbed the laptop from the small round table under the window, and crawled back into bed.

Adel sat up against the headboard and pulled Evan against him, his arms around his waist.

Evan opened the laptop and the screen came to life with a beep. The program showed a message received from his contact:

Stone
locker 138/sundown
YMCA/Sample
JudassaninC

"What does that mean?" Adel asked, reading the message over Evan's shoulder.

"I'm not sure, but I think we need to get to the Y and find whatever sample my contact is sending us." Evan leaned over and kissed Adel softly on the lips, then got up. A wicked grin crossed his face as he crooked a finger in Adel's direction.

Adel's lips curled back from his teeth and a lust-filled growl erupted from his throat.

Evan knew exactly what he wanted—more of Adel—and they'd just enough time to play a bit before they needed to get to the YMCA before sundown.

EVAN AND Adel parked the truck in front of the large abandoned building. The YMCA sign hung precariously on one side, swinging in the breeze, chased by dust devils that danced through the street. This would be the third YMCA Evan and Adel had visited, but the first abandoned one. This part of the city resembled a ghost town, left behind by humanity to return to nature.

Evan eyed the sign nervously as they ducked under it and into the archway. The door dangled from the upper hinge and fell as Adel pushed it aside. Adel reached back and took Evan's hand, pulling him behind him as they progressed into the dark interior of the building. They found the locker room with ease. Adel led the way through the decaying refuse that littered the hallway. The fading sun filtering in through the small, dirty windows above the lockers left the room in eerie twilight. Evan doubted anyone had been here in decades.

"There." Adel pointed to the row of lockers along the far wall. They walked over and looked at the rusting lockers, many with their number plates on the floor in front of them. Adel grabbed the handle of 138, and the screech of his claws piercing the metal door before he pulled it from the rusty hinges sent goose bumps spreading across Evan's skin.

At the bottom of the locker sat a large, unmarked cardboard box. Unlike the locker and everything around it, the box appeared pristine, new, and unsoiled. Evan reached down and picked it up. It was surprisingly heavy. He figured whatever it contained was probably made of stone. He handed the box to Adel, and the two of them left the building. Evan rubbed his hands up and down his arms, trying to get rid of the goose bumps as they climbed back into the truck.

As the last rays of the sun disappeared, Cela uncurled from around Adel's neck, sat on his shoulder, and crooned.

Evan smiled, reached over, and scratched the ridges on his face and between his wings. "Good evening, Cela." Evan smiled. Then he squeaked and jumped back when the box between him and Adel began to rock on the truck seat.

Adel growled and the box stopped moving. Claws extended, Adel sliced open the top and pulled back the cover. Inside sat a birdlike creature: a miniature gryphon. The head and front legs were that of a dark brown raptor, while the back looked like a sleek tawny lion. Its wings were folded tightly against its body, and feathers ran from the nape, along the backbone, and down over the rump, where they turned into a mix of flaxen fur and feathers at the tail. Golden eyes peered up at Evan and Adel. The gryphon chirped and crooned at Cela, who sang right back and jumped down into the box to rub up against the gryphon. At almost twice the size of little Cela, the gryphon seemed entranced and sang happily as Cela snuggled into its tawny fur and feathers.

"What do we have here?" Evan carefully held out his hand, allowing the gryphon to smell him before gently running his fingers over the crest of the bird and down between its wings. Evan reached for the red bow tied to one of its front legs. A small envelope attached to the ribbon had the name

"Stone" written on the outside. Evan pulled one of the ends of the ribbon and the envelope came with it.

Adel reached into the box, brought the little gryphon out, sat him on his lap, and stroked the birdlike creature until it purred like a kitten.

Evan opened the envelope to find a note.

> *To Stone,*
> *This is Skye. I'm sending him to you as a show of good*
> *faith. I'd like to meet up to discuss the recent destruction of*
> *Skye's brothers and sisters. Skye knows where to find me.*
> *Please come alone. Truly, I mean you no harm.*
> *JudassaninC*

"What does it say?" Adel asked, petting Skye and lifting Cela up so he could curl around his throat.

"My contact wants to meet and has left Skye to show us the way. I don't usually meet with any of my contacts in person. We're safer if we stay anonymous. If I don't know who the contact is, then I don't have information the Bishop's Service can force from me. I can't reveal and hurt those who've helped me." Evan frowned but reached over and scratched Skye under the chin.

"I would think your contact is aware of the danger of meeting as well. It must be important if he is willing to take the same risk you are. Maybe the information is only safe to discuss in person? Besides, my heart, I can keep you safe from any human. None can touch you with me at your side." Adel grinned, drawing his lips back to reveal a dangerous set of teeth.

"All right, my love. We'll follow our new little friend here and see where he leads us." Evan leaned in and kissed Adel deeply before sitting back in the seat. They got out of the truck, Adel holding Skye in his arms, and walked toward an overgrown parking lot.

"Skye, can you take me to your friend?" Evan asked.

Skye whistled and chirped, and then Adel threw him into the sky. Wings unfurled, Skye flew in slow circles overhead.

Adel took Evan into his arms. With a powerful downstroke of his wings, they were airborne, and Skye, his charges following, turned to the north.

Chapter 11

GARGOYLE LORE

As written by the scribes and entombed in the Church Archives:

Immortal:

1. Gargoyles are immortal and will live as long as their stone body remains whole. To destroy the stone is to destroy the gargoyle.
2. Gargoyles can be killed when they are flesh and blood.
3. If mortally wounded, a gargoyle may voluntarily turn to stone to heal itself. It will awaken whole with the next sunset.
4. A gargoyle will never leave a charge unguarded and will sacrifice its life to protect its charge before it will turn to stone to protect its own life.

ADEL KEPT Skye in view as he flew, but stayed far enough away so as to remain unnoticed and hopefully unseen against the dark horizon. They'd decided to conceal Evan behind Adel, under his wings, so Adel could meet the contact first. Evan didn't know if this would work, but he hoped to at least get to see the person before being seen himself. If things looked suspicious, they could still cut and run, hopefully with little Skye in hand. They hadn't traveled far when Skye floated down toward what could've once been a park but now looked like a small meadow in the center of an old, wild forest.

Adel hung back, landing silently in a tall redwood where they could see into the clearing but not be seen themselves. A young man in black jeans and a dark-colored trench coat stood alone in the center of a grassy ring. Adel carefully moved from branch to branch of the enormous tree, landed silently on the pine-needle-covered ground at the edge of the curtain of trees, and wrapped Evan in his wings behind his back. Then the two of them stepped forward as one into the open area.

Skye sat on the ground at the man's feet. Adel walked forward and opened his arms to Skye, who came bounding across the grass to him and leaped into his arms.

"Hello, Skye. Who do we have here?" Adel asked as he watched the scowling man warily. The man was quite a bit shorter than Evan, but well proportioned for his size. His hair hung in a thick, dark auburn curtain with black streaks, to fall just beyond his shoulders. His skin was a pale cream with a light dusting of freckles, giving an innocent cast to his deep, seafoam-green eyes.

"You are not who I expected."

"I am Stone," Adel answered.

"You are not the Stone I'm here to meet. Sorry to have bothered you."

"What do you want with Stone?"

"You aren't him. I can only speak of this with him."

"I can pass the message to him. He appears only to me in person," Adel replied.

"If that's true, then he has nothing to fear. But if he has even the smallest connection with anyone in the Bishop's Service, especially Father Michael, then he's very much in danger."

"What danger?" Adel growled in agitation.

"I'll only speak of it with him. I will not risk either of our lives by giving my information to anyone but him."

Evan placed a hand on Adel's shoulder, and Adel unfurled his black wings, allowing Evan to step out from behind him.

The man gasped audibly as Adel's great wings must have seemed like living shadows, indistinct and blending with the darkness around them. Evan materialized out of the blackness from nothing, as he walked around his protector.

Adel slid an arm around Evan's waist, keeping physical contact between them. He fluffed his wings out, stretching slightly to relieve the kinks after having held them still and the wrong way around for so long, before folding them snugly against his back, where they disappeared completely from view.

"What danger?" Evan asked.

"My God! What are you?" The man stared at Adel.

"What danger?" Evan repeated a bit more sternly.

Adel snarled in warning.

Skye cheeped, then leaped from the crook of Adel's arm and ran across the grass to stand defensively in front of the man.

He bent down and picked up the little gryphon and scratched behind his feathered ears while he stared at Adel in awe. "I've been investigating

Father Michael, and you've become a person of interest, Evan Halvard. I suspected you might be the Stone I've been in contact with for a number of years, and I wanted to warn you and ask you for your help."

"Who are you?"

"Just a concerned friend with similar interests. Look, Father Michael's been doing extensive digging into the background of your friend. I understand now why you had me set up the file for him." The man began to nervously pace back and forth while he spoke. "Unfortunately, the file I created won't hide him indefinitely. You'd need access to files that can only be created in Rome. If Father Michael requests records directly from Rome's master-file database, which he will if he's suspicious at all, there won't be anything for him to find, and that'll be the end of the ruse." He stopped pacing and turned, locking gazes with Evan directly. "You'll have some time because the Vatican databases aren't connected to the net. Which makes accessing any information formal and slow, but I've only bought you a few months at best before he will know the file is forged." He paused, then looked pointedly at Adel. "What is he, exactly?"

"He's like Skye, but more than Skye. A gargoyle." Evan turned a loving gaze up at Adel, but Adel's eyes never moved. He continued to growl menacingly at the man he perceived as a threat to his mate.

"You're him, aren't you? You're the Maker. The Earth Elemental," the man asked, his voice an awed whisper.

"Who are you?" Evan asked again, frowning. He wouldn't be tricked into revealing anything before he knew more about who he was dealing with. This man seemed to know way too much for comfort. Evan hadn't revealed anything to any of his contacts before he'd met Adel, much less what he might have become since meeting him. He'd taken the information given to him and utilized it to save lives and save history. When he came across things that were outside of his expertise, he passed them on to others to take care of as best they could. So how did this man know so much, or was he just guessing? He just stood there, staring at Evan as if he'd discovered the Holy Grail.

"Who are *you*?" asked Adel.

"I'm a Jesuit Inquisitor of Rome. My name is Peter Judas Jamison. Please call me Jude."

Both Adel and Evan nodded.

"What are you doing here?" Evan scowled.

"As a Jesuit, my allegiance is to the Pope, and as Inquisitor, my duty is to seek out corruption. My current assignment is to find that corruption within the Church, gather proof, and report to His Holiness directly."

Evan rubbed his hand over Adel's protective arms, wrapped around him as much to soothe himself as his mate.

"I'm here on orders from Rome to investigate Father Michael. We suspect he is a member of a group trying to discredit the Church and eventually overthrow Rome. His dealings with the people of the diocese have been very severe and not in Rome's best interests. We believe this renegade group has committed crimes in the name of Rome against the people. We suspect he's dealing with dark powers, and we want to stop him and apprehend him for trial in Rome. I'm also here to seek out the Maker and return him to Rome for his own protection."

"And you think I can help you with Father Michael and that I'm this… Maker?"

"From our previous communications, I know you're struggling against Father Michael. There are complaints and petitions to Rome lodged against him. Unfortunately, by the time we were able to launch an investigation, those filing the complaints had disappeared. We wish to preserve your safety. Rome has no wish to harm you. This is especially true if you are the Maker. Rome would like to offer you sanctuary and a safe place to awaken the gargoyles." Jude smiled, continuing to hold Skye and pet him gently.

"Why would Rome suspect me of being this 'Maker'? I'm just a stonemason, like my father before me." Evan trembled slightly. He'd done everything he could to keep a low profile. He didn't want the attention of Rome on him. Having to deal with Father Michael's attention was bad enough. To have an Inquisitor watching him, looking for his every mistake, would be tantamount to a death warrant.

"We've suspected for some time that you could be the Maker, Evan Halvard. Ironically, Father Michael's investigation into you and your background is what first drew our attention. The Church doesn't view gargoyles or the Maker as evil. On the contrary, the Church only wishes for your safety, to protect you." Jude stroked his hand over Skye's feathered head.

"The Church has never shown an interest in my welfare before. Do you really believe I will trust them now?"

"The Church is not perfect. There are zealous men who crave power and disagree with anything they can't control or understand. We believe Father Michael is one of these corrupt people." Jude smiled down at the little gryphon in his arms and scratched behind his ears, eliciting croons of pleasure from Skye, who gazed up at Jude with obvious affection. "Father Michael feels comfortable with you, and most likely will continue to, as long as he believes he can control you. When he realizes he has no control over you and can't force you to do his bidding, he'll destroy you as he has others."

"I do appreciate your warning where Father Michael's concerned. I wish you could do something about the documents in Rome, but I don't expect you to, knowing you're part of the Church. I hope you understand my reluctance to trust you."

"I've never once steered you wrong or betrayed you. I've helped you and sent you contacts whenever I could for years now," Jude begged. "Why can't you trust me?"

"I've found too many living-stone gargoyles destroyed at the hands of the Church, and not all by Father Michael or in the diocese. I've no reason to believe you or Rome." Evan shivered uncontrollably at thoughts of friends taken by the Church for inquisition. Father Michael handed down rulings in the name of Rome, and the punishments he dealt ran from debilitation to death.

Adel snarled when Evan shivered, wrapping Evan protectively in his wings.

Evan smiled up at him, patted his arm, and then laced the fingers of one hand through Adel's, giving them a squeeze to reassure both of them.

"Your friend is very beautiful. He's the largest of his kind I've ever seen. The only others I can think of even remotely like him are in Europe. A couple guard the Papacy, and there are some in Russia, Japan, Egypt, and, of course, Notre Dame, but they all sleep. They've been unmoving for centuries. Only a few, like Skye, are awake." Jude's voice held awe and reverence for Adel.

"Notre Dame stands?" Adel asked hesitantly, his voice trembling with excitement.

"Yes." Jude grimaced slightly. "I've seen the gargoyles there in the daytime, when I passed through the city. The Papacy fears they are dead. Nobody knows how long your kind can sleep before they die, or how much evil they can take on before it kills them. The Papacy is hoping you'll come to Rome and help those who sleep to awaken." Jude sighed sadly, shaking his head and staring at Skye, still softly crooning in his arms.

"Betrayal is all I've known from the Church. I'd expect them to destroy my friends, like Father Michael has. Kill me, like they killed my father. These are the actions I've been raised to expect of the Church, not protection and security," Evan scoffed.

"This country isn't safe for gargoyles or the Maker. Many rule here in the name of Rome, but the Church has very little actual control over them. They aren't protected here, but gargoyles are protected in other countries." Jude shook his head, sounding defeated. "The Papacy would like to have you in Rome for your safety, but if not there, France would also be a good choice. Japan and England should also be safe, for the most part. Russia isn't safe, nor is Africa, Egypt, or Australia."

"Why would I even begin to believe you? After watching what happened to my friends, my family, in the name of the Church? Even if the Church didn't know or have any control over what's happening here, which I have no way to prove, why should I believe what you're saying is true?"

"Please, Evan, I've never steered you wrong or betrayed you. I never would."

"I don't know that it's any safer anywhere else. I know what's happening here, who my enemies are, and how to protect my family and myself. Why should I gamble on the unknown you're offering?" Evan frowned, looking at Jude.

"I'm the one who sent you to the cemetery, where I believe you found your large friend. I've tried to send you warnings every time I learned you were in danger. I've tried to let you know if Father Michael found any living stones, with the hopes you could rescue them. Please, won't you consider what I've told you is true? Consider the possibility that I'm not the enemy," Jude said, frowning slightly. "I'd hoped you'd grown to trust me, at least a little."

"I trust you more than most, because I've never met with any of my contacts before. You're the first. Adel calls me a Maker, and I've discovered a few things I can do. I'm still learning." Evan sighed, then looked up at Adel, with Cela curled around his neck, not moving under the scrutiny of Jude. "Skye, come here." Evan stepped forward.

The miniature gryphon looked up at Jude and crooned sadly, but Jude gave him a final scratch and let him go.

"Keep him safe for me. He's been my best friend, my partner, since I found him just out of the seminary, ten years ago." Jude watched Skye reluctantly leave his arms and slowly walk across to Evan, looking back at Jude.

"If that's so, then why are you sending him to me? I understood you were looking for sanctuary for him." Evan opened his arms and Skye leaped into them, keening mournfully, to the point where Cela, who never moved in the presence of strangers, uncurled from Adel's neck. He jumped to Evan's shoulder and began cooing and rubbing against Skye, trying to console him.

"It's true. In this country, Skye's at risk, but I can protect him during the day. I hide him, keeping him close to me. When he's awake, if he needs to hunt, I take him to abandoned fields or to uninhabited areas where he can fly freely and sing. He sings so beautifully when he's happy. He's been my only companion for a very long time." Jude smiled sadly as he looked at his empty hands, then hung his head.

"Adel, what does he say?" Evan handed Skye to Adel, and Cela followed, curling again around Adel's neck.

Adel crooned to Skye softly and purred, listening intently. "Skye's very young, my heart. Maybe a century or so. He doesn't understand the passage of time as we do, but he likes this man. Skye protects him while he sleeps and believes he's a good man. All he remembers is hunting, flying, and his protector. He's very sad and doesn't want to leave Jude. Skye worries he won't eat well or get enough rest. He's afraid Jude will be hurt without him in the night. Jude has enemies who hunt him as well, it seems," Adel said in a surprised voice.

"You're not safe? Who'd come after an Inquisitor?" Evan put a hand to his head. He didn't want to leave Jude unprotected, but he wasn't sure he trusted him to protect Skye. On the other hand, Jude had proven he could be relied upon, more so than any other contact he'd ever worked with. He'd never betrayed Evan's trust. Evan felt torn, wanting to continue to believe in this man, yet fearing for his family.

Skye continued to keen softly, mourning his separation from Jude.

Sighing, Evan turned to Adel in frustration, speaking so only Adel could hear him. "What do you think? I'm tempted to bring them both back to the cabin. Worst case, we have to abandon the cabin and go into hiding, possibly leave the country. Best case, he's genuine and we might be able to get the others to safety and get rid of Father Michael." Taking Jude to the cabin constituted a risk, but if Jude was right, Father Michael would be on to them soon anyway, and they'd be on the run.

"From what Skye has said, I do feel they have been together for years. Skye has traveled around the world with him. They have rescued many people from injustice and have many enemies as the result. They work covertly and rarely spend more than one night in any one place. The pursuit of them has become increasingly intense of late, and they have been in hiding, traveling on foot occasionally in order to cross diocese borders without being interrogated. Skye has hunted for both of them. Jude doesn't like to kill, even for food, so Skye shares." Adel purred reassuringly.

"So you think we should trust him?" Evan didn't want to put Jude at greater risk by separating him from Skye, so the logical conclusion was to take them both home. Once there, they'd soon discover where their loyalties lay.

"I think he is a good man, Evan. I do not know about his connection to the Church, but if he is who this little one says he is, my duty is to help to protect him as well. We were created to protect the people of the Church. There is something about him…. I am not sure what it is, but just like you, there is something special about him."

"I want to believe in his intentions, but they're so contrary to what I've always believed of the Church. If I'm the Maker or Elemental, I need to learn what I am, what to expect of my powers. Maybe he knows?"

"You are the Maker. You create and awaken my kind. Every century in which the Maker is killed or lost to us prevents my kind from reawakening. The Maker has a spirit of renewal, and with his death, that renewal is cut short. Jude's right. Eventually even creatures made of stone will deteriorate and cease to exist. Evan, the fact that you live—your life force—is calling to us. The very existence of the Maker is awakening the younger gargoyles. For those like me to awaken, you need to call us, talk to us, as you did to me. I remember hearing your voice calling to me that first day, feeling your power drawing me from my sleep."

"So you think we should trust him?"

"He's a man of the Church." Adel nodded as he spoke, with certainty, as if he were doing something that felt positively right to him. "I was created to protect him and those like him. Skye believes in him, and I want to believe Skye."

"All right. Let's go back to the truck and take him and Skye back to the hotel. If we leave within the hour, we can be back at the cabin shortly after dawn," Evan said, sighing and petting Skye. He turned his attention to Jude. "Jude, would you like to come with us? You could continue your investigation of Father Michael, up close and personal, and you'd have a home, at least for a while. Skye would be safe, and I'd be able to get to know you. Maybe we could work together and see how things go," Evan offered.

Adel put Skye on the ground and made gentle cooing noises. Skye cackled happily and bounded across the grass, back toward Jude.

"You don't trust me, but you're going to take me to your sanctuary anyway? That's a big risk." Jude eyed Evan and Adel with suspicion, but opened his arms to Skye, who leaped into his embrace and rubbed his head against Jude's chest.

"Yes, but one worth taking. If you're really an Inquisitor sent here to help us with Father Michael, then I owe it to all the people he's hurt to help you. If you really are trying to help and risking yourself for our benefit, then by working together we will accomplish much more."

"Thank you for giving me the chance to prove that I'm not here to hurt you," Jude said.

"Prove to me you're trustworthy and who you say you are, and Adel and I'll consider coming with you to Rome to awaken the gargoyles." Evan sighed and trembled in Adel's arms as fear of this deal washed through him. Just the thought of going to Rome and risking Adel's life terrified Evan more than losing his own life did. He'd find a way to free Adel completely of his forced sleep before he ever agreed to travel to Rome. At least then Adel wouldn't be at their mercy when he slept.

"You've nothing to fear from me. This is far more cooperation than I expected or dared to hope for. Are you sure you want to do this? The people who are after me because of what I am to the Church are very powerful. Harboring me won't make you any friends in their eyes. They claim the sanctity of the Church and their own righteousness, but they abuse that gift. They fear and hunt me because once I have the proof I need of their activities and my report reaches Rome, reinforcements will be sent in to remove them from power. Father Michael will have people hunting me because of the danger I pose to him. Officially, my investigation can destroy him, but not before I can prove his activities."

"Won't Rome come to your rescue if they try to hurt you? If they—" Evan frowned and stuttered.

"Of course, if they can get to me before he kills me and reports my death as an accident or accuses me of attacking him—whatever trumped-up charges he can create to cover for himself. Rome would send officers to collect him and remove him from power, but they can do nothing without proof." Jude frowned and shook his head in frustration. "You'll be at a greater risk with me there."

"Come on. Let's go. We can discuss this better back at the hotel. Better yet, back home." Evan smiled. "Do you have transportation or did you walk?"

"I have my own car. We haven't been on foot for about two years." Jude smiled as he walked toward Evan and Adel. Skye began to sing, his voice ringing over the area. "Shhh, Skye. I know you're happy, but it isn't safe for you to sing here."

"Well, then, lead the way." Evan grinned. With his decision made, he felt so much better. He'd decided to trust Jude, so he'd do so unconditionally until proven wrong. Jude had already earned Evan's trust over the years with the tips he'd given. Evan had trusted Jude to set up an identity file for Adel, and he'd done so without questions. What was the difference between keeping their secrets from afar and keeping their secrets in person? The possibility that they could be rid of Father Michael by helping Jude was too great an opportunity to pass by.

Chapter 12

ELEMENTAL LORE

As written by the scribes and entombed in the Church Archives:

To date, the Church has recognized five types of Elementals:

1. Earth, being the rarest and least-often born. Only two known in all of Church history.
2. Air, being the second rarest.
3. Spirit.
4. Water.
5. Fire, being the most prevalent, most destructive, and most volatile of all the beings.

No other information is contained in the archive as to their purpose or powers.

THE SUN began to peek over the horizon just as the truck, followed by Jude's tan, two-tone El Camino, pulled in to the dirt driveway that led up to the cabin. The night had been long, and although Adel had driven most of the way home and allowed Evan to sleep, they'd traded places as morning came upon them. Adel needed to get down into their bedroom before he became stone.

Evan had no sooner parked the truck than Adel made a dash for the cabin.

Evan's connection with Adel, that tingling sensation he felt every time Adel awoke or went to sleep, told him Adel had made it to their bed with but a few seconds to spare. He hated cutting things so closely. He needed to start working on extending the amount of time Adel could be in the sunlight. Maybe if he began with small enough increments of time, the drain on him wouldn't affect him to the point where he'd sleep for weeks.

If he could convince Jude to help Adel make his excuses to Father Michael, he'd start working on those changes as soon as possible. Evan climbed out of the cab of the truck and made his way to the front porch of the cabin.

Jude climbed out of the El Camino and smiled at him. "Do we need to hide Adel? I imagine he's harder to disguise than Skye." Jude grinned, then frowned when he didn't see Adel sitting in the passenger seat of the truck.

"Nope, he made it to the cabin and into our bedroom before he turned to stone." Evan chuckled.

"How? The sun rose at least half an hour before we stopped. Skye's been stone for at least that long." Jude frowned.

"Well, it's a bit of a long story. Let's get you settled, and I'll take you below and explain how Adel can be awake after sunrise and before sunset. I'm hoping you can tell me what you know of the Maker and his powers, and I'll tell you what I've experienced."

Jude handed Evan a box from the front seat that held Skye and grabbed a bag from the back of the vehicle. Jude turned and looked at the small log cabin.

"Come on in and welcome to our home," Evan said.

"Thank you." Jude smiled, followed Evan into the cabin, and looked around.

"Well, I don't believe Father Michael did any breaking and entering since we left. You'll need to use one of the bedrooms upstairs until we can get you a room prepared downstairs. I mainly use the upper levels of the cabin for show. I keep things simple up here. It keeps Father Michael off my case. He hasn't discovered the caves and mines below because of the naturally occurring iron ore in the hills," Evan explained as he led the way through the living area. He pointed out the hallway and the guest bedrooms.

"Wow, I never thought something naturally occurring would jam up their instruments. You're sure they aren't on to you?" Jude asked, frowning, seeming unsure if Evan was brilliant or misguided.

"Well, I've been here saving gargoyles for a couple years now, and Father Michael has never set foot below or even questioned me about the possibility of a basement."

"That's brilliant. I'm impressed you got one over on the walking skeleton."

"Well, my dad is the mastermind behind this place. He bought the cabin and didn't tell anyone. He willed it to me upon his death. I found a letter from him waiting here for me. Back in the late 1800s, a gold rush hit this area and prospectors honeycombed the Black Hills, searching for gold.

Now all the mines are shut down, but they left behind the tunnels, which have been long forgotten."

"That's unbelievable. How could they not know?" Jude asked, crossing his arms over his chest.

"The 1800s were a violent time, and most of the documents, including prospecting records, mineral rights, and mining records, were destroyed."

"Unbelievable. Your dad was a genius."

Evan led the way toward the back of the cabin and the bedrooms. "There are three bedrooms. Mine is on the right. The one at the end of the hall I've made up to look like Adel's, but take your pick—you can have either one. We should be able to get you a real room set up downstairs soon."

"Don't trouble yourself too much. I've never really stayed anywhere too long. I don't want to bring trouble down on you." Jude rubbed at his eyes, frustration coming off him in waves.

"Don't worry. This place is more secure than your mother's arms. After you see the setup, I'll gladly put in place any other security measures you can think of, but wait till you see my security. Like I said, this level is mainly for show. Bathroom is on the left. Make yourself at home. The kitchen and everything in it is fair game. There's a garden out back and a few fruit trees, but the main kitchen is below." Evan set the box with Skye inside on the dresser as Jude set his bag on the bed with the hand-sewn quilt bedspread.

Evan went into the kitchen and heated a pot of water for instant coffee. Despite wanting desperately to go lie down with Adel and sleep the day away, Evan struggled to stay upstairs with Jude. They had too much to talk about and get done before Father Michael's inevitable visit. For example, they needed to discuss the role Jude would be playing in front of Father Michael. Evan looked into the freezer and found some home-baked cookies his mom had sent as a gift. He grabbed a few and put them on a plate to thaw. He went out to the living room and turned on a local radio station to wait for Jude.

He didn't have to wait long. Jude hadn't brought much with him. He returned, self-consciously carrying Skye's box under his arm.

Evan handed Jude a cup of coffee and settled down on the sofa. He motioned for Jude to have a seat and offered him the frozen cookies. "Help yourself. You've got to be hungry and exhausted after the drive. I know they aren't much, but dunked in the coffee, they soften quickly and taste pretty good."

"Thanks. I had snacks in the car, but that's one hell of a trip." Jude sat, placing Skye's box beside him.

"I thought we'd better get our stories straight before Father Michael shows up, and I want to give you a tour of the rest of my place. Then you can get some rest, if you like."

"Well, as far as Father Michael and our story goes, he won't recognize me on sight. Very few of the clergy know what I look like. If they did, I wouldn't be able to do my job. Do you want to introduce me as another cousin, or maybe just someone who came to you to apprentice as a stonemason? Either story would be fine."

"I don't think another cousin is a good idea. I don't think even Father Michael would be stupid enough to believe two cousins just dropped out of nowhere."

"If I can log in to your system, I should be able to create documents to back up either story." Jude sipped his coffee and picked up a cookie.

"Well, since Adel recently became a new cousin, I think being an apprentice would probably be the most viable option. I don't want Father Michael to dig around and try to contact my family to ask questions. Father Michael's been less than pleasant to them in the past." Evan tiredly ran a hand through his hair. Sometimes the fear for his family's safety could become overwhelming, because he knew if Father Michael decided they threatened his plans, he'd have them killed.

"There's a significant risk in staying close to your family, given your hobbies. I think you're pretty good at doing everything you can to protect them. I'll also petition Rome to adjust the records in the database for Adel. If Father Michael requests the records, they should be able to stall him until the record is adjusted. I know Rome will do whatever they can to protect you and Adel." Jude slowly nodded, a look of deep consideration on his face.

"Good, I'd really appreciate that. I'm not sure I can trust Rome, but I guess if they do help us, maybe I'll be able to start believing that Rome isn't the enemy, but the one being wrongly blamed for everything done in their name."

"It'll be all right. You'll see. Rome isn't your enemy."

"So, you're now an apprentice stonemason. Cool. That'll give me an excuse to take you around to various sites—cemeteries and such." Evan chuckled softly, thinking of the many frowns he'd see on Father Michael's face as yet another man moved in to his house. "Just so you're aware, Father Michael practically had kittens when Adel moved in. And Adel's a bit protective and possessive. He didn't take well to Father Michael's attempt to lay claim to me. I'm sure Father Michael will be even more unhappy about you living here."

"If he is part of the group I am searching for, then he is not above using dark magic to make himself more powerful. If he suspects you're the Maker, he may want to possess you, own you for your abilities, use you to increase his own renown among his peers. He'll want to force you to demonstrate your power and then destroy whatever you create, making him seem more powerful and godly. If he can keep you from understanding that you are the source of the power, all the better. He'll see the two of us as interfering with those plans. The mere fact that we're living here and influencing you will make us a threat. He won't like our presence, which could work in my favor."

"Oh? And how will pushing Father Michael be a good thing? He's dangerous. I've always worked to keep him calm so he wouldn't have any reason to suspect me," Evan said.

"If he's unstable, then maybe he'll make a mistake. When he does, I'll be there to catch him. We'll have the undeniable proof the Church needs to put him away—permanently." Jude nodded thoughtfully.

"Another thing you should know. Adel's and my relationship isn't simply one of friends, or even Maker and guardian. Adel's chosen me as his mate, and I really love him. He's mine and I'm his, for as long as we live. I just wanted you to be aware. If you're going to have a problem with us being together, then we need to make alternative living arrangements for you. Neither Adel nor I will tolerate being looked down upon because we love each other."

"I don't have a problem with it. I think we're all seeking someone special to spend a lifetime with. If you've found that with Adel, then who am I to dictate differently?"

"Well, the Church hasn't been the most accepting of gay relationships in the past," Evan scoffed.

"Unlike the Church in the past, Rome encourages same-sex relationships. Love is celebrated as a gift, wherever it's found." Jude smiled gently, a touch of sad longing in his eyes. "Unfortunately, even though that is the stance of Rome, many dioceses still do not fully embrace and endorse the attitude."

"Thank you. I didn't know how to tell you, but I know Adel won't restrain himself, as we're relatively newly mated. I didn't want you to misunderstand his attention. We truly love each other." Evan sighed. He stood, setting his cup on the coffee table.

"Don't worry, Evan. I envy you, finding your true love. I hope to someday find mine." Jude stood.

"Why don't I show you the rest of the cabin?"

Leaving his half-drunk coffee behind, Jude followed Evan to the open trapdoor in the kitchen floor. The lights were on below. Evan led the way into his basement.

"Welcome to my home and sanctuary." Evan grinned at the surprised look on Jude's face as he stood in the small room at the base of the stairs. He took a right into a large, spotlessly clean living room. Conservatively decorated, with large rugs covering the rock floor and bookcases against the walls, the room felt warm and homey even though there were no windows. "This is the living room and library. Feel free to read anything you find interesting. Adel and I share the bedroom on the right, which is directly below my bedroom up in the cabin." Evan went down a corridor to the left to another open cave. "This cave is directly beneath the bedroom you chose in the cabin. We'll get a nice rug and some furniture moved in. Just let me know what all you need. Adel and I have discussed putting in another trapdoor. I didn't want to take the chance that he might get stuck in a room upstairs, unable to get below. I hope you don't mind. I'd still like to install it, and I'd appreciate any help you might be willing to give. There are doors going both ways from the main rooms in the cabin down here, as well as tunnels going out to the shop."

"This is phenomenal, Evan. This place is perfect. You've got everything set up. Now all you really need is a good security program and a computer network," Jude remarked, looking around at the cave with a smile.

"Right this way." Evan chuckled and led Jude into his bedroom. Adel lay covered in the bed, waiting for Evan to join him. Evan kissed Adel on the cheek. "I'll be with you soon, my love. I'm just showing Jude around a bit," Evan whispered into Adel's ear. Then he returned to Jude. "These are the security-cam relays and they are all piped into these computers. I have security cams at all the entrances to the property. They're motion sensitive, so occasionally the alerts will be animals, but I've been saved from more than one surprise visit from Father Michael by this system. I'm the only one really using it. Adel's learning, but there's a lot he doesn't quite understand yet, although I'm surprised how quickly he's adapting to modern technology. There's no reason we can't run hardline cable into your room and the living room for access to the system. I'd prefer cable to a wireless network. Don't want anyone picking up on us accidentally, as Father Michael doesn't even know I own a computer, much less this system."

"I can imagine he would enjoy thinking he caught you unsuspecting and off guard," Jude said.

"Oh yes, surprise is one of his favorite techniques. I used to let him believe he surprised me a couple times a week. With more people wandering around, he'll probably find it harder to do."

"And don't we feel sorry for him? I'm guessing that would be a no." Jude's voice dripped sarcasm, and they both laughed.

Evan flipped screens to show the other camera angles. "There are also views of the shop, the garage, and each of the rooms in the cabin. The link to the Internet is by a remote nearby satellite uplink, and so far has remained stable. It used to be a network tower, but it's unused and nobody knows I've commandeered it."

"Wow, you've got quite the setup. Thank you so much for trusting me with this. You've got a really great place. It truly is a sanctuary." Jude looked around in awe. "You've literally carved yourself a place to feel secure out of the very stone surrounding you."

"My dad did most of the excavating and connecting the mines to the caves before I inherited the cabin. I've updated security and set up and installed the net connections and the cameras, but he did the manual labor. If you ever go out beyond the lighted portion of the network, take one of the gargoyles with you, or you could get lost in the labyrinth of mines and caves." Evan was proud of what he'd achieved and grateful for the special gift his father had left for him.

"He gave you the perfect location, and you've made it safe." Jude yawned. "If you don't mind, I really could use some rest. I think I'll keep Skye with me for the time being."

"I'm sorry. I know you must be tired. I just wanted you to know the layout. Please feel free to come down whenever you wish. While you're living here, I want you to feel at home. You'll be comfortable and safe here. Skye's free to roam the property. The others will show him around when they all awaken." Evan led the way back up the stairs and through the trapdoor. "The kitchen on this level is stocked mainly with instant coffee and easy-to-make, microwave-type meals. The real food is below."

"Thank you. For everything." Jude put a hand on Evan's shoulder. "Really, thanks. I don't believe anyone has ever trusted me like this. I won't let you down."

"I know you won't. This is your home now for as long as you want it to be. Go get some sleep." Evan smiled.

Jude walked down the hallway to the bedroom and closed the door.

Evan went back down the trapdoor to his bedroom. He checked the security cams and made sure everything was in place and the alarms were set, then headed to the bathroom for a shower.

Thoughts of Adel floated through his mind as he washed away the travel dust and exhaustion. He emerged from the bathroom feeling much more like himself and climbed into bed. He stroked Adel's face, the silky smooth, cool texture of the white stone gliding under his fingers. He could feel Adel's sleeping mind, silent and restful, yet filled with love for him. Evan smiled. He couldn't imagine a more beautiful sight than Adel. Asleep, Adel had more allure than any other carved effigy he'd ever seen. Just the sight of him, waiting for Evan to join him, soothed his soul.

"I want you to be awake longer, my love, when you wish to be awake, and asleep when you wish to sleep. I want to give you the gift of this freedom from the demands of the day and the night. But I can't give you that freedom all at once. I just know in my heart that someday you're going to need it. I don't know how long I'd sleep or if I'd ever awaken if I tried to do it all at once. I don't want to put you at risk for my whim, so I'm going to try to do this a little at a time, my love." Evan swept his gaze over the stone body of his lover. He ran his fingers from Adel's shoulder, then along his arm to his hand. "Tonight, my love, I'll try to give you half an hour more of daylight. This is half an hour more that you control, where neither the day nor the night can force you to be alive or remain stone." Evan took hold of the blankets at their feet and covered both himself and Adel, then snuggled into Adel's chest. "I want you to have the freedom to choose."

JUDE PUT the box with Skye on the dresser in his room and then closed the drapes. He wanted the darkness, and even though they were out in the middle of nowhere, he needed the feeling of privacy. He looked around the room, noticing the large, comfortable bed. He ached to lie back on the soft pillows and relax, but the opportunity to use the shower called to him. He hadn't had a real shower or running water in what felt like months. Clean water tended to be a scarce resource in some dioceses, and expensive. They hadn't splurged for the extra charge to use the only functional shower at the motel the previous night, so Jude had made do brushing his teeth and washing with water that had been provided in a bucket next to the sink.

He entered the bathroom and found folded towels sitting on a shelf. This would be a treat—to have a real shower, complete with soap and shampoo. Jude stripped to the skin, piling his dirty clothes in the corner and stepped into the shower, drawing the curtain. As he turned on the water, dirt ran from his body and hair. It felt so good, numbing his already-exhausted senses and muscles that had long needed release from the tension of being on the run.

When he finished, he couldn't believe how incredibly good it felt to be clean after having been filthy for so long. After pulling on a fresh T-shirt and a pair of sweatpants he'd brought into the bathroom with him, he hung his damp towel on the hook on the back of the door and returned to his bedroom. His body felt practically boneless as he dropped to the bed and crawled under the covers.

He couldn't remember the last time he had actually slept in a bed. He'd been sleeping in his car, not wanting to chance being traced to a motel room. He'd given Evan cash for his room when they had stopped on the way from California, but it had been in Evan's name. Although he'd tried to sleep, doing more than just resting his eyes had been impossible. He'd felt completely exposed.

Jude took hold of the quilt and curled into the thick, warm blanket. He felt bone tired but strangely safe for the first time in years. Evan had risked a lot letting Jude get close, when their previous relationship had only been one of impersonal net messages. Jude was grateful. Evan's trust gave Jude the chance to bring Father Michael down and hopefully give people some justice. Whether Evan really believed or not, the raw power of the Maker existed in him. The Papacy viewed him as an extremely powerful entity, and one they revered. One they wanted to control as much or more than Father Michael did.

Jude closed his eyes as he remembered what the Pope had told him before sending him on his mission and giving him Skye. Only one Elemental—be it Earth, Fire, Water, Air, or Spirit—was born in a century, and there hadn't been an Earth Elemental born for more than a millennium, which made Evan extra special. He'd be safer with the Church to protect him than out here in the wild. But for all the Pope's good intentions, the Church was imperfect and the corruption Father Michael represented went deep. Father Michael and others like him wouldn't wield their power so freely without support from someone high up within the Church. If Evan ever agreed to go to Rome, he would need to be made fully aware of the political posturing and the games played for power beneath the mantle of purity and godliness.

From the little power Evan displayed, Jude didn't understand the need to control him. Protect him, yes, but not control. So he could breathe life into stone statues, turning them into living stone gargoyles, and awaken them from their hibernation if they were already alive? If there was more to his power, Evan clearly didn't know what it was, and since his only teacher was a gargoyle himself, the extent of those powers might have been lost forever. Was Evan a threat? Probably. Indirectly, at least. The purists would see his power of creation as an attempt to become a god, for only gods could create life. Since the form that life took was a gargoyle, which again the purists saw as a personification of evil, then Evan must clearly be evil since he gave life to evil.

Evan seemed only to want to love and be loved, to protect his family and the gargoyles in his care. Jude might not be able to hide Evan from the Church, but he'd try to keep him safe from those who'd use and abuse his power, or even have him killed out of fear of that power. If he couldn't do that, at the very least he could rid Evan and the rest of the souls in this diocese of Father Michael.

Chapter 13

JUDE AWOKE late in the afternoon. An alarm sounded softly in the cabin, and Adel shook his shoulder.

"Jude, wake up. The perimeter alarm is sounding, and I don't know how to turn the thing off. Evan's still asleep, and I believe he probably will be for a while." Adel looked quite worried.

"Okay, first things first. Let's get the alarm off." Jude got up and followed Adel back to the trapdoor in the kitchen and down the subterranean corridors into the main bedroom. Evan, gently snoring, was wrapped in blankets, oblivious to everything around him. Jude shook Evan's shoulder gently. "Evan…. Come on, buddy, wake up."

"He will not awaken. My little Maker has no idea of the extent of his power, and what going against the natural order of things costs him. I have tried to explain, and I thought he understood the consequences, but still he continues to risk himself." Adel snarled his frustration. "Will you please refrain from touching my mate? I do not wish to kill you, but if you do not desist, I may attack you anyway." Adel glared at Jude, who quickly pulled back his hand as he noticed the curl of Adel's lips and his tightly clenched hands.

"Sorry. Didn't mean to upset you. Okay. Alarm first, story later." Jude sighed and looked to the computer system and the monitors flashing their alarms. The monitor showed a car pulling up in the front yard. It parked next to the truck and the El Camino. Jude opened the alarm program and clicked on the mute button, which silenced the alarm but did not turn the system off entirely. He'd come back and look over the program later when they had more time. "Come on, Adel. You need to introduce me to Father Michael, and we need to make Evan's apologies. We can tell him Evan stayed to visit his mother. You brought me back to help around here, and Evan will be returning in a week. I think that should keep him off our backs, at least for a little while."

"Perhaps. That may keep him away, but will we be sending him to Evan's mother?" Adel worried aloud. With Jude at his heels, Adel ran for the trapdoor and up into the kitchen.

"Damn! I don't know. I think Father Michael mainly comes here because he had complete control over Evan before you arrived. Now he doesn't have that control, but his best chance for alone time would still be here and not at Evan's mother's. I think our odds are pretty good that if he knows Evan will be back soon, he won't go after his mother," Jude said, hoping he was right.

"I shall see to the door. You go make coffee. He was very hostile when I moved in with Evan. I cannot imagine he shall be accepting of another moving in as well."

"Oh, I don't know. There's less suspicion of sexual misconduct when three guys are roommates than when it's a couple. Let's just see where he goes with it." Jude chuckled and watched the rug straighten out automatically over the trapdoor as it closed just as pounding began on the door.

"Good evening, Father Michael. Please, come in," Adel said simply, holding the door open for him to enter. "Evan isn't here, I'm afraid."

"What do you mean, he isn't here? The truck is here, and a vehicle I've never seen before is here. Did you boys get a new car?" Father Michael's words were conversational, but his tone accusatory.

"No, the car belongs to the new apprentice stonemason. We met him when we were in California purchasing rock," Adel said matter-of-factly as he led Father Michael to the living room and waved him to the sofa.

Father Michael glared around the room, staring into all the corners as if looking for things hiding in the shadows.

"Father Michael, it's so nice to meet you in person. Evan's told me so much about you, I feel like I've known you for years." Jude came out of the kitchen carrying three empty cups and a carafe of hot water, which he set on the table. He turned to shake hands with Father Michael. "I'm Jude Jamison. Do you take cream or sugar?"

"Yes, both." Father Michael scowled at Jude, but reluctantly took his hand in a firm handshake.

"Be right back, forgot the coffee crystals. All Evan drinks is instant." Jude smiled and popped back into the kitchen, then emerged with a jar of instant Folgers, powdered creamer, and sugar, while Adel poured the water and handed a cup to Father Michael. "Evan should be back in about a week. His mother's health isn't good, but he didn't want to leave things here unattended any longer, so the two of us returned. Evan will be home when his mother is well enough to be on her own." Jude set it all on the coffee table and picked up his own cup.

"So he just left his business to the two of you untrained apprentices?" Father Michael scowled in confusion and anger.

Jude laughed. "Oh no, by no means."

Nerves skittered along Jude's spine, but he made small talk as he fixed his coffee. Adel sat back and watched as he put on his act for Father Michael, and hopefully the priest would buy his story.

"I know which chores need to be done, and Evan showed me how to run the grinder," Adel said, his eyes never leaving Father Michael.

"We can do some of the basics around the place, so when Evan returns, we can begin immediately with the more difficult work." Jude moved his hands about as he spoke with exaggerated expression.

"We are to clean up the workshop, tend the garden, and prune the fruit trees," Adel added as Father Michael's attention turned from Jude to Adel and back, as if he couldn't decide which of the two he disliked the most.

"If you have so much work to do, why are you both in here instead of working?" Father Michael accused.

"Actually, we just arrived ourselves, not long before you. I just finished getting settled into my room."

"And I unloaded the rock we purchased in California into the hoppers behind the shop." Adel picked up his coffee and added sugar and cream.

"Would you like to join us for dinner, Father? I'm not a great cook, but I can make something simple and filling for the three of us." Jude smiled but prayed he would refuse.

"Ah, no, that's not necessary. I just wanted to check on Evan and make sure his trip went well. I've more pressing duties to perform." Father Michael stood and set the coffee cup back on the table untouched. "Adel, Jude, may God be with you," Father Michael said as a cursory blessing as he turned suddenly to leave.

"Thank you, Father. Feel free to drop by anytime." Jude smiled and waved, following Adel and the father out onto the porch.

Father Michael got into his car and took off down the driveway.

Jude and Adel closed the door and returned to the kitchen.

"This way," Adel said, ducking down the trapdoor, and then back into the bedroom with the computer monitors.

Jude tapped on the screen and watched Father Michael's car pull out of the main gate. Once the vehicle turned toward town, it could no longer be seen on camera.

"That went far better than I'd imagined," Jude mumbled, half to himself and half to Adel. He reset the alarms, took the system off mute, and sighed, resting his head in his hands. "Okay. You mind telling me what's going on and why Evan is sleeping like the dead?"

"Yes, I suppose now is the time for explanations. I'm hungry. Can you cook?" Adel asked, eyeing Jude, tipping his head to the side.

"I do all right as long as it isn't fancy," Jude said with a crooked smile.

"Good. Come, then. Evan has taught me a couple of things, but not everything. The others should be awake in an hour or so. Shall we see what we can find in the kitchen?" Adel motioned toward the door, then turned back to the sleeping Evan. "Sleep well, my heart. Awaken soon." Adel stroked Evan's hair and kissed his cheek, while Jude got up from the computer and strolled out to the kitchen.

Jude opened the refrigerator and pulled out cold cuts, cheese, and the fixings for sandwiches. "Okay, talk. Evan seemed fine yesterday. What happened?"

Adel sat at the breakfast bar and watched as Jude put together the sandwiches. "I believe he decided to extend the amount of time and control I have over when I am awake and asleep. He wishes to give me the freedom to decide when I turn to stone and when I am awake."

"That's quite the gift if he can pull it off."

"He does not like having things like yesterday's near mishap of me almost turning to stone in the truck rule my life. Previously, I never had to worry about when I turned to stone, but then I lived with my own kind and life was simpler—we all have the same sleep patterns, so there is no problem."

"But Evan wants to be with you always, not just at night."

"Yes. I live with my mate. I want to protect him all of the time, and not being able to control my cycle is very… inconvenient." Adel sighed, watching Jude intently as he prepared the meal.

"So you think he tried to do something about it?" Jude shook his head in amazement.

"Yes. He told me as I slept what he planned to do. I heard him make the statement, and I felt the power drain from him into me. I also awoke earlier today because of the change he wrought. He intends to continue with this until I'm able to decide with complete freedom when I awaken and when I sleep."

"So he sleeps to recover from the power drain," Jude mumbled, half to himself.

"I appreciate his gift, but the amount of power necessary to make this change is incredibly taxing for him. He does not seem to grasp the fact that he is going against a gargoyle's natural state, which is more than just awakening a half an hour earlier than before."

"He's ambitious, that's certain. How long do you think he'll sleep?" Jude asked.

"Last time he did something like this, he remained unconscious for a week." Adel shrugged. "This time it wasn't quite as taxing. I can tell he does not sleep as deeply this time."

Jude pushed the plate of sandwiches to the center and took one off the top to put on his own plate, just as Cela uncurled from around Adel's neck, stretched, and crooned happily as Adel stroked his eye ridges.

"Greetings, Cela. Will you go and fetch the others and bring Skye down here so he knows where Jude is? Evan is in the bedroom sleeping." Adel smiled at Cela, who cheeped and leaped off his shoulder and disappeared.

Yin and Yang came bounding in to sit at Adel's feet, their deep-throated growls causing Jude to back up against the refrigerator.

"Who are these fine fellows?" Jude glanced furtively between Adel and the lion-dogs.

"Easy, boys. This is Jude. He's living here now, so be nice. Evan says he can stay." Adel laughed and greeted each gargoyle separately. "The one on the right is Yin and the other is Yang. They're lion-dog gargoyles who were placed in Evan's care by the monks before the Church demolished their temple. Come on, guys. Give Jude a break."

"Hi, guys. Sorry I didn't make enough for you too." Jude let the two lion-dogs nuzzle his hands.

"They prefer to hunt for themselves over eating prepared foods." Adel watched the lion-dogs bound down the hallway into the darkened corridors.

"What's beyond the rooms?"

"Mostly tunnels where the other gargoyles find their places to sleep during the day. They prefer the natural tunnels to having their own rooms. The musketeers should be showing up next, unless they have already gone out for the night. They like to watch the entrances to the property and run the perimeter marking our territory."

Cela glided down into the kitchen with Skye close behind, twittering and singing happily. He spotted Jude and landed on the countertop, rubbing into Jude's hand.

"Hello, Skye. I'm happy to see you too. Did you sleep well?" Jude asked as Skye sang happily and Cela sat in front of Adel.

"Are the musketeers already on patrol?" Adel asked Cela, who crooned softly in reply. "I see. Will you please show Skye around? Introduce him to the four and the lion-dogs. He may need to hunt as well." Adel smiled at Cela, who nuzzled Skye and then took off on wing, heading down the hallway, with Skye following after a farewell nuzzle against Jude's hand.

"Cela seems to understand you quite well." Jude watched the two fly off until they were out of sight, lost in the darkness of the tunnels.

"Cela understands perfectly. He just doesn't have the ability to speak. His vocal cords are not capable of it. He's very young, younger even than your Skye, but Evan called him and gave him life. I think Cela has the understanding he has because Evan expected him to. That's Evan's power. Eventually, Skye will understand more language as well, especially if he continues to hang around Cela." Adel chuckled, but then sobered quickly.

"Jude, are you sure we have nothing to fear from the Church? I want to believe you, but I cannot take any chances with my mate. I love him, and he is the hope for my kind." Adel watched Jude so carefully he felt as if Adel's eyes could bore holes directly to his soul and assess his honesty.

"No, Adel, I don't believe you have anything to fear from the Church itself. These are very dark times. Humanity is struggling in darkness. We've lost so much, our spirit as a people is broken. The war cost us families and friends to the point where it was uncertain whether humanity would survive or become just another extinct species." Jude picked up a napkin and wiped his hands. "I can't imagine how horrifying it would be to see everyone around you succumbing to disease and then experience the aftermath of trying to bury or burn the dead, all the while wondering if you were damned or blessed because you survived while others died." Jude scowled, narrowing his eyes as he contemplated the horror.

"Yet mankind perseveres." Adel sat back in his chair.

"Yes, but at what cost? The governments fell into disarray. Humanity went through a very black period, during which we were no better than animals. Those who survived did so through force of will alone. There were no sanctuaries and nobody to help, no law. No justice." Jude frowned slightly.

"Survival of the fittest is a harsh mistress."

"After a few years, pockets of humanity drew together. We're a social species, you see, and communities of survivors formed. At the center, the Church, consoling those who lost loved ones, encouraged people to believe God hadn't forgotten them." Jude rubbed his forehead as if these thoughts pained him.

Adel nodded. "The Church has always been there to console the living when a loved one passes on to the next life."

"The Church drew together and began organizing humanity, with the Papacy in Rome extending through the various dioceses under the control of the Cardinals, Archbishops, and Bishops to guide and rule the world. Those who represented the Church followed the rules set out by God's law, which even in the past had always left much to the interpretation of the reader. Wherever humanity resided, dioceses were created, and Rome gave the local ruling regent the religious title of Bishop, leaving him to govern with little or no interference." Jude's eyes became unfocused as if he was remembering something unpleasant. "Thus Rome allowed these priests the right to interpret the Law of God as they saw fit, with the idea that they'd do so in the best interests of their communities. In some cases, the local ruling body allowed the people to flourish and grow. In others, evil took root and the Church found itself in need of a military force, a police body, to step in and rescue the people from tyranny."

"And you are a part of this police force?"

Jude nodded. "The Papacy is getting stronger. It's attempting to put a stop to the misuse of power it so benignly bequeathed without consideration of the people it was giving that power to. If I didn't believe… if I didn't think the Church means to be a power for good, I wouldn't be here."

"So you think Evan should go to Rome?" Adel tipped his head to the side.

"Yes, I think he'd be safest there. I think he'd be free to learn about his power and free to use his power as a force for good. Even in Rome, though, not everyone is a good person or in agreement as to the purpose of the Maker or the Elementals, but I think Rome holds his best chance to be safe and to learn about himself."

"Why are you doing this? Why are you here, Jude?"

"I'm doing this because I lived in one of those places. The Church freed me, but not before I lost my baby brother. I dedicated my life to freeing others from those who abuse the power the Church bestows." Jude sighed as if a great weight were dragging down on his shoulders.

"Why do you not have someone to assist you? You should have a partner, someone to look out for you."

"A great man saved me, and because of him, I went to school and became part of the JIS, the Jesuit Inquisitor's Service. I wanted to spend my life helping him. He felt protective of me and died saving me instead of allowing me to do my job."

Adel frowned. "I am sure he felt he was doing the right thing. He sacrificed himself to save you. That is what a partner does. They are willing to pay the ultimate price."

"I know, but after that I refused to have another partner. His death still haunts me, and I feel responsible, as though I let him down—I failed him."

"If he willingly sacrificed his life to save yours, I cannot believe he blames you or felt you let him down. He gave his life that you might live on. It is not right to live in guilt. Your partner would not have wanted that for you. You dishonor his sacrifice by belittling yourself."

Jude sighed, refusing to meet Adel's eyes. "The Pope, it would seem, agrees with you. The Church encouraged me to take another partner, but I refused, so the Papacy gave me Skye."

Adel chuckled. "I'm sure it must have been a shock to you when Skye awoke."

Jude nodded. "At first I didn't know what to make of the statue placed in my care. I thought someone had played a really bad joke on me, telling me this was a partner I couldn't kill, till the first night Skye awoke. I've never looked at statuary in the same way ever again. I'm not sure why, but he's different. He's loyal, more so than any other in my life, and I'm so glad he is." Jude stared into Adel's eyes as he tried to convey his feelings.

"I am glad the Church found you a partner you were able to accept. Skye is in good hands, and he is very protective of you."

"Yeah, well, the feeling is mutual."

"Thank you for alleviating my worries and telling me about yourself." Adel rose. "Make yourself at home. I need to hunt, or we'll run out of meat. I suspect one of the lion-dogs, if not both, will be in with Evan while I am out. They understand speech as well as Cela does, and will help you if you need anything." Adel put a hand on Jude's shoulder, then turned and ran down the hallway, his wings appearing briefly before he disappeared into the darkness.

JUDE HAD begun to clean up the dishes when he heard a jingling sound and turned to see one of the lion-dogs sitting, watching him, from the end of the counter.

"Sorry, no leftovers." Jude smiled and went back to cleaning up the kitchen. When he was done, he went into the cave beneath his bedroom and looked at the ceiling, making plans for a trapdoor into the room. "What do you think? We live in a cave beneath the house. What better way to install a trapdoor than to make one like the heroes of old?" He chuckled to himself as he remembered a program he had once seen on an entertainment forum, where the hero had slid down a pole into a subterranean lair. He couldn't remember the name of the program exactly, but it had to do with bats. He liked the thought of the pole and maybe a ladder, all hidden behind a sliding panel in the bedroom closet. He went to the main trapdoor in the kitchen and then back to his bedroom to see about the logistics of creating his escape tunnel.

Chapter 14

EVAN AWOKE with a start. Instinctively he knew the sun was already up, even though there were no windows in his belowground bedroom to allow in any light. He hoped his attempt at adjusting Adel's sleeping patterns hadn't caused him to sleep for too long this time. He had no idea how long he'd slept, but the sound of a hammer banging away incessantly reminded him that he had a guest. Adel's stone form, spooned up tightly against his back, reminded him that, even with that guest, he was warm and safe. Evan carefully climbed out from Adel's arms and headed for the bathroom. He felt gross, and wanted at least a shower before going to find Jude.

Evan sipped the steaming cup of coffee he carried as he followed the sound of hammering toward the guest room. Jude must be working on something in his room, probably starting the trapdoor up into his bedroom. The room he entered was brightly lit and strewn with electrical and computer wires. Glancing around the room he spotted what could only be Jude's jean covered ass, with what appeared to be white hand prints on the back pockets, on a ladder. The rest of him disappeared into the square hole in the ceiling.

The trapdoor Jude had created amazed Evan. He'd have thought Jude would build something simple, but the elaborate setup looked far more sophisticated. The tunnel up to the bedroom above had been excavated vertically, and Jude was in the process of lining the walls with hardwood. If Evan remembered correctly, the trapdoor would come out in the closet of the bedroom. The pole extending up through the center of the space made Evan want to laugh. Jude had anchored the pole into the stone floor, and the other end had to be anchored into the roof support beams of the cabin itself. He'd never have thought to use a pole in a trapdoor, but this was ingenious, and Evan could hardly wait to slide down it. He stood next to the ladder and looked up at Jude.

"How's it going?" Evan asked. He didn't want to surprise Jude, but Jude hadn't noticed him, and Evan thought touching him would've been more of a shock than just speaking.

"Oh!" Jude jumped and almost fell off the ladder, but Evan had hold of it and put up a steadying hand against Jude's legs. "Ah… hi. Sorry, I didn't see you there. Did you just wake up?"

"Yeah, grabbed a shower and some coffee."

"Adel didn't know how long you'd sleep this time." Jude moved down the ladder to stand beside Evan, color returning slowly to his pale face as he shook his head in embarrassment.

"Sorry, didn't mean to make you jump. How long have I been out?" Evan asked, grinning at Jude.

"Three days. I hope you don't mind. I figured I'd get things started." Jude motioned to the pole. "I began the rewiring as well, as I need access to my computer, and with Father Michael nosing around, I wanted to get the trapdoor completed. I figured this was kind of a priority. Sorry things are a bit of a mess at the moment." Jude waved around the room at the work in progress.

"No, I'm glad you feel comfortable enough to get started. I'm hoping the gargoyles have been helping. The lion-dogs love digging, and nothing cuts through this granite like the claws of a gargoyle."

"Yes, they've all been very welcoming and good at lending a claw." Jude laughed.

"Good. Glad to hear it." Evan hadn't seen Jude look relaxed and genuinely happy before. "Any problems? I'm sure if I've been asleep for three days, Father Michael's already made an appearance."

"Oh, you mean the walking skeleton who visited the day we arrived? Yes, he's been here. He thinks you are still at your mom's, and Adel and I are here on our own till the end of the week. He left quite quickly once he found out you weren't here. He has no interest in either of us. He has eyes for you alone. Watch yourself. I have no idea what he might do if he feels desperate," Jude warned Evan with a derisive roll of his eyes.

"Yeah, he's been after my ass for years now. At first the only things in his way were my parents. I'm not really sure what kept him from attacking once I moved out, but he stayed away, keeping things friendly but never crossing that line. But when Adel showed up, he seemed to go a bit nuts, and he's become more aggressive. He's usually shown up early in the morning or late evening, and Adel's been awake to keep him off me." Evan smiled, remembering Father Michael's reaction when Adel had first appeared and possessively drawn him away from Father Michael.

"Well, with me in the picture too, I'm sure he's even more agitated. He is probably wondering what our relationships are, so watch yourself. He may try to get details from you to figure things out. How are you feeling?"

"I'm fine. A bit stiff, and I'm starving. I think I'm going to go make something to eat. You hungry?"

"I could eat."

"You keep working, and I'll call you when lunch is ready."

"Okay." Jude moved back up the ladder and began to work again on his trapdoor.

Evan moved out to the kitchen and went through the cupboards. There were limited choices, but Evan wanted fresh produce; the spring greens in the garden were calling to him and would make a wonderful salad. He didn't say anything, but went up the trapdoor and out into the late-morning sun. Evan smiled into the warm morning air and walked through the grass to the garden. He hummed to himself merrily as he plucked at the fresh lettuce and tender greens growing in abundance. The cucumbers and tomatoes were far from ready, but the radishes would make a nice addition.

He didn't hear the car pull up into the drive. The remote in his pocket never vibrated. When Father Michael grabbed him around the waist and covered his mouth and nose with a cloth saturated in a sickly sweet-smelling substance, he never even got the chance to scream.

Adel is going to be pissed, thought Evan as he slid into darkness.

JUDE WALKED out of the bedroom upstairs in search of Evan. He'd completed working on his trapdoor and had waited for Evan to call him to eat, but he'd heard nothing. He walked into the living room and found the trapdoor open. Why would Evan leave the door open?

"He knows better than to do that," Jude mumbled to himself, feeling incredibly vulnerable. Evan must be around here somewhere. "Evan?" he called, looking into each room of the cabin. Something was wrong. Jude could feel it. He walked outside the cabin and looked over the forest, then around back to the garden.

"*Evan!*" Jude hollered at the top of his lungs. *I'm going to kill him if I find him lounging around or sleeping somewhere. I will kill him for making me worry like this!* His unease increased the longer he couldn't find Evan.

He stared around the yard. There was something out of place. *Where is he?* It made him nervous, but he just couldn't put a finger on what.

He walked around to the front of the cabin. His El Camino and the truck were parked as they had been since they'd arrived. Nothing looked out of place. Everything looked the same as any other day. He turned slowly as scanned the distant tree line and the forest beyond. *"Evan!"* he called again, as loud as he could. The name was swallowed by the whisper of the wind through the pine trees. He walked back around the house and pored over the meadow and garden. Then he saw what he'd been missing.

He ran toward the vegetable beds. Greens and lettuce had been picked and were lying neatly at the edge. Radishes had been scattered about as if dropped. Young plants had been stomped into the ground. There'd been a struggle. Evan would never treat the garden this way. Jude squatted beside the plants and picked up a radish.

"Evan!" Jude called again. He dropped the radish and ran back to the cabin and down into the bedroom, where he skidded to a stop, sitting heavily into a chair in front of the computer. The screen flashed the alarm, but no sound came from the system. He'd been working on it earlier in the day and had completely disconnected the system so he could run the wires out into the living room and his room.

"Damn! Damn!" Jude cursed as he brought up the camera footage that showed Father Michael's car pulling through the gates and parking in front of the cabin. Father Michael got out of his car and walked toward the back of the cabin. Jude clicked a couple of keys, and the view switched to a different camera as Father Michael appeared behind Evan. Jude could only watch helplessly as Evan was chloroformed and picked up. Father Michael hoisted Evan's inert form over his shoulder, carried him back to his sedan, and laid him in the backseat of the car. The last camera showed the car charging out of the gates, a cloud of dust rising behind it.

"Fuck! Goddamn! Fuck!" Jude spewed an unending stream of curses as he ran his hands through his hair, before banging his fists on the desk.

"I warned him. I told him Father Michael wanted him. Goddamn!" Jude mumbled as he rested his head helplessly in his hands. He had no idea where Father Michael was holed up, and he had no way to track him. He'd just arrived and had no contacts in the area to even begin to draw on for clues. *What the fuck am I going to do now?* Jude thought. He looked at the clock. The gargoyles wouldn't be up for a couple of hours yet, and he didn't know if they'd be able to track Father Michael or Evan in a car.

Time to call in a few favors. He wouldn't let Evan get hurt because of his negligence. He had to find out where Father Michael lived. He had to give Adel at least a place to start looking for Evan. They didn't have the luxury of time, for the longer Father Michael had Evan, the greater the chance he'd be dead when found.

Jude's fingers flew over the keys as he sent out a multitude of messages to his contacts, pleading for information on Father Michael's whereabouts. He also searched the records of the Papacy and any other databases he could think of. The bad part was he'd already searched these databases for hints of where Father Michael resided, and the man was a ghost. He never really settled anywhere, but would appear when you least expected him.

Jude prayed he'd have some leads before Adel awoke.

Chapter 15

JUDE'S INQUIRIES had brought back little information. He'd even addressed the Papacy directly, seeking a contact address for Father Michael from their directories. The one supplied was, of course, fake. It ended up being a complete dead end—a residence he'd researched months ago. He sat with his head in his hands in front of the computer, waiting for the last of his contacts to reply. He had no other ideas about what to do next. Waiting for his contact to respond, waiting for Adel to wake—just waiting drove him crazy.

He'd even gone into the kitchen, put a roast in the oven, and set the timer, hoping that by keeping busy time would flow faster. Patience wasn't one of the virtues fate had gifted him with. He needed Adel.

Jude sighed loudly and turned around, looking at the gargoyle.

"Adel, if you can hear me, I need you to awaken as soon as you can. Father Michael has kidnapped Evan and I need your help. I'm drawing blanks here. He grabbed him in broad daylight, right out from under me. I had no idea the guy was even here. By the time I started looking for him, Father Michael had taken him and disappeared. So, if you can hear me, you need to wake up, now. He needs us." Jude stared at Adel lying in the bed. Evan should have been resting with him, safe, and not in the hands of a madman. Jude cursed as he turned his back on the gargoyle and hung his head in his hands. "Please, Adel, I don't know what else to do."

A crackling sound, like static electricity snapping and popping, caught Jude's attention, followed by a roar so loud, Jude had to cover his ears. He turned to see Adel take a breath and sit up in the bed. His eyes were red with anger. The hair on his body seemed to stand out from his skin. His lips drew back in a fierce grimace, and his wings extended fully behind him. The sight chilled Jude's blood. Adel looked like an avenging angel, or an enraged demon from Hell. Maybe both.

"When?" Adel snarled, staring at Jude, panting.

"According to the time stamp on the computer footage, about five hours ago."

Adel leaped from the bed to all fours, streaking through the caverns and up the trapdoor into the kitchen faster than Jude could process and run after him. He found Adel with his nose to the ground, sniffing around the porch, then the garden and over the vegetables scattered at the edge of the grass. He snorted violently, retaking his feet and sniffing the air. "He picked Evan up here and carried him." Adel snorted again. "God, he stinks like death."

"Can you follow his scent?" Jude asked quietly, standing behind Adel, watching as he furled and unfurled his wings in agitation.

"Yes. It is very distinctive, and with Evan's scent added to it, I can follow. I'll stalk him and feast on his evil."

Adel inhaled deeply and then turned to Jude. He took two steps, lifted Jude in his arms, and with a stroke of his wings, they were airborne.

"*Shit!*" Jude screamed, throwing his arms around Adel as he felt the ground drop away below them.

"Be calm. I won't drop you, even though I should for your failure to protect Evan. But it is not right for me to blame you for not doing something that by rights is my job. He's my mate and I failed to protect him." Adel growled as he flew over the road, the miles disappearing.

"Adel, this isn't a good idea. We need the truck. If we find him, we'll need to bring him back with us. I know you can fly carrying one of us, but surely not carrying both of us." Jude smacked Adel on the chest.

Adel snarled and turned around in midflight, winging back to the cabin. "Why didn't you say so sooner?" Adel huffed and landed in the bed of the truck, setting Jude down roughly in the dirt. "Get in. Drive. I'll tell you where to go."

Jude climbed into the cab of the truck, and as he turned over the ignition, Adel sank his claws into the roof of the cab above him and peeled the metal back so he could look directly down into the cab.

"I hope Evan wanted a skylight," Jude commented as he threw the truck into reverse. A cloud of dust rose around the tires. He turned the truck around and drove down the driveway and out onto the highway in the direction he'd watched Father Michael go on the camera footage. He floored the gas, going as fast as the truck could manage, hoping they didn't come across anyone else on the road. They didn't need to try and explain Adel, standing in the bed of the truck. Jude had to admire Adel: he was glorious in his rage, in a monstrous kind of way.

"You getting anything up there?" Jude called, glancing up through the hole in the roof of the cab.

"Yes, you are going the right way," Adel snarled. "Faster, go faster!"

"This truck can't go much faster. It's old. I'm giving it all she's got, and this road is horrible," Jude hollered up at Adel over the noise of the wind whistling through the cab. He tried to press harder on the gas, and the engine whined, but the truck sped along at its top speed and would go no faster. Twilight had fallen and the darkness grew. He hoped Adel could find Evan before that maniac Father Michael did something they would all regret.

"Wait. *Stop!* Go back!" Adel's voice reverberated about the cab.

Jude hit the brakes, slowed, and stopped. He turned around in the middle of the highway—not a simple feat, as the truck had not been made to turn on a dime—and slowly drove back the way they'd come. Adel launched himself into the sky, and Jude followed, barely able to see him shrouded in the night. Adel flew in slow circles, then landed in front of the truck and paced back and forth. A dirt road bisected the pavement. Adel went first to one side of the intersection and then the other as he searched for signs of Evan and Father Michael's passage.

"Evan's scent ends here. They had to have gone in one of these directions, but I'm not sure which," Adel said in frustration as he stood beside the truck. "The scent is just cut off, as if something has swallowed it, hiding him. There is strong dark magic at work here, to hide my mate from me."

"Okay, let's try this from a different angle, then. You said strong dark magic is hiding him from you. You can sense the magic, right?" Jude asked. "Your kind hunts dark magic?"

"Sort of. We hunt evil—demons, the soulless ones from Hell—not magic, and even though a human may do evil things, as long as they have a soul, we can't hunt them directly." Adel's face scrunched up as if he'd tasted something rotten. "This magic is full of blood, and I can sense the evil being generated by it."

"Blood… can you identify whose blood? Not Evan's blood?"

"No. Not Evan's blood. Regardless of how his blood were used, I'd be able to follow and his blood would smell sweet to me. This is horrid, evil, probably Father Michael's blood used to summon a demon who is hiding Evan from us." Adel hissed as he said the name of the vile man who had kidnapped his mate. Father Michael would die for this.

"Okay, so, can you follow the magic? If the magic is covering or hiding Evan, can you follow or trail the magic?" Jude asked, looking at Adel as he watched the idea register on his face.

Adel walked immediately away from the truck and began to prowl back and forth; a deep snarl arose from him as he took off down the dirt road on the right. Jude hoped this would work. Even if the magic didn't take them directly to Evan, it might lead them to someone who could tell them more.

Adel pulled away from the truck until he appeared as a speck, glinting in the dimming light of the setting sun. Jude struggled to see him. He barreled down the road as fast as the truck would allow and tried not to think about what would happen when Adel caught up with whomever they found at the end of the magic trail.

EVAN AWOKE, his head pounding. The sound of chanting rang in his ears, and the assault of burning incense and blood, filled his nose and singed his throat. He wanted to cough. Something made him remain quiet. His hands were bound above his head. His arms ached with the need to move, but he didn't want to draw attention to himself. The words, an incantation, grew in intensity and made Evan's skin crawl. They called to something evil and powerful from the depths of Hell.

Slowly Evan opened his eyes and struggled to focus. He found himself sitting on a mattress on the floor, with his back against the wall and his arms over his head, manacled into the cement of the wall.

He sat in the far corner at the back of a large basement room. A man in black robes knelt before a stone altar, upon which incense burned and a brazier steamed and smoked. Evan struggled not to cough.

Evan twitched and trembled. He felt as if insects were creeping across his body, just under his skin, as the evil being drawn and controlled by the man grew. A dark, swirling cloud of power churned and rolled like a possessed storm cloud overhead. The screams and snarls of creatures hidden in the depths of the darkness came from the cloud and increased in ferocity and volume with each droplet of fresh blood that fell from the man's wrist into the brazier.

The chant suddenly stopped, and the man slumped over the altar as the cloud of power divided into three parts. Each part coalesced and solidified. Claws reached out from the clouds and wings tipped with talons pushed their way through. Each cloud shrank in on itself, forming a body, muscles, sinew, bone, arms, legs, scales, muzzle, teeth, tail, and iron restraints that clamped into the cement foundation. From each of the three clouds appeared a demon covered in scales that glinted in the dim light, the color of old, blackened blood. The middle demon stood upright on two legs and was markedly taller, while the other two appeared more doglike on all fours. Manacled to the floor, hissing and snarling, they stood before the altar. The demons struck out at the man who'd called them, but some kind of barrier stood between them and the man, and their claws sparked and flashed as they hit it.

The demons looked around the dark room. Evan stifled a scream of horror as one of them noticed him and lunged in his direction, coming up short because of the restraints. The other two demons then focused on Evan. All three pairs of red eyes stared at him as if they could kill and eat him by looking at him alone. Evan sat up in his corner and drew his legs closer, trying to make himself as small as possible. Pure terror washed through him as he watched the demons staring back at him. Vile black fluid flowed from their fangs as they salivated to get at him.

Oh God, please, someone, help me! Evan begged, sending the plea silently out from himself. He put every bit of his fear and terror out into the dark, willing every bit of power Adel told him he had along with it. He prayed help would find him and save him from the evil glaring at him hungrily.

"We are here." Evan heard the answer in his head. *"Fear not, Maker."* The voice sang musically in his mind. Evan tried to will his body to stop shaking.

The three demons never looked away, licking their lips as if in anticipation. The tall demon stroked the heads of the two doglike demons, which lunged against their manacles and snapped their teeth in Evan's direction.

Evan closed his eyes. His hands tingled from lack of circulation, but he gripped the rings as tight as he could while he rocked minutely forward. He struggled to control his breathing and calm down to no avail. When he opened his eyes, he saw the stone below the demons cracking under their constant attempts to pull the manacles from the floor.

A massive tremor shook Evan and the foundation of the building, further cracking the cement that held the demons. He felt the tremor again and again through the cement behind him and realized something large on the other side of the wall was trying to get in.

His mind froze. He couldn't take any more. Whatever wanted to get in had enough power to destroy cement. One of the rings fell forward out of the wall with the next tremor, freeing his right hand. Evan couldn't even think enough to try to pull away before another quake shook the wall and the second ring fell, freeing him. Unfortunately, in the process the remaining foundation shattered, leaving a spiderweb of cracks across the floor, baring the earth below.

Instead of seeing his life pass before his eyes as he'd always been told would happen, Evan saw everything move in slow motion. What took only portions of a second felt like minutes, hours, an eternity. The doglike demons lunged at him, their restraints clanking loudly, while the tall demon raised its arms in a silent roar. Somewhere he thought he heard Adel screaming his rage, but he had no idea how his love could be here. He saw his death coming straight for him and could only cry for want of seeing Adel one more time. He didn't want to leave Adel, but he couldn't defeat the demons. His death would come at their fangs.

ADEL FELT Evan's fear radiating from the building. He could almost hear him pleading for help. Built into a hillside with a large graveyard that extended behind the building on the lower level, the church stood alone, surrounded by a meadow. The crumbling building was run-down, a lost relic of a forgotten time. Adel, with Jude in the truck trailing behind him, approached from the front. He didn't even pause at the door but collided with it, shattering the wood to pieces as he scanned the entrance for stairs to take him to the lower level. He roared his frustration as he ran down a hallway lined with doors. He threw them open, one after another, only to find musty, decaying rooms filled with books. Adel yanked open yet another door and found the stairway leading down just as Jude ran into the hallway.

At the bottom of the stairway, Adel entered the room and roared his challenge as he saw the wall behind Evan crumbling and the demon-dogs attacking. The man in the black robes lay inert over the altar; Evan was curled in a ball against the far wall. The tall demon turned to face Adel.

ANOTHER TREMOR, and the wall behind Evan crumbled completely. An enormous gargoyle forced its way through the rubble. It stood on all fours, with the body of a tiger, huge clawed paws, a deep, broad chest, and a bull's head and horns. Midnight-blue fur with white streaks covered the animal, whose eyes were black as coal.

He watched in awe as the bull-tiger bellowed and stood between him and the attacking demon-dogs. The demons barely paused in their forward motion as their focus turned from their intended prey to the large gargoyle defending him.

A second gargoyle came through the hole in the wall, joining the fight. Evan would have smiled at the sprite standing between him and the attacking demons had the circumstances been otherwise. He stood just slightly taller than Evan—who sat on the floor—and practically glowed with defiance. His hair fell in white curls to his shoulders, with just a touch of red at the tips. The pointed peaks of his ears poked out of his hair, and a soft mossy-green tinge colored his skin. He appeared delicate and fragile. Evan didn't think the creature would be able to fight any better than he himself could, but he assumed wrongly. From behind his gossamer butterfly wings, the gargoyle drew a sword from its scabbard and met the charging demon-dogs with a snarl as fierce as any Evan had ever heard come from Adel.

ADEL COLLIDED with the large demon. The sound reverberated through the room like a crack of thunder. Claws and teeth snapped, ripping into flesh and muscle. The cacophonous snarls and roars filled the room as the blur of clashing bodies and rending flesh mixed with the stench of blood.

JUDE ARRIVED at the base of the stairs in time to see the battle between the gargoyles and the demons begin. He spotted Evan against the far wall, curled into a fetal position, watching the fight unfolding before him. Jude's gaze locked on the man in black, who had started to rise from the altar. He considered the gun at his hip, but feared he'd hit Adel or one of the other gargoyles by accident. Jude pulled out a large hunting knife and, careful to avoid the gargoyles, advanced on the man who gleefully watched the carnage going on around him. He seemed oblivious to Jude's presence and began to chant again, relighting the brazier.

Jude attacked before he could call the evil power to him.

EVAN WATCHED the battle with a sense of helplessness. He watched Jude struggle to subdue the robed figure, and trembled. He had no idea how to defend himself. His friends and his beloved were fighting for him, and he sat curled in on himself, unable to help. *No, I can help.* He wouldn't allow this evil to harm those he loved. He reached deep into himself and, with determination, stood. He could feel the power building in his heart, in his soul, calling to the earth around him. He felt the power of life and death pooling in his chest, rushing down his arms, crackling like electricity. The shackles snapped from his wrists as the power hit the bindings, sending them flying. He stepped forward and stood staring at the fighting before him.

"Evan, get back!" Adel hollered, distracted. The demon he faced snarled and lunged, latching teeth and fangs onto Adel's throat. Its feet struck his unprotected gut, attempting to eviscerate him. Adel screamed in agony and clawed wildly at the demon latched on to his throat.

Evan dug his feet into the ground beneath the broken foundation of the church. His power increased with the touch of the bare soil. It erupted from the earth and stone, flowing through his body as if he were the volcano and the power the molten core of the earth. Evan dropped his head back and gasped for air as the power surged in him. His fingers shone with a golden mist as the gathering power manifested in his hands. He flung his arms toward the ceiling. The power flew from his fingertips, blasting through the ceiling and out through the roof till the night sky and the stars above shone down on him.

Panting, trying to catch his breath, and struggling to contain the power, to control it, Evan again faced the room, his hands in fists, the power building within his body. "You will not harm *my Adel*!" Evan screamed while pointing at the large demon latched on to Adel. The power flew from Evan's hand into the demon, exploding on impact. Bits of flesh and blood flew in all directions.

Adel slumped to the floor.

Evan turned to the demon-dogs, still fighting the large bull-like gargoyle and the sprite. Evan screamed again as the power coursed through his body and out his hands toward the demon-dogs. They burst like overfilled balloons, sending gore and blood splattering over everything.

Evan stared at the altar and raised his hands. He once more released his power into the stone of the shrine, blasting it to vapors.

The destruction seemed to break the man fighting with Jude. As it crumbled, so did the man. "*Master!*" the man screamed as he collapsed to the floor like a marionette with its strings cut.

Dazed, Jude reached down and uncovered the face of Father Michael. With the center of his dark power gone, his life force, which apparently fed on the evil flowing through the altar, had faded away. He lay at Jude's feet, dead.

The building around them began to tremble and quake. With the foundation cracked and broken, the supports were failing. The evil power, so violently destroyed moments ago, had broken what was left of the building, causing the remains to fall in on themselves.

"Out! Everyone out now!" Jude hollered as he grabbed the sprite gargoyle by the arm and tried to get him out, away from the collapsing building.

Evan sprinted to Adel, who was slumped on the floor. He was bleeding profusely from his throat, the jugular torn. Gashes covered his abdomen; his bowels barely remained contained. Evan fell to his knees.

"My Adel," Evan cried, tears flowing down his face as he watched Adel's eyes glaze over and close. "*No!*" he screamed and placed both glowing hands to Adel's chest. "*Adel!*" Evan's head flew back and his remaining power flowed into Adel in a rush, then flowed outward from them to touch everything in the room.

Evan collapsed, unconscious, to the floor as the church crumbled around them.

Chapter 16

EVAN'S CONSCIOUSNESS returned slowly. At first he seemed to float as his mind attempted to rejoin his immobile body. Unsure if he was even alive, he concentrated on trying to feel himself breathe. Deciding that somehow he must have survived, he worked at listening to his surroundings, trying to discover where he was. Closest to him, he heard a continuous rumble. He loved that sound, so familiar, so soothing. Then he remembered. His body went rigid with fear.

"Shhh, my Maker… my mate." Adel's voice soothed him, relaxing him as he caressed the curve of his ear with a sweep of his tongue. "You are safe, Evan."

With a sigh, Evan relaxed as Adel tightened his arms around him. Adel held him. He was safe; the where didn't matter anymore.

Slowly their bedroom came into focus. They lay in their bed at home. Memories began to overpower him: the kidnapping, awakening, the evil coalescing into the demons, the fighting, and Adel getting hurt. Evan's eyes flew open, and the light in the room assaulted him, making him squint. He twisted around and looked over his shoulder into the open eyes of Adel, who gently caressed Evan's face.

"All is well. Peace." Adel sighed. "I'm so glad you finally opened your eyes, my heart. I've been very worried."

"Adel! Oh!" Evan gasped and threw his arms around Adel's shoulders and snuggled up tightly, leaning into Adel as if he might disappear.

"I'm here. You are so strong, my heart. You're my miracle." Adel clutched Evan against him and nuzzled his hair. "We're all fine. We all got out. Jude got the gargoyles you called from the church cemetery out before the building collapsed. The bull still sleeps. He's in a healing hibernation. I imagine he'll awaken in a week or so. His injuries were severe, but when he awakens, he'll be whole. Jude has named the sprite Fin, but he refuses to acknowledge the name and says he'll only be named by you."

"How long this time?" Evan asked, feeling his muscles and not noticing any overwhelming tightness as he had many times before.

"Not long. Two days. I've held you the entire time." Adel purred softly. He stroked Evan's back, raining kisses down on his hair. "I've been so worried. You really scared me. I love you so much, my heart."

"I thought you were dead. I saw your eyes close and—" Evan couldn't continue as he buried his face in Adel's chest to hide the tears that threatened to escape.

"With the power you wielded, you healed me. You also changed all of us. When you dumped the earth energy into me to heal me, you also completed what you began before Father Michael took you. The excess earth energy flowed out from us and caused the same change in the sprite, the bull, Skye, and Cela. You are so strong, my heart… my mate." Adel nipped at Evan's shoulder.

"Oh. Ah," Evan gasped, trembling with desire in Adel's arms, his libido awakened by Adel's skillful hands and tongue.

"Umm," Adel hummed as Evan laved kisses across his chest, brushing his lips over one of his taut nipples, kissing the pink nub lightly before running his tongue around it in slow, wet circles. "We are no longer tied to the night. I now can choose when I sleep. In fact, I seem to need very little sleep. I have held you these past two days without going to stone, and I have yet to feel the need to sleep. I am content just to have you in my arms." Adel snuggled his face deeply into Evan's hair, inhaling his scent, sliding his hands around to cup his ass. Adel brushed his fingers along the crack, gently stroking till he elicited a soft moan.

"Adel." Evan arched into his lover's arms as Adel's fingers drove all thoughts from his mind.

"Promise me, Evan. No more changes! None!" Adel insisted, humming deep in his chest. The sound reverberated through his body as he brought his hand around to scoop Evan's chin up to look him in the eyes. "I am quite serious, my love. No more. I know how important it is that I am able to be with you whenever you need me, and I agree—especially with the dangers we face—that I need the freedom to choose when to sleep. The fact that Father Michael preyed upon you during the daytime while I had to remain stone almost destroyed me. Never again will my nature put you in harm's way. So please, my love, stop now."

"I didn't change you because I thought you were less or not good enough. You know that, don't you? I've loved you from the minute I saw you. You're magnificent and perfect. I just wanted to be with you always." Evan sighed as he stared into Adel's eyes, trying to make him understand how much he loved and needed him. "I promise I won't make any more changes, ever again."

"That is all I needed to hear. I love you, my heart." Adel's voice deepened with need. He massaged Evan's ass, gently drawing the cheeks farther apart. He danced his fingers over the skin.

"We need the lube, Adel." Evan moaned as Adel brought one hand around his hip to enclose both their cocks, slowly stroking their lengths together.

"I have it." Adel chuckled. "What did you think I thought about as I waited for you to awaken? With you in my arms, I could practically feel my cock sinking deep into your ass."

Evan moaned again as the snap of a bottle caught his attention, and then cool liquid flowed between his ass cheeks. He shivered as Adel rubbed gently around the tight ring of his entrance.

Adel moved him to one side and sank one slick finger into Evan, stroking him, working the muscle until a second finger slid alongside the first, scissoring and stretching his opening.

Evan moved down Adel's chest, kissing and licking his beloved, spurred on by the fingers in his ass to find what he needed. Rewarded by Adel's deep growl of satisfaction, Evan wrapped his mouth around Adel's shaft, laving the bulbous head as he swirled his tongue around the glans in wet circles. Evan matched his pace to the rhythm as Adel fucked his ass. He took the shaft deep into his throat, struggling to ignore his gag reflex, then drew back. He sucked strongly, hollowing his cheeks to swallow down the length until the head struck the back of his throat.

"Evan... so good. Please." Adel trembled.

Knowing he caused Adel to shiver and beg made Evan feel like a giant. Evan groaned as Adel brushed his prostate, and he struggled to maintain control as he bobbed his head along his shaft. Evan loved Adel's cock. *So perfect*, he thought, as he sucked it down his throat, humming on the upstroke, breathing through his nose. He worked Adel's cock, swallowing the length farther, till his nose felt the tickle of the silky-soft fur covering Adel's crotch. He sucked even harder as he drew back.

Adel growled. "Evan, stop. I want to… I need to be in you when I come."

Evan came off Adel's erection with a pop, grinning as he wiggled his ass, then moaning as the motion caused Adel's fingers to brush his prostate. "I want you, Adel," Evan whispered. He dropped down to rest on his forearms, pointing his ass to the ceiling and spreading his legs to give Adel better access.

Adel withdrew his fingers, got up behind Evan, and stroked his hand along Evan's spine, caressing and kissing the small indentation in his lower back. "Beautiful. You are so beautiful when you present your ass to me." Adel's words were barely more than a growl. The snap of the lid on the lube made gooseflesh rise up on Evan's arms and legs.

"Adel, can't wait—"

"As you wish, my love." Adel pressed the thick, blunt head past the ring of muscle at Evan's entrance. A wave of heat swept over him from the press of Adel's hot body, and he panted, perspiration beading on his skin. Adel froze, giving Evan's body time to adjust before sinking slowly in to sheath himself deep inside. Both men groaned their pleasure as Adel bottomed out. Adel ran a hand over Evan's lower back, soothing tight muscles until they relaxed under his soft, gentle touch.

"Move," Evan begged as he wiggled his hips wantonly, needing Adel.

Adel, unable to hold back longer, snarled and pulled back until only the head remained inside, then slammed his length back in. Evan thrashed and moaned, fisting the sheets as Adel's pace steadily increased. His thrusts became more erratic, but the angle of his hips caused Adel's cock to peg Evan's sweet spot with each thrust. Adel grasped Evan's cock with a slick-covered hand and stroked him in time with each thrust.

Evan's screams grew in volume as he neared his climax. "Gonna come! A-Adel," he gasped.

"Come for me, my heart," Adel ordered as he pulled Evan's back against his chest. Adel bit lightly into the tender flesh between Evan's shoulder and neck, barely breaking the skin. He quickly sucked up the blood of his mate, absorbing his essence.

Evan shot a ribbon of spunk up against his chest and out over the sheet as his muscles clamped down on Adel's shaft.

Adel roared as he thrust deeply once, twice, then found his climax. He filled Evan with his seed. He collapsed, pulled Evan down with him, and snuggled him tightly against his chest as he kissed and licked the wound on Evan's neck.

"DON'T TELL me what to do!" Jude yelled at the sprite standing at the end of the counter, hands on his hips.

"It tastes better without them!" the sprite yelled back, stamping his foot in irritation.

"It does not! Besides, how would you know? You'd never eaten cooked food before yesterday!" Jude growled in frustration as he held the onion he had yet to peel and chop.

"Because we ate them yesterday. I can smell them from over here, and they burn my nose and eyes. Why would anyone think such a foul-smelling thing edible!" The sprite screeched and threw his arms wildly about him as he spoke, his eyes flashing at Jude.

"You don't know anything about cooking, so just shut up already!" Jude snarled back, and Skye looked concerned as he jumped about on the countertop, trying to calm Jude. Anger flowed through Jude. His face flushed red, and sweat beaded on his forehead. His breathing was irregular, as if he couldn't catch his breath or had just sprinted up several flights of stairs.

Adel and Evan entered the room in time to see the onion in Jude's hand burst into flames.

"Whoa!" Jude hollered and dropped the onion into the sink. Shock covered his face. The flames on the onion went out immediately, but blue flames continued to dance along the skin of Jude's hand.

"Jude!" Evan ran over, turned on the sink, grabbed Jude's wrist, and thrust it under the flowing stream of water.

"Wait! It doesn't hurt. I'm not burned." Jude stared at his hand in wonder, turning it over as he watched the flames lick up and down his skin. "The flame isn't really on the skin. It's hovering just above and around my hand, but not really touching me. I feel a bit of warmth, but nothing else." Jude moved his other hand through the flames, and the fire spread till both hands flickered, ablaze.

"Jude… um… can you control those flames?" Evan asked.

"I don't know. Maybe. I can't believe what I'm seeing," Jude whispered, his voice filled with awe.

"Jude, concentrate on putting the fire out. Visualize the flames getting smaller and colder, then gone altogether." The sprite spoke softly, his entire demeanor changing with Jude's need for help. He moved to stand beside Jude and put a hand on the small of his back.

Jude took a deep breath, calming himself, and closed his eyes. The flames on his hands flickered brightly at first, then dimmed and disappeared entirely. Jude opened his eyes, looked at his hands, and sighed. Relief flooded his body and the adrenaline faded away. Jude wavered on his feet, and his eyes rolled up into his head.

"HE'S GOING to faint," the sprite said quickly, a touch of panic in his voice as he reached for Jude, catching him before he hit the floor. Despite his size, the sprite cradled Jude, who was only slightly shorter, but broader in the chest than the gargoyle. The sprite looked down into Jude's unconscious face. "I'm sorry, young one," the sprite whispered into Jude's ear, brushing the red hair back from his brow.

"I can carry him for you." Adel stepped forward to take Jude from the sprite.

The sprite snarled, flashing a wicked set of teeth. He growled at Adel as he clutched the man to his chest.

"Okay, brother, we aren't going to take him from you," Evan said softly, stepping in front of his mate. "We just want to make sure Jude's all right."

"Maker?" The sprite's attitude changed to immediate subservience. He whimpered in apology but continued to gently cradle Jude.

"It's all right. Do you need assistance carrying him?" Adel asked, staying behind Evan but obviously ready to defend him from the sprite if necessary.

"No, I'm fine," the sprite said haughtily, as if daring Adel to try to take Jude from him.

"Okay. Come on, then. Let's take him to his room so he can rest." Evan led the way, and Adel followed while Skye trotted along ahead of the sprite, who carried Jude into his room and gently lowered him to the bed.

The sprite stared down at Jude's face, then looked up at Evan and dropped to his knees. "Maker, you need to name me."

Evan knelt in front of the sprite and laid a hand on his shoulder. He put a hand under the sprite's chin and drew his gaze up. He peered into the luminous sky-blue eyes for a moment, then smiled warmly. "You are Fin... short for Finton, meaning 'white fire.' I think it fits." Evan stroked a hand through the white hair with its unique red tips and then stood.

"Thank you, Maker." Finton closed his eyes and smiled softly, then gazed back at Jude, where he lay in the bed.

"Come on, Fin, you're my friend. You defended me. You saved my life. Stand and be proud." Evan smiled warmly as Finton slowly rose, meeting Evan's gaze and returning his smile. Evan sat on the edge of the bed, stroking Jude's hair gently. "Fin, Jude needs a very special touch. He means a great deal to me. He needs a guardian, a partner to look out for him. Will you watch over him for me? Skye watches over him, but I believe he has a rough future ahead of him and will need help he can trust."

"Thank you for giving him to me, Maker. I won't let you down. I'll protect him, always. I'll guard him with my life," Finton whispered, as if in prayer to a deity instead of Evan, who stood beside him.

"Fin, I may have awoken you, but you owe me nothing. You don't have to do this, but I'd be very grateful if you would."

"It's my honor to watch over him, Maker."

"Take good care of him. I know he's special." Evan put his hand on Adel's arm, and they left the room, closing the door behind them.

"What's going on, Adel?" Evan asked when they were back in the kitchen. He went through the refrigerator to finish cooking the meal Jude had begun.

"I do not know, my heart. But Jude is not as he appears. Our friend harbors a very strong power. If I did not know that you were the Maker, I'd swear Jude had the power of the Maker, a Fire Elemental."

Adel stood behind Evan as he cleaned, peeled, and chopped the onion Jude had dropped into the sink. The pieces went into the frying pan with the cut-up potatoes. Then he put marinated steaks onto the rack and turned on the broiler.

"Something dark is coming, Adel. I can feel it. I think it felt my power when I destroyed the altar."

"If it does, we will face it together." Adel snuggled into Evan's neck, breathed deeply of his mate's scent, and purred to soothe him.

Epilogue

Evan, Adel, Jude, Fin, Skye, and Cela stood at the base of Notre Dame, looking up at the enormous church as the sun set, leaving the city of Paris in twilight. Tourists were exiting the building, and workers were closing the church to the public.

"It was nice of His Eminence to send his personal jet for us. I hope he understands why I'm not quite ready to set foot in the Vatican just yet." Evan stared at the multitude of gargoyles hidden in the architecture of the church.

"He understands, but hopes that you'll understand his good intentions by his gesture." Jude stared at the building in front of him. The thought of all those gargoyles coming to life once the sun set… it would be a sight unlike anything he'd ever experienced before. "You had to get out of the States. It wasn't safe anymore. Here at least you'll have some protection."

"I hope you're right. The Pope knows where I am, and after the fight with Father Michael, he knows what I'm capable of." Evan shook his head. They'd been over this so many times, it was like a well-worn trail to nowhere, circling back around on itself. Was he safer with the Vatican knowing where he was and that he was protected by stone warriors? Or was that just another reason to get rid of him? Adel felt sure that with the gargoyles of Notre Dame at his beck and call, the Vatican would leave them in peace. He hoped Adel was right.

"The Pope isn't after you, Evan, but someone within the Church is, and it's my job to find out who."

"Yeah, well, it's his job now to see to it that you don't get yourself killed." Evan grinned as he glanced at his friend who was shadowed by Fin. He'd bid Fin to keep his friend safe, and Fin was taking his job very seriously.

"Don't remind me. He barely lets me go to the bathroom alone. Are you sure you're ready to do this?" Jude looked at Evan and then back up at the enormous structure and the gargoyles that covered the church from one end to the other.

"It's why we came. I need to do this. I can feel them calling to me, pleading for me to awaken them," Evan whispered, his voice as soft and reverent as a prayer.

"My brothers and sisters wait for you, my heart." Adel gazed at the church, an excited grin on his face. "This is something only you can do. The gift of awakening is the one gift that will take nothing from you but will mean life to them."

Evan watched as, unbeknownst to the few people still wandering about the church, Skye and Cela flitted from gargoyle to gargoyle as if they couldn't wait for them to awaken and come play. He looked around, slipped out of his shoes, and stood in the grass, feeling the power of the earth beneath him. He closed his eyes and channeled the earth power, drew it into himself. The many lights within the church and those all around it flickered and went out. The surrounding lights for blocks around flickered and switched off, one at a time, enshrouding the church in the darkness of the night. Evan smiled, hearing more than a few curses as people fled the darkness for the still-lit parts of the city. Evan welcomed the darkness, the freedom to safely awaken the gargoyles of Notre Dame unseen.

"Father in Heaven, awaken these guardians. Awaken these spirits of love and protection. Fill them with your love so they can fulfill their duty and honor your will. Guardians, awaken!" Evan prayed, his head bowed in reverence to the Creator, the spirit of love he felt, the power of the Lord of Heaven and Earth from whom he gained his power. "Come, my children. The night is young and you've slept long enough. Awaken. The world needs you." Evan held his slightly glowing hands out toward the church, palms up. His words were barely a whisper, sent with his mind, aided by the earth power he drew to him from beneath his feet.

The power danced in a wave, bathing the church and then farther out to the city of Paris as a whole, calling to the gargoyles to awaken. An electrical shiver rent the night air like the static electricity before a thunderstorm, yet it didn't make a sound.

"They awaken." Adel's voice filled with awe as he stared at the cathedral covered with his brothers and sisters. "Come, my love. We're done here."

Evan slipped into his shoes and walked back to Adel, who wrapped Evan into his arms.

"Will they be okay on their own?" Jude asked, watching as he caught glimpses of the stone moving, yet having the eerie feeling the shadows of the night played tricks on him.

"They have been alive much longer than you, young one. They will be glorious." Fin laughed, patting Jude's arm reassuringly.

"We aren't done yet, but we can't meet with the clutch out here in the open. They will join us at the hotel. We can meet them on the rooftop and answer their questions about this century. There are still several places we need to go before we go to Rome." Evan smiled at his friends, trying to stifle a large yawn.

"You are not yet awake, my heart," Adel said teasingly and lifted Evan into his arms.

Evan snuggled into Adel's embrace and rested his head on his lover's strong shoulder, closing his eyes.

"Let's go back to the hotel and let the Maker sleep. Tomorrow will be soon enough to figure out the mysteries of Rome," Fin said, taking Jude's arm. He whistled shrilly and led the way to the lighted streets.

Evan knew Skye and Cela would follow in the air above as they returned to their hotel. As the small party got farther away from the church, the streetlights in the surrounding blocks, and then on Notre Dame itself, slowly flickered and came back to life. The low light showed a slightly different cathedral, one only those most familiar with the structure would notice. Here and there about the building, the stone gargoyles were staring down at the new world into which they'd awakened.

NICO'S
FIRE

To my family and friends who keep encouraging me to chase after this sometimes elusive dream. I can't say "Thank You" enough.

Prologue

March 22, 2216—Café courtyard. Paris, France. Midmorning.

"Are you sure you have to go?" Evan picked up his croissant and bit into the flakey pastry.

"He's my boss. When the Pope calls, I go. He did say you and Adel weren't required to come to Rome. In fact, it almost sounded like he'd prefer you remain in France." Jude sipped his espresso, enjoying the dark brew. He glanced around at the nearly vacant streets and the number of abandoned buildings just beyond the little market square. But where they sat, beneath the budding trees, Paris was beautiful in the spring.

"He doesn't like that I refused to go to Rome. Now he's taking it out on you by making you go to him. Should I be wary of being attacked when you leave?" Evan glanced about the courtyard.

Jude had already checked for hostiles. It was automatic for him. It came with his line of work. There were a few shoppers, but mainly the morning was pleasant and quiet. "No more than usual. Besides, even he knows with Adel and all the gargoyles of Notre Dame surrounding you, there isn't a safer person in this world," Jude teased. "I'm the one who needs to be careful going to Rome. I can't be spotted there and then again back in the States—I could blow my cover if I'm recognized."

"I want you to take Fin with you. Regardless of what you think, you need a keeper, Judas Jamison. If nothing else, do it for me, so I know you are safe. Running secret intel operations for the Church is about as dangerous as it gets," Evan grumbled.

"Hey, not so loud," Jude hissed and looked around as if he were concerned about being overheard. There wasn't a person within earshot of their conversation. He just liked teasing Evan.

Evan stubbornly folded his arms over his chest. "I really wish you'd consider getting out of the Jesuit Inquisitors branch. Better yet, get out of the church service all together."

"Um…." Jude hesitated, looking at his friend, trying to determine if this was an argument he could win. These days it was getting harder and harder not to say yes. His job was becoming incredibly dangerous, and not just for him, but for those around him as well.

"I know that isn't going to happen anytime soon." Evan chuckled at Jude's grimace. "Take Skye too, because I know he won't be happy if you are gone and he has to stay with us. Pout all you want. You can even say no if you like. I'm still sending them with you, so deal with it."

"Fine… whatever you want, oh mighty Elemental. Your word is my command." Jude picked up his cup and sipped his espresso. Although he wanted to be mad at Evan for insisting, he really did like Fin and would appreciate the company.

"Just keep an eye on them while in Rome. I don't want to hear that they were crushed while you were in a meeting with your boss."

"I get it. Keep the gargoyles safe. I won't let you down, Evan."

"Really, it's not the gargoyles I'm worried about. I want *you* to stay safe. You're my friend, this fire thing is unnerving, and nobody seems to know what's going on with you. I want you to be careful and come back."

"I will." Jude looked down at the table.

"I'm serious. Promise me you'll contact us if you need anything," Evan insisted, reaching over and grasping Jude's wrist.

Jude looked up, plastering a confident smile on his face. "I promise. If there's anything you can help with, I'll contact you right away. Besides, it's probably going to be a quick trip, and I'll be back bugging you about croissants and peanut butter before you know it."

"I like putting peanut butter on my croissants, especially when they're hot. The peanut butter just melts all over." Evan grinned, allowing him the subject change, even though he must have known Jude's issues were far from settled.

"But you get all sticky," Jude complained. "How can you eat that and still not get all messy?"

"Practice." Evan laughed as Jude just shook his head.

Chapter 1

ELEMENTAL LORE

As written by the scribes and entombed in the Church Archives:

1. To date, the Church has recognized five types of Elementals:
2. Earth, being the rarest and least-often born. Only two known in all of Church history.
3. Air, being the second rarest.
4. Spirit.
5. Water.
6. Fire, being the most prevalent, most destructive, and most volatile of all the beings.

No other information is contained in the archive as to their purpose or powers.

July 12, 2216—
Present. Burned-out abandoned building, New York City.

THE DISTANT crunch of tires on gravel should've been alarming, but it wasn't. They'd been on the run practically from the moment they'd left Evan and Adel in France. *I hope they're all right.* Jude was the eternal worrier. He hadn't had a chance to contact them, to see if they were being hunted as well. At first there just wasn't time—they'd needed to stay ahead of their pursuers. Now time had run out. As he lay, broken and bleeding, he prayed Evan was okay, but exhaustion overrode everything else, and he felt too tired to really care.

Jude's mind wandered aimlessly in a numb haze. In his efforts to destroy the demons that had attacked him, he'd expended way too much energy in the firestorm that had torched the building above him. He thought of Finton—last time he'd seen him, Fin had swung his sword and decapitated a vile-looking creature that'd kept coming even without its head. It must've been some sort of zombie. Fin had been defending the entrance, but he'd eventually fallen to the ever-increasing number of hell's denizens as they swarmed like vultures over a kill. Jude couldn't remember where Skye had gotten to. He prayed the little gryphon gargoyle was okay. Evan would have his hide if either one of them had been hurt. *So tired.* It was becoming a mantra, going round and round in his weary mind.

If only I could pass out. Jude felt as though he was waiting for something—maybe death. *That particular entity must be having a busy night, since he hasn't come to collect my soul yet.* Jude closed his eyes and groaned as something sharp from the rubble beneath him poked him in the back. His senses registered the pain, yet he was so far beyond mere sensation that Jude's mind could barely acknowledge it.

A decidedly masculine voice floated through the fog of Jude's thoughts. It was deep and warm and made him want to curl up into it and sleep for an eternity. *Is that the voice of death?* A familiar sing-song warble and the sound of flapping wings accompanied the voice and made him want to smile. *Ah, my Skye. Good. He's okay.* Jude would know Skye's song anywhere. He was here, somewhere close by.

"Come on, you beautiful bird. This place isn't safe for a gargoyle. You're too young to be on your own," the man's voice crooned softly. Even in his less-than-stellar condition, the velvety sound of it touched something deep inside Jude. "Oh God!" the voice shouted. Jude would've winced if he could've moved. He felt a hand touch his arm and forehead. "What happened?" That touch, so warm and gentle—he felt bathed in the heat of it.

The urge for this person to possess him, the desire to touch and fuck, was primal. A basic, instinctual part of himself reached for this other man blindly. He wanted to whimper and rub himself against those fingers, but that would take too much effort, although the aching need to do so hurt almost more than his battered body. The desire to answer the voice just wasn't enough to do more than force him to open his eyes. There was nothing left, but the last thing he saw was going to be the owner of that melodic voice. His gaze latched on to the most beautiful brown-black eyes he'd ever seen. He reached up with one hand and touched the man before him. He sighed as peace overwhelmed him for only the fleetest second before darkness closed around him.

"No!" NICOLAS Daemarkus screamed.

The gryphon gargoyle perched nearby screeched, rising up on his haunches, flapping his wings furiously.

Fate is truly a bitch. How could that fickle woman play with me like this? Nico thought.

He had questioned the urge to follow the gargoyle when he'd first seen it circling the abandoned building, but gargoyles were so rare these days and the creature was small and clearly unable to defend itself. Now he couldn't be happier he'd given in to his instincts and the gargoyle, but he'd also never been more distraught over his discovery, all at the same time.

The man he knelt beside was a mess of wounds and infection, blood, and dirt. For all that… he looked incredibly beautiful and fragile. The man's temperature was cool to the touch, but all humans tended to feel cool to Nico. *Still, for a human, he's too warm, probably feverish.* He brushed long red hair out of the man's face, wishing those beautiful green eyes would open again.

"My poor little human, what's happened to you?" Nico practically whimpered with distress, something he hadn't done in centuries, as nothing touched his heart anymore.

He knew he needed to get the man to safety. To call the burned-out building hazardous was an understatement. The structure barely held itself together, still smoldering in places. He didn't know if he dared pick up this beautiful human—he might have broken bones or internal injuries, which could be made worse by Nico's interference. He trembled with indecision, but he saw no other way. He had to get help for him, and there'd be none if they remained here. He carefully ran his hands along the thin arms and legs. Nothing was obviously broken.

Nico growled, decision made. He gently slid his arms beneath the man and drew him against his chest. He could feel the bones poking from under practically translucent skin—far too thin, but again his mind registered the bones weren't broken. Thin, Nico knew how to fix. Now, if he could just get the man to safety and get him to open his eyes. The steady, fluttering heartbeat reassured him his prize was very much alive, and Nico intended for him to stay that way.

The gryphon gargoyle flew out of what had once been a third-story window after glancing out and seeing no one below. Nico followed, clutching his precious cargo securely, tight against his chest to keep from jostling him. He landed on the ground with the gentle grace and ease of a dancer stepping from one room into the next. He sprinted to the car, where he strapped the guy into the passenger's scat. Nico couldn't resist the urge to nuzzle his passenger's neck as he secured the seatbelt. He smelled wonderful: like burning cedar in a fireplace, and spice, overlaid with strong male musk. The scent spoke to Nico, confirming what he'd known on sight. This man belonged to him—well, he did if he survived.

"Easy, little one," Nico whispered more to himself than to his unconscious passenger. His instincts were screaming at him to take and claim, but the human was in no condition to satisfy the flaming lust flowing through Nico's veins like molten lava. He adjusted himself, trying to relieve the strain on the raging erection that pressed against the zipper of his black dress pants. His protective instinct was the only thing keeping him from ravaging the guy on the spot. He'd protect this man, even from himself.

"Don't give up on me." He couldn't resist the briefest brushing of his mouth against plush red lips. His human was handsome, his skin soft and pale as alabaster, with just a smattering of freckles across his high cheekbones and nose.

Nico straightened and closed the car door, then ran around to the driver's side. Pulling onto the street and heading toward home as quickly as he could, Nico was never so glad that traffic became nearly nonexistent after dark, thanks to the mandates of the Church. Even here in the heart of New York City, people were careful about moving around after the sun went down—not that the night would ever hold any dangers for him.

He hit a button on the dashboard of the car and called his brother. "Doc."

"Hey, Nico, what's up?"

"I need a favor. A friend has gotten hurt. I'm taking him home to the penthouse. Can you meet us there?"

"Sure, Nico, but maybe a hospital would be a better choice?"

"No!" Nico growled. "This is personal, Doc. Please—"

"Okay, Nico. I'm on my way."

"Thanks, Doc. I owe ya."

"Yeah—so what else is new, bro."

Nico hung up and glanced at his passenger, reaching out and touching his face with a shaking hand. "Please—hold on."

IT WAS quiet, warm. Jude couldn't remember the last time he'd truly felt warm. Where was he? Evan and Adel? No, he'd left them in France months ago. Jude struggled through the haze surrounding his thoughts, trying to bring himself to consciousness.

"You're safe, little one."

Damn, that voice. It definitely had him struggling to wake up. That deep bass reached out and stroked Jude's soul with every syllable. A vision of brown-black eyes reflecting concern and worry filled his memory. He *had* to see those eyes again.

The bed dipped as someone sat next to him. Yes, it had to be a bed. It felt too good to be anything else.

"Come on—open those beautiful eyes for me."

Jude wanted to obey the pleading sound in that voice. A warm hand engulfed his, and he felt lips caress his knuckles. That did it. A deep breath, and Jude forced his eyes open.

"That's it. Come on back."

"Bright." Jude squinted and mumbled in a voice so raw, it was barely recognizable as his own. His hand was momentarily laid upon the blankets. The bed moved, and the rustle of fabric and dimming of the light signaled someone had drawn the curtains. Jude blinked rapidly, trying to focus his eyes and thoughts. The warm hands returned, engulfing his once more.

"Better?"

"Yes. Where?" Jude glanced around the room, then back at his host, meeting those amazing eyes. The man's hair was long and black, flowing like glossy silk to a point just beyond his shoulders… and damn, didn't he have just a fabulously broad chest and wide shoulders? His host was drop-dead gorgeous—the epitome of tall, dark, and handsome, the kind that made Jude want to scream, "Take me home, Daddy." And here he was, laid out, looking like hell, and barely able to pull together the energy required to speak to this ministering angel.

He vaguely noted he was in a large bedroom, which was comforting. It was a peaceful room, and for some reason, it had a calming effect on him. Even though he knew he should've been at the very least nervous, having awakened in a strange place, he wasn't. He felt safe. Jude gave himself a mental shake. He couldn't afford to feel safe anywhere, especially in unfamiliar surroundings with an unknown number of people who could be hostile. Although there was one who he didn't wish to remain a stranger for long.

"You're in my home. I found you and brought you here and had you looked at by a doctor."

"No doctors!" Jude struggled to sit up, instantly awake, panic overtaking him. There wasn't a human doctor alive who'd consider him normal in any sense of the word. His body screamed in protest as he forced himself past the pain, trying to make it obey.

Strong hands stopped him and gently pressed him back into the mattress. "Shhh… it's okay. You're safe here. Relax. Rest."

"No doctors!" Jude tried again, but it was futile to fight against the strength that held him in the bed. The internal heat was building with his rising adrenaline. Jude closed his eyes and worked to control his emotions and the rising heat.

"Okay, no doctors. Calm down before your fever spikes. I can feel your temperature rising with your agitation."

"Please—no doctors. They'll kill me. I can't—" Jude opened his eyes to plead with the gorgeous man.

"Shhh… no one will hurt you. What's your name?"

"Jude…. Jude Jamison."

"Okay, Jude. I'm Nicolas Daemarkus. Friends call me Nico. You're in my home. No one will hurt you here." Nico brushed Jude's hair back and tucked the errant strands behind his ear.

Jude wanted to believe him, and he thought Nico probably did believe it, but he had no idea how powerful the people hunting Jude were. Jude relaxed into the pillows. He really had no choice. He wasn't strong enough to leave. Exhaustion had quickly overwhelmed his momentary surge of adrenaline-fueled strength.

"You have a very devout guardian. I haven't seen his kind awake in many decades," Nico said softly. "He sleeps now, of course, but refuses to leave your side. He appeared on the balcony the night I brought you here."

Jude found Skye curled up on the blankets by his side, secure in his stone sleep. Evan was going to kill him for letting Skye reveal himself like this. Jude moaned softly and ran a hand over Skye's sleeping marble form. "What have you done? Skye, protect yourself, you silly bird," Jude mumbled.

"He's in no danger here. He knows I'm no threat to him or you."

"And why is that? Why do you welcome and care for a stranger with a pet gargoyle? For all you know, the Bishop's Service is after me, and police officers from that division will soon be knocking on your door. You could be putting a price on your head by helping me." Jude's strength was gone; depression and helplessness flowed through him. He couldn't fight anymore. He was beaten down, with no way to return to France, to his friends.

"That's true, although the Church tries to avoid my kind as much as possible." Nico chuckled.

"Well, that may not last long with me being here." Jude hissed as he moved a hip and a searing pain shot through his back.

Nico reached for Jude, helped him to arrange himself more comfortably, and held a glass of water with a bent straw so he could drink. "Why would the Earth Elemental bestow one of its guardians on you?" Nico asked, cocking an eyebrow at Jude.

"How do you know about the Earth Elemental?" Jude tried to smile, but his cracked lips smarted, turning it into more of a grimace. Evan would cringe at anyone who referred to him as an Elemental, even though it was the truth.

"Word of the Elemental's discovery has spread like wildfire. The paranormal community is a small one, but you also mumble in your sleep. The awakening of the gargoyles of Notre Dame was felt throughout the community by those sensitive to the ebb and flow of magic. A person with a gargoyle guardian is someone who could only be favored by the Elemental."

Awakening gargoyles from their hibernation was just one of the powers Evan held as a Maker—which was his preferred title, if he was forced to acknowledge one. "The Earth Elemental… Evan… is my friend. I was given Skye before I met him. Later Evan gave me his blessing to keep the little gargoyle. We each had our calling to attend to and went our separate ways in France. He bid Skye and another, who I fear is lost, to watch over me. Or left me to watch over them, depending on how you look at it."

"Gargoyles are hard to lose. I bet the other one shows up yet. It's good to have strong friends." Nico placed the water glass on the nightstand and picked Jude's hand up again.

Jude felt a bit uneasy, holding hands with Nico—it felt very intimate—but he also didn't want to let go. "Yes. Evan's very strong." He chuckled but ended up coughing more than laughing. "But Adel's stronger."

"You're strong—"

"I'm not safe to be around. Skye is the only one who's safe for me to be near. I can't hurt him—at least, I can't hurt him when he sleeps."

"That remains to be seen. Rest now. We can talk more later. When you wake, I'll bring you something to eat."

Jude hadn't realized he was struggling to keep his eyes open. Somehow Nico's voice made everything all right, even though he knew it wasn't.

Nico's hand comforted him; he didn't feel so alone. It might be okay not to be alone, at least for a little while.

HOURS LATER, Skye's soft song awoke Jude. The gargoyle swayed to his own music as he crooned, his eyes closed. He gave a sharp chirp when he realized Jude was awake and began to purr and rub against him, eliciting a smile and a bit of a laugh. The room was dark other than the glow from the fireplace in the corner.

"Are you hungry?" Nico's voice from the door startled Jude. A dark outline changed into Nico walking into the room. Jude realized from the rattle of china that he was carrying a dish-laden tray.

"I think I could eat." Jude pushed himself up, stifling a groan as his arms and ribs protested the move. He leaned against a multitude of pillows between his back and the black metalwork headboard for support.

Nico set the tray on the nightstand. "Here, let me help you." He straightened the slipping pillows and carefully drew Jude back against them, then turned on a dim lamp next to the bed.

"Why?" Jude shook his head in confusion. After all the sleep, he was finally able to begin thinking clearly and couldn't figure out why this— admittedly, ruggedly handsome—man continued to help him.

"Why what?" Nico sat beside him on the edge of the bed. He pulled a napkin from the tray and tucked the edge into the neck of Jude's T-shirt. His fingers lingered on Jude's throat for a brief moment before picking up the tray and laying it across Jude's lap.

"Why are you helping me?" Jude mumbled.

"Because you're special." Nico looked at the tray, not meeting Jude's eyes.

There was something else, something Nico wasn't telling him. But it wasn't a good idea to force a gift horse, especially when you couldn't move out of the way if it decided to give you a good, swift kick in the ass. "There's nothing special about me." Jude turned away from Nico, trying not to get angry at his host. It wasn't his fault—he didn't know Jude's fire was volatile and at times uncontrollable.

"There is, but you don't have to tell me. I don't mind. I can wait until you trust me. I'm just glad I found you." Nico pointed to a bowl of soup.

"Now eat. You are way too thin. Do I need to feed him as well or will he hunt on his own?" Nico looked at Skye, curled against Jude's side.

A range of emotions flew through Nico as he glanced at Skye— jealousy, anger, longing, need—none of which made any sense to him until he focused on Jude. Then he saw the desire and lust, a hunger aimed at him, burning brightly before they gave way to a more peaceful glow of compassion and kindness.

"Skye will hunt if he needs to, but he likes table scraps when he can get them. If you leave the window open during the night, he'll come and go as he pleases." Jude sipped at the chicken noodle soup hesitantly at first, but when the rich broth hit his stomach, it elicited a ravenous growl, and Jude inhaled the meal like a starving man.

"Where is your friend the Elemental, Evan? Does he know someone's trying to kill you?" Nico seemed upset, but Jude wasn't sure why.

"It's been awhile since I last contacted him. He's in France… or was. He is negotiating with the Vatican to stop the killing of the gargoyles and trying to ensure the attempts on his life stop as well. Evan wasn't thrilled with the idea of going to Rome in the first place, and he refused to go without me. But the Pope insisted I return to Rome, and once there, he assigned me to a new investigation. I had to return to the US. I haven't had access to a computer to check on him since." Jude pushed the tray back, feeling stuffed and lethargic. He was talking too much, giving away secrets like they were normal conversation to a pretty face—no, a gorgeous, wet dream, drool-worthy, and totally masculine face. He just couldn't seem to guard his tongue around Nico. He felt too safe and content… something he couldn't afford to feel.

"Okay, if you decide you want to try to contact him, you can use mine— when you're better. Right now I'm just glad I'm able to help you." Nico took the tray and set it on the nightstand. He scooted closer and picked up Jude's hand. "Whether you contact your friend or not, I'll be here to help you."

"I-I'm sorry—I…." Jude stuttered, relaxing back into the pillows as his eyes began to lose focus, exhaustion once again pressing to the fore.

"Shhh…. There's nothing to be sorry for. You're perfectly safe and you need to rest, *mein Feuer*." Nico brushed Jude's hair back from his face and helped him ease down beneath the blankets.

"You don't understand. By helping me… just by being here, I've put you in danger. There are people—the Bishop's Service—" Jude rambled, trying to get his mind to focus. He wanted to warn Nico, but he wasn't having any of it.

"Rest now. You can tell me later who's after you. Nobody will touch you here. I won't let them, *mein Feuer*." Nico stroked Jude's face.

"What does that mean?" Jude mumbled as sleep began take him.

"*Mein Feuer?*" Nico asked and Jude nodded, struggling to keep his eyes open. Nico leaned in and nuzzled Jude's cheek, drawing a deep breath, and he whispered in his ear, "My fire."

"You have no idea…." Jude chuckled sarcastically. "No place is safe for me, Nico. No one's safe around me. If I thought they could actually end it, I'd go to the Bishop's Service myself, but all they can do is torture me as they try to kill me, and when that doesn't work, they'll use me against Evan."

"Enough talk about killing. The Church can't reach you here. They have no power over me, so there's nothing to be afraid of."

"They have power over everyone. But they aren't the only reason you aren't safe. I'm a danger to you as well." Jude sighed, his eyes closing against his will.

"No, not to me," Nico assured him.

"I am—" Jude insisted.

"Just rest," Nico whispered as Skye softly sang, lulling Jude back to sleep.

"Not safe," Jude mumbled in his sleep.

Nico rubbed small soothing circles on the back of Jude's hand. "Sleep. For now, just rest."

"HE'S RIGHT, Nico. The Church won't stop just because they fear us," Doc said from the doorway. "There are those who they employ who are suicidal enough to go against us. If they attack in large enough numbers, they can overwhelm even you, big brother."

"I know. But for now, he's safe. He needs to rest and eat. He needs to get his strength back so I can tell him about us, and I can claim my mate. Right now, that's my priority. I need to get him healthy, and then we can deal with the rest." Nico growled, turning to glare at Doc. His natural urge was to drop into a protective crouch between his brother and his mate, and it took every ounce of his control to keep from doing so.

"Easy, Nico. I'm not after your man," Doc said softly, not moving an inch from the doorway.

"I know, little bro. It's just he's so weak, and I can't claim him like I need to until he's stronger. I can't hurt him. My instincts are riding me hard." With a last reluctant glance at Jude, Nico led the way out of the bedroom and into the living room, putting some space between them. Motioning for Doc to have a seat, Nico paced around the room.

"Are you sure he's the one? I mean, humans are so fragile, and he may not survive if you were ever to lose control." Doc sat on the loveseat across from the fireplace, then crossed his legs and laced his hands together in his lap.

"Don't you think I've thought of that! He's been here all of four days. It's insane, but—he calls to me. Everything about him pulls at me, and it's getting stronger every damn day." Nico ran his hands through his hair in frustration. "The irony is that he thinks he's the dangerous one and will hurt me." Nico dropped into a chair across from Doc. "It's all I can do to just sit there, to be content holding his hand or helping him move about the bed. Every second I'm touching him, I *have* to be conscious and in control so I don't burn him." Nico struggled not to yell, knowing Jude slept fitfully just down the hall.

"Okay, breathe, Nico. Calm down."

"Yes—I know—I'm trying." Nico met Doc's eyes. "It's just... you didn't see the place where I found him."

"So tell me."

Nico rose again and strode to the tall glass french doors that led to the large stone balcony. He stared out into the night, not really seeing it. "It started when I was sitting on the balcony just after sundown. I'd been sipping coffee and considering going out for the night. I was about to leave when I saw the gargoyle flying around, over that tenement building that's been smoldering. You remember the one: it had gone up in flames the day before and you accused me of causing the fire." Nico half smiled at his brother.

"I remember. It was a strange fire. According to the news, there were no accelerants and no explosives, yet the upper two floors of the building were blown clear off, while the rest simply smoldered but never really caught fire." Doc frowned and tipped his head to the side in consideration.

Nico nodded. "The gargoyle was such a small one, and I figured he had to be pretty young and defenseless. I wondered what he was doing there by himself, just circling the building. I was afraid he'd attract attention if he kept it up, so I went to see what the deal was and if I could keep him from revealing himself and being hunted."

"Yeah, I'd probably have done the same." Doc smiled at Skye, who'd followed them from Jude's room and was now perched on the balcony, peering out into the night.

"So I get to the building, and even though it's still kind of smoldering, it looks more like ground zero of some kind of explosion rather than a place that's been set on fire. Even with the kind of power we put out, that place had its top blown off—the flames licking at the edges were secondary to the explosion." Nico paced across the living room floor agitatedly.

"You know the newspaper quoted the fire marshal saying that whatever caused the explosion, the temperature was so high it basically vaporized the upper two floors, and there was hardly any rubble, just ash. But when the fire department arrived, it was only slightly smoldering and no major fires were found—the building was practically cool to the touch. They didn't even go in because they were afraid the structure was too weak, and the building had been abandoned shortly after the war and was unused."

Nico nodded. "That explains why they never found him."

"Nico, with temps high enough to vaporize the upper floors, I'm sure they felt if anyone had been in the building, they'd be dead."

"I get that. It's just really strange. I'd never seen anything like it."

"So you get there, the place is ground zero... then what?"

"I'm calling to Skye, trying to get him to come down so I can bring him here to roost. I follow him up to the top floor, and that's where I found Jude. He's lying in one of the rooms on a pile of rubble and the gargoyle's standing guard. The instant his scent hit me, I knew who he was."

"So you just grabbed him and put him in the car and called me." Doc laughed, putting a hand to his face. He snorted, his amusement getting away from him, as Nico tried to ignore his brother's behavior.

Nico felt his face warm as a blush colored his cheeks. "He's so beautiful." He spoke more to himself than Doc as he gazed off into space, picturing Jude lying in his bed.

"Nico, this is reality. He's human. That makes him fragile and a liability."

"He's my mate, Nero!" Nico stood, and in two steps, was leaning over his brother, his arms braced on the back of the chair.

Doc put up his hands, palms out in a placating submissive gesture. "I know, Nico. Please—you know I hate it when you call me Nero. And get a breath mint, man—you forget to take care of yourself while worrying about him? Consider brushing your teeth." He hissed in annoyance as Nico stood and stumbled a step or two away. "Look, if you intend to keep him, I'd say stock up on burn cream and really try to never ever lose control or you will kill him. Be ready: there will be those that may not accept a human into our world so easily."

"I know," Nico mumbled, dejectedly shaking his head. He turned to walk back to his bedroom, paused at the door, and gazed in at Jude, sleeping in the oversized dark mahogany canopy bed. Nico returned to stand at the bedside, and Doc followed him into the room standing just inside the door. "You're sure he's just human? I mean, would Fate be that cruel to give me a mate who I can't ever truly be with, a mate who can't take the heat?"

"I'm sorry, Nico. His scent is purely human. Although… he does seem to run a little warmer in temperature than your average human, but he isn't well and they run fevers to kill infection in their bodies. From what I can see, he's all human." Doc put a hand on his shoulder.

Nico closed his eyes. "All I smell says human too. He's a beautiful gift, but like a bird in a gilded cage. He's so fragile, and I'm a tiger. I could kill him without even thinking about it, completely unintentionally, just by closing my eyes for the briefest second. Beautiful, sexy, fragile—human. My human, but still… human." Nico looked at Jude, his red hair flowing over the black silk sheets of his bed.

"Control—that's going to be the key to a happy future for both of you. Fate is insuring you learn complete control, big brother." Doc smiled. "Are you going to be okay?"

"No. I'm not. I'm terrified. The need… this desire to claim my mate is increasing steadily every day. But he's so sick and so fragile. He's barely conscious, and I want to ravish him."

"With a human as a mate, this is just the beginning." Doc clenched his hands into fists, revealing his frustration. "I wish there was more I could do or tell you that would help, but…."

Nico silently walked around the bed and knelt beside it so he wouldn't jostle its occupant. He cupped Jude's face in his hand. Jude mumbled in his sleep and turned into the caress, sighing softly. Nico whimpered, leaned in, and tenderly kissed him on the forehead. He gently picked up Jude's hand, rubbing slow, soothing circles on it with his thumbs. "I know, which is why I'm forcing myself to sit here and be content just to touch him like this."

"So it will be a fight that you will have to win, brother, for both of you."

"He's so alluring. I find myself drawn to him, and even though it may be the death of us both, I can't reject my mate. Who could? I even think his freckles are cute. He's so young."

Doc walked over and put a hand on his back. "He should be much better soon. Give him something solid to eat when he next wakes—it'll help him build his strength. Fluids are a must. Keep him hydrated, and he'll heal soon enough. His injuries are fairly minor. He's mainly fighting malnutrition and exhaustion. If you need me, call." Doc headed for the door.

"Thanks, Doc." Nico rose and accompanied him.

"Everything will be fine, Nico. Congratulations on finding your mate. Most of us never do."

"I know. I'm just scared shitless. I don't want to kill my mate. I can't…," Nico whispered.

Doc left, and Nico returned to his vigil. He couldn't resist the pull of his mate. He carefully eased himself onto the bed to lie alongside Jude. Nico rested his head on his hand, running his fingers through Jude's long red hair. "So what am I going to do with you?" Nico brushed a kiss across the top of Jude's head and watched a sleeping Jude snuggle unconsciously into his chest, eliciting another wanton whimper from Nico.

He knew it'd be a damn long night.

Chapter 2

DAEMON LORE

As written by the scribes and entombed in the Church Archives:
Angel (daemon as known by pre-Christian history):
a.k.a.: Messenger of God
a.k.a.: Nature Spirits
a.k.a.: Spirit Guides
a.k.a.: Muse
a.k.a.: Demigod

CARDINAL SWIFT sat in his office, impatiently drumming the fingers of one hand as he waited for the last of the archbishops to arrive. The sweltering temperatures had caused the air-conditioning to kick on, ruffling the papers on his desk. The climate was relentless in Phoenix, and the rising heat mirrored his anger and frustration with each passing moment of forced delay. They were waiting on Kennedy: he always seemed to arrive late. Of course, he did have the farthest to travel, as his territory covered all of the mid- and upper-Northwest dioceses, and he actually worked out of Portland.

A knock at the heavy oak door heralded the arrival of his wayward archbishop.

"Come," Cardinal Swift called.

Archbishop Luke Kennedy entered the room and gave a short bow. "Your Eminence, my apologies for my tardiness. The plane was late in landing."

"Sit, Kennedy. Let's get on with this already," Swift growled, motioning for him to take a seat.

"Yes, Your Eminence." Kennedy sat beside the two other archbishops who worked under Cardinal Matthias John Swift: Archbishop Patrick Henry O'Flaggan, who controlled the East Coast dioceses, and Archbishop Thomas Mark Mason, who was in charge of the Southern dioceses. Between the three of them, they controlled the Church in the United States, all under *his* benign benevolence.

"Report!" Swift barked at his men.

"I used three of my elders to send out twenty-one demons to get the man. But it didn't work. That damn Inquisitor must be guarded. There's no way he could've survived the attack alone, much less prevented even one of the demons from returning with news about his person, without help." O'Flaggan glared at the other two priests, daring them to contradict him.

"Of course he's guarded. His Holiness the Pope sent him after the Earth Elemental, and he was able to send the Elemental to France, where he woke the damn guardians over Notre Dame Cathedral in Paris. After that, you really think his friend the Elemental didn't send a couple of the guardians to watch over him?" Kennedy scoffed.

"You should've killed them both before they escaped to France, for God's sake! Your man—that sniveling weasel, Father Michael—had them, and he only succeeded in scaring them out of the country and getting himself killed in the process," Mason hissed.

"Enough! You bicker like old women. I don't care about who did what. I want results. I want the man dead, or at the very least, I want to know who he is before he can disrupt our plans for the Pope." Swift stared at each man, his penetrating gaze leaving no question as to his intentions.

"How's that part of the plan progressing?" Mason asked.

"I was able to get a couple of men into his personal guard. They've begun to poison him. It's a slow-acting substance. It must be if we're to remain undetected and take over without anyone the wiser." The upturn of Swift's lips was far from a smile, closer to a sneer. "By the time it kills him, I'll have taken over most of his duties and will be leading the Council of Cardinals."

"You'll be next in line for the Papacy." O'Flaggan laughed. "You'll rule the world."

"Yes, I will. And no sniveling, ass-kissing Inquisitor is going to ruin my plans." Swift banged his fist on his desk. "Find him! Kill him! Can I be any plainer? I hope I don't need to draw you a map?"

"No, Your Eminence," parroted all three archbishops.

"No…," MUMBLED Jude in his sleep, tossing his head from side to side. "No, you can't!"

"Shhh… easy, *mein Feuer*. It's okay, Jude," Nico whispered softly into his hair.

Jude had been asleep for twelve restless hours while his body knit itself back together. Nico left his side rarely, if ever. Repeated cycles of nightmares would almost wake him as he struggled with his demons, crying out and thrashing restlessly. Nico would whisper, gently taking Jude's hand, making promises he hoped he'd get the chance to keep. Jude would relax as if drawn by the soothing words and tone before slipping into a more restful sleep until the cycle began again.

Nico ran his fingers through Jude's hair and caressed his face, kissing him gently as he inhaled his scent. "Sleep, Jude. You're safe now," Nico reassured him over and over, listening as Jude sighed, a soft smile gracing his lips.

The ringing of the doorbell caused Nico to frown. He didn't want to leave Jude, and he had no idea who could be at his door. Regretfully, he had no choice, as the ringing was becoming an insistent knocking.

Nico quietly crept from the bed and headed out to the front door. He looked at the security camera and was shocked to see a sprite—or rather, one of the Fair Folk. He had white-and-red hair, pointed ears, green skin, and gossamer wings that were folded tightly against his body.

Damn, I've never seen such a creature in the flesh. So they do exist.

Nico pressed the button. "Yes?"

"Hello, lad. You want to open the door. I know Jude's in there, and he's needing me."

"Who are you?" Nico frowned, noticing the large sword handle poking over the top of his back from between the curled wings.

"My name is Finton. I'm his guardian."

"He already has a guardian."

"Oh good, I've been worried that Skye was injured and lost somewhere."

"Skye is fine. He—"

An ear-wrenching scream echoed through the apartment. Nico turned and ran for the bedroom. The sound of panicked pounding on the front door echoed behind him. Nico stood in the doorway of the bedroom, staring in shocked surprise at Jude.

Jude stood on the bed, blankets having fallen at his feet, his eyes glazed over, clearly lost in the torment of his nightmare, precariously balanced on the mattress. His hands were held out in front of his body, red-orange flames engulfing his bare arms from elbow to fingertips. "No! Get back!" Jude screamed at his nightmare assailants.

A crash came from the front room and Finton stood beside Nico. "What did you do to him?" he yelled.

"Nothing! He was sleeping before you showed up!" Nico snarled in accusation as Finton ran into the room, leaped up on the bed, got in behind Jude, took his arms above the elbow, and held them away from their bodies and the bedding.

Skye cooed and sang softly, trying to calm the screaming Jude.

"Jude, calm down, boy. Wake up for me. I'm here. You're okay." Finton spoke loudly, his voice sounding much calmer than his frantic actions.

Jude came unhinged. He spun on the bed, his legs getting caught in the bedding as he reached for Finton, the menacing flames moving toward him.

"Now, come on. You know you don't want to hurt me. Wake up for me, Jude. Please," Finton begged softly, keeping his voice gentle and not panicked.

"No! Get away from me!" Jude screamed.

"Get out of my way!" Nico roared and shoved Finton off the bed. A smile lit his lips as he realized that, unlike Finton, he had nothing to fear. Likewise, he no longer had to worry about hurting Jude either. Nico scooped him up in his arms, held him against his body, and instantly burst into blue flames. He matched the intensity with Jude's, the blue mingling with the red, fire with fire. The flames engulfed them, hovering just above their bodies but not burning skin or clothing as they danced on the air. Nico controlled the warm blue fire as he cooed to Jude, nuzzling his neck. "Shhh, Jude. You're safe," Nico whispered repeatedly as he absorbed the blaze from Jude.

"No...," JUDE whimpered with less conviction as he came out of the nightmare. "Nico." Jude sighed in relief as he felt the strong arms wrapped around him, holding him to a broad chest. He opened his eyes, gazing up into Nico's dark eyes, before realizing they were on fire. Jude squealed and struggled, pushing against Nico, his eyes filled with terror.

"Shhh, Jude. You're safe, and so am I. Calm down." Nico hugged Jude tightly. "I'm controlling our fire. You concentrate on calming down, and it will burn out. You're safe." Nico rocked Jude like a small child, cooing nonsense.

The realization that he wasn't hurting Nico and they were okay registered in Jude's mind. The adrenaline flowing through his system abated, and he collapsed against Nico's chest.

"That's it…. Good. See? Everything's okay."

"What are you?" Jude asked softly as the flames died around them.

Nico sat on the bed, with Jude on his lap, snuggling against Nico's chest. "I'm a fire daemon."

"A demon!" Fear and confusion hit Jude with another rush of adrenaline, engulfing them in a renewed wash of fire as he struggled against Nico. He was far too weak to get away.

"No, little flame, not demon. I'm a daemon—a nature spirit, an immortal. Similar in kind to the sprite there, although I wasn't aware that the Fair Folk could leave the land of fae anymore. I'd been told that gateway was shut, unable to be reopened." Nico looked at Fin curiously but then turned back to Jude, nuzzling his neck.

"I'm not one of the Fair Folk." Fin relaxed his stance. "I'm a gargoyle, like Skye. We were assigned to Jude as guardians by Evan Halvard, the Maker. Skye is… he's very young and not exactly strong enough to protect Jude. I've come to realize I'm not strong enough to protect him either. This last attack nearly did me in," Fin admitted, frowning.

Skye leaped up into his arms and cooed, rubbing against Fin.

He smiled down at him. "Nice to see you too, birdbrain."

"I'm really sorry, Fin…. 'Thank you' seems not nearly enough. Are you okay?" Jude relaxed, temporarily assuaged by Nico's answer. The fire surrounding them dimmed, then went out entirely. Jude leaned toward Fin, looking at him closely. "Evan would have my ass if anything happened to you."

"I'm fine. I should sleep more, though. I'm not nearly a hundred percent, but I needed to make sure you were safe." Fin stroked Skye, drawing forth a purr.

"I'm okay, Nico. You can put me down," Jude tucked his head against Nico's chest, hiding his embarrassment. He couldn't believe he was letting this man, this daemon, hold him like a child. "I'm not a kid… really."

"What if I don't want to put you down? I kind of like having you in my arms." Nico pointedly kissed the top of Jude's head.

"Oh… I guess that's okay," Jude's jaw cracked as he yawned, relaxing more than he knew he should. "I'm just so tired."

"It's all right, *mein Feuer*. You aren't recovered yet, and creating fire takes a lot of energy. Sleep, and I'll bring you something to eat when you wake," Nico whispered.

"Okay. Will you take care of Fin too? I know he's an ass, but he means well and he's very protective of me. Besides, Evan will kill me if I try and send him back to France—again," Jude mumbled, a mischievous smile on his face. His eyes closed as he drifted off to sleep.

"I heard that, you brat." Fin pretended to growl as Nico laid Jude in the bed and tucked the blankets around him. "I won't fall for you telling me to sleep in a crate for safety ever again, so don't even try it."

Skye jumped from Fin's arms and curled against Jude's body, and Fin motioned Nico to follow him out of the room.

NICO WINCED at the sight of the broken front door—it hung precariously on one upper hinge—and pushed it closed. He'd need to contact building maintenance to have someone sent up to repair it as soon as possible. Then he led Fin to the kitchen, where Nico dug around in the refrigerator, pulled out the fixings for sandwiches, and turned on the coffeemaker.

"So the two of you are mates," Fin said.

Nico's head snapped up so quickly, he was surprised he didn't give himself whiplash. "You know?"

"Of course. If you were any more affectionate, it'd be intolerable to be anywhere near you. As it is, it's only slightly nauseating," Fin teased.

"And you're with him because…?"

"I'm his guardian. Where else would I be?"

Nico sighed as Fin grinned mischievously. "Please, enough with the taunting. Why does Jude need a guardian? Who's attacking my mate?"

"Jude… Peter Judas Jamison… is a Jesuit Inquisitor of Rome, and he reports directly to the Pope. All of the clergy are aware of the Jesuit Inquisitors, but their identities are extremely guarded. The only person who knows what Jude looks like is supposed to be the Pope himself. The Council of Cardinals knows him by title and name—Inquisitor Peter Judas—and by his reputation, but not by his appearance." Fin picked up a sandwich and began eating.

"So nobody is supposed to know what he looks like, but somehow he's still being attacked? And you were barely able to keep him alive to the point that you actually left him lying out in the open, unprotected?"

"No, it wasn't like that. Evan gave Skye and myself a gift—we can control when we turn to stone. But when mortally wounded, the only way

I could prevent my death was to let hibernation take me. When Jude goes off like a Roman candle, not even a gargoyle can take the heat. Luckily, the enemy can't either… at least, so far." Fin looked at the coffee Nico poured. "Do you have milk and sugar?"

"Yes." Nico grabbed the sugar bowl from the counter and the milk from the fridge and set them on the table.

"Thank you."

"So what happened?" Nico sat at the table with a sandwich of his own.

"When it became obvious we weren't going to win, Jude's self-preservation instinct overrode his fear, and he blew like a bomb. His fire is so hot, it vaporizes everything it touches. He burns until he collapses from exhaustion. Even in our stone form, Skye and I'd be nothing but ash and rubble if we came too close." Fin added sugar and milk to the coffee.

"You left?" Nico asked, trying not to frown but definitely not happy with the thought of Jude lying defenseless amongst the smoldering debris.

"When he gets like that, we hightail it because we can't protect him if we're dead. I hid in the sewers below the building and went into hibernation to heal. Since I'm larger, I find the sewer is the easiest place to roost in the city and not attract the attention of the clergy. Skye takes to the air and finds a place on a rooftop, out of sight."

"So you just abandon him and, what, return when it's over?" Nico struggled to control his mounting fear for Jude.

Fin sipped his coffee, set the cup down, and stared into Nico's eyes. "I try to stay as long as I possibly can. But when he lets go, there's no control—everything caught in the flames dies."

Nico nodded his understanding. "I'm sorry. Go on."

"Sometimes Jude expends so much energy that he seems to fade into a smokelike state. I've watched him from a safe distance. The edges of his body blur in the heat, becoming pure white in the center, radiating outward as if he's literally becoming fire."

Nico rubbed his hands across his face, trying to control his agitation. Only the thought that Jude would never have to go through this alone again made him feel better. He'd always be there for him from now on. It was a miracle the gargoyles hadn't been killed.

"When it's over, he's exhausted but alive. I don't know what it means when his edges blur. I've my suspicions, but…." Fin took another sandwich from the platter and a few chips from a bowl in the center of the table.

"I get that you can't be at his side when he burns. It just upsets me to think how long he lay—alone—in that building when something could've found and killed him." Nico frowned, trying to prevent his lips from curling back and snarling at Fin.

"Found him—tortured him—sure. Killed him? Won't happen. Boy's pretty much indestructible as far as we can tell. That's why he's so afraid of the Bishop's Service and whoever's hunting him. If his secret were discovered, some of the clergy would see him as evil, as a demon of the highest order, straight from the bowels of Hell, because of his control of fire."

"He's *not* evil! Just because you wield fire doesn't make you evil!" Nico snarled, struggling to calm his anger.

"I know that, and I think he's coming around. The clergy who've been trying to kill him—when and if they were to discover he is not only the Jesuit Inquisitor of Rome, but also has the power to create fire? They'll make his existence Hell on Earth."

"Ignorance be damned."

Fin sighed sadly. "He's already pretty much tried everything to kill himself since we left Evan. Nothing works. He just keeps coming back, exhausted and usually unconscious. If they capture him, they'd torture him into insanity." Fin tipped his head back and stared at the ceiling, blinking rapidly.

"But why? Why would he try to kill himself?" Nico reached out and grabbed Fin's arm. "Why is my mate suicidal?"

"Because *he* isn't sure they're wrong. He grew up believing in the Church's teachings. In the same environment as the assholes who are after him. He is an officer of the Church, beholden only to His Holiness the Pope. His faith is at odds with his existence." Fin stared into Nico's eyes, as if he were trying to make him understand. "He's afraid he's becoming evil. He says he can feel the fire consuming him from the inside. It's terrifying him. I don't know what to tell him. I know something happened to him that night I was awakened and Evan destroyed the demons. He'd pulled so much power from the earth that, when he released the excess, the blast washed through all of us. It awoke fire in Jude." Fin stifled a yawn.

"Fire isn't evil. If it were, my kind would be no different than the demons of Hell. But we *are* different. Fire is an Elemental power, no different than the power of the Earth his friend Evan employs."

"You and I know that. Now you just have to convince him that the fire he feels devouring his soul each time he lights up isn't making him evil."

Fin's head was starting to drop, and he'd end up a statue sitting at the table if he didn't move soon. "I really need to sleep. Just point me in the direction of a dark corner where I won't bother you and I'll turn to stone. I'm really exhausted and not as well as I may look."

"Oh sure. The guest bedroom is down the hall on the left. You can use the bed, chair, or whatever. Make yourself comfortable. No one will bother you." Nico absentmindedly pointed down the hallway. He was shocked Jude would think himself evil just because he controlled fire. It seemed so illogical to him that Jude could even consider himself evil.

"Thank you. I should be completely back to normal by tomorrow night." Fin got up and walked down the hall.

Nico cleaned up the remains of their repast and wandered back into his bedroom, where Jude slept peacefully. "You'll never be alone again. I'll burn with you, my mate."

Chapter 3

DAEMON LORE

As written by the scribes and entombed in the Church Archives:
Physical Attributes:
1. Immortal but can be killed.
2. Strength, speed, and agility significantly greater than mankind.
3. Wings, which can appear or disappear.
4. Can choose to be seen or unseen in their observation of mankind.

JUDE AWOKE feeling warm and safe. He could see this becoming a habit, one he might actually enjoy. He hadn't felt this relaxed since before he and Evan left for France, after they'd left Evan's cabin in the hills of South Dakota. Nico must have taken the time to strip him of his clothes, leaving him in a pair of soft cotton sleep pants and a T-shirt.

"Good morning. Are you hungry?"

The deep voice sent tingles through his body, pooling in his cock—it instantly sprang to life every time Nico spoke. Jude barely contained the moan that begged to escape as tiny kisses rained down on his ear and neck. He tipped his head to the side, giving Nico more room to work. "Wait, stop. We can't do this. I owe you for saving me. I understand that, but—"

"I'd never hurt you or do anything you don't want, and I'd never take payment from your body." Nico growled his annoyance. "You're not well, so don't panic, just enjoy the morning." Nico snuggled closer, drawing Jude against him.

"I didn't mean it that way. I don't understand your attention to a vagrant injured man you found in a burned-out abandoned building," Jude mumbled. "Guess you know I'm gay, but I don't usually react like this… I don't just curl up with guys like this." Jude snuggled into Nico's chest, unable to resist giving in to his desire to be closer.

"I should hope not." Nico smiled down at Jude, evidently finding humor in his confusion. "There was nothing to figure out. You're just feeling the pull. There's no fighting it. Fate doesn't put together incompatible mates… and you are mine."

"Mates? You mean like… marriage mates? Like Evan and Adel are mates?" He'd heard them say as much, and he'd envied their loving relationship. He'd halfway hoped, in a silly, lovelorn moment, to find a mate himself someday, but then he began to burn and he'd thought he'd be alone forever. Until now.

"Yes, a gargoyle would be a good mate for an Earth Elemental. Gargoyles are fiercely strong and loyal almost to a fault. Adel will protect and love Evan for a very long time, and when Evan finally passes this world, Adel will go to stone and never return to life. It's the nature of gargoyles when they lose their mates to never return. They cannot live without their bonded."

"You said we're mates." Jude shifted so he could look into Nico's deep brown eyes. "How do you know?"

"For my people, we know our mate on sight and by smell. When I saw you in the remains of that building, I instantly knew you were my mate, and your scent confirmed it for me." Nico ran his fingers through the silky strands of Jude's hair. "I have waited for you for a very long time."

"So am I becoming one of you?" Jude asked hesitantly.

"No, you must be born a daemon. You're human." Nico nuzzled against Jude's neck, his words soft and gentle. "But not just any human. You're special."

"Nobody seems to know what's happening to me or what I'm becoming. They don't understand it, but His Excellency says I'm a child of God and my soul is good, that I need to trust in God's plan for me." Jude sighed. "Problem is, he doesn't know what this feels like."

"I can honestly tell you that you're not becoming anything else. If you were, your scent would be changing, and it isn't. Even when you were all aflame, you were still you. One hundred percent human, that's all. Nothing else," Nico reassured Jude and ran his hands down Jude's arms and back, gently rubbing the stress away.

"So what, then? Humans don't generally burn and not get hurt."

Nico paused as if considering his words carefully. "You, my flame, are an Elemental, like your friend Evan. If I had to guess, I'd say the power was dormant, but when you were exposed to Evan's raw energy wave, it awoke the fire in you."

"But I can't be an Elemental. There is only one Elemental power at a time." Jude frowned in confusion.

"Who says there's only one?"

"Well, Adel said that there was only one power at a time, and His Excellency seemed to agree." Jude placed a hand on Nico's chest, feeling his heart beat beneath his palm.

"I'm afraid Adel and His Excellency are wrong. Adel may be a very old gargoyle, but they aren't awake all the time. They tend to hibernate for decades. It certainly is rare for there to be more than one power active at a time, but not unheard of. It usually heralds an era of great instability in both the world of man and the paranormal world." Nico sat up a little straighter in bed and drew Jude with him.

"But you're saying it's happened before, that more than one Elemental has been alive at once?" Jude asked.

"Yes, this isn't the first time and probably won't be the last." Nico grinned, leaned over, and kissed Jude gently before continuing. "There are five Elemental powers—"

"Yeah, I know. Earth, Air, Fire, Water, and Spirit."

"Right. Earth is your friend Evan's power. Fire is you." Nico pressed the palm of his hand gently against Jude's chest, and Jude's rapidly beating heart fluttered beneath his fingertips. "Air, Water, and Spirit are the other three. Don't be afraid. I'll teach you everything you need to know about your fire."

"So what're you... exactly?" Jude reached up and ran the back of his hand against Nico's face, turning it over to cup his jaw.

NICO HAD been expecting this conversation but was still apprehensive about it. He was bonding with Jude and wouldn't survive separation if rejected, yet he needed to come clean and explain the nature of the bond. He struggled to maintain control, to keep from frightening Jude, while every cell of his being was screaming to claim him and never let go. Jude was human and wouldn't understand the mating instinct completely, although it helped that he'd seen Adel and Evan. Jude must feel the compulsion himself, or he wouldn't be practically trying to climb into Nico's skin, despite his misgivings.

"I'm a daemon." Nico couldn't resist rubbing his face into the tentative caress. His body felt starved of attention and his control was slipping, but allowing himself to indulge in these little touches seemed to help appease the need to claim him. Feeling Jude's skin on his instantly took him to the heights of heavenly desire and lust.

"A day-mawn... not dee-men." Jude spoke carefully.

"Yes. It depends on your beliefs as to how you see my people. Truly, we are known as beings with a link to the Earth and the gods, each of us born with a special gift. The early Greeks believed us to be messengers of the gods. Some see us as go-betweens. Christianity dubbed us angels. Some named us demigods... although I'm not fond of that version, as I don't see myself as any type of god."

"Angels?" Jude frowned, grasping at the most familiar definition.

Nico nodded. "I can honestly say I've never spoken with any god, and I've never left the earthly plane. I'm strong... much stronger than you, little one. I can manifest wings and fly, although it's been a while since I've done so. I can control fire—that's my gift. Each of us has a different one. We're immortal, much as Adel, Fin, and Skye are immortal."

"Immortal... you'll live forever?"

"Yes, but we can be killed. You, as my mate, will live as long as I live, and I'd live as long as you live. When we leave this world, we go together. Our lives and fates will be forever joined." Nico spoke slowly, letting the weight of his words sink in. He wanted Jude to understand clearly what being mated meant.

"Forever. We'd be together always...."

Nico thought he heard a touch of awe in Jude's voice. Humans had such short lives—even Elementals, who could exist longer than most, were deficient in comparison to the daemon and gargoyle races, who were considered immortal. It made choosing lovers very hard for Nico and his kind. Whom would they choose when they always outlived their partner, and in the end, would have to watch them age and die? It'd never happen again, not to him. Only one man from this point on, only Jude, and they'd die together. With luck, in time he'd fall hopelessly in love with Jude. If his growing need to protect and his lustful possessiveness were anything to go by, falling in love would be the easiest part of this relationship.

"You really think I'm an Elemental?" Jude hesitantly asked.

"Yes. The fact that you're human and you can manipulate fire pretty much cinches that fact for me." Nico placed little kisses along Jude's jaw and nuzzled his ear.

"I... I never thought that I could be like Evan. I never asked him what his power felt like." Jude's gaze focused far away, appearing to be caught up in his thoughts. "Do you have any family?"

"I have a brother, Nero. You may or may not remember him. He's the doctor who checked on you when I brought you to my home. His power is healing, and he's the only member of my family I've seen in a very long time. He and I have stuck together through the centuries. Even though we don't always see eye to eye, we rely on each other."

"Why do I feel like whenever I use fire, something is coming to life and eating my soul when I burn? It… it feels like an animal is trying to consume me from the inside out."

Nico caught a glimpse of barely restrained fear in Jude's eyes before he ducked his head against Nico's chest. He put a finger under Jude's chin and raised his eyes to meet his. "Because you're afraid. Normally when an Elemental awakens to his or her power, it's as a child. The power and the child grow together. You're an adult, and your power is rushing to catch up with you, while you struggle to learn to control it."

"But Evan never said anything about feeling like his power was eating his soul."

"I suspect that Evan grew up with his power, and Earth is a quiet element—a steady, solid power that's always there but not necessarily always volatile. His power is reflected in the beings he is able to create. Gargoyles are naturally an unshakably strong presence, but not dangerous unless irritated, and then all bets are off." Nico chuckled. "Fire is a completely different type of element."

Nico pushed the blankets back and extended one hand, lighting a fingertip so the flame could dance along his fingers. He held them before Jude. "Fire can feel like a living being. It breathes—for without oxygen, it cannot burn. It consumes—for without fuel, it cannot grow. It has been said to dance and roar. It gives light in the darkness and heat in the cold. But in and of itself, it has no will but to exist… to burn." Nico closed his hand and the fire went out.

"You think what I feel—the thing that's eating at my soul—is just the power of the fire trying to become part of me." Jude hesitated. "But it feels like it's trying to consume me, not join me. It really scares me, Nico."

Nico tried to reassure him. "I know you're scared. Fire is an unpredictable element at times."

"When the fire consumes me, like it did in the battle before you found me, I feel like I'm becoming lost in the flames. There's nothing holding me together. I try to stay in control, but I feel like it wants out, and I'm terrified of what'll happen when it does."

"I'm your center now. I'll teach you, and when you feel like you're going to lose it, you focus on me. Even if your fire sets me alight, I can take the heat. We'll do it together. Okay, *mein Feuer*?" Nico kissed Jude on the tip of his nose. He wanted to kiss his lips—he ached for the touch—but he feared if Jude showed even the slightest hint that he desired Nico as well, he may not be able to stop.

"Yeah, okay." Jude hesitated.

Nico leaned forward, making sure he had a tight grip on his control. He gently brushed his lips across Jude's in a soft, lingering kiss, eliciting a moan from Jude. "We need to get out of bed, or I'll do things that we'll regret later. We need to get you something to eat. You need to get your strength back. I ache to claim you as my mate, but I won't hurt you." Nico pushed himself upright and out of bed. Jude's gaze stayed glued to his hands as Nico adjusted the obvious erection tenting his boxers. He usually slept in the nude, but having Jude in his bed, he felt it appropriate to at least appear modest. He wondered what thoughts flowed behind those lust-filled green eyes. "Please, *mein Feuer*, stop or I won't be able to control myself. You make me burn hotter than any fire."

Jude blushed, and his color deepened when Nico swept him off the bed, into his arms, and headed out the door, carrying him to the kitchen.

"I could've walked." Jude sighed into Nico's chest before being set down at a small table.

"Probably, but then you'd have been too exhausted to eat." Nico moved about the kitchen, preparing coffee and putting together a light lunch. "Besides, I like carrying you. You'll be well soon and then I won't have an excuse for having you in my arms, and I find I rather like having you there."

"Sure. I'm a grown man. That's just what I wanted to hear—another man likes to carry me around like a child. You've shredded whatever remained of my manhood. Thanks." Jude rolled his eyes as he teased lightheartedly.

Nico set a plate of cold cuts, bread, and fixings on the table for sandwiches and let Jude choose his own. "Eat already, funny man," Nico countered, pouring coffee into two mugs and placing them on the table before taking a seat and putting together his own sandwich.

Jude picked up his sandwich and nibbled at the center, avoiding the crust.

"So tell me, who or what is chasing you?"

Jude choked and coughed at the sudden question, the mood changing immediately as a wash of fear poured from him. He caught his breath and sipped his coffee, attempting to dampen his distress. "I'm not exactly sure who it is. I have suspicions, but that's all they are. No proof. The creatures that keep finding me are demons—the real, red-skinned, black-eyed, horns and ugliness kind of demons from the pit. Skye and Fin have been very apt protectors up until the other night when the demons attacked in a swarm. There were so many of them, we were simply overwhelmed."

"So the enemy keeps sending demons after you, but doesn't attack you directly. Why?"

"I don't think they know where I am and probably don't even know what I look like."

"They're hunting you with demons blindly? Without anything to link you, but they're finding you anyway?" Nico asked.

"They must know my name and just enough to send creatures from the hordes to hunt me. I think they hope to exhaust me enough that some of their minions will be able to kill me, or at least survive to return to their masters with information about me."

"But why? What do they hope to gain?"

"I'm an officer of the Pope. It's my job to uncover corruption within the system. When there is suspicion, His Holiness sends me to discover the truth and bring back the proof." Jude put together another sandwich and sat back, watching as Nico did the same.

"So you're, what? On a mission? Trying to discover what?" Nico didn't like that Jude was risking his life. Even with all the secrecy, it seemed a very shady business.

"His Holiness sent me to find out if Father Michael, the man who tried to kill Evan, was working alone or is in league with others. We suspect he was taking his orders from much higher up in the Church. We need to know where the corruption stems from and stop it." Jude bit into his sandwich, groaning softly as roast beef and mustard hit his palate.

"Like the sandwich?" Nico watched it disappear rapidly and smiled with satisfaction at being able to care for Jude.

"Yeah, thanks. It's been a while since I've had something I didn't have to scrounge or steal. My money ran out a couple weeks ago, and I haven't been able to send a request for more to the Vatican." Jude grabbed a third sandwich from the platter and applied mustard liberally.

Nico hated the idea of Jude being forced to beg or starve, and made a vow to himself that never again would he go without. "So these men… they know you're after them, or at least suspect you've been sent?"

"Yes, the Council of Cardinals is aware of all of my missions. If the corruption goes high enough into the Church, then someone on the council could be the source." Jude took a bite and chewed slowly. "If the demons return, they can report who I am and what I look like. With that information, they can prevent me from doing my job as Inquisitor. If they know who I am, I can't infiltrate their group and get the proof I need for Rome to stop them." Jude set his sandwich down and pushed the plate back, looking like he'd suddenly lost his appetite.

"Oh no you don't. Eat." Nico pushed Jude's plate back toward him. "You must eat more than a couple bites. I'm sorry this conversation upsets you, but you need your strength back."

Jude sighed and looked at Nico. "No, you're right. I do need to eat." Jude picked the sandwich back up and took another bite. "So far I've been able to ensure that none of the demons have returned to their masters. But the other night, they almost succeeded. If you hadn't found me, they probably would've returned, and I—"

"No, Fin would've got to you before that happened. But I'm glad it was me."

"Me too."

"So who do you suspect is behind the attacks?" Nico reached out and grasped Jude's trembling hand.

JUDE'S NERVES subsided as his mind latched itself on to the mundane, like the threats to his life. When had the idea of being with someone become more nerve-wracking than his own murder? Was he seriously considering telling a man he'd just met a scant few days ago his theories? Apparently, yes. How could he not? Nico was completely sincere and looked at him with such desire that Jude wanted to lay everything out on the table for him. His troubles, his past, his… well, let's just say lay it all out, including himself wrapped up with a big bow, preferably naked on Nico's lap with a bottle of lube nearby. If that didn't make him feel like a complete slut for being so wantonly carnal….

"So how much do you know about the Church?" Jude asked.

"The basics, I guess. We tend to ignore them and they leave us alone. When we do interact, it's on a very basic level. We abide by the law and they don't disturb us. I have a number of humans whom I employ, and I treat them like they're family. The Church leaves them alone as long as we don't openly defy them. It's kind of a live-and-let-live relationship."

"I have a feeling that may not last much longer, at least if you continue to allow me to remain with you. Because it'd really be in your best interest for me to leave here as soon as possible."

"Not happening." Nico's confident smile encouraged Jude to continue. "I want you to stay. I hope you'll stay, although I won't force you to if you really wish to leave me."

"No. I don't want to go. But—"

"No buts." Nico flushed red, quickly looking away in apparent embarrassment. A groan escaped him. "Don't say it… just go on with your story," he practically pleaded, shifting a bit in his seat.

"Okay." Jude cleared his throat. "I'm a Jesuit Inquisitor. My only boss is the Pope."

"Yeah, got that part."

"I answer to and can be sent on assignment by the Council of Cardinals or the Apostolic Delegates Council, but neither council has ever seen me without my robes, which completely hide my appearance. I never appear before any of them in person, always on closed-circuit video. The only member of the clergy who's supposed to know who I am is His Holiness."

"So, do you think someone has found out who you are and is trying to kill you?"

Jude paused before answering, considering the possibility that his cover had been blown. "No, I don't think so. If they knew who I was, they'd be more direct about it instead of sending demons after me."

"How can the demons hunt you without knowing who you are?" Nico scowled.

"The more info the conjurer has about his target, the easier it is, but with only my name and position, a random hunt can be sent." Jude closed his eyes and rubbed his face with his hand. He could only feel pity for the poor souls used to call the Hellspawn. "It takes a lot out of the person wielding the magic, and they can only send as many as their soul is able to support. The person slowly corrupts their soul. The sensation of power they receive from the demons they call becomes addictive."

"So whoever is after you is willing to corrupt their soul in order to kill you?" Nico asked incredulously.

Jude nodded. "The magic they use ensnares their soul and they become the slave. The larger the demon they call upon, the more power the creature possesses and the better chance they have at either killing me or getting the demon to return with information about me. But also the quicker the demon will take their soul." Jude stared at the table. Now he'd really lost his appetite, but he forced himself to eat another couple of bites. "From the sheer number and size of the demons, there's more than one person sending them. Somebody must be orchestrating the hunt, using others to send the creatures of Hell after me."

"I don't like this at all, Jude. I mean, you've got a powerful enemy and you have no idea who it is." Nico's growling increased in volume as he became more upset.

Jude sipped his coffee. He placed a calming hand on Nico's, drawing his attention back from his musings. "It isn't that I don't have an idea who my enemies are. There've been many whom I've turned over to the Inquisition since I accepted this position, and I'm not the only Jesuit Inquisitor." Jude pushed his plate back.

"It's worse, isn't it? Whoever's hunting you could just be sending demons after the job title, instead of you specifically." Nico shoved his plate away from him.

"I don't believe it's that vague, but—essentially, yes." Jude squeezed Nico's hand gently. "But I don't think it's someone from my past. The Pope has had several attacks on his person. Nothing fatal, but deadly enough that if they should succeed, they could seriously incapacitate him."

"You believe the attacks on the Pope and yourself are connected. Was he attacked by demons?"

"No, nothing that direct. So far his loyal guards have been able to thwart the attempts." Jude shivered as he remembered the skeletal creature that had been after Evan. "We know Father Michael was just a pawn—someone else was pulling his strings. We also suspect that, in his own twisted way, he was protecting Evan from the people he answered to, but ultimately his soul fed the demons he was forced to summon to kill Evan."

"But if the men who are after you want Evan, isn't he also in danger?"

"I think Evan's in the clear, for now. He'll be hunted, but with all the gargoyles of Notre Dame at his disposal and ready to defend him, nothing short of a direct attack will touch him, and even then, Adel is a power to be reckoned with." Jude smiled, thinking of how much Adel loved Evan. He found Adel's devotion sweet, if a bit possessive. He would often wrap Evan in his wings, protecting him from the world. "I should check up on them. It's been months. I'm sure they're worried."

"At least your friends are safe. I think he's right in staying away from the Vatican. With the Pope himself under attack, he can hardly guarantee the safety of the Earth Elemental."

Jude nodded his agreement. "Yes, which is why I was sent on another mission. Evan told me he wouldn't go to Rome without me. His Holiness is aware of this. I think it was a subtle way for the Pope to keep Evan away from Rome."

"So what do we know for sure?" Nico asked.

"Father Michael was a bishop in charge of a fairly large diocese in the upper Midwest. He was in league with several bishops in numerous dioceses across the US. I've tracked a number of them to an archbishop by the name of Luke Kennedy. He and Archbishop Patrick Henry O'Flaggan and Archbishop Thomas Mason all report to Cardinal Matthias John Swift."

"Okay, so this Cardinal Swift. You think he's the one in charge of the assassination attempts?"

"If I had to place a bet, I'd say he's the ringleader. He controls the entire US Church in his benevolence, and does so with a cast-iron fist. Even the Apostolic Delegate from the US answers to Cardinal Swift." Jude scowled and shook his head in frustration. "And he should be an independent delegate voted in by the congregation, not under the cardinal's control."

"But you don't have any proof to back up your theories." Nico shifted restlessly, a scowl furrowing his forehead.

"That's what I'm here to find."

Nico sighed and went for the pot of coffee to refill their cups. "So what are you going to do?"

"I need to find a direct line of orders from the bishops who are the small fish in this pond up to the ringleader. We know that the little guys aren't doing this on their own." Jude took another sip from his refreshed cup. "They're the cannon fodder."

"Couldn't they have banded together to create this mess themselves?" Nico asked, playing devil's advocate.

"They're too organized and uniform in their proclamations. To the point that even their punishments for crimes against their version of the Word of God is the same." Jude watched as Nico nodded his understanding. "It gives the people nowhere to turn and sets everyone against the Church and His Holiness. Everyone believes that it's him doing this, when the Pope has no idea what's going on unless a complaint is lodged. By the time he receives notice of possible wrongdoing, it's often too late. When someone from the Jesuit Inquisitor's division of the Service arrives, the persecuted person has often disappeared and the locals are terrified to say anything, or they are deceased, as it was with Evan's father." Jude sighed. He'd eaten his sandwiches and exhaustion was kicking in. He couldn't believe how little it took to drain him. If just talking about his problems could leave him wrung out, how could he even begin to handle them?

"We'll think of something. Right now, you're tired. How about a quick shower, a change of clothes, and then more rest?" Nico suggested, sweeping Jude into his arms.

"Sounds wonderful." Jude's head fell against Nico's chest with a sigh. He didn't even have the energy to complain about being carried.

Chapter 4

SIN EATER LORE

As written by the scribes and entombed in the Church Archives:

1. A person born with a physical deformity that has marked them as being a punished reincarnate soul. In order to redeem themselves in the eyes of God and earn His divine forgiveness, they take on the punishment for sins done by others, absolving the person who has sinned. Through these deeds they earn a place in Heaven.
   a. Body must be pure, chaste, and innocent of sexual desire.
   b. Mind unsoiled by modern convenience or influence.

ARCHBISHOP O'FLAGGAN threw open the door to his study and swept everything piled on his desk to the floor with a roar. "That fool Kennedy is going to get us all killed. He couldn't even take care of one young man. Thanks to him I have gargoyles to deal with. Demons running amok in stone skins, uncontrolled by the grace of God or the restraints of Hell. France is going to be a Hell on Earth for at least a hundred years. Even if we succeeded in eradicating him now, the damn gargoyles are awake and the Pope…. His Holiness is a blind fool!"

Samuel curled himself into a ball in the corner where he'd been asleep before the Archbishop stormed into the room. He'd tried to make himself as small as possible. He had no desire to catch the Archbishop's attention now, even though he'd been told to wait in this room for His Grace's return. When the Archbishop was in a rage, his punishments were life-threatening.

"Damn!" Archbishop O'Flaggan screamed as he grabbed a book off the desk and threw it at the first of his monks coming into his office. He hit the man squarely on the head, and he crumpled to the floor.

His fellow monks soon had him by the arms and were dragging him from the office. There was a scrambling of people as everyone hurried to comply with Archbishop O'Flaggan's desires. Nobody wanted to bear the brunt of his fury.

"Samuel!" O'Flaggan screamed at the top of his lungs.

"Here, Your Grace." Samuel stood but knew better than to look at anything but the floor in front of his feet. He was a young man dressed simply in ragged jeans, the remains of a dirty, stained T-shirt, and bare feet. He clutched at his own arms across his chest, rocking slightly in place as he tried to console himself. Sammy was holding himself together by the barest margin of control.

"Clean up this mess!" O'Flaggan ranted as he paced in front of the bookcase.

"Right away, Your Grace." Samuel rushed to pick up the papers and books on the floor. When he heard the soft click of the door latch catch, he knew nobody would come to his rescue. Whenever His Grace came back from his trips, his rages were far worse than any other time, and as the "accursed one," the "Sin Eater," it was Samuel's job to take on that rage. He'd be beaten—again. One day the archbishop would beat him to death. Maybe then God would forgive him for his existence and he'd be allowed peace. Maybe tonight would be the last.

NICO CREPT from the room. Jude had finally fallen asleep and seemed to be undisturbed by dreams for a change. Maybe talking it all out with someone had given him some peace of mind. Having all that pressure lying on his shoulders and no one to share it with must've eaten away at him. Hopefully he'd be able to recover more quickly and peacefully now.

Nico walked into the living room and sat. His brother sat across from him, along with Nico's two other lieutenants, Gabe Windslow and Lira De'Forrest.

"How is he?" Doc asked.

"Sleeping."

"Who?" Gabe frowned, looking from Doc to Nico.

"He's the reason I asked you all here. We need your help, but I won't force you into this with us. There's a cardinal that's after my mate, and I won't let anyone hurt him."

"Mate?" Gabe and Lira parroted at the same time, smiles coming over both their faces.

Nico softened slightly at their enthusiasm. He was the first of his family—Gabe and Lira included—to ever find his mate in the centuries they'd known one another. He grinned at his friends. "Yes, I found him a few days ago. He's an Elemental. Fire Elemental, to be exact. He's just coming into his powers, so his control isn't the greatest, and he has horrendous nightmares. He's been through a lot, and from what he tells me, it isn't likely to end any time soon." Nico worriedly shook his head.

"Fire Elemental…." Doc offered him a shit-eating grin. "See? I told you Fate wouldn't set you up with a mate who couldn't take the heat. Once he fully comes into his power, it may be you who has trouble keeping from getting scorched," Doc laughingly teased.

"Shut up. Wait until you find your mate, so help me…." The threat was toothless and they both knew it, as Nico would only celebrate the occasion when his brother found his mate and rejoice at his good fortune. Doc's existence was difficult and lonely, just as Nico's had been. Still, he couldn't deny his brother a little good-natured teasing.

"So what's the story, Nico, and do I really want to get involved in this? Is it likely to get me killed?" Lira rolled her eyes. She always was the hard one of the bunch. Lira, a dryad, stuck close to her trees and wanted little to do with humans. As the world had become more civilized and populous, she'd withdrawn into the forest. She'd only returned to the fold as the forest began to once again reclaim its place in the world after the war.

"My guess is, no, you won't want to be involved. Yes, it does have the potential to get us all killed. And yes, I expect you'll get involved anyway when you hear the whole story." Nico's dry chuckle contained no humor, watching as Lira's deep forest-green skin and hair paled to a seawater hue due to her increasing concern.

Gabe shifted uncomfortably. "Nico, you know we're always behind you, but are you sure we need to get involved in this? I mean, I'm starting to have the dreams. My mate is close. Lira is just starting to get back to her normal self." Gabe scooted to the edge of his seat, his hands pressed tightly together. "I don't want to miss meeting my mate because of some quest you've got us all tied up in."

"How do you know that helping me isn't what brings you to your mate? You don't!" Nico growled.

"Calm down, brother. Gabe is just worried. You'd be too if you were dreaming about Jude and didn't know how to get to him." Doc stared intently into Nico's eyes until he calmed down.

"You're right. I'm sorry, Gabe, it's just that…. Jude was almost dead when I found him, and I can't lose him. I'll do whatever it takes to ensure his safety. You can't ask me not to." Nico's pleading glance begged his friend for patience.

"Nobody's asking you not to protect your mate, Nico," Lira grumbled. "Why don't you just tell us what's going on before we all get bent out of shape speculating without knowing what the problem is? If it's in our best interests to help you, we will. Even if it isn't, we've been through a lot over the years, and we'll still probably help you. So trust us and tell us what the deal is."

"Of course, you're right." Nico sighed and explained everything, from Evan and Adel's problems with Father Michael up to his suspicions regarding Cardinal Swift and Jude's involvement. When he'd finished, they all sat and stared at him with varying degrees of worry and doubt.

"Are you sure your mate isn't mad? I mean, seriously, to attempt to take down not only a cardinal, but one bent on assassination? Even if he's an Elemental and his friend is also an Elemental… a cardinal using the powers of Hell…. Seriously, you want *us* to go against that?" Lira rubbed at her face, winding her fingers in her long pale green hair.

Gabe rose and paced the length of the room. Nico watched as he prowled about. He knew the part of Gabe that was a lion thought best when in motion, while the part that was an eagle hated being enclosed in a room. He admired Gabe's form—he was a tall man, with wide shoulders, a broad chest, long white-blond hair that hung past his waist, and eyes as blue as the sky. They'd once been lovers for a short time, but it hadn't worked out well. Gabe's animal needed to be in control, and Nico couldn't seem to relinquish it. They'd battled more than loved.

Fin walked out of the back bedroom and stopped in the doorway, looking shocked. He crouched and pulled his sword, ready to attack the various beings assembled in the living room.

"Fin, please. Calm down. These are my friends. Come let me introduce you," Nico beckoned.

"A sprite!" Lira exclaimed. A look of wonder spread across her face, and she practically clapped her hands in delight. She hadn't seen a member of the Fair Folk in a long time and was clearly overjoyed at the prospect.

"No, I'm sorry, my lady. I'm not a sprite, although I do resemble one," Fin apologized.

Lira, as well as the other two newcomers, frowned.

"He's not a sprite, but considering it's daytime and what my senses tell me… he shouldn't be here." Gabe's head tipped to the side, looking at Fin with curiosity.

"You're right. He's a gargoyle!" Doc exclaimed.

"But it's broad daylight. How?" Lira frowned, watching Fin as he sheathed his sword, still standing in the hallway.

"Right now, I'm more concerned about Jude. I need to see him first, then I'll come back out and answer whatever questions I can." Fin looked at Nico.

"That's fine. He's asleep and getting stronger. He was up for a few hours earlier. I was able to get him to eat a few sandwiches and take a shower." Nico nodded his permission for the visit.

"Okay. I'll be back." Fin retreated down the hallway toward the bedroom.

"He's one of the gargoyles that the Earth Elemental transformed, isn't he?" Doc said softly, watching Fin's retreating back.

"Yes. There are five gargoyles with the ability to be awake both night and day. They were there when Evan destroyed Father Michael, and the power wave gave them all the ability to sleep and wake as needed."

"Unbelievable, the amount of power he'd have required to produce such a result! It's a miracle the Elemental survived." Doc shook his head in awe. "I honestly didn't believe it was possible until the gargoyle walked out here."

"We can't go against the Elementals. I mean, in our world, they're practically looked upon as gods. We're all children of nature, but they have a direct line to the raw power all around us. We can't deny the will of our mother," Lira said softly. She peered down the hallway, as if lost in thought.

"No, we can't. So we need a plan." Gabe, having come to his decision, sat and looked to the other three.

WHEN FIN walked into the bedroom, he saw Jude sacked out in the bed asleep, tossing and turning, sweat dripping from his forehead. Fin sat beside him and stroked his arm. He murmured softly, soothingly, trying to lull Jude into a deeper sleep so he could rest outside of the nightmare realm.

Instead, Jude flinched at Fin's touch and his eyes flew open in a panic.

"Shhh, young one, it's only me." Fin hoped his familiar voice would reach beyond Jude's fear.

"Fin." Jude sighed and relaxed into the blankets.

"Yes. You're safe. Go back to sleep."

"Is Nico here?"

Fin smiled. "He's out in the living room with his brother and a couple other guests, attending to his business."

"Okay, I guess I've been keeping him away from his work. He's been so good to me, allowing me to stay. We're going to have to leave soon or else we'll bring everything down on him," Jude mumbled, frowning and rubbing his chest as if the thought pained him.

"No, young one. You can't leave your mate. The separation would kill both of you. The reason you're upset is because it's me you woke up to instead of him." Fin chuckled.

"But… my job?" Jude shook his head.

"It'll all work out in time. You're always in a rush, but these things don't happen overnight. I guess it must be in your nature. Or maybe the red hair," Fin teased.

"Fin," Jude whined and rolled his eyes.

Fin chuckled. "Fire's always in a hurry to consume. This time, young one, you must be patient. You're no longer alone. We'll figure this out. Your mate will help you. And I will too."

"Okay." Jude sighed. His eyes closed once again and he sank into a more restful, healing sleep.

"Be at peace, young one… all in due time," Fin murmured. He ran his fingers through Jude's red hair, making sure Jude was well asleep before rising and leaving the room to rejoin the others.

"HOW IS he?" Nico asked Fin as he walked into the living room.

"He was a bit restless and woke briefly, but he's sleeping now."

"Good." Nico nodded, forcing himself to resist the urge to go check on Jude, and motioned for Fin to take a seat. "Please, tell us what you know."

Fin joined them, sitting next to Lira, who seemed to feel reassured by his presence. He told them much the same story Jude had recounted to Nico. Of their suspicions of the cardinal, of Evan and Adel, of his belief that Jude was becoming the Fire Elemental, but that he hadn't wanted to mention anything until he knew for sure.

"What do you mean, until you know for sure?" Nico growled. "Jude would've been so much more comfortable if you had at least shared your suspicion. Instead he's been floundering and thinking he was becoming evil."

"I was afraid to tell him. Elementals don't always survive coming into their powers late in life. He feels like the fire's consuming him, and in a way, it is. It's changing every cell of his body, burning off the human cells as his body realigns to his Elemental powers. The fact that he's had to use his fire to defend himself is speeding the process along, but eventually every part of him that is human will be changed into the Elemental."

"But I don't smell any change in him. He smells the same today as he did when he arrived." Nico practically hissed at Fin.

"You're wrong, brother. I can smell the difference." Doc spoke softly. "You're with your mate constantly. The change is subtle, but it's there. When we're finished here, I'll check him over and make sure he's recovering well. He's young and strong—he'll be all right."

"So, what… you think he'll reject this change you see happening?" Nico's voice contained a deadly controlled calm.

"If he rejects the change, the fire will consume him uncontrolled. He's right that there's a beast within him. I don't know the nature of the beast—there've been many over the centuries." Fin shrugged his shoulders. "The Fire Elementals have reappeared much more often than Earth Elementals or even Air Elementals. When he's using his power at its fullest, he'll be one of the creatures of fire."

"What kind of creature?" Gabe asked.

Fin looked at Gabe. "There've been fire horses, wolves, big cats, dragons, and, of course, the greatest of all the firebirds, the phoenix. He needs to become one and accept the beast within in order to fully control his power and survive."

"So he's becoming a type of shifter?" Gabe frowned slightly, trying to understand.

"Not really. The beast is the fire, but he needs to choose a form for it. For a Fire Elemental, their power can be like a living thing, and his body chooses the form. It'll overlay his own body, but he doesn't actually shift into another form. Once accepted, he can project and fight with the form, but his body must be protected so his spirit has a place to return to once the fight is ended."

"How can fire be a beast?" Nico shook his head. He'd just explained to Jude that fire was not a sentient creature.

"For a Fire Elemental, fire is a living thing. Just as for the Earth Elemental, rock becomes a living thing. Even if he doesn't breathe consciousness into all rock, they all still live for him. For Jude, fire lives," Fin explained. "Usually child and fire beast grow together, slowly, each learning of the other, the child learning to control the beast and trust it."

"But Jude hasn't had the opportunity to bond with his fire beast." Gabe nodded his understanding. "This sometimes happens amongst our people. Usually when a halfling child is born outside the community. Our people first change at puberty, but with a halfling, they can't feel the beast until after puberty. There's really no knowing if they'll even be able to shift. But if the change comes, without someone to teach them, they rarely survive."

"Yes, exactly. His beast has been dormant, asleep all his life. He needs to learn to accept it. They need to become one and understand each other." Fin nodded.

"Does the beast have a voice or is it purely a natural force?" Gabe asked.

"In the past, Elementals have said the beast has a will and mind of its own, usually one based on primal need more than cohesive thought, but no less demanding," Fin answered, cocking his head.

"Maybe some of the things we teach our halflings will help your Elemental connect with his beast and ease his transition." Gabe looked over at Nico. "I'd need to spend time with him, alone, to teach him how to reach his beast. They need to learn of each other before the change occurs, so they can become one and he can learn control."

"You think this will really help?" Nico was afraid to hope. He didn't want to think of Jude being consumed by his own fire. If that were to happen, the fire would consume them both because Nico wouldn't let go. If he could just get Jude to accept his fire beast, then they would have a chance at a happy, eternal life. Of course, that was barring someone assassinating Jude. Elementals didn't just have short lives because they were born human. Usually some idiot insisted the power belonged to them, the power was evil, or any number of stupid reasons people found to fear what they couldn't understand.

"Yes." Gabe smiled and walked over to him, put a hand on his shoulder, and squatted down in front of him. "Nico, you've been my friend for centuries.

I wouldn't steer you wrong, not with something like this. I can help your mate reach his beast, and we can find out what he'll become. I can teach him how to accept that part of himself, and the two will be stronger for it."

"Please, Gabe... I don't know how to help him. To me fire is power, nothing more." Nico rested his elbows on his thighs and covered his face with his hands. "He's my mate. I—"

"Shhh, brother. You may not know how to help, but I think I do. We'll prepare him as much as possible. Sometimes with really strong shifters, the beast actually has a sentient voice and the two can be introduced on the spiritual plane."

"Okay." Nico tried to rein in his scrambled emotions.

"We'll begin as soon as you've completed your mating and he's able." Gabe patted Nico on the shoulders and retook his seat. "Otherwise you won't be able to allow me close enough to him for us to work."

Doc took over as Nico struggled to regain his composure. "All right, things are squared away as far as Jude's transformation is concerned. I think we need to start investigating these bishops and that cardinal. We need to find out as much information about their dealings as possible."

"I'll check with the families and the villages near the forest to see what the black market has to say," Lira said, thinking aloud.

"There's always talk around the docks about what's coming and going in the world. I'll see what I can find. There might be rumors of deaths or strange happenings. My informants might know something." Gabe nodded to Doc.

"I can ask around at the gentlemen's club uptown, see what the social gossips have to say." Doc smirked. "It's been a while since I socialized. I could do with a little dancing."

"Brother, I don't think—"

"You'd be surprised by the number of things people will tell their doctor that they wouldn't reveal to others, even in a social setting outside the office. These are powerful men—they have to have some standing among the rich. If they do, when I start asking and being my charming self, someone will say something." Doc radiated confidence, and Nico knew his brother could be charming. It was a skill the daemon had cultivated when becoming a doctor. He needed his patients to trust him, and nobody was better at getting it.

"Thank you all so much for your help. I know I wouldn't be able to do this without you." Nico looked around at his friends and brother, knowing they would do everything in their power to help him, as he would do for each of them. "I don't socialize much anymore, but I do have a large number of corporate contacts." Having lived for centuries, it had become easier to own banks and change his identity, making himself the beneficiary of his fortune, than to start over each time in a different field of business. Having seen many nations rise and fall, he backed his business solidly in gold and jewels collected throughout his lifetimes and lent money and gave jobs to as many as he could afford to help. "I'll contact as many as I can. Some still owe me favors," Nico said half to himself. "Where there is power, there is money. When money is changing hands, there are corporate bloodhounds sniffing around, trying to pick up the loose change. Someone has to know something."

The group rose, and Nico saw Gabe and Lira to the door, giving each a hug and receiving congratulations on his mating.

"Fin, if you don't mind, I know Jude's your charge." Doc put a hand on Fin's shoulder. "But I'd appreciate it if you could sit down with me and tell me everything you know about Elementals and their powers. It'll help me to have as much information on hand as possible."

Nico smiled as Fin and Doc walked down the hallway toward his bedroom, where Jude rested. They were both intent on helping as much as possible. It warmed Nico's heart to know his family and friends would be there to support them.

Chapter 5

DAEMON LORE

As written by the scribes and entombed in the Church Archives:

Mating Habits:

1. Mates are believed to be Fate assigned.
2. Mates are recognized immediately on first sight or smell, without any prior contact.
3. Mating is a permanent bond believed to last throughout eternity, beyond this world.
4. The life force of the mated individuals is said to be combined, thus a mortal mate becomes immortal when joined.
5. At the time of death of either partner, both will die.
6. Mating can be a heterosexual or homosexual partnership, as daemons are not born of procreation but created through a joining of power. A daemon comes into this world as a fully formed adult.

THEY WALKED into the bedroom to find Jude asleep in the armchair alongside the fireplace, with Skye curled on a blanket that covered his lap. Nico admired him in the flickering glow of the firelight. *My sweet Jude must've awakened long enough to get out of bed, then fallen asleep in the chair.* Nico smiled as the light from the blaze shot across Jude's gleaming red hair as if it was aflame. He looked at Jude's fine features and tried to imagine what beast lurked in the recesses of his mind, but he couldn't quite match him with any animal.

Doc approached the chair and placed a hand on Jude's shoulder, awakening him.

"Wh-What…," Jude mumbled as sleep fell away.

"Hi, Jude, remember me?" Doc looked down at Jude with his most professional doctor smile.

"No… should I?" Jude glanced around for Nico, who sat at the edge of the bed and nodded reassuringly, but he didn't really relax until he spotted Fin standing in front of the glass doors that led to the balcony.

"I'm Dr. Nero Daemarkus, but you can call me Doc. I'm Nicolas's brother. I saw you when he first brought you here a couple days ago, but you were pretty out of it. It doesn't surprise me that you don't remember."

"Oh, hi. Sorry… I don't even remember him finding me." Jude yawned a bit and blinked, stretching his arms over his head.

"I just wanted to check in on you and see how you're doing. You're looking stronger. How are you feeling?"

"Better. But it's like all I do is sleep and eat."

"From what Nico tells me, you've been on the run for a while and your body's trying to recover. You should be stronger soon." Doc placed a gentle hand on Jude's forehead.

Jude smiled reassuringly while Nico dug into the edge of the bedding, forcing himself to remain seated instead of throwing Doc across the room, away from his as yet-unclaimed mate.

"Good, you're no longer feverish. That's a relief. I think next week you should be ready to begin your training." Doc stepped away and leaned against the mantle of the fireplace.

"Training?" Jude asked.

"It's time for everyone to leave now. You've seen him. He's better. Now please, Doc," Nico said between gritted teeth. "Get out. I don't want to hurt you."

Doc chuckled and walked slowly toward the door. "Easy, Nico. I have no designs on your man. In fact, I think I'm going to head home and see what information I can pull out of Fin here."

Fin walked away from the glass doors and moved toward the doctor. "Are you okay with me going with Doc, Jude? I can stay if you'd prefer." Fin smiled at Nico, who'd quickly taken up a position between the two men and Jude.

"I think I've got all the protection I can handle for one evening. Thanks." Jude snickered, taking Nico's hand. "Why don't you take Skye too, and see to it he either goes hunting or gets fed. No use me getting stronger if he isn't eating."

"As you wish. Skye, come on, birdbrain," Fin called.

Skye chattered and leaped off Jude's lap, ran across the room in a couple of bounds, and jumped into Fin's arms.

"Thanks so much," Jude said as they headed out the door, closing it behind them.

Nico leaned down and gently brushed his lips across Jude's, sending electrical shocks racing through his body. Before Nico could pull away, Jude wrapped his arms around Nico's neck, holding him in place, opening up to him, seeking a deeper kiss. Nico groaned, feeling Jude's desire, and plunged his tongue into the recesses of Jude's mouth, tasting his kiss for the first time. Nico silently demanded Jude's submission, and he gave it willingly.

Nico swept his tongue across Jude's teeth and along the roof of his mouth, stroking his tongue with his own. He teased and thrust into Jude's mouth, coaxing him into an intimate dance that drowned out all but the exquisite touch of each other.

Finally breaking apart, Nico swept Jude into his arms and carried him to the bed. "You need to be sure. Because I'm not certain I can stop," Nico panted as they crossed the room, setting Jude on the bed like he was the most precious treasure in the world.

"I want you, Nico. Everything I am screams out for you. I need to feel you. I don't know about the mate thing."

Nico eased up onto the bed and pulled Jude into his arms. There was nothing he wanted more than to ravish Jude, but he knew it was important for him to listen to him and not rush. "For a daemon, to be a mate is a lifetime commitment. There's no halfway. If we mate, I'll always want you, desire you." *I want to fall in love with you and only you for as long as we both live.* But it was too early to talk of love just yet, wasn't it?

"I've never had anyone who wanted to spend their life with me." Jude tried to hide his face in Nico's chest, only to have Nico draw back, catching his gaze.

"That's okay. I've been alone for a very long time. So we'll learn together."

"Okay," Jude whispered, trembling slightly in Nico's embrace.

"I don't want to mislead you. We'll probably have arguments and fights. That part's no different from any other relationship. We can be happy together—or we can fight and make each other miserable. The one thing I can guarantee is that there'll always be an 'us.'" Nico stroked the side of Jude's face and nibbled his ear. He couldn't not touch his mate, knowing Jude desired him, but he had to make this clear.

Jude stared at the comforter, picking at the edge. "So once we're mated, it's forever. There'd never be anyone else for you or me, for as long as we live."

"Yes, it'd be us against the world. You'd never be alone. The strands of our lives would be intertwined, and when Fate cuts one, she'll cut both. As we live together, we would die together."

"If I say no, that I don't want to mate with you, what happens?" Jude asked.

Nico trembled, a wave of almost palpable panic engulfing him.

Jude quickly rested a hand on him and stroked reassuringly down his arm. "I'm not saying I'm doing that, I'm just asking what if?"

Nico closed his eyes and took a deep breath, trying to hide the wave of desolation, rejection, and fear he'd felt at Jude's question. "If you reject me and we don't mate, there'll never be another mate for either of us. Fate gives us only one. If we don't consummate the relationship, then both of us will be able to continue to have sexual relations with others, but there'll never be another mate for either of us."

"But you wouldn't go crazy, start killing people, and crap like that?" Jude asked, trying to make light of the situation, but Nico refused to make a joke of it.

"I'd probably go mad without you. You already own a piece of my heart, whether we are mated or not. If you stay and we don't consummate our relationship because you need time to get to know me…." Nico paused and nuzzled into Jude's neck. "I wouldn't be thrilled, but you'd be here, in my bed, where I can hold you. I'd be able to prove to you that I may not be perfect, but I'd do my best to see you safe and happy. If you left—I don't… I don't want to pressure you or say something to make you think I'm trying to trap you, but I don't want to lie to you either."

"Are you saying you'd die if I were to leave?" Jude pushed Nico back so he could look him in the eyes.

"Probably, yes. I'd survive for a while, maybe even a year. I'd fall into a depression and more than likely wouldn't come out of it. I don't say this lightly or to make you feel guilty or anything like that—it's the nature of mates for daemons. We can't survive without them once we find them. I can hold off and I'll happily wait forever for you—as long as I'm close and can see you and touch you. Without you, I'll be half a being. I wouldn't survive." Nico closed his eyes, fearing he'd just lost his mate, that Jude would feel manipulated and want to leave.

"My parents died when I was young, and I was saved by a great man, Jaren Thomas. I went to school and later became part of the service so I could work with him." Jude hesitated, and Nico waited to see what he'd say next, hoping it wouldn't be a rejection. "He became my partner at the Vatican. I admired him greatly. He died saving my life."

"You cared about him a great deal." Nico wondered if Jude pined for this lost man.

"He was like a father to me." Jude reached up and cupped Nico's face, looking deeply into his eyes. "Everyone who's ever mattered to me—everyone I've ever loved—has died, leaving me alone. My greatest fear is… if I give you my heart, you'll leave me too," Jude confessed.

Nico interlaced their hands and brought the back of Jude's hand to his lips. "Not possible, Jude. If we mate, you'd have me forever. For better or worse, you'd never be alone again. Even when we die, we'd go together."

Jude studied Nico's eyes. "Then I'm ready. I can't say I love you, but… I like you… a lot. I trust you, probably more than anyone else in my life." Jude paused, as if trying to discern his feelings. "I want you. I can't stand it when you're away from me, even when you're just in the next room. I need to feel you touching me. If you're okay with claiming me but waiting for my heart, then I'm yours."

"*Mein Feuer*, I'll happily take whatever part you're willing to give me. This is a two-way street here, Jude. You're my mate, but that means I'm yours as well."

Jude ducked his forehead against Nico's chest. "A mate—my mate. Someone I can't kill with my fire, who won't burn if I lose control. Someone to be with me forever and never leave," Jude whispered into Nico's chest. "Yeah… I want that."

JUDE DIDN'T want Nico to see how afraid he was to admit to how much he desired those things. How much he needed someone—*No, not just someone*, he corrected himself, *Nico*. How much he hated being alone. Nico said he wanted to be with him forever, to give him a part of his soul, to tie himself to Jude for the rest of their lives, so neither one would be alone. Jude could barely contain the budding feelings of—dare he consider it?—*love*. He couldn't say it, but the speed and depth of his feelings took his breath away.

Nico put a finger under Jude's chin and lifted it so he could meet Jude's eyes. "I won't rush you. If you're not ready, it's okay," he whispered.

Jude realized if he was going to accept Nico as his mate, he needed to let Nico see his emotions. It was hard to trust someone with his passions, to be honest about his pain and fear. "No, Nico, I want this. I know we'll grow and learn about each other. I do have feelings for you. I just don't know— I'm scared. But I'm not willing to let this go, not because of my own fears." He wanted Nico to be his mate. Nico couldn't burn, and Nico made him feel wanted and desired. That was enough for him. Maybe love would come later. Maybe sooner than he thought.

Jude leaned up and kissed Nico tenderly and a bit tentatively—a brushing of warm lips, a nibbling, a touch of his tongue on the crease between Nico's lips, requesting a deeper connection, a deeper kiss.

Nico opened immediately, groaning in wanton desire, his igniting lust reflected in his eyes. "I want you so badly it hurts," he pleaded as he stroked Jude's shoulders and back, his fingers following the line of Jude's spine to the crack of his ass, caressing him through the soft cotton material of his sleep pants.

"Yes, Nico. Make me yours…." Jude sighed into his kiss.

"Too many clothes." Nico leaned back and unbuttoned his shirt.

Jude tugged up on Nico's shirt tails, pulling them from his trousers. Jude went to work on the belt, unbuckling it. He stroked the enlarging bulge with the flat of his left hand as his right popped the button at the waist.

"Oh, that feels so good." Nico sighed, tossing the shirt to the floor.

"You like that, do you?" Jude smiled. "Then you'll love this."

"Jude!" Nico gasped "Ahh… yes," he moaned as Jude slipped down the zipper and slid a hand in, freeing his cock from the confines of pants and underwear. Nico shimmied, helping to lower his pants, and he tugged at the hem of the T-shirt Jude wore.

Jude had to stop long enough to take in the beautiful sight before him. Nico was thick and long. Jude licked his lips; he ached for a taste. Easing down along Nico's body, Jude sampled Nico's chest and rippled abs with kisses and swipes of his tongue. He'd been dying to taste Nico since the first time he awoke and saw the black-brown of Nico's eyes filled with concern. He had handsomeness in spades, and Jude wanted to lick and touch every inch of him.

Jude grasped Nico firmly and let the flat of his tongue caress the dark red mushroom-shaped head. He lingered, fluttering his tongue over the crease as beads of precome dotted the slit. Jude locked his lips around the shaft and sucked, moaning his pleasure at the salty flavor mixed with just a hint of sweet ash, like marshmallows toasted almost black over a campfire.

He slowly bobbed his head up and down Nico's rod, fondling his balls, rolling them, and giving them a gentle squeeze.

Nico panted and put a hand on Jude's head, his fingers knotting in his hair. Jude was glad he didn't guide or push—it was more of a connection, as if Nico had to touch him.

He glanced up, catching Nico's smoldering gaze as he released the head and his lips slid along the side of the shaft, following the heavy vein down to his sack. Jude gently sucked first one ball, lapping it, and then he moved to the other, giving it the same loving care. He followed them down to the perineum, laving the flesh gently, teasing a strangled moan from his mate... *his mate*. He'd never thought he'd actually use those words. Now that he had a mate of his own, Jude intended to never let him go.

"JUDE... NEED you." Nico spoke softly, pulling gently back on Jude's hair. He wanted to allow Jude the time to explore his body, but not now. His need to claim Jude was too strong. His hunger for his mate was pulsating through his blood. Nico drew him up alongside his body and rolled, pinning Jude beneath him. "Let me do the work. For both of us."

Jude squirmed under him while Nico aligned their cocks, feeling Jude's humping upward creating a delicious friction as he kissed his way down Jude's neck. He slowly moved across Jude's collarbone, then farther down to one of his russet nipples. As Nico laved the nub, it hardened and darkened to a deep brown-red under his attention. Nico bit down gently, pulling on it and rolling it about between his teeth.

"God, you're beautiful. I love that everywhere I touch you, you come alive beneath my fingertips," Nico whispered as he tweaked and pinched one nipple while blowing cool air over the other. Nico could watch Jude's enflamed desire all day. It was more beautiful than anything he'd ever seen.

Jude's eyes rolled back into his head and his back arched up off the bed. The sounds coming from him stoked Nico's lust; the wanton cries and moans had him burning hotter than any flame. "Nico... oh!"

Nico kissed his way farther down, following the sternum and midline of Jude's chest to his belly button. He rimmed the little crater and dipped his tongue in and out, eliciting a frantic, ticklish giggle amid the moans before he continued on to Jude's engorged and leaking cock. He didn't have Nico's size, but he was well endowed for a rather small man. When Nico's lips wrapped around him and the hot silk of his mouth encased him to the root, Jude screamed, "Nico!" His climax clearly took him by surprise as his seed shot down Nico's throat. Nico hummed happily as he swallowed everything Jude gave him, continuing to work him through the aftershocks. He came off Jude's still-hard cock with a pop, gazing down at him, those piercing green eyes were half-lidded and burning with carnal need.

Nico rose up, reached for the nightstand drawer, and pulled out a bottle of lube. The snap of the lid and the touch of his fingers had Jude moaning. Nico gently massaged the guard muscles, encouraging them to relax and let him in.

"Condom?" Jude's voice was barely above a whisper.

"We don't need anything between us. I can't get or transmit disease," Nico assured him as he rubbed the gel between his fingers, warming it.

Jude nodded his understanding. "Nico…. Please."

"I know." Nico slowly slid in to the first knuckle. As he felt the gentle suction drawing him deeper, he added a second and then a third finger. He moved them around, stretching. With a tight grip on his control, he determinedly sought out and caressed Jude's prostate.

Jude fisted the sheets and rocked his hips uncontrollably, fucking himself on Nico's fingers and panting. "More…. Nico…."

Nico pulled away and slicked his cock with more lube, then grasped Jude's legs, placed them over his shoulders, and lined up, pressing gently against Jude's quivering pucker. "Ready for me, my mate?" Nico asked, leaning forward with his hands braced against the mattress on either side of Jude's head.

Jude grasped his biceps and looked into Nico's eyes. Beyond coherent words, Jude nodded, and Nico grasped the base of his cock and eased himself in.

He paused once the head passed the guard muscles, trembling as he stretched the last remnants of his control. He wouldn't rush this. "Ah… you feel so good." Nico growled, staring into Jude's eyes. Jude slid his legs off Nico's shoulders to lock around his waist and wiggled beneath him. Nico continued to press in slowly with short thrusts until he was completely seated, his balls nestled against Jude's ass.

"Fuck…. Nico!" Jude panted.

Nico leaned down and captured Jude's lips in a soul-searing kiss that went on as Jude's body relaxed, accepting his lover. Nico drew back until his cockhead was all that remained inside, then pressed forward again in one long thrust, pegging Jude's sweet spot. "Just for me… all mine." Nico stared into

Jude's lust-glazed eyes. He kept the pace slow and sensual, steadily increasing in speed and force, the two of them gradually finding their rhythm.

As Nico looked at Jude, he began to glow with their combined fire, a lavender blaze that spread until they were both bathed in rich purple flames, proof of their mating. Nothing around them seemed to be touched—not the bed, nor the bedding or anything else about them smoldered. Nico's arms braced on the outside while Jude's clutched at his shoulders, they held tight to each other. Just the two of them bathed in the mixing shades of amethyst fire, the color of Nico's sapphire blue combined with Jude's ruby red, their mating fire, which danced along the surface of their sweat-slicked skin. Where Jude's arms touched Nico's, the flames painlessly and freely burned along the surface of both. Where the flames touched, they left behind black swirls of interlocking flames from fingertips to shoulders on both of them, leaving a tattoo on both as one being, one fire, joined for life.

"Come for me, my mate, *mein Feuer*," Nico ground out between bliss-filled thrusts. His climax upon him, he wanted to feel Jude come from the inside.

"Nico!" Jude screamed, spattering their stomachs with white ribbons of jizz, the muscles of his ass clamping down hard on his lover.

Nico's orgasm hit him with an intensity he'd never felt before. He cried out Jude's name and coated his passage with hot seed.

The mating fire extinguished with their fading passion. Nico wrapped his arms under Jude's shoulders and lay down with him until the tremors of their love were spent, then rolled to the side, his cock slipping from Jude's body.

Soft snores told Nico that Jude was completely satiated and asleep. Groaning softly, he climbed out of bed, went into the bathroom, and cleaned himself. Then he brought a warm washcloth back and cleaned Jude. After tossing the cloth back into the bathroom, he climbed into bed and wrapped himself around Jude, snuggling him tight against his chest.

Never again would either of them be alone. Nico could feel the bond between them—the tendrils of Jude's sleeping dreams unwound in his mind, indistinct and pleasant. He didn't know if Jude would be able to know his thoughts, but he hoped this would be a mate-gift they'd both share. With a gentle fingertip, he outlined the black swirls of flames that trailed up from the tips of Jude's fingers to his shoulders and back down to his fingertips. The markings were beautiful and distinct, except for the matching swirls that moved along his arms. These were the mating marks of a daemon, flames for his gift, marking them as one, as mates, forever.

Chapter 6

Daemon Lore

As written by the scribes and entombed in the Church Archives:

For a time, daemons were hunted by humanity. Their blood was believed to be the fount of youth that would give the drinker immortality. This has since been proven a fallacy, and by Papal decree, any person or persons said to have murdered a daemon will be sentenced by the Inquisition to immediate death.

JUDE WOKE slowly. He felt more relaxed and energetic than he had in days. Nico belonged to him, and he knew he'd never be alone again. That thought was practically intoxicating. He actually awoke with a smile instead of screaming from his nightmares.

He also felt a degree of control over his inner fire that he'd never had before.

"*Good morning, mate.*"

The thought teased at his mind, and his eyes flew open. He reached out to touch the bed beside him. It was empty, but then the sound of the shower came to him and he relaxed. Nico was in the shower.

"*Yes, mein Feuer, I'm in the shower. Want to come and join me?*" The thought tendril had a teasing quality but was filled with warmth and desire.

"*Nico?*" Jude hesitantly thought. It wasn't that he feared having Nico in his mind, sharing his thoughts—it was more surprise and shock.

"*Yes, my mate.*" Nico's reply was clear as day.

"*You're in my head.*"

Amusement bounced around inside Jude's skull. "*Yes, Jude. We're mates. I'm sorry I didn't tell you, but I wasn't sure, with you being human, that you'd be able to hear me or reply, and I didn't want it to hurt your feelings if you couldn't. I can't tell you how happy it makes me that you can hear me and I can hear you. Can you feel my emotions as well?*" A wave of joy, longing, and desire washed over Jude, and his cock began to fill. A vision of Nico fucking him in the shower had Jude scrambling out of the bed and practically running into the bathroom.

He stared at Nico behind the glass doors. The sight of Nico's bronzed skin and long black hair, his face upturned into the spray, water cascading down his hard body, little rivers following the cut of the muscles across his back and buttocks, practically had Jude salivating and blowing his load right then and there.

Nico turned, laughter welling at the sight of Jude playing Peeping Tom. "Come on. Join me."

Jude, still naked from their night of lovemaking, opened the glass door and joined him. He marveled at the black swirling flames that danced over Nico's arms, matching his own. Reaching for Nico, Jude traced each black line as it flowed along Nico's skin from shoulder down around his wrists with his fingertips. The tender caresses were full of awe as the warm water trickled down their bodies and sent visible shivers through Nico.

"What are they?" Jude looked up into Nico's eyes.

"They're our mating marks. As a daemon, when I mate, the marks appear on my arms and those of my mate. It shows to all potential rivals that we are a pair."

"A ring would've done just as well—" Jude chuckled, "—but these are stunning."

"No, a ring can be removed. We're far more permanent than that. Like these marks, we are forever joined." Nico wrapped his hands around Jude, one to the small of his back and the other up into his hair, pulling his head back, as Nico descended and captured Jude's lips in a kiss that seemed unending in its exploration. If there was one thing on this planet Jude had discovered about Nico, it was that he was exceptionally good at kissing. No, not just good—Nico was a kissing god.

They both relaxed in their slow exploration, the heat of their passion building, sending out billows of steam, filling the bathroom with the scent of sex, and later the sandalwood-scented body soap Nico used to clean them.

Thoroughly ravished and bathed, Nico carried Jude from the shower, dried him off, and wrapped him in warmed cotton towels. He sat Jude up on the counter while he dried himself off. Then with a towel draped about Nico's waist and Jude in his arms, they returned to the bedroom.

Jude pulled on a pair of Nico's sweatpants and cinched the drawstring tight about his waist. The pants hung on him like a sack. Nico's clothes definitely wouldn't do for long. Taking the T-shirt Nico handed him and pulling it over his head, he noticed Nico was trying hard to disguise his snorts of laughter by clearing his throat. Stepping in front of the mirror, he had to laugh himself. He looked like a child who'd gotten into his father's clothes. The crotch of the sweatpants practically hung to his knees and the T-shirt stopped just above them. All he needed was a pair of oversized shoes and a red rubber nose, and he'd be set. *Send in the clowns*, Jude thought as Nico burst out in great guffaws.

"I think we need to get you some clothes, my mate." Nico wiped a tear from his eye as he wrapped his arms around Jude, hugging him, then led him out to the living room.

"I don't have any money," Jude hedged. "Everything I had was lost. I don't have any credit cards or even a cell phone. No accounts, nothing. They're all too easy to trace. I live off cash, and I don't have any right now. I'm broke 'cause I've had no safe way to access my accounts in Rome."

"You're my mate. What's mine is yours. Besides, if we draw the money from my accounts, nothing can be linked back to you. I've been around a lot of years and I have plenty. Let me take care of you."

"Fine, but I'm not a charity case. I do have money in Rome. The Vatican pays me quite well for my service. I just can't access it here without drawing attention to myself," Jude grumbled.

Nico smiled and kissed him. "So when we're in Rome, then you're buying."

"Huh," Jude snorted. He followed Nico down the hallway into the kitchen.

Fin was bent over, reading the packet of a gourmet ground coffee as the hiss and aroma of fresh brew filled the kitchen with its hot black goodness. He glanced up, stared at the tattoo-like marks on their arms, and grinned. "It's good to see you up and about. How are you feeling?"

"Like I've been claimed by my mate." Jude squeezed Nico's hand.

"Congratulations. I'm very happy for you." Fin poured coffee for them and took a deep breath. "I have a confession to make and I'm hoping you'll be able to forgive me."

"Fin, we've been friends quite awhile now. Whatever it is, it can't be that bad. Talk to me. We'll figure it out." Jude looked from Fin to Nico, trying to control his anxiety. Fin was a friend, one of the few he had due mainly to his job. Friends were usually very short term. The span of one job, while they were useful to him. After that, he would disappear and the friendship would vanish as well. Everything depended on being able to trust the few people who knew his secrets, and betrayal was a constant fear and nightmare.

"Why don't you go into the living room if you're going to talk and I'll make breakfast?" Nico kissed Jude's temple before shooing them away.

Fin sighed as he walked from the kitchen into the living room and took a seat in the armchair across from the sofa.

Jude followed before making himself comfortable on the sofa. He sat, looking at his friend, trying to figure out what this was all about. Fin was a gargoyle, and that was truly a good thing. He'd taken the brunt of things while Jude had struggled in the beginning to learn to control his fire. At first he flared up with even the slightest bits of emotion. Now he had a little better control, but not much. He'd singed the sprite's wings more times than he cared to think about. But Fin was clearly upset, and Jude struggled not to fear the worst—something that would get, if not him, then all of them, killed.

"I know what you are and what you're going through." Fin stared at his hands, not meeting Jude's eyes.

"Nico told me. I'm an Elemental like Evan... sort of," Jude said with a grimace.

"Yes, but I've suspected as much almost from the beginning and I didn't tell you. I was afraid. I've been hoping that I was wrong, but it's well beyond the point of being merely coincidence. I'm so sorry. I just didn't know how...." Fin wrung his hands in agitation.

"You knew?" Jude scowled. He felt betrayed by the one who was supposed to be protecting him.

"Sort of, well I suspected."

Jude closed his eyes, trying not to get upset with Fin. He needed the whole story. "Just tell me, Fin. It'll be okay."

"I hope so. I.... Okay." Fin closed his eyes and gathered himself, then began. "Fire Elementals aren't like Earth Elementals. The Earth Element is silent, enduring, sustaining. Fire... fire is volatile, consuming—some see it as the essence of life itself. The beginning—the first spark. The end—the smoldering ash. Fire Elementals aren't singular beings. They're ultimately similar to shifters in that their power manifests itself in a primal fire being. Some speculate this difference is because fire is so volatile and consuming, that without the other presence, the power of fire would subdue its host Elemental."

"Other presence… primal being… you're talking about the feeling I have of being consumed." Jude leaned back on the sofa, running his hands through his hair, trying to contain his fear and irritation.

"Yes." Fin looked up, his gaze captured by Jude. "You're feeling the stirrings of your fire being. Most Fire Elementals grow up knowing they're different. Having years to get to know their fire beast. The fire spirit and child grow up together. Evan's power burst must've awakened the fire beast within you."

"Why? Why didn't you tell me?"

"At first I wasn't sure, at least not right away. I thought maybe it was a power spike, or maybe someone in your background, an ancestor, might have been one of the Fair Folk and you were just unaware of it. I hoped that with time the power spike would wear off and you'd return to normal." Fin dropped his head in shame. "When you started talking about how you were feeling consumed from the inside and that you felt something was trying to get out… I started to guess that you were becoming an Elemental."

"You… you should've told me," Jude whispered.

"Even then I thought maybe it'd stop. Maybe the beast wouldn't awaken fully because, even if it was within you, it'd been dormant for so many years. But your power's increasing and I realized you're a Maker, same as Evan, only your power is Fire, not Earth." Fin kept his eyes on the floor. "Then we were being attacked and you were so exhausted all the time. I…."

"You should have told me!" Jude screamed, his hands igniting into balls of red flame. "All this time! You've known! I've been going slowly insane thinking I was going to burn in Hell!" Jude rose and stood over Fin, screaming down at him. Jude knew Fin could turn to stone and he wouldn't be hurt by the fire, but he also knew Fin wouldn't do it. He'd take whatever punishment Jude unleashed upon him for the betrayal. "You lied to me! You lied!"

"Shhh…. Easy, Jude." Nico was behind him. He didn't restrict Jude's hands, just wrapped his arms round his waist. "He meant no harm. He wanted to protect you, but instead he screwed up. We all screw up from time to time."

"But he knew, and he never told me. I was right. I'm going to become some beast, and I won't be me anymore." Jude's rage was fueled by his fear of becoming something uncontrollable… inhuman… evil.

"No, Jude, that's not it at all." Nico took a seat on the sofa and pulled Jude into his lap.

The flames slowly went out as Jude's anger and fear gave way to Nico's calming influence.

"Continue, please, Fin. He needs to hear it all." Nico's voice was low, reassuring.

"Fire Elementals have an animal spirit. When you call on your power to its utmost, you'll free the fire beast." Fin spoke quickly, as if he was afraid this would be his only chance to tell Jude what he knew before he was sent away for failure in his duty—a failure to Evan and Adel.

"We've always believed there was only one Maker—you couldn't be an Elemental because Evan was the Earth Elemental. But your power kept getting stronger, and the nightmares... and the damn demons were there every time we thought we could relax. We were always on the run. There wasn't time to figure it all out. Then when it became obvious that there could be no other answer for it, I was too afraid to tell you." Fin glanced at Jude, then turned away, unable to face him.

Jude trembled. "Is that everything?" he asked, his voice deadly cold.

"Yes, that's all I know. I'm sorry. I don't know how to help you bond with your beast spirit. The only Fire Elementals I've ever met were already adults and bonded," Fin said softly. "I was just a simple guardian, not a friend. They didn't confide in me as to how it felt."

"I want you to leave, Fin. I'm not ready to see or speak to you right now. I don't want to hurt you, but my control isn't the best when I'm angry," Jude practically hissed.

"Yes, my Maker." Fin rose and headed for the door, instantly obeying without question.

"Fin?"

"Yes, Maker?" Fin didn't turn from the door, but paused.

"I will forgive you. I don't want you to go away permanently. I just need some space from you for a bit," Jude said, allowing his tone to soften to give Fin hope that their friendship could be repaired.

"Go to Lira, Fin. She'll look after you. Remember, Jude does expect you to come back in one piece when he calls you. Take care of yourself," Nico chided gently.

The sound of the closing door was the only sign Fin had left.

"Who's Lira and will she really look after him? Maybe I was too hard on him." Jude immediately second-guessed his actions. He hadn't been separated from Fin for more than a night or two at the most, and he'd never sent him away before.

"Yes, Lira will look after him. They met the other day and she took an instant liking to him. She's a dryad. She lives in the forests around the city. Fin reminds her of the long-gone Fair Folk. She'll treasure the time she's allowed to spend with him. It'll also give that headstrong sprite some time to rethink his ways." Nico nuzzled Jude's neck; the affectionate motion sent a wave of relaxation through Jude's tensed muscles. "Evan gave him to you to watch out for you and be your confidant, not to keep things from you."

"He made a mistake. He didn't do it on purpose." Jude rolled his eyes, realizing he was now the one defending Fin.

Nico chuckled softly. "You have a very big and forgiving heart, my mate. Fin will be fine. When you're ready and won't singe his gossamer wings, I'll call Lira, and she'll bring him back."

"Okay." Jude began to relax. His anger released, he shuddered with apprehension. "How do I accept a fire beast? I've barely been able to accept that I can control fire. How do I give half of myself to an animal made of fire?"

"I don't know. But I know someone who does. His name is Gabriel Windslow, and he's a shape-shifter. Having a fire beast may not be identical to what he does when he shifts into his animal form, but I think he might have some ideas that might help, so it's worth a shot." Nico tightened his hold on Jude.

Jude felt so safe, like nothing could touch him or break through to hurt him within the circle of Nico's arms. "Okay, call him. I'm willing to try anything to get a handle on this." He clutched Nico just as tightly.

"Good, 'cause I just found you. I'm not about to lose you now," Nico vowed.

Chapter 7

SIN EATER LORE

As written by the scribes and entombed in the Church Archives:

2. A practice followed by very few in the modern age of genetics that explains away many of the physical deformities that plagued humanity in the past.

   a. Some religious zealots remain who believe, even though genetics has explained the disfigurement, the souls of these misshapen beings are impure. They argue that the accursed individuals need cleansing for their own well-being, and therefore use them when performing the dark arts. The acts perpetrated are supposedly paid for by the self-sacrifice of the Sin Eater.

   b. Some are used in the name of sin-eating when it is an excuse to perpetrate violence on the innocent, as well as perverted sexual deviance.

3. It is the Church's belief that these beings were a means to an end in a time when fear of the unknown bred contempt. The Church does not recognize Sin Eaters as anything other than abused individuals, and condemns those who claim to vindicate their violent actions on the blood of so-called Sin Eaters.

ARCHBISHOP PATRICK O'Flaggan paced about his office, waiting for the phone to ring. His people in different parts of New York had noticed questions were being asked. Questions were a bad thing. Questions about paranormals being kept prisoner and priests participating in the dark arts were even worse. They made people think, and he preferred the people in his diocese to obey, not think.

Theirs was a sect that lived in the shadows. Most people were unaware of their existence, and they preferred it that way. The archbishop's sideline activities had delved into the dark arts for many of its more sinister applications. They used those arts to grow and control the population base in his diocese—under Cardinal Swift's direction, of course.

O'Flaggan hated dealing with the paranormals. They were all demon spawn. The only difference was the demons summoned from the pit were obedient and did what they were told and no more. They burned out of existence once their task was complete, returning to the Hell from whence they came.

Paranormals were different. They hid themselves in society, but the Church ignored their existence. They generally kept to themselves and stayed out of the Church's way, not wanting to draw the wrath of God down around them. He couldn't understand why they were surfacing now and why in his diocese.

O'Flaggan stared out of the window. The phone rang. He crossed to the desk and answered it. "Archbishop O'Flaggan."

"You needed to speak with me, O'Flaggan?" Cardinal Swift got right to the point.

"Yes, Your Eminence." O'Flaggan struggled to keep his cool. Cardinal Swift could unnerve him just by the sound of his voice alone. "There's been a marked increase in the activity of the paranormals in my diocese of late. I'm not sure of the reason. They seem to be asking a lot of questions…."

"Oh? What kind of questions?"

"Nothing earth-shattering, really. Questions about the Church. About some of our comings and goings. Asking about missing paranormals, I suppose because of the recent abductions. Those questions weren't unexpected. It always happens when we send some of their number back to the pits. I was more concerned with their increased activity than the actual questions."

"Where are these questions being asked?" Swift seemed more curious than concerned.

"Oddly, I'm getting them from a lot of different quarters—the docks, the black market, business interests…. Even the society gossips." O'Flaggan shook his head in confusion. "I mean, what do they care as long as they aren't sent back to the pits themselves? They usually avoid our dealings. Why this sudden interest?"

"Did it never occur to you that the guardian gargoyles are paranormal creatures? Hell, even the Elementals themselves are paranormal. The fact that they're protected by the Papacy doesn't make them any less monstrous. They should all be destroyed. For the purity of mankind. We are created in the image of God. The Pope is supposed to be the most pure and godlike of us all, yet he cavorts with monsters." Swift snarled. "How am I supposed to become a god if we can never reach absolute purity and righteousness because of the scourge of these beasts from Hell? The Papacy grows weak because he allows such creatures to live. Whether they ignore the Church or not is irrelevant. Inevitably, we'll need to destroy them all, or, regardless if I achieve the Papacy or not, humanity will never reach its ultimate goal to become one with our creator and become gods ourselves."

"So what do you want me to do?"

"Track down who's asking the questions and find out why. Any news on the Inquisitor?" Swift growled.

"No, Your Eminence. I haven't attempted anything. I was trying to—"

"I don't care what you were trying to do! I want that Inquisitor dead! Get the job done, O'Flaggan, or maybe I need to find a new archbishop who can." Swift ended the call.

O'Flaggan hissed as he hung up. He'd wanted to give his monks more time to recover after the last round of sacrifices. He'd found three of his dark arts monks dead at their altars. Demon work was painful and exhausting, but when the cardinal demanded results, he had no choice but to do the same.

"Samuel, go prepare yourself. I'll require you to become a physical sacrifice before dawn." O'Flaggan picked up the phone receiver and punched in the number for his secretary as Samuel crept from the room. "Father Abe, please assemble the monks. The cardinal has set a task for us. I fear it shall not be easy."

"Yes, Your Grace."

O'Flaggan hung up the phone and sat down, elbows resting on the desk, hands clasped. He prayed tonight they'd succeed in, if not killing the Inquisitor, capturing him. At least that would please His Eminence.

NICO SAT in the living room. He stared out at the balcony, where the morning sun bathed Jude and Gabe, who were doing tai chi. The two had been meeting every morning for several hours: exercising, meditating, working at joining mind and body in order to reach Jude's beast.

The sun danced across Jude's sweat-glazed skin and glinted off his red hair, the beauty of the sight causing Nico to burn hotter than the fires of Hell. Both men were shirtless and barefoot, clad only in silk pants, going through the slow-motion moves like synchronized dancers. Gabe claimed tai chi would help Jude with his control and calm his mind—the better to reach a meditative state.

It was Gabe's assertion that going into such a state helped shifters reach their beasts while in puberty and reduced the amount of pain involved in a physical shift. Fin had said he wasn't sure if Jude would actually experience a physical shift, but Gabe wanted to be ready for anything. If Jude and his creature could come together, they might be able to bond and ease Jude's fear.

Nico needed them to bond; he didn't want to lose Jude, having just found him.

He growled softly behind the glass door, watching. Every fiber of his being told him to keep Gabe away from his new mate. Nobody should be practically naked with Jude except him. Seeing them move together—beautifully, gracefully—made him want to rip Gabe to shreds and burn the pieces. He couldn't stop watching, not just because of the urge to scream *mine* like a caveman and drag Jude away, but because Jude's movements were so smooth and effortless. Watching him was more breathtaking than witnessing the finest ballet, performed by the most skilled terpsichorean.

They would exercise and then sit and discuss Jude's feelings about the fire creature. Sometimes Nico would be a part of it, but lately Gabe had asked him to keep his distance. He didn't like it. Gabe called him a distraction. Which, admittedly, he was. He couldn't keep himself from getting between Gabe and Jude when they needed to work together.

The glass door to the balcony opened. "There's my mate." Jude grinned. A week had made all the difference in the world. He looked vibrant, strong, and happy. Jude strolled across the living room and sat in Nico's lap, planting a passionate kiss on his lips.

"How was tai chi?" Nico tried to keep the snarl from his voice.

"Good. I really wish you'd join us. It's so restful, and every time I'm done, I feel so alive and invigorated." Jude placed one hand on Nico's heart and wrapped the other around his neck.

Nico tightened his arms. "Maybe once you don't need Gabe's help anymore, but the space is too small or I'm too big. I'd take up all the balcony and there'd be no room left for the two of you," he joked, trying to cover the hurt of being excluded.

"We could move inside." Jude frowned, sensing Nico's pain.

"No. Later… just the two of us. Then I'll join you." Nico plastered on a smile for Jude's benefit.

"Come on, Jude. Break time's over. You need to meditate while your mind's clear." Gabe moved toward the guest room that they'd converted into a meditation space, complete with a fountain and the sound effects of nature. Nico had spared no expense; he'd even purchased a couple of beautiful bonsai and filled the room with oversized pillows. Anything to make this as easy on Jude as possible.

Jude sighed. "Sometimes I think this'd be so much easier to do at the cabin I shared with Evan. Out in the middle of nowhere. If I messed up there, nobody would be hurt or killed. Nothing there for miles."

"We can go there if you want to." Nico nuzzled Jude's neck. "Spend some time in the mountains alone, just the two of us. If you think Evan wouldn't mind us borrowing his cabin."

"You'd leave the city? You'd go with me?" Jude moved to look up into his eyes.

"In a heartbeat. If that's what you want and what you need to make this easier for you, I'd take you anywhere. We could even go to France if you think doing this with Evan and Adel nearby would help." Nico rubbed Jude's back. He wanted to support Jude in this. He just wanted to feel—needed to feel—like he was helping.

Jude wrapped his arms tightly around Nico's neck and leaned in for a soul-searing kiss. "I don't need to go anywhere. I can do this as long as you're with me."

"Come on, Jude. Let's get this show on the road. You need to be thinking peace and tranquility. This is about your beast within, not the beast between Nico's legs." Gabe leaned against the wall, rolling his eyes impatiently.

"He'll come when he's ready, Gabe. Why don't you just leave us alone for a fucking minute!" Nico snapped.

Gabe put his hands up in surrender and moved out of the room, disappearing down the hall.

This wasn't the first time Nico had lost control of his baser emotions at Gabe's restlessness. He knew he was the first amongst them to find a mate. They'd all known one another for so very long, through centuries of loneliness. It was hard on Gabe, but Nico wasn't about to give up Jude so his friend could be more comfortable. If push came to shove, Jude would win every time.

"Hey… hey now. Easy, big guy," Jude whispered softly.

"I'm sorry, *mein Feuer*. This goes against everything I know and feel. My instincts say to kill him. That he's getting way too close to you. To keep you for myself, hold you close, keep you safe."

"Shhh… I know. It's okay. I'm here. He's not touching me." Jude ran his fingers through his hair.

Nico couldn't suppress his moan and leaned into the caress. He loved feeling Jude's hands on him. Nico had been having a hard time sleeping. He hadn't been taking good care of himself the last day or so. The time Jude spent with Gabe was eating at his psyche, and he felt very close to the edge.

"You know what I think? I think that Gabe should take the afternoon off. We've been making tons of progress." Jude rested his head on Nico's shoulder.

"Oh yeah? It's working?" Nico took hold of the thick red braid that ran down Jude's back and played with it. He'd plaited it earlier that morning for him. Jude had considered cutting his hair, saying it was always in the way, but Nico was totally against it. He loved the feel of those fire-red locks as they flowed through his hands, and he craved sinking his hands in all that hair, using it to control Jude when he fucked him into the mattress. It shimmered iridescently in the sunlight, as if it were made of flame, and Nico felt he'd never get enough.

"Yeah, I think so. I can feel my beast lurking at the edges of my consciousness. He's here with me now, you know. Just there, at the edge. Watching. It's like seeing something out of the corner of your eye, knowing it's there, but if you turn to look, it's gone."

"If it's working, maybe you should keep up with the lessons," Nico reluctantly admitted. He didn't want to let Jude go into that meditation room. He wanted to keep him right here on his lap, not send him behind closed doors with Gabe.

"No, I don't think so. Gabe says I need to listen to my instincts and learn to listen for my beast. Right now, they're both saying my mate needs my attention, not my teacher. Gabe says—"

"Gabe says…. Gabe says… I'm so sick of what Gabe says!" Nico stood abruptly, dumping Jude onto the floor.

"Fuck!" Jude hollered as he landed on his ass.

"Oh, I-I'm sorry, b-baby. I-I—" Nico stuttered, reaching down.

"Don't touch me. Don't help me." Jude put up a hand and scooted away from Nico before standing. "You've done enough!"

"No, really Jude, I'm sorry. I didn't mean…."

"Just shut the hell up! I've been putting up with your goddamn jealous rages ever since your friend came to help. I think I've been supportive and tried to be understanding. You think I like any of this? You think I enjoy spending time with Gabe when I'd rather be with you? Well, do you?" Jude snarled.

"I—"

"No! I don't want this! I've got a beast to tame inside my head, and I don't need to be trying to tame your damn demons too!" Jude screamed. He stormed past Nico, shoving him back as hard as he could.

Nico barely moved, but it was enough for him to hit the backs of his knees on the edge of the chair, and he abruptly sat. He watched a fuming Jude head down the hallway. "I'm sorry."

"Yeah, well, so am I." Jude slammed the door to the meditation room.

"Fuck!" Nico yelled. He picked up his phone from the coffee table and called his brother. "Hey, Doc."

"Nico! How's mated life treating you?" Doc asked.

"Not so good at the moment. I've pretty much pissed off my mate because sometimes I'm a jealous ass."

"Sometimes, big brother? You've been a jealous ass over anyone that even says hi to your mate since you found him." Doc chuckled as Nico growled into the phone.

"I know. I just can't seem to stop."

"Some say knowing's half the battle." Doc tried to calm him, consoling his pain.

"Do we have anything new?" Nico asked.

"Yes, actually, Lira said she's got some news on the history of Elementals."

"Why don't you call everyone, and we can meet here this evening? It'll give Jude some time to cool off. And maybe he'll forgive me for being an immature, overbearing brat."

"You got it. See you later," Doc said.

"Make it around seven. And make sure Fin comes."

"I'm on it. Bye." Doc hung up.

Nico stared out onto the balcony, wondering how to apologize to his mate.

NICO HAD spent most of the afternoon in his office attending to his business, which he'd been neglecting lately. It wasn't that his business interests needed all that much hands-on attention, but there were some decisions he needed to make. When seven arrived and the doorbell buzzed, Nico rose and let in Doc, Lira, and Fin.

"Have the two of you made up yet?" Doc asked as they all proceeded to the living room.

"No. He's been in with Gabe since this morning. I took them sandwiches and drinks at noon, but Gabe said Jude didn't wish to speak to me."

"I think I'll go make some coffee." Lira turned and headed for the kitchen, leaving Doc and Fin to sort out Nico.

Nico shook his head, trying to clear it. "I… I'm not sure what happened. I think my mate… I don't know…."

"You had a jealous fit again, didn't you, brother?" Doc chuckled. He patted Nico's shoulder compassionately, then took the chair across from him.

"Yeah, I guess I did."

"You know, for being an old bastard, you really are stupid when it comes to loving someone. You know that, don't you?" Fin plopped down on the loveseat.

"I never said I'd be good at this. It's just eating me up inside that I can't help him and Gabe can. He's *my* mate, damn it! Why can't *I* help him? Why does he need someone else?" Nico raged.

Lira entered the room with a tray of mugs and set them on the coffee table. "Do you even listen to yourself?"

"What's that supposed to mean?" Nico hissed.

"All you say is… I, I, I. Me, me, me. Mine, mine, mine…. Selfish much?"

"But…."

"She's right, lad. Jude's terrified. He's dealing with a world he's barely tapped the surface of, trying to figure out a way to survive before the fire creature that's been awakened inside of him destroys him. He's reaching out to everyone, grasping at straws just to stay sane. What are you doing to help him? Hmmm?" Fin asked.

"I—"

"Exactly… you." Lira stood hipshot with her hand at her waist. "You accuse him of desiring Gabe over you, instead of supporting him and encouraging him. You glare at him, sulking in here, while he tries to better his understanding, doing what he's told by the one person who may be able to help him. The person *you* told him to trust and listen to."

"I know—"

"What do you know, exactly, big brother?" Doc asked. "Have you talked to him? Asked him how things are going? Have you spoken about the beast? Listened to him reason out for himself how he feels about being part of a creature of fire?"

"No.... Damn, I'm a bastard. I want, I need... you're right. I'm consumed with what I feel." Nico leaned forward, resting his head in his hands. "I don't know what to do." He sat back abruptly, wanting to get up and pace, struggling to remain in control.

"Ah, but you see... you've finally made your first right move all week." Doc grinned at him.

"What... what move?"

"You've admitted you don't know what to do. That's the first correct thing you've done. Now, when Jude comes out after meditating with Gabe, you're going to *ask* your mate to accompany you into your room. You're going to sit down and *talk* to your mate. You're going to *ask* him what *he* needs, and if it's nothing more than to have you sit and hold him or listen to him... by God, you're going to do it. And you'll do it with a goddamn smile on your face, because you're providing for your mate. If he talks about Gabe or his beast or the fucking man on the moon... you *will* listen to him. If he asks you to rub his feet or wash his hair so he can relax, you *will* do it. Do you understand me, Nicolas Daemarkus?" Lira scolded.

"Damn, you're quite the pistol when you get riled up, aren't you, missy?" Fin grinned at Lira, who flushed, a dark green color rising to her cheeks.

"Knock it off, rockman. I'm on to you," Lira taunted Fin, giving him a mischievous grin as she headed toward the kitchen.

"Not yet you aren't, but there's always hope," Fin hollered after her.

"I get it, I do. When he and Gabe are done for the day, I'll talk to him and really apologize." Nico knew his friends were right. He and Jude were mates and there is no "I" in mate.

"Now that we have your love life taken care of." Fin smiled at Lira as she returned from the kitchen and placed a carafe of coffee on the table. "Lira has a story to tell you."

"Oh, what's the story?" Nico turned and glanced down the hallway before he shook his head and focused back on those around him. He picked up the cup of coffee that sat untouched in front of him.

"I checked with some of the forest residents and the black market folks to see if I could find anything out about the cardinals and the Church.

Although I struck out for the most part, I did learn an interesting myth about the Elementals."

"Really? Do you trust the source?" Nico stood and headed toward the hallway.

Lira nodded. "Yes, actually. The forest witch is a very resourceful gal. She has many of the old books that were burned during the Church's purification of history. They contain the myths and legends long gone from everywhere else in the world."

"I'll go get Jude. He should hear this." Nico walked down the hall and knocked on the door to the meditation room, only to have Gabe answer it.

"What?" Gabe snapped.

"Fin, Doc, and Lira are here, and they have news for Jude. Lira's learned some things about Elementals and I think he should hear it firsthand from her." Nico forced himself to speak calmly, fighting against the feeling that Gabe was deliberately keeping Jude away from him.

"Fine… fine. It's not like he was getting anywhere with his meditation today anyway." Gabe stepped back and allowed Nico to enter, walking past him. "Come out when you're ready."

"Thank you, Gabe." Nico put a hand on his shoulder. "I know I haven't acted like it lately, but I do appreciate everything you're trying to do."

"I know, but thank you for saying it." Gabe left, closing the door behind him.

The soft scent of pine and sage filled the room. Nico hadn't been in the meditation room since he'd helped move the furniture out and the fountain and pillows in. Jude was sitting cross-legged in a lotus position, his eyes closed, his faced scrunched into a frown of frustration instead of the relaxation he needed.

Taking a deep breath, Nico moved around behind Jude and sat on the pillows. Jude tensed. There was no fooling him. He knew Nico was there and probably didn't want anything to do with him. But Nico needed to make this better, even if he wasn't forgiven. He put his hands on Jude's shoulders and massaged the tense, tight muscles, working them until he felt Jude relaxing beneath his ministrations.

"I owe you a big apology. I truly am sorry that I've been a complete bastard. I let myself get tied up in my own petty insecurities. I forgot the most important thing, and that's you," Nico whispered gently.

"I'm not the most important thing," Jude's head lolled on his shoulders as he relaxed to the point where his muscles and bones felt like Jell-O.

"Ah, but you are, Jude. See, you're my mate, and to me that means you come first before anything and everything else. My jealousy doesn't even get to be a consideration when your life is at stake." Nico gently eased Jude around so he was lying across his legs, arms outstretched above him. He worked on the muscles of Jude's back.

"But I need to be more considerate. I know how much it bothers you to not be included. Even though I'm distracted by your presence, I think I need to try to meditate with you in the room. Maybe together, with you to lure the beast, I can connect with it."

"Maybe. You know, I've been thinking too. Maybe you should stop referring to the fire spirit as a beast. Yes, it's an animal spirit. A flaming animal spirit. But listening to the way you say beast, it's like you're comparing it to a creature from the deepest pits of Hell or some scourge. Ultimately, love, this fire spirit's a part of you. And I can tell you, there's nothing in you that comes from the pits of Hell. And that includes this fire spirit." Nico rubbed his thumbs along each side of Jude's spine. Jude grunted as Nico pressed firmly down, the heels of his hands forcing air from Jude's lungs, aligning his spine.

"You really think that might help?" Jude groaned as Nico worked a particularly tight spot.

"I really do. How would you like it if I started sneering and calling you *that human* in a derogatory manner? You wouldn't be jumping at the chance to get to know me better, would you? You'd be pissed that I looked down on you and treated you like less than you are. Your fire spirit is a sentient part of yourself, living within you."

"You're right. I wouldn't want anything to do with someone who treated me like that." Jude slowly sat up and leaned back against Nico's chest, into his embrace. "Thank you. That felt wonderful."

"Good. Fin and our friends are waiting for us. Lira has news about Elementals, and I thought you'd want to hear it."

"Okay, let's go find out what she has to say." They rose from the pile of pillows, and Jude took hold of Nico's shoulders and drew him down for a searing kiss. "I forgive you. Let's not talk about arguing anymore."

"Yes, my mate." Nico grinned and led Jude into the living room and their friends.

Chapter 8

JUDE HELD Nico's hand as they entered the living room and joined the group gathered there. A new person had joined them. He was a large man, his short blond hair in a military haircut, with piercing ocean-blue eyes.

"Oh good, I was hoping you'd be able to join us," Nico said. He released Jude's hand, moving his to the back of Jude's waist. "Jude, I'd like you to meet my head of security, Cole Gentry. Cole, this is my partner and mate, Jude Jamison."

Cole stood, shaking first Nico's hand, then Jude's. "Nice to meet you." Cole nodded. "When the boss calls, I'm here." He retook his seat as Nico claimed the loveseat and pulled Jude down alongside him.

"I want to thank you all for helping. I know it's dangerous for you. I just wanted you to know I appreciate everything you're doing." Jude's gaze traveled to each as he spoke.

"Jude, you're Nico's mate. We'll do everything we can. We know that if it was one of our mates in trouble, Nico would be there to help. He'd grumble a lot and pitch fits, but he'd do everything in his power to ensure the safety of our mates." Lira smiled and placed her hand in Fin's.

Jude cocked his head to the side and grinned at the intimate gesture that hinted at a budding relationship. She'd be good for Fin, and as a dryad, Lira would make a good mate for a gargoyle. Both were immortal, tied to the power of the earth, and they seemed to be compatible. Jude knew how long his guardian had been alone and couldn't be happier they'd found each other.

He almost laughed when he noticed Gabe had settled in another armchair with Skye in his lap. For some unknown reason, Skye seemed rather attached to Gabe. In all the conversations he'd had with Jude about beast spirits and shifting, Gabe had never once told him about his own creature. Jude assumed it must be a wolf or maybe a cat of some sort. Still, Skye was an excellent judge of character, and he snuggled up quite peacefully on Gabe's lap, lending credence to Jude's confidence in him, regardless of what his beast might be.

"You have some information for us?" Jude asked Lira.

"YES, IT'S more of an old legend, really. It starts out that in the beginning, the world was filled with God's creations, and all lived in harmony and filled the planet equally, sharing the world. Then mankind began to multiply faster than the others, filling the world with his offspring, leaving no corner unpopulated. He became selfish, wanting the world for himself, and he intended to have it so. Humans tried to take over, subjugating the other races and destroying those who wouldn't be controlled through sheer force of numbers. He believed himself better than the others, special in the eyes of God. He called himself a 'child of God,' when we all were. He believed himself made in the image of God—again, we all are, for an omnipotent, omnipresent being can be and is all things. But in his mind, man was most beloved of all." Lira paused.

The room was silent, all eyes upon her.

"God was unwilling to hurt one of his creations. He viewed humanity as a child, for they were much younger than some of the other races and slow to mature. He punished mankind by giving them what they wanted. A world to themselves. He blinded them to the magical and wondrous beings that were God's other creations. The only time the blinders were removed was when one of us revealed ourselves to them, for mating or some other purpose. So mankind in his infancy turned on himself, dividing himself into factions based on territory, wealth, skin color, belief, or whom he loved. Pretty much any reason seemed good enough to incite hatred and killing." Lira paused again and looked at her hands, then directly at Jude before continuing.

"But God didn't want mankind forever separated. His creation was not whole while mankind was kept apart from his brethren. Those who knew the secret of the magical creations kept the secret and passed it on to their children, in stories and fables. And God gave mankind a gift: the Elementals. The gift was to be given to one special child of the human race, a piece of creation. Earth, Fire, Water, Air, and Spirit. Each a power that could be born into a single child. It was a special gift, because while the child with that power lived, those who possessed that magic could be seen by mankind. It gave man a chance to accept the magic world and his place in it."

"You mean, since Evan is an Earth Elemental, now all humans can see gargoyles alive at night because he lives to share the magic?" Doc asked.

"Precisely, yes. As well as other creatures that live by Earth magic, such as myself, unicorns, centaurs, gnomes, elves, trolls, and many others—all creatures who thrive on Earth magic. They've always been here. They're just no longer hidden from human eyes, should humans choose to see and believe."

"Is there more?" Jude asked.

"Only this: God made the Elementals immortal. The belief being that when all five Elementals live and come together, all of the creatures of God's creation will be revealed to mankind once more that he might rejoin the fold of all creation."

"Okay, so then as long as man is stupid about magic and kills the Elementals, then he'll never rejoin the others, but if he leaves the Elementals alone and all five live, then magic is returned to the world? But he has to overcome his fear and self-righteousness first?"

"Yep, that's the legend as told by a three-thousand-year-old forest witch." Lira stood. "Would anyone like some more coffee? I know I would." A number of yeses and nos answered her as she moved to the kitchen.

"So Evan and I are part of some plan to bring humanity back into the fold of the realm of magic. That is, if mankind doesn't kill us off as abominations and can get over his self-importance." Jude shook his head. He tried to laugh it off as being ridiculous, but he failed miserably.

"Shhh, it's okay, love. It's going to be okay." Nico rubbed Jude's back. "Most of that myth isn't really any use to us now anyway. There are only two of you. You and Evan. So let's just deal with the here and now and leave Fate to her weaving."

"Listen to your mate, Jude. Don't go borrowing trouble where there isn't any. Leave tomorrow for another day. Right now, concentrate on you." Fin stood. He patted Jude's shoulder as he passed into the kitchen to help Lira with the coffee.

"So, how are things going, Gabe?" Doc asked.

"It's coming along. We've made progress."

"Except we still don't know what animal I'm going to become," Jude grumbled.

"The animal spirit comes closer when Jude's upset, but it hovers at the edges of his consciousness. I'm not sure if we're getting through to it or not." Gabe shook his head. "I've taught him all the meditation and relaxation techniques we teach our young when they're learning to shift. But

I'm not sure how much it's going to matter. The relaxation is to help with a physical shift. When you're relaxed and accept your beast, the physical changes come naturally. When you're nervous and upset, muscles tense up and it's painful to the point of being life-threatening. I'm not convinced a physical shift like we go through is what Jude will experience."

"You're right there." Nico nodded.

"You don't think I'm going to become a fire creature?" Jude tipped his head to the side and looked up into Nico's eyes.

"Yes and no. Remember when Fin was telling us about how some Fire Elementals burned up because they didn't accept their fire spirit? It occurred to me that their fire spirit overlaid the Elemental."

"Yeah." Jude nodded. "I remember."

"They were both there, the Elemental and the fire spirit both present at the same time. The Elemental didn't shift into the fire spirit—they were both present in physical form at the same time."

"So both of us are there. So I don't become the beast—we're both in the same space?"

"Essentially, yes. Just as you are now. Both of you are inside your mind, but only you control the outside. If you need to call upon your power, it's not like Evan. You can't stand in dirt and channel the power directly."

Jude considered the source of his power. It was strongest when his emotions were riding high or when he was threatened. "No, you're right. I have to create the fire. It comes from within me."

"Do you see, that's where your fire spirit is as well. It's why you feel like you're being consumed when you really cut loose. You draw on him when you need your power, and he comes to you."

"I understand where you're going with this. I think you're right." Doc smiled grimly at his brother. "The power for both comes from within him. If one or both doesn't accept the other, then both perish in the flames, because a fire turned against itself burns out."

"Yes, you've got it." Nico smiled.

"But if we work together as one being, then the fire doesn't fight itself, and we'll end up twice as powerful," Jude reasoned, feeling the rightness of his words resonating deep within. He sat back, leaning against Nico's side, pillowing his head on his shoulder, and closed his eyes.

He turned his gaze inward, following that feeling of rightness, seeking. He could feel his fire spirit; it agreed with the conclusion he'd drawn. A deep, contented, internal thrumming reached him and he smiled. The fire spirit was happy. He was still not coming out to be seen, but he was sharing a feeling of understanding and acceptance. Jude suddenly felt if he were to lose control today, everything would still be all right—his fire spirit accepted him. He tried to convey that same feeling of trust back to it.

"He's happy," Jude said, opening his eyes. It was the first solid feeling he'd gotten from the spirit since he'd begun his lessons with Gabe.

"See, it's all going to work out just fine." Nico leaned forward and brushed a quick, chaste kiss against Jude's lips.

"You know, I think you're right." Jude returned Nico's smile, feeling for the first time in months that he just might have a chance to survive and not be consumed by the fire. Jude stood and gave Nico a peck on the cheek, then went into the kitchen to help Lira and Fin, realizing they'd disappeared some time ago. He needed to talk to Fin and forgive him for holding back on him. It wasn't as if it'd been altogether intentional, but it had hurt a great deal. They needed to bridge the gap forming between them and move on.

When Jude got to the kitchen, he was shocked by the sight of Fin wrapped in Lira's arms, engaged in a serious lip-lock. It was almost comical to see Fin up on his tiptoes, butterfly wings fluttering, kissing the tall, elegant woman. She so resembled a willow tree, with her slender body and her long green hair, bowed like a tree in the wind to reach Fin.

Jude cleared his throat, startling the pair. "Excuse me. Um, Fin… a word?"

"Y-Yes… ah…. Of c-course," Fin stuttered. His light green skin flushed a deeper shade.

They really did make quite a stunning couple: her deep emerald green next to his much lighter, more minty-colored skin. Jude hoped they'd be good for each other. Fin deserved to have a loving mate.

Lira grinned and picked up the coffee carafe. "I'll just go join the others."

"Thanks, doll," Fin whispered.

She leaned down and brushed a sweet peck across his lips once again. Giving him a wink, she walked out of the kitchen, hips swaying seductively.

"Fin—"

"Just hear me out, please." Fin's eyes were riveted on the floor at Jude's feet.

"Okay."

"I'm so sorry. I really didn't mean any harm. I never meant to keep what I knew a secret. But once I figured it out, you'd gotten hurt and all hell had broken loose. Time got away from me. I know it's not right, and I know I should've told you, but I really didn't...." Fin tried to apologize and explain himself at the same time.

"Fin. It's okay. I understand. I don't blame you anymore. I was scared and angry." Jude walked over to Fin and wrapped his arms around him. "My control is for shit, man. Fear and anger are definite fire emotions. I needed you to leave, not so much that I didn't want you around, but because I didn't want to hurt you. I needed to calm down so I wouldn't inadvertently lash out at you."

"It wasn't because you hated me and—"

"God, no. Fin, you've seen me through some of the worst parts of my life—being able to start fires, the demon attacks. You were there even when I tried to end things because I was sure I'd become a creature from the pits of Hell." Jude squeezed him tighter in his arms. "I could never—ever—hate you. I'll always want you around. You're my guardian, and it sounds like I'm going to be needing you, my friend."

"Are you sure? I can go back, you know… to France. I'm sure Evan would assign you a different guardian." Fin turned his head away.

Jude could feel the waves of desolation coming off his friend. He knew Fin felt guilty for not having come clean earlier, feeling as though he'd prolonged Jude's suffering. "I'll accept no other guardian but you. You're my friend, as well as my guardian. You and Skye are my family. Nico's my mate and I love him with all my heart, but you're like my brother. He has Doc, I have you." Jude let go and smiled down at him.

"So we're good?" Fin hesitantly asked.

"We're good. Just please, please, don't keep secrets from me again." Mischief glinted in Jude's eye. "At least things that pertain to me. Now, if there's a tall, green-haired woman who captures your heart and turns out to be your mate, then you don't have to tell me…. We've all guessed that one."

"Brat!" Fin snarked, but he grinned.

"Happy to be of service," Jude teased.

Chapter 9

"WHY HAVE you called me here? You know I don't have time to be chasing you all over the damned countryside. I have the Northwestern Diocese to govern!" Kennedy stalked into the office of Archbishop O'Flaggan.

"Good morning to you too," O'Flaggan sneered at his guest.

"I don't have time for pleasantries," Kennedy snapped.

"I need you to tell me everything you can about the information that puppet Michael got from Evan Halvard."

Kennedy's eyes narrowed with suspicion. "Why do you need to know what Michael discovered? Evan's out of our reach. He's in France, and I don't care how many sacrifices you're willing to commit to the effort, you won't get them past that force of gargoyles he currently surrounds himself with."

"Of course not." O'Flaggan scoffed, closing the file in front of him and motioning for Kennedy to take a seat in front of the desk. "But the boy was there and vulnerable. He should've been easy to destroy. Even a crazed fool like Michael should've been able to take care of him before he became so damned untouchable. I'm sure he had help, someone beside those small pet rocks of his." O'Flaggan steepled his fingers as Kennedy sat before his desk in the center of a dark windowless study, the dusty bookshelves loaded with ancient tomes on all four sides. It possessed all the ambience of a tomb. Only a few of the volumes were cared for, and those were kept behind the archbishop's desk, securely locked behind glass doors.

"I know Evan had help. We were in telepathic contact with Michael throughout the ceremony. He was the focus, but my monks were helping him to draw those demons. Michael didn't have enough soul left to call them himself. What Evan had was no pet rock—it was a monster of a gargoyle. I saw it through Michael's eyes just before he was destroyed," Kennedy hissed, taking his seat.

"Yes, yes, yes, I know. I saw that in your report. My question is, where did the creature come from? Have there been any other new events? Changes in his schedule? New people in his life? We need something we can go on, something concrete," O'Flaggan grumbled as he ran his hand down his rather substantial black goatee, stroking it in a contemplative gesture.

"Now that you mention it, yes. There were a number of new things going on at the time. I'd received a request from Father Michael to check out some relative… a cousin of Halvard's who had evidently moved in with him as an apprentice stonemason. I can't recall the name. Shortly after that, another man joined them. He also claimed he was an apprentice. Having two apprentices move in with him in such a short time is what alerted Michael that something more was going on. He'd been investigating them before he was killed. Afterward, Halvard met with the Pope's people in France." Kennedy crossed his legs and set his hands in his lap.

"All three men went to France? Are they currently under the Papacy's protection?"

"To be honest, I don't know. After Michael was killed and Halvard had escaped, Cardinal Swift ordered me to back off, and we lost all connections to him."

"Damn it all to Hell!" O'Flaggan pounded on his desk. "Find out the names of those two men. I want them…. Now!"

"What good would that do?" Kennedy picked up his phone and called his office.

"Because one of those two men must be connected to the Papacy. How else could he get gargoyles out of the country without my knowledge? I control the docks and the airports. My priests handle all security. Only a direct order from the Papacy would've circumvented my control. I think if we find out who those men are, we'll have our Inquisitor." O'Flaggan's smile was a humorless sneer.

NICO AND Jude followed their guests to the underground parking garage, seeing them to their cars. The lights flickered in the hallway in front of the elevator as they joked and chatted.

"The power grid must be heading for another brownout. So few people are using power, and they *still* can't keep the supply of electricity constant," Doc complained.

"At least we have electricity here. Much of the country is without power unless they create their own." Jude rolled his eyes.

"You're going soft, little brother. How many centuries did we spend without electricity?" Nico teased.

"Doesn't mean I want to go back to that. I like modern conveniences." Doc grumbled but smiled at the ribbing.

They walked toward the steel door leading out to the private parking area set aside for the residents and their guests. Doc, needing to get home, had moved ahead of the group, while Jude walked with Fin, Lira, and Cole. Gabe and Nico brought up the rear in a more leisurely, social pace. There was a chill in the air, and the musty odor of car exhaust and oil hit them when they opened the door.

All in all, it had been quite the evening and they'd learned a lot. Jude felt good about reconciling with Fin, and he enjoyed seeing him with Lira. She was quite a statuesque woman, and it was easy to see Fin was completely taken with her.

Doc had chosen a parking place closest to the door, so he was already in his vehicle and headed for the outside ramp. Nico, Gabe, and Cole were grouped together off to one side. Jude could hear them talking—Cole was filling them in on some of the information he'd discovered from his business contacts.

Jude stood beside a black limo next to Fin, who held the door for Lira as she slid in and took a seat. The driver had gotten out and waited discreetly on the opposite side. Fin turned to Jude. "Keep working on your meditation and trying to get in touch with your fire spirit. I think you're doing exactly what you need to do in order to prepare yourself." He patted Jude on the shoulder.

"I know. I'm really starting to feel good about—"

A clank echoed around the empty garage. The sound of metal canisters hitting the cement, rolling toward them, and the hiss of released vapors.

"Gas!" Cole shouted, pushing both Nico and Gabe toward the hallway and shoving them inside as demons emerged from the corners of the garage. Cole hit the lockdown code on the security keypad at the door, trapping both Nico and Gabe in the hallway.

"Demons!" Jude screamed, his hands lighting up at their presence.

Fin slammed the door to the limo as he pulled his sword from the scabbard between his wings. "Get her out of here!" he yelled at the driver.

The man sneered before he pulled a gas mask over his face. "No!" Fin screamed. He leaped toward the car just as the demons struck. They came in all sizes and imaginable designs: black horns, tails, gnashing teeth, and claws that scraped over the cement. A cacophony of snarls and hissing rose as they emerged from the shadows, closing in on their prey.

Cole pulled out two guns and fired into the midst of the demons, working his way through them to Jude and Fin's side. He motioned for them to get down as he scanned the area.

"Get the human!" snarled one of the larger demons, wielding two blades that flashed malevolently.

"Which one?" one of the smaller creatures asked, raking its talon-like hands along the cement with an eerie screech.

The larger demons looked between Cole and Jude, snarling at one another as they crept forward, forcing the smaller demons ahead in front of them.

"Get them both!" the largest of the bunch finally decided, kicking one of the little monsters that didn't quite move fast enough. The smaller demons surged forward, grabbing and slashing at anyone who got in the way, charging toward Cole, Fin, and Jude.

Fin's fierce battle cry echoed off the cement walls as he rushed into the fray, his sword flashing. Jude's fireballs lit up the garage, adding smoke to the increasing number of gas canisters that had been set off. His fireballs flickered and the flames became harder to create. Jude struggled for breath. Cole fell to his knees, gasping for air, as the three were overrun.

"The master wants the human! Put them in the car!" the largest of the horde snarled, punching Jude in the face and knocking him to the ground.

Darkness threatened to engulf Jude as he saw a net had been thrown over Fin, immobilizing him. He was dragged into the limo. Cole lay unconscious beside him; more nets were thrown over them both, while somewhere an explosion reverberated. The scream of an enormous bird of prey and a roar Jude recognized as Nico's battle cry echoed through the parking garage.

Don't die… please, God, don't let him die. Jude pleaded with the powers that be to protect Nico from the same fate that held him as consciousness evaded him and darkness fell.

NICO BURST through the door that kept him from Jude, an enormous white gryphon following on his heels. The beast barely fit through the door. It screamed as it attacked, leaping and covering Jude and Cole's bodies where they lay on the garage floor.

"We'll be back for them!" the largest demon hissed as he faded into the shadows, disappearing the same way they'd arrived.

"We'll be ready," Nico snarled just as loudly, sending waves of flame at the demons. The horde retreated after their leader, their forms melting and disappearing into the haze-filled darkness. The limo careened out of the parking garage, tires screeching, with Lira and Fin in the back. Nico burned with a white-hot fury that consumed any remaining demon within reach, but they were soon gone. There was little he could do but return to Jude and lick his wounds.

Nico slowly turned. He saw the gryphon, cut and bloody, with dead demons shredded around him. He trembled with the effort required to stay on his feet. The distinctive stench of carbon dioxide gas was taking its toll, even as it dissipated out of the open doors leading to the night streets above. If they had all been human, the demons would have easily captured Jude and everyone else would have died from the exposure to the gas. As it was, being paranormal didn't ensure you were immune to the gasses affects. "You all right, Gabe?" Nico warily approached.

The great white eagle's head shook, as if to clear its mind. The white lion's body, covered with gashes from demon claws, was already beginning to heal as he stretched his enormous wings, reaching up until only his back paws remained on the pavement, and beat the air with such power it forced the remaining gas from the garage. He landed on four legs once more. He stepped carefully away from Jude and Cole and shifted back into his now-naked human form. "I'm good. You?"

Nico quickly threw off the net that covered Jude and Cole. He sat on the cement and gathered Jude in his arms, holding him close. "He lives. He's passed out, but I think we're good."

Gabe knelt over Cole and placed a finger on his neck. "He lives as well. Why did he push us into the hallway and lock the door?"

Nico sighed, the adrenaline leaving his system now that the fight was over. He didn't want to think about Cole. "He's my chief of security and a private investigator. I pay him to keep me safe. He was just doing his job, but the man's only human. I'm not sure he realized he was in far more danger than we were."

"Can you take care of them? I think if I go now, I may be able to track that limo and find out where they're taking Fin and Lira." Gabe watched Nico carefully.

"Yes, go. I'll call Doc back and he can make sure these two are all right." Nico stood with Jude in his arms. "Can you put him over my shoulder before you go?"

Gabe stood, and with a strength that belied his size, he picked up Cole, who was a much larger man by several inches and as much as a hundred pounds. He placed Cole carefully over Nico's shoulder, making sure Nico had a good grip on the man. Gabe shifted back into his gryphon—the beast, clearly at least fifteen-hundred pounds, stood a few inches taller than Nico's six-foot-plus height and well over five feet long, not including the lion's tail. His wingspan was an impressive six feet from shoulder to wingtip. He eyed the area and carefully picked up a dropped cell phone from the cement with his talons, cocking his head at Nico.

"I think that's the phone I gave Fin so he could keep in contact with Jude," Nico said as he made his way toward the door. "Take it with you and call me if you discover where they're keeping Fin and Lira."

Gabe bobbed his head up and down, resembling a parrot in its antics. On three legs, with one talon clutching the phone to its breast, he charged out of the open garage door and up into the overcast, starless sky.

Chapter 10

NICO HAD never been so glad for his superior strength as when Gabe laid Cole over his shoulder while he was carrying Jude. Daemons were far stronger than they appeared, but Cole was not a small man. With Jude being close to a hundred thirty pounds, he needed every ounce of strength to get them all up to the penthouse. Nervous that their attackers might've broken into their home, Nico set Cole down outside the door, and with Jude snuggled close to his chest and armed with a handful of flames, he entered the silent apartment. He quickly scanned everything. Finding nothing suspicious, he laid Jude on the bed in their room and ran to retrieve Cole from the floor, carried him in, and set him in the armchair across from the bed.

Nico needed to be able to help both men, but he wasn't about to lay Cole in the bed alongside Jude. They seemed to be all right, just unconscious. Nico grabbed his cell and dialed his brother. "Doc, get back here. You just missed the party."

"What're you talking about, Nico?" Doc sighed as if he was being put upon, but Nico could hear the sound of the car's tires squealing as Doc spun the vehicle around and the horns of disgruntled drivers.

"You'd barely pulled out of the garage when we were attacked. They got away with Lira and Fin. Jude and Cole are unconscious. Gabe went after the limo in his shifted form."

"Damn it all! I'm on my way. I should be there in five minutes."

"Front door is open. Just come on back to the bedroom when you get here. I'm waiting for Gabe to call—he took a cell." Nico sat on the edge of the bed, moving a lock of red hair from across Jude's face and tucking it behind her ear.

"Hang in there, Nico," Doc said, then disconnected.

Nico leaned over and gently kissed Jude's forehead. A groan drew his attention to Cole, who'd put a hand to his head and seemed to be coming around. "Cole?" Nico moved swiftly to his side.

"Wha… what happened?" Cole mumbled, blinking his eyes and struggling to consciousness.

"We were ambushed. You locked Gabe and me in the hallway by the elevator."

"Oh… yeah… mmm…." Cole shook his head, then dropped his chin to his chest. He placed a hand to his temple and moaned, obviously regretting the action.

"Easy, big guy. You're human, not a hero." Nico went to the bathroom and brought back a glass of water.

"I'm your head of security. It's my job to make sure you're safe." Cole took the water and sipped it.

"Cole, I'm only going to say this once," Nico snarled, enraged fury and fear for Jude's life burning through his veins like molten lava. Flames burst along his upper torso and arms. "My safety is secondary to my mate's. If you want to live, never again prevent me from helping Jude, no matter what my personal risk."

Cole shrank back in his chair. Never before had Nico turned his abilities on him. Cole had never feared him—until now.

"Are we crystal clear?"

"Ye… yes." Cole managed to force the word from his lips, his fear palpable.

"Nico, stop scaring Cole," Jude's faint voice said from the direction of the bed. "You don't mean it and he was just doing his job."

"Jude!" Nico spun so quickly, he fell to his knees by the side of the bed. Fire extinguished, he reached out to him with tentative hands as Jude's green eyes blinked slowly back at him.

"Hi."

"Oh God, baby, you scared the crap out of me. How are you feeling?" Nico's fingers trembled as they brushed through Jude's hair.

"I'm going to be fine. I have a massive headache. Please tell me you have painkillers in your bathroom, because my head's about to split open." Jude raised a hand to his forehead.

"It must've been the gas. One minute I'm fighting to get to Fin and Jude, and then it was like everything had started to go numb. Next thing I know… lights out." Cole sipped his water as Nico went to the bathroom for a glass for Jude.

"Yeah, at first it seemed to just make everything foggy. Then my arms started to feel like lead and I was having trouble breathing and my fire wouldn't stay lit. It was like trying to burn in a vacuum." Jude pushed himself up to a sitting position, leaning against the headboard, moaning as he did.

Nico handed him a glass of water. "I called Doc. He should be here soon to check you out. I'm also hoping to hear from Gabe. He went after them. Hopefully, he'll call with good news." He sat on the edge of the bed and gathered Jude in his arms. He needed to feel him, to know he was safe.

"They were demons, weren't they?" Cole asked. "And they got away with Fin and Lira."

"Yeah, and they were a lot more organized and intelligent than the ones I've run into before. These guys knew… they came prepared." Jude relaxed into Nico's arms.

"I have painkillers, but I don't think you should take any until Doc gets here and checks on you." Nico rubbed Jude's back. "I was so scared I was going to lose you."

"So, were Fin and Lira the targets?" Cole frowned. "Lira keeps to herself. I can't imagine she'd have angered anyone to the point they'd send that many high-level demons after her."

"No, I suspect they're after me." Jude sighed.

"I'm here!" Doc hollered as he came charging through the door, surprising Nico, who almost threw a fireball at his brother. "Hey, watch it! I'm on your side!"

"Sorry," Nico growled, panting a bit as he struggled to regain his composure.

Doc went over and checked Cole out first, allowing Nico to calm down before he approached Jude. "How're you feeling now?" Doc asked, looking into Cole's eyes before checking his pulse.

"I have a pounding headache, like I was kicked by a mule, but other than that, I feel okay." Cole sat forward, letting Doc check the deep gouges and scratches from the claws of the demons who'd gotten close enough to slash at him.

"I need you to get in the shower and really scrub these wounds and cuts. Demon claws are filthy and can leave serious infection behind. After you shower, I'll treat the wounds with some strong antibiotics, which should help." Doc helped Cole to his feet.

"Doc, can you help Cole to the guest bathroom? That way both of them can get cleaned up at the same time." Nico clutched Jude to him as if he was about to leap to his feet and run to the bathroom in his hurry to get him cleaned up. The idea that the demons had touched Jude drove Nico toward the bathroom.

"Yes, I think that's a good idea." Doc smiled at Nico's protectiveness. Wrapping an arm around Cole, he led the man from the bedroom and toward the guest room. "We'll get you all cleaned up, and then we'll talk about all this and see what we can figure out."

"Let's get you in the shower." Nico nuzzled Jude's hair, and Jude groaned with pain rather than pleasure. "Your head hurt?" Nico gently probed Jude's scalp.

"Yeah. I think it was either that last punch or maybe I struck my head when I collapsed to the floor, but my ears are still ringing." Jude flinched when Nico brushed a rather nasty bump forming on the back of his head.

"I believe you probably have a concussion. There's a pretty nasty bump here." Nico carried Jude into the bathroom, carefully putting him on his feet and making sure he was steady before he turned and started the shower. "Okay, shower now, then Doc can look at the bump while we're dealing with the cuts."

"You've got a fair share of those cuts as well." Jude pulled his T-shirt over his head with a pained hiss as Nico adjusted the temperature in the shower.

"Yes, but daemons don't get infections. I suspect you may not be vulnerable to them either, now that your Elemental powers are awakened, but I don't want to chance it. Cole is definitely vulnerable. Humans really are exceedingly fragile." Nico returned to Jude's side and helped him remove the light cotton pants he wore while meditating and doing tai chi.

"Well, then, it's good that Doc is seeing to Cole's injuries first." Jude pulled at Nico's shirt. "Why don't you join me in the shower? I really can't… don't feel up to much. I just want your arms around me."

Nico grabbed his shirt and pulled it off, then dropped his jeans just as quickly. "I'd be happy to help you shower and hold you, my love. That's something you never have to worry about. I'll always hold you, whenever you need or want me to."

"Thanks, Nico." Jude blushed as Nico helped him into the shower, letting the hot water wash away the stink of demons and the pain and pounding in his head.

AN HOUR later, Nico and Jude sat in the living room with Doc and Gabe, dressed in clean T-shirts and jeans. Cole had fallen asleep after the shower and having his wounds tended, his human physiology exhausted. Doc thought it was best to let him sleep and heal.

"The limo pulled into the warehouse district, into an abandoned building. From the outside, it looks like the place hasn't been used for years. I'm not exactly sure what happened. I was all of a few seconds behind. I landed on the roof and went in through a broken window. But it was empty. No limo, no men, no demons. No Lira or Fin. The only things moving were the rats."

"What the hell?" Doc gasped, staring at Gabe.

"After I realized nobody was there, I went around to the front and then in the same door they drove through. Nothing. The place even smells like it hasn't been used in years." Gabe stood and paced in front of the balcony doors.

"It must be a portal of some kind. That's magic the Church hasn't used before." Nico stared at Jude as if for confirmation.

"I've never heard of such a thing. I mean, demons appear and disappear through portals, but I've never heard of them taking things from this world into Hell with them." Jude trembled, closed his eyes, and took a deep breath to steady his nerves. "Can I use your computer? I think it's time we call for backup. I hope they can return to the States or that at the very least I can talk to Evan and Adel. We need to pool our resources and they're the most powerful allies we have."

Nico stood, walked from the room, and returned with a laptop, handing it to Jude. "What are you hoping for?"

"Maybe Adel can tell us what happened to our friends. He's been around for a very long time. It's a long shot, but maybe." Jude began frantically typing, tapping the old, secure, anonymous underground message system he and Evan had used long before they'd met.

Stone
SOS
New York
Need talk or visit ASAP
JudassaninC

"Please hurry up and answer," Jude said as he sent the last message. "Has anyone seen Skye?"

It was almost comical as everyone glanced around the room looking for him.

"I'd guess he's out hunting, my love." Nico frowned slightly.

"He was with me before we left and were attacked." Gabe tipped his head to the side and went to the glass sliding door to look out over the deck, but Skye was just gone.

Chapter 11

THE SOUND of weeping filled the darkness, but it took a while for Samuel to realize he was the one who was crying. The agony of muscles held almost motionless in shackles for far too long sent burning waves of pain throughout his body. He felt hot and cold at the same time. The chatter of his teeth, even as sweat dripped from his forehead, was enough to convince him his body was in less-than-stellar condition. The archbishop had probably succeeded in signing his death release from this world with his last bout of punishment.

A soft sound reminded him he wasn't alone in his prison. After he'd done his duty by submitting to Archbishop O'Flaggan, he'd been left in his dark cell to recover or die as God saw fit. He prayed he'd endured enough to be acceptable and God would allow him to die.

The sound was like music—singing, but more like the song of wind through the leaves on a summer day. Yet it was a woman's voice, gentle and sweet. "Hush, little baby, don't say a word…." it crooned as gentle hands cleansed his damaged back.

Memories of the horrors he'd endured—the crack of the whip and the pain of leather on breaking skin, the trickle of blood as it seeped down his back in rivulets, mixing with sweat, searing as the salty fluid leeched into fresh wounds—flooded him. He was no longer able to keep them back, not in his weakened state. Tears flowed uninhibited down his cheeks, soaking the scraps of material that posed as bedding on his pallet.

"Rest easy. I'm just trying to clean you up a bit."

She sounded so unbelievably kind, even to a freak of nature like himself, whose ugliness of soul was physically visible. He'd seen very little kindness since he'd been taken from his grandfather eleven years ago, when he was ten. Everyone steered clear of Archbishop O'Flaggan's Sin Eater, his cursed one, lest they become infected with his deformity. As if that were even possible. Just because he had webbed hands and feet didn't mean he was contagious. Still, nobody in the service of Archbishop O'Flaggan would come anywhere near him, much less speak to him. He was a nonperson, which suited him most days, except when he was called to do his duty. Then he hated his existence.

"How's he doing?" a male voice asked.

It seemed to be coming from behind him, toward the door. His pallet lay against the far wall. He was well aware of his surroundings and where he'd been left to rot, amongst strangers—others Archbishop O'Flaggan deemed unworthy to see the light of day, whom he kept hidden in the dank bowels of his own personal dungeon.

"He's been severely beaten. He has what can only be the scars of multiple beatings and healed lacerations all over his body. This boy has been someone's punching bag for a very long time, Fin." The woman's voice was sad, yet so gentle, as she worked to clean his wounds.

He tried not to moan, but it was impossible not to as she gently probed a particularly bad injury.

"Do we try to take him with us?" Fin asked hesitantly.

"We can't leave him here, love. If we leave him behind, he's as good as dead. With injuries this extensive, I can't guarantee he'll live through being moved either. If we were only in a room with light, I might be able to do more and help heal some of the damage, but as it is, I can only give him so much before I could do myself harm."

"I know, my love. I know you want to do more. And we will as soon as we can, but I need you to not drain yourself. We don't know what they want with us or how long they plan to keep us here," Fin whispered. He sounded like he was standing right over Samuel.

"How long?"

"I slept last night. My kind generally sleep during the day, but a few of us were blessed by Evan and we can choose when we want to sleep, but when I sleep, I will turn to stone. I can keep from sleeping for about two, maybe three days tops. Then I'll have to start napping or I'll go into complete hibernation and be out for at least eight continuous hours." Fin sighed and sat beside the woman. "There's no way that they can look at either of us and not realize we aren't human, but I'm not giving away what I am any earlier than I have to."

"We'll have to get out of here soon, then. I'll only survive forty-eight hours without light of some sort, and then I'll start to weaken and die." The woman's voice became muffled, as if she were being held against someone.

"No escape. No will but the master's is done in these walls." Sammy's voice was hardly recognizable, even to himself, as it croaked out in a raw-edged whisper.

"Hush, child. Use your energy to rest and heal. Leave all else to us." Her singsong humming began again, joined by a soft, birdlike trilling, gently sending him beneath consciousness into the dreamless darkness. His last thoughts were of the joy of never having to open his eyes again.

JUDASSANINC
Worried Sick! Bad Dreams
At home
Meet 24 hours—Ancient Empire State
Stone

"He's coming." Jude leaned into Nico's warm body, sitting with him on the sofa. He'd just read the message from Evan and was thrilled to find out he'd returned from Europe. It hadn't even taken a full twelve hours for Evan to respond. Jude had sometimes spent weeks waiting for him to see his message in the old days. Now it was as though Evan had been waiting for him to call.

"Good. We need all the help we can get. Maybe he can track Fin and we can find out where our people are being held. I want our family back." Nico growled in frustration. He had never felt so helpless in all his life. The only thing that kept him from burning everything in sight until his friends were found was knowing Jude was safe. Nico's grip on Jude's shoulders tightened, momentarily reassuring him that they would figure out a way to make this right.

"He's going to be so pissed at me. Fin saved him from the demon-dogs Father Michael conjured during that last fight. And I lost him…."

"You're making Fin sound like a runaway pet or a thing you misplaced. He was kidnapped, along with Lira, and you did everything you could to try and save them, to keep them from being abducted. It's not your fault. We'll get them back."

Jude stood and paced back and forth in front of the glass sliding door that led out onto the balcony, trying to burn off his agitation. "It's still my fault. I'm an Elemental. I should be able to protect him," Jude snapped. His eyes burned with his anger and his fear.

"Evan is your friend. He knows you'd never intentionally hurt Fin. He knows you'd do everything you could to keep him safe." Nico stood and crossed to Jude, attempting to console him.

"But that's just it. It's never intentional with me. It's why I stayed alone for so long. I can't have a partner. I hurt the people around me. They end up dead and I end up alone—again. It's always been this way and always will be. The only way for me to keep the people I care about safe is to stay away from them." Jude stormed down the hall into the bedroom that had been Fin's before he'd gone to stay with Lira in the forest, and slammed the door behind him.

Nico followed, standing outside the closed door. Everything in him screamed to go in and wrap his arms around Jude. He knew Jude really wasn't angry with him, just scared Fin wouldn't survive his abduction. "You're wrong, you know." Nico spoke loud enough to be heard through the door. "Yeah, you've had it rough, and you've been alone more than you should've been. But there's a difference between being alone because you choose to be and being alone because you're afraid to be anything else." Nico rested a hand against the cool wood of the door. "Regardless, you'll never be alone again. We are one soul now, *mein Feuer*. And I'm a little more hardy than your average partner." Nico sighed and shook his head. "The only thing between us is a door. You are not alone."

He heard the sound of soft sobbing, muffled by the wood. He debated between stepping aside and letting Jude come to terms with his feelings alone, or going in and holding him. He leaned toward the latter. It ripped his heart out knowing Jude was going through such wrenching pain, both from past losses and the fear of another. The echoing tendrils of Jude's distress reached out to him, and Nico felt them as acutely as if the feelings were his own and not Jude's.

"Please, Jude, let me in."

"Come...." The answer came so softly that if it hadn't been for their bond, Nico wouldn't have known Jude had asked him to enter.

Nico eased the door open. Jude sat on the bed, his head in his hands, his breathing coming in little gasps as he struggled to control his emotions. Nico sat beside him, then drew Jude into his lap and set his head against his chest, cradling him like a child.

"When I was little, my father was murdered because he defied the Church. My parents refused to be separated when my mother had no other children besides me with my father." Jude paused, turning his face into Nico's chest.

Nico could feel Jude's pain radiating through their link as he relived the past, memories flowing like water over them both with the dull ache of an old injury.

April 8, 2199

JUDE STAYED in the closet where his dad had left him. They'd long ago talked about him needing to hide from the priests when they came. He knew his parents were breaking the law by staying married when his mother hadn't gotten pregnant in years. Although she knew it was her duty to find another partner and bear children, she loved her husband and family and didn't want to leave them. The alternative made their lives dangerous. So Jude tried to make himself disappear amongst the coats, but he cracked the door so he could see and hear what the adults were doing.

"Now, Maggie, we've gone over this. You don't have a choice here. It's the law. All able-bodied women need to reproduce if the human race is to continue. It's God's wish for all mankind to flourish." Father Jefferies stood at the front door to the small ranch-style house.

"We've been trying, Father. But the good Lord hasn't blessed us with any more children since Jude. It mustn't be in his plan for us." Maggie reached over and clasped her husband's hand.

"You know that isn't your choice, Maggie. It's been taken away from you. Your marriage with Dennis has been dissolved and another man of good, producing bloodlines has been chosen for you by the Church. He'll be arriving from Texas in the morning. He's already fathered quite a few children. We expect he'll be able to give you the child Dennis is unable to."

"We have an exclusive marriage!" Dennis snarled at the priest.

"No, Dennis. You applied for an exclusive and it was denied. Maggie's too good a breeding female for her to be granted an exclusive. She'll be taken to the hospital, the conception of the child will be monitored, and she'll stay on Church grounds, observed by the Church, until the baby's born. If she chooses to return to you after that time, she may until her body is required to bear another child." Father Jefferies waved a hand and two armed men approached from behind. "Take her away."

"No!" Dennis yelled. He pulled Maggie behind him as the men stalked toward them, brushing past the priest.

"Don't make this any harder than it already is, Dennis. It's the way of our world. Procreation is blessed by God. It's necessary for the continuation of our race. This is a sacrifice we all must bear. It's her duty."

"No! You can't make me! Dennis!" Maggie screamed and fought as one of the men grabbed her and dragged her from the house. "Dennis!"

"You can't do this!" Dennis yelled as he attacked the other armed man.

The crack of a gunshot echoed around the room. Jude's ears rang as he watched his father slump to the floor, dark blood spreading through his shirt and pooling around his body.

"Dennis! Dennis!" Maggie screamed loudly as they dragged her from the room, out of sight.

"There's supposed to be a child?" Father Jefferies looked around.

"I would guess he's in school, Father." One of the guards glanced around the living room.

"Look about for him and see if you can find him. It'd be best if there weren't any witnesses to this fiasco. The woman has been claimed by the bishop. He's one man you don't want to cross." Father Jefferies turned and disappeared from Jude's sight, followed by the sound of a slamming door.

In the closet, Jude shivered, his body quaking with fear. He couldn't move, couldn't breathe, couldn't think as the guard walked through the house, searching for him. He was going to be found, he knew that, but he couldn't force his body to function, to move out of the closet, past his dead father, to run away. Instead, darkness overtook him, and he sank silently into the nothing that cradled him from the horror, taking him away, even temporarily, from the evil around him.

Present

"ALL I remember after that was waking up in Jaren's arms as he carried me from the house to his car. I found out later I'd lost four days. I remember nothing that happened during those days. Jaren hid me in a different diocese while he continued his investigations and later came to visit and to tell me of my mother's death. She'd committed suicide, taking my unborn half sister with her into the afterlife."

"I'm so sorry, Jude." Nico rubbed Jude's back in soothing circles.

"Jaren always watched out for me. He was like a big brother and mentor all in one. I idolized him. I worked my way through school doing everything I could to get myself into a position so I could apprentice to him. I wrote letter after letter to the Pope, requesting an apprenticeship while I attended university." Jude paused, letting his head fall back onto Nico's shoulder, grasping the arms that held him as if ensuring he wouldn't be let go.

"I'm glad he was there for you when you needed him."

"See, that's just it. He was always there for me, and the one time I was supposed to be there for him, I failed him. He died." Flames hovered along Jude's fingers and arms. "It was supposed to be routine. No big deal. Just a meet and greet, then back on the plane to Rome. Hell, it wasn't even a hostile takeover. The former bishop of the diocese had retired, and a new bishop stepped in to take his place. We were to meet the man and get a feel for him. We were to be the eyes and ears of His Holiness the Pope."

"So if it was so easy, what happened?" Nico kissed Jude's temple.

"To this day, I'm not exactly sure. I wasn't allowed to be on the investigation team. All I remember is walking up to Bishop Gleeson's home and hearing gunshots. We went on the offensive and broke down the door. The bishop and his wife were already dead, right there in the living room. I saw four armed men. It only took us minutes to subdue them because they were untrained. We took them all alive, but we knocked three unconscious. Jaren wanted to question the fourth." Jude turned his face into Nico's chest, hiding his expression, trying to suppress the grief that still remained. "I should've gone and checked the rest of the house. I should've made sure that those men we saw were the only ones. Instead, I stayed with Jaren when he began asking questions. We were so focused on the prisoner, we didn't see the other man. He took us unaware. Jaren must've heard him, because suddenly he was spinning, pushing me behind him. Shots rang out. More men from the Bishop's Service were flooding the house, but it was too late for Jaren."

"He saved your life. It's what partners do." Nico carded his fingers through Jude's hair.

"I should've checked the rest of the house. We had the others subdued. I...."

"Which of you was the more experienced agent?" The movement of Nico's hands had a calming effect on Jude, even when he felt so upset he couldn't think straight.

"Jaren. I was barely out of my apprenticeship training. I'd only been partnered with him for a year."

"He didn't tell you to check the rest of the house?"

"No. He was intent on the prisoners."

"Nobody's perfect, Jude. We all make mistakes. You can't live your life feeling like you're cursed when things are just beyond your control. He was the more experienced agent. He should've thought to check the rest of the house. But he made a mistake that almost killed you both. In the end he did right by you. He saved your life. If he loved you like a brother, he wouldn't want you going through life afraid to care about others because of 'what if.'"

"No, he wouldn't want me to be alone." Jude shook his head and softly chuckled. "He was always harassing me about finding someone. I remember when I came out to him and told him I was gay. I'd already known where my preferences lie, but I wanted him to know. I was seventeen and I wrote him a letter, mentioning being aroused by some of the other boys in the locker room. Next thing I knew, I had a phone call I had to take in the dean's office. Jaren actually called me, long distance from Rome, to talk about the birds and the bees."

"See? He really must've cared about you. This isolation is unhealthy. You can't keep punishing yourself for other people's actions. You can't keep blaming yourself for the *what ifs* of this world, Jude. You can only do your best in the present and go forward from there."

"You're right. I know you're right. It's just hard to let go."

"So let me help you, *mein Feuer*. Be with me. Let me love you."

"Nico," Jude whispered as Nico's hands began to stroke his body with a purpose. Nico's hot lips nibbled on his ear as nimble fingers slipped beneath the hem of his T-shirt, stroking the skin beneath, sending shivers of delight all over as he arched into Nico's body.

"You're mine, Jude. You're my fire." Nico pulled his T-shirt over his head and let it fall to the floor. He laid his arm alongside Jude's. "Proof covers both our arms. Never will we be apart. We'll always burn together." Nico scooped Jude up. He left the guest room, carried him into their bedroom, and gently sat him on the edge of the bed, then knelt before him. He reached up and held Jude's face gently between his hands, his thumbs brushing Jude's jawline slowly, soothingly, back and forth. "We will survive this, Jude. We will get our friends back and we will live for many years to come, the two of us together."

"How can you be so sure?" Jude clutched the edge of the bed, fisting the blankets.

Nico's hands dropped to Jude's and rubbed into the back of the fists, coaxing them to relax before reaching for the hem of his T-shirt. He tugged it over Jude's head and let it drop to the floor. "I have faith. Faith in you… in our friends… and in Fate." Nico punctuated each phrase with a brushing of his lips across Jude's. Sweet, coaxing kisses, stoking the fire of Jude's hot lust, tenting his jeans.

"Fate?" Jude's voice dropped an octave, deepened by want. He watched as Nico trembled, his control shaky as bits of blue fire danced along the black tribal flames that tattooed his arms.

"Yes. She holds the strings of all our lives and weaves the patterns of the universe. It'd be cruel of her to put us together just before the end… before we even have a chance to get to know each other. I need to have faith that she knows what she's doing and sees the pattern she weaves, and that we'll have a long, happy life together."

"You really believe…?" Jude tugged at Nico's clothes ineffectually.

"Yes. Because without the hope for a better tomorrow, what is there? Everything in life is temporary. The good and bad equally come and go as we live day to day. The only thing not temporary is you, my mate. We are bonded. Whatever Fate has in store, it will be for both of us, and knowing that, I can deal with everything else." Nico placed a tender kiss on Jude's forehead.

"I can live with that." Jude grinned and leaned forward to capture Nico's lips.

Chapter 12

NICO'S LIPS closed over Jude's, silencing all further conversation. His tongue slid along Jude's bottom lip, requesting entrance. Jude opened for him, and Nico plundered the depths of his hot mouth, running his tongue along his teeth before drawing Jude's tongue back into his own mouth, where he began gently suckling. He could feel their temperatures rising along with their lust, could hear Jude's heartbeat pounding out his need in sync with his own. Jude was everything to Nico—his whole world now revolved around him—and he'd let nothing hurt him ever again.

Nico ghosted his hands along Jude's shoulders, tracing along the black flame markings, sliding from shoulder to fingertips. Sharing the lavender flames, the fires of his heart that danced along his skin to warm Jude's, he kissed down Jude's neck, gently pressing him back until he lay on the bed with Nico bent over him. Nico laved along Jude's collarbone, laced fingers drawing Jude's hands over his head, changing his grip so he held both of his wrists with one hand. He nuzzled his way across Jude's pecs and buried his nose in Jude's armpit. Here was the essence, the scent he hungered for. His tongue lapped lightly at the russet-furred skin, heady with musk that was all man, declaring, "*Mine, you're all mine.* Mein Feuer. *My mate.*" Nico nipped at the skin and moved down and across to the hardening nub of Jude's nipple.

Jude squirmed beneath him, and sparks of flame burst from his skin, to be absorbed by Nico. "Oh God!" Jude groaned, thrusting his hips up, grinding himself against Nico. "Yes, yours!"

Nico blew gently against Jude's chest, sending little blue flames dancing across the surface of his sweat-beaded skin—tickling, tantalizing, gently warming everywhere they touched. Jude hissed softly at the heated touch, like another set of fingertips stroking along his skin. Nico gave Jude's hands a last squeeze, letting him know to keep his hands above his head as Nico moved down along his body until he knelt on the floor between Jude's knees. He rained wet kisses along Jude's thighs, spreading them to give him better access.

Jude's cock throbbed with the beat of his heart, the angry purple head weeping viscous droplets of precome onto his tight abs. Jude had put on a little weight since Nico had found him, but Gabe's intense mind-body workouts insured those pounds were muscle, and Nico enjoyed outlining each one with his tongue.

"Beautiful," Nico murmured. His tongue was met by a neatly groomed patch of tight russet curls that flowed about Jude's groin at the base of his cock, and over his heavy balls. Nico nipped at the curls, rolling Jude's scrotum in his hand, kneading it gently, eliciting gasps with each tender touch. "Hold your legs for me."

Jude grasped his thighs and held himself open as Nico kissed first the left, then the right testicle. He let his tongue caress the perineum before circling Jude's hole. "Nico!" Jude cried out as Nico's tongue speared past his guard muscle.

Nico grasped Jude's thigh to steady himself, loving the taste that was uniquely Jude's. After drenching two of his fingers in his own saliva, he slowly pressed them in. He worked them around, scissoring them back and forth, loosening the tight hold. When Jude began to meet him with each thrust, Nico added a third, curling them to brush against Jude's prostate.

Jude came undone in his pleasure, grinding his hips, seeking to impale himself deeper—harder—lost in his ecstasy. "More… I need more." Jude's movements were becoming frantic, and Nico released his thigh and encircled his erection.

"I know, love." Nico withdrew, rose to his feet, and reached for the lube in the nightstand drawer. "I have what you need." Nico squirted it into his hand, spread it over his shaft, and then added more to his fingers. He reinserted them and spread the liquid over the muscle on the inside, making sure there'd be as little pain as possible.

Jude reached out and took hold of Nico's arm, drawing him closer as if to pull him into his body. "I need you!" he whimpered.

"I'm here." Taking his cock in hand, Nico pressed forward until his tip spread Jude's pucker. It fluttered against his invasion, challenging his control.

Jude panted as Nico shifted Jude's legs over his shoulder. Leaning forward over Jude, he pushed in until his cockhead passed through, then remained motionless, allowing Jude's body time to adjust. He kissed Jude, devouring lips, tongue, and breath, until the tension in his body moved from burning pain to need. He broke the kiss when he felt Jude squirm beneath him, trying to lift his hips to get more of him inside.

Bearing down, Nico eased the rest of his length into Jude's tight channel, both of them groaning as his balls brushed against Jude's ass. "God, you feel so good wrapped around my cock." Nico pulled out. Jude whimpered at the loss before being impaled slowly. Nico set a slow, steady rhythm, Jude rising, milking his cock with each thrust. He worshiped Jude's body, stroking the back of his fingers along Jude's jaw, down over Jude's chest, tweaking his nipples. He drove Jude's passions higher with each caress of fingertip and swirling of purple heart flames.

The blaze surrounded both of them. Flaring at the edges in light lilac, shifting to periwinkle and magenta as their bodies pressed together, it danced along the tattoo, over sweat-slicked chests, along their thighs, appearing to consume them both as their rapture drew them higher toward their climax. As the dance of their bodies became frenzied and the slap of flesh against flesh sent them toward bliss, the light burned ever brighter.

"Come…. Jude," Nico gasped, his hips jackhammering into Jude, body trembling with the effort to hold back his orgasm.

"Nico!" Jude screamed, sending ribbons of spunk across his stomach and chest.

Jude's body clenched Nico's cock as he roared, filling Jude with his essence. The aftershocks drew every quivering drop from him as he collapsed to the side, drawing Jude with him. Holding them together, unwilling to leave Jude's body just yet, he savored the feeling of being joined. "I love you, my fire."

"Love you too, my angel," Jude's eyes were half-closed and passion dazed as he looked up into Nico's gaze. A sigh of pure contentment escaped him. He snuggled into Nico's arms and drifted off into an exhausted but sated sleep.

Nico wasn't quite as ready to succumb to the wiles of sleep. His mind struggled over the portal where their friends had disappeared. As he gently brushed the hair from Jude's eyes, he contemplated how lonely Jude's life had been. Nico had been around a long time and lived much of that alone, but Doc had always been there for him. Jude didn't have anyone. Thoughts of Jaren Thomas produced a tangle of emotions for Nico: a combination of anger that Jaren had died and left Jude alone, as well as the green of jealousy because of the love Jude had for his mentor. In the end he was grateful the man had been there when Jude needed him.

L<small>IRA</small> <small>SAT</small> on the pallet, the boy's head in her lap and Fin's curled wings pressed against her legs. He sat on the ground in front of her, staring at the locked door. "They won't leave us be forever." Lira's voice trembled. She tried to feign nonchalance while stretching tired arms over her head to ease the aching muscles. She needed sunlight to live. Staying in this darkness would steadily weaken her, although she could tap into Earth magic and it would sustain her for a time.

"No, they won't. I can only assume our treatment may be similar to the boy's—if not more so, as the boy appears to be human. I can't for the life of me guess as to why they'd treat one of their own like this. What could a human boy possibly do to deserve this kind of punishment?" Fin placed a hand on the boy's thigh. He radiated heat, the efforts of his body struggling to heal itself.

"What do they want?" Lira asked as she carded her fingers absently through the boy's short, curly black hair.

"I can only guess they want info about the Maker." Fin kept his answer vague in case someone was listening, but he knew Lira would know he meant Jude.

"I'm growing weaker. It's been two days. If they don't let me have some light soon, I'm going to pass out from exhaustion," Lira reluctantly admitted.

"I don't know how long I'll make it if we get separated. I'll try to hide…."

"You're fae. Maybe we can use that. I'm sure they've never seen your kind. You know the legends—use them."

"Yes, but Lira, I can't do the things in the legends." Fin frowned, not really sure what she wanted him to do.

"Of course not. With the gateway to the courts closed, most of your power's been cut off. They only know what you tell them." Lira's smile was grim. It was a long shot playing the part of a one of the Fair Folk, but he did have the wings for it, and if it helped deter their kidnappers from killing him or Lira, then maybe it was worth a try. A little smoke and mirrors to keep the enemy guessing couldn't hurt. The longer they were uncertain, the better chance their friends had of finding and rescuing them from the windowless basement they were being held in.

"Fae… it's worth a go. Seelie or Unseelie, would you suppose?" Fin fingered his white and red hair.

"Oh, Seelie, of course. Unseelie are supposed to be the dark fae and, my love, for all your fire, you're not a dark fae." Lira chuckled and tweaked one of Fin's pointed ears.

"Good to know." Fin grasped her hand and squeezed it gently. "I'm going to take a nap."

"Okay." Lira watched as Fin draped his arms around his legs and turned to white marble.

In the darkness of their cell, unless someone looked closely, he could pass for being asleep. The only problem was, if their jailors entered and tried to rouse him, they'd discover his stone gargoyle form. It was a chance, but if he took naps of five to fifteen minutes, he'd be able to hold off a full regenerative sleep for a couple of days. But like Lira, eventually he'd be discovered—it was only a matter of time.

IT WAS early evening when Nico and Jude made their way to the top of the Empire State Building. It was one of the few office buildings still in use. The ancient skyscraper stood as a beacon, proof of what human ingenuity could create. Many of the old towers had fallen to ruin and only the lower levels were safe to use. With human population levels one-third of what once filled the Earth, and most of that now scattered across the globe, New York's population was a mere fraction of its former millions. People tended not to congregate in the large numbers they once had in the glory days of the human populace.

The pair stepped off the elevator onto the viewing level at the top and approached the railing to watch the last of the daylight disappear as true night enveloped the city. Some electric street lights at the core glowed brightly in the darkness. The rest of the lights came from the scattered residences.

Gabe walked out into the night with Doc on his heels; they stood on either side of Jude and Nico.

Jude looked around. Seeing they were alone, he let two short bursts of flame up into the dark night.

The sound of wind preceded Adel's landing, with Evan in his arms. He was followed by four large gargoyles, all of whom were smaller than Adel but powerful, if less human in appearance than he. Adel set Evan down in front of him, eyeing Nico carefully, as well as Doc and Gabe.

"Jude!" Evan grinned, pushed out of Adel's wings, and moved toward them as Jude stepped out of Nico's arms to meet him and hug him close. "It's so good to see you. I've missed you, and you don't stay in touch like you should."

"Oh God, Evan. I've missed you and Adel so much. Things are so messed up." Jude rested his head on Evan's shoulder.

"Introduce us around. There's a rather large man whose hands are catching fire and who's glaring daggers at me," Evan whispered into Jude's ear.

Jude pushed back and grinned up at Evan. "That would be my mate, Nicholas Daemarkus."

"Really! Wow, you found your mate! We have *so* got to catch up."

Jude moved from Evan's arms to give a brief hug to Adel. "Hey, big guy! Still keeping my friend safe? I see you brought a few friends along."

"The city is not a safe place to be. These are a couple of warriors from Notre Dame. Upon awakening, they pledged their service to the Maker." Adel patted Jude's shoulder. "Where are Fin and Skye?"

Evan walked with Jude along the catwalk overlooking the city, pulling the two groups closer together as they followed in their wake.

"That's part of the mess we're in. Skye's been gone for two days now. We thought at first he was hunting, but he seems to have disappeared. Fin and Lira, his mate, were kidnapped." Jude stepped back to Nico's side, feeling Nico's arm snake around his waist and pull him up against him. "Nico, this is Evan and Adel. Guys, this is Nico, my mate, his brother, Doc, and Gabe Windslow, our friend."

"Nice to meet you. I'm so glad Jude found someone to look after him." Adel grinned, extending his hand as he pulled Evan against his side.

"Likewise. It's good you could come. I fear we're in over our heads here. We'll need all the help we can get." Nico shook Adel's hand and gave a tight smile to them both. "Let's get home and we can fill you in."

Adel's wings disappeared and his appearance became decidedly human as he took Evan's hand. "I'll call when we arrive, and you can take up point on the rooftops," Adel said to the four gargoyles standing back in the shadows.

"Our building is to the north of here, about twenty-five blocks." Nico hesitated, looking at the gargoyles. "Gabe?"

"I'll lead them." Gabe stepped into the shadows, shedding his clothing. With the sound of wind through dry leaves, a large white gryphon emerged from the darkness.

"Wow! I've never seen a shape-shifter before, much less a gryphon. He's magnificent." Evan beamed as Gabe stepped up to the four winged gargoyles, and with a cry that sounded like that of an eagle on the hunt, he launched himself from the rooftop, followed by the four.

Adel growled, wrapping his arms around Evan possessively.

"Damn, he's going to beat us back home." Nico rolled his eyes, leading them to the elevator that would take them to the parking garage and his car.

Chapter 13

EVERYONE SETTLED into Nico's living room as Jude explained the kidnapping and their suspicions to Evan and Adel. The gargoyle guards concealed themselves on the nearby rooftops, keeping watch through the heart of the night.

"I never imagined there could be more than one. We search for the Maker all our lives. Our duty to protect him is one of our primary bonds in life. If I'd known, I never would've allowed you to leave." Adel crossed the room and fell to his knees before Jude. "I'm so sorry I failed you."

"Adel, you didn't fail me. I have a job to do. How could you know what I am when I didn't even know? Fin had his suspicions, but he was very closemouthed about it. When it became obvious what I was becoming, we were inundated with demon attacks, I was injured, and Nico found me. Everything's been happening so fast." Jude put a hand on Adel's shoulder.

Adel looked up and nodded, his gaze locking with Jude's. "We won't fail you again, Maker." Adel returned to his spot on the sofa, and Evan snuggled against him.

"He's not your concern, gargoyle. I guard my mate." Nico pulled Jude tightly against him, gripping him in a viselike hold.

Jude rolled his eyes at the warning sparks Nico inadvertently shot like mini fireworks. "Can we please get past the pissing contest? We have friends to rescue."

Gabe stood next to the glass sliding doors, staring out into the night. "Has anyone seen Skye? I still haven't found him, and I'm really starting to worry."

"Do you think he followed Fin or maybe he's tracking him?" Jude looked to Adel. "Gabe followed the limo until it passed through a gateway. Could Skye have somehow gone through to the other side?"

"He's young. If he chased after the limo, he may have traveled through the portal without knowing he'd done so." Adel frowned, stood, and walked to the glass doors, staring out into the darkness. A cheeping trill came from around Adel's neck and a small dragon uncurled and ran down his arm to perch on his wrist, his tail wrapped around his arm. "Do you think you can find Skye?" Adel asked Cela.

The little dragon tipped his head and stared out into the night.

"How can he?" Jude watched intently as Cela crooned, weaving slightly on Adel's wrist.

"Cela has incredible tracking abilities. He's familiar with Skye, and he likes the little gryphon. If anyone can track him, Cela can," Evan reassured Jude, as they all watched Adel and Cela.

"Be careful and don't take any chances. If you find him and he can't come with you, come and get us." Adel opened the glass sliding door, and Cela launched himself into the darkness, disappearing almost immediately, swallowed by the night.

"Your enemy obviously knows where you're staying or they wouldn't have been able to stage the attack in the garage." Evan frowned in thought as Adel returned to his side.

"If someone has figured out that I'm a Jesuit Inquisitor, then I'm no good to the Pope. My job has been compromised." Jude sat forward, dropping his head into his hands, as he rested his elbows on his thighs.

"To be honest, I think your position as an Inquisitor was over anyway. You're an Elemental with a mate. It's not like you'll be able to keep your identity a secret. Your position within the paranormal community will be your main duty." Evan grinned. "At least we'll be doing it together."

"Yeah, you're probably right, but in the meantime, we need to get our friends back before I have to figure out what my role as the great Fire Elemental means." Jude looked up and met Evan's glance, rolling his eyes as he settled back against Nico's shoulder.

"Is there any way to track a portal that you're aware of?" Gabe walked across the room to lean against the fireplace mantel.

"Not after it's closed. For all we know, the gateway you saw could've led to the warehouse next to it, or to the other side of the world. However, the larger it is, the more power it takes to create." Adel rubbed the back of Evan's neck as he considered the possibilities. "Judging by your description, I don't think it would've gone any great distance. Maybe outside the city limits… twenty- to thirty-mile radius at most, I'd think, but not much farther."

"That's a lot of land to cover." Nico frowned.

"If Skye did go through, he may be disoriented and not sure how to get back, suddenly finding himself in a strange place. If Cela can find him and bring him back, we may be able to find the others and rescue them." Adel tipped his head to the side in thought. "We need to hurry. It's already been two days. Fin won't be able to hold off a full sleep cycle for much longer." Adel paced back to the glass sliding doors.

"How many men can we count on when we're ready to go, if Cela comes through for us and finds Skye and our people?" Nico looked to Gabe and Doc.

"There are a few in the forests who'll help, those who know Lira. Ten to fifteen come to mind. It will be morning soon. Some of our people will be about to sleep and others will soon be waking. I'll start making calls and putting people on alert." Gabe grabbed his phone and moved off to the kitchen.

"Cole has about another fifteen on the payroll as security. They're a mixed batch of humans with military backgrounds and paranormals, mostly wolf-shifters and a couple of large cat-shifters," Nico said. "He is usually an early riser and should be awakening soon. When he does, I'll have him make some calls."

"I don't think we can count on him to be recovered before we'll be making any sort of assault. His human body needs longer to heal." Doc leaned forward in his chair.

"Even without him specifically, if we can use his contacts, that'll help. Adel, can we count on you and your gargoyles?" Nico eyed the large man.

"Of course." Adel scowled, looking affronted. "Gargoyles serve the Maker. Jude is as much a Maker as Evan. Fin is also my friend. I do not wish to see him being held captive or killed."

"I might be able to raise a few more gargoyles here in the city. I doubt that there'll be any of the guards' size, but there may be some of the smaller ones who've gone unnoticed by the Church. If you can show me a place where I can meditate?" Evan stood, Adel coming to stand behind him.

"Sure, let me show you to my meditation room. Nico created it for me to help me get in touch with my inner fire spirit." Jude rose and headed down the hallway, with Evan and Adel following along.

IT WAS midmorning and the penthouse had gone silent since some had left and others had found different places to get some sleep. Evan and Adel retired to the meditation room for some much-needed rest. Doc took over the guest room previously occupied by Cole, who had gone to organize his security force. Jude retired with Nico to their room, leaving Gabe to stand watch with a few of the shifters. The gargoyle guards had scattered about the nearby rooftops, taking refuge where they could find it, keeping hidden from view as they slept.

Gabe gazed out over the city. Two small birds hovered in the distance, steadily coming closer. Periodically one would dip lower and the other would follow, until both would once again regain altitude and continue.

Can't be..., Gabe thought as he stared at the birds. Torn between shifting and leaping out to make sure his hunch was correct—that the "birds" were really the missing gargoyles—and running to wake Nico and Jude, he opted for the first: stripping, shifting, and launching himself from the deck. He closed the gap between them in minutes. He carefully scooped a rather bedraggled Skye out of the air and clutched him snugly between his chest and a paw. Cela seemed no worse for wear. He landed on Gabe's shoulders between his wings and wrapped his tail about Gabe's throat. It was an unnerving sensation even though the tail only reached part way around, but Cela seemed content to relax there, letting Gabe do the work of returning them to the balcony of the penthouse. If his flight appeared odd, the gargoyles on the rooftops didn't so much as budge when Gabe alighted on the terrace and shifted with Skye now safely in one hand and Cela about his neck.

The sun topped the horizon and both of the gargoyles turned to stone. "Won't be getting much from them today," he mumbled as he set Skye on the kitchen counter, but he could find no way to unwind Cela from his throat. "Guess I've got a new necklace until you decide to let go." Gabe dressed, poured himself a mug of coffee, and returned to his post at the balcony, knowing the others would be joining him before too much longer.

As he looked over the buildings, he noticed the absence of the other gargoyles—they must have taken refuge from the sun. It wasn't as if they couldn't stand the sun, but they'd be vulnerable to attack, having turned to stone as the first rays topped the horizon. He wondered where they'd disappeared to and hoped they'd chosen their refuge wisely.

Hearing movement, Gabe turned around.

A relieved yell came from the kitchen. "Gabe! Nico! Evan! Adel!" Jude hollered.

Gabe entered to see Jude petting Skye.

"Skye's back!" he yelled as pounding footsteps announced everyone rushing into the kitchen.

"Oh, thank God!" Nico reached out and brushed a hand over the gargoyle's stone form.

"Skye and this little one—" Gabe fingered Cela about his throat. "—approached just before dawn. They were exhausted. I met them and carried them the last bit. They turned to stone almost immediately. I figured I'd let everyone sleep, as there's nothing they can tell us until they awaken."

Evan walked over to Gabe. "Do you mind? I can remove him without hurting him for you."

"Please. It isn't that I don't like him there, but… I'm really not used to having anything about my neck like this. It's uncomfortable." Gabe chuckled nervously as Evan reached up and Cela became pliable beneath his fingers. With easy movements, Cela was uncurled from Gabe's throat and wound back around Adel's.

"He does take getting used to." Adel gave Gabe a knowing grin.

"Your guards have retreated. I'm assuming they must've gone somewhere to wait out the day." Gabe nodded toward the glass doors.

"Yes, they've probably retreated to a nearby abandoned building or to the sewers." Adel walked into the kitchen, took two mugs down from the cupboard, and poured two coffees, one for himself and the other for Evan.

"There's milk in the fridge and sugar on the table." Jude waved a hand.

Nico ran his hands up and down Jude's arms. "Why don't we go try get some more sleep? Then when we get up, you can do your meditation and tai chi. You'll be primed for this evening when we storm the castle and free our friends." Nico gave Jude's shoulders a reassuring squeeze.

"Okay." Jude relaxed back into Nico's chest.

"Help yourselves to whatever you need. We'll join you after we've had a bit more rest." Nico guided Jude down the hall and into their room.

Chapter 14

IT TOOK most of the day for them to contact everyone and get the group organized. The penthouse apartment had become a combination of Grand Central Station and a sort of gathering place for both the curious and their allies. A more eclectic group of people surely had never been assembled in one room at the same time. There were many different species: centaurs, trolls, gnomes, will-o-wisps, dryads, and a forest witch, as well as varying types of shape-shifters. There were even a few who Jude had to ask Nico what they were. The most striking of those was a kitsune, or fire-fox shifter, whose flaming red hair was almost as bright as his own but significantly different, having white-and-black stripes running through it as well.

Amongst these paranormal creatures were human men with military backgrounds. Dressed all in black, they were heavily armed with everything from automatic weaponry to knives, crossbows, and hand grenades. The idea being, if all else failed, blow it up.

Jude hoped it didn't come to that. He just wanted his friends back.

He stood by the glass sliding doors. Evan had joined him there, and they watched the chaos in the living room. Nico, Gabe, and Cole—who insisted he was fine, although Doc's frown claimed otherwise—planned and strategized, without knowing what they were actually getting into. They could assume resistance, more than likely demonic, but if they were fast enough and undetected, it would most likely be humans. The proper ceremony to raise a demon and have it not turn against the summoner takes time. In a surprise attack, they wouldn't have a lot of that at their disposal.

"I don't think it's going to get any better in here," Jude said as he turned to look at Evan.

"Nope. They're just spinning their wheels until Skye wakes up. I would've tried to wake them earlier, but they are both so young, they just don't have the endurance Fin and Adel have to stay awake for long periods of time." Evan glanced out of the window at the setting sun. "The other gargoyles will be awakening soon. I think it should be safe to wake Skye and Cela now." Evan pushed away from the wall and headed for the kitchen counter, where Skye remained unmoving.

Adel came in from the terrace, following Evan and Jude. Evan touched Cela first, and he awoke and stretched around Adel's neck, crooning as Evan scratched his neck ridges.

Silence fell over the group as Evan turned to Skye. "Wake, Skye." Evan placed his hands on each side of his body, which immediately turned from stone to feathers and fur. Skye shuddered and stretched, but appeared decidedly droopy, wingtips resting on the counter instead of held snugly against his body in his usual manner.

Jude brought out a plate of cold chicken wings from the refrigerator—they were Skye's favorites—and a bowl of water. Skye eyed the wings and cried mournfully. He looked to the plate and then to Jude. Wherever he had been, he'd obviously not hunted. "Go ahead. They're for you." Jude smiled, taking a seat at the counter on a stool, as Skye virtually attacked the chicken wings, making little grunting, happy sounds as the meat disappeared amongst the snapping of bones, purrs, and lapping water. When he was finished, he plopped down on Jude's lap and closed his eyes.

"Oh no, you don't." Evan ran his fingers over the feathered crest on Skye's head, and Skye looked up at him, cooing, tipping his head to the side.

Adel stood behind Evan and looked down. "He's tired and doesn't understand why you don't want him to sleep."

"Skye, do you know where Fin is?"

Skye turned and looked up at Jude. He trilled and fluttered his wings, sitting down on his haunches, cooing in a mournful tone.

"He says Fin is very tired and in a dark place. He wanted to help Fin, but he couldn't find us." Adel placed a hand on Evan's shoulder.

"We need to find them. Skye, can you take us to Fin?" Evan scratched behind one of Skye's feather-tufted ears while Skye crooned, closing his eyes and leaning into Evan's touch.

"He's tired but willing to try." Adel reached out and picked up the gargoyle. "I'll fly, carrying him. He can tell me where to go. You'll need to follow with our people, but stay far enough back that you aren't discovered. We don't know what we're going to find when we reach our destination."

"Adel's right. We need to go about this carefully. If they go ahead and we follow, Adel can tell us what he finds before we go in with guns blazing."

Hopefully we can surprise them and get our people back without too much trouble." Nico rested his hands on Jude's shoulders. "But rest assured, we *will* get them back."

ADEL HAD landed on a rooftop in the warehouse district. Although Gabe had scoped out the structures around the gateway, the warehouse district was vast and he hadn't checked them all. The portal truly hadn't gone far—the building Skye had guided Adel to sat farther back from the main thoroughfare, closer to the shipyard and the waterfront, away from any others currently being used. The building itself was in ill repair, but the number of cars parked in the parking lot belied its ramshackle appearance. They wanted it to appear unused, but obviously they didn't expect to be noticed in the middle of the night and had done nothing to conceal themselves.

"*Skye's brought me to a warehouse farther back from the main road,*" Adel told Evan through their mating bond, showing him the location in his mind. He also pointed out a place to meet. With this number of vehicles, they'd need to be ready for more than a few people in the warehouse, and they'd need all the help they could get to rescue their friends.

"*We're coming, Adel.*" Evan's mental touch set off a purr inside him like nothing else in this or any other world could.

Adel glided in through the hole in the roof of the warehouse next door to the one they planned to attack. Paranormals appeared inside in various ways: walking through the shadow realms, teleporting, and flying in, much as Adel himself. SUVs and cars poured through the open doors and unloaded humans dressed in black clothing. Adel held open his arms as Evan jumped from one of the vehicles and ran to him. Nico and Jude followed right behind, with Gabe, Doc, and Cole at their backs.

"Skye says there's a basement beneath the warehouse next door. Nothing's in the actual warehouse—everything's below ground. There are about ten cars parked in the lot next to the warehouse, so we're going to have company." Adel handed a weary Skye to Evan.

"Sleep now, Skye. You've shown us everything you can." Evan cradled the miniature gryphon as he cooed and visibly relaxed, then turned to stone.

"I'll put him in the SUV. He'll be safe there until we return." Gabe took the stone gryphon and carried him away.

"He has a real soft spot for Skye, doesn't he?" Evan watched Gabe snuggling Skye gently against his chest as he headed for the parked vehicles.

"I think Skye reminds him of his people." Doc shook his head slightly as he watched his friend. "A white gryphon is ostracized from the pride as a pariah because its coloration is not the normal golden or mix of gold, brown, or black. It's against their beliefs to kill one of their own, so they made Gabe's life miserable, harassing him until he left. I hardly know the whole story, but he's doomed to a solitary existence, and it wears on him. I'm guessing that even though that gargoyle isn't really a gryphon, Skye's close enough that he feels as though he could be part of his pride. A cub, maybe."

"Well, if Skye makes him feel better, then I'm all for them spending time together." Jude smiled up at Nico. "I know what it feels like being alone. I'm glad I'm not anymore."

"No, and you never will be again." Nico growled hard. "Let's go get our friends back."

HAVING DISCUSSED their plans at length in the penthouse, everyone had their instructions. They crept through the night and made their way into the warehouse. The building appeared to be completely empty—a stadium-sized, rundown shack of a place with a few lit light bulbs hanging on bare wires from the ceiling. Two guards paced the length of the building, appearing bored and unconcerned about possible intruders. They were dispatched before they could alert anyone or even knew that the gargoyle guards had fallen on them from above.

Evan paused with closed eyes, reaching out with his senses into the earth below them for a moment, before he pointed out the entrance to the lower levels. The trapdoor in the floor at the center of the warehouse was covered by a rather large mat. The door opened to a staircase, which allowed passage for two at a time, but the tunnel below the stairs reduced them to single file as they proceeded into the maze of corridors.

After dispatching the guards at the entrance of the first level, they found passages leading to hallways lined with five cells and another stairwell. Evan guessed the complex sank four stories into the ground. As they explored, they discovered each level seemed to contain a single type of paranormal, like a sick collection of beings kept by an insane collector who cared nothing for the well-being of his toys.

"We've got to get these people out of here!" Gabe snarled as he looked into a room on the first level and found two female shifters, a lion and a deer, obviously starving. It was as if the collector wanted to see if the starving lion would eat the deer. The sick man didn't consider shifters to be beings with souls who would no sooner commit cannibalism than any other.

"Gabe, you and Cole work to get these shifters back to the other warehouse." Jude caught each man's eye as he spoke softly. He hoped that by beginning a large-scale rescue, they wouldn't be leaving themselves shorthanded if a battle broke out. "Doc, help them and take a couple of the human men with you to prepare a triage there so we can save as many as possible."

Doc nodded and pointed at two of the humans, grabbed the keys from the downed guards, and handed them to the men, who unlocked the cells and got the injured moving.

The second level contained Earth creatures, gnomes, and trolls. Most were in good shape, if starved. They must have been too fierce for the collector to handle easily, because they hadn't been beaten like many of the shifters from above. One of the dryads and the forest witch hung back to release the captives and guide them to the surface.

The third level appeared to contain humans, all severely abused, possibly workers being punished or people who dared to oppose the madman and left to rot here like all the others.

As they sank deeper into the recesses toward the last level, they relied on Evan's feel of the Earth to guide them. Unerringly, he led them to what could only be described as the bowels of Hell. Paranormal beings were manacled to cement walls, many in conditions that barely sustained life. They were bloody and beaten into submission, though whether it was for information or sport was impossible to tell from what remained. Some were beyond help, already deceased, their bodies left to rot in the chains. Others needed immediate medical assistance.

Their rescue mission took on new meaning as being after being was released and moved to the building next door. They worked to help as many as possible. Some just escaped into the night, refusing any assistance, not trusting even their rescuers to help them past the door.

FINALLY, NICO called to Jude. "In here!" He melted the lock on the door and shoved it open. Lira sat on the dirty pallet, cradling a boy's head in her lap. She looked ashen, and the boy appeared emaciated, his dark skin caked with grime, dried blood and scabs.

Jude ran in and squatted down beside Nico, each of them taking one of Lira's hands.

"I've got him." Gabe practically growled as he scooped the boy off Lira's lap and disappeared out the door.

"Nico…. Jude?" Lira's eyes opened. Once viridian, they were practically clear and appeared almost sightless.

"We're here, Lira." Nico held her hand very gently.

"You have to find him. They took my Fin." Her voice sounded like dried leaves on the wind, a crackling whisper, and she appeared parched, withered.

"We will. Go with Cole. He'll get you out, and we'll go look for Fin." Jude gently kissed her cheek as Lira's eyes closed. Jude's fearful gaze met and held Nico's. They were running out of time. The dryad was close to death.

Nico picked her up and handed her to Cole, who frowned at her lack of weight—she should have weighed close to one hundred seventy pounds, but she felt closer to one hundred and ten. Nico took Jude's hand, and they headed out of the cell and down the corridor. Most of their force was now doing triage in the warehouse next door, but a few of the gargoyles, Adel, Evan, and a few humans still continued the search for Fin.

At the end of the corridor, they came up against a closed door. Through the barred window, they could see an enormous natural-rock cavern. The ceiling appeared to be three or more stories above and made of solid rock. Fin slumped in a chair in the center of a large circle. Spaced at equal distance from one another around the circle were five chanting priests dressed in red hooded robes, their arms outstretched toward Fin. A man Jude recognized immediately as Archbishop O'Flaggan paced impatiently about the outside of the circle. Abruptly he turned to another five figures who were off to the side.

The scent of blood permeated the room from the five priests in the corner. Hooded and cloaked in black robes, blood dripped from multiple wounds on their arms into chalices on individual altars. Periodically one or two would scream and slump forward, their bodies shaking, wracked with convulsions.

Jude shivered in horror. He was amazed that, while they remained prone over the altar, somehow not a drop of blood spilled.

"Now! Damn you all! Now!" the archbishop screamed at the bleeding priests.

Jude realized their error a moment too late. While he and his friends had been occupied taking out the few guards who'd opposed them and rescuing the prisoners, the archbishop was already aware of them and had used the time to have his priests perform the blood ceremony—the one designed to draw demons into service.

"Fuck!" Nico gasped as a horde of demons coalesced from billows of black smoke—from the smallest of gremlins, no bigger than a lapdog, to some that stood taller than Adel—all with black razor-sharp claws and teeth, black eyes, and horns. Some had multiple pairs of arms, rows of spikes running down their backs, and tails. They came on two, four, and six legs. Some looked mammalian, some reptilian, others appeared insect-like; all were ugly and repulsive. They gnashed their teeth and yanked at the chains that bound them to the floor, preventing them from escaping until the spells were complete, thus binding them to their tasks.

Together, Nico and Jude threw out their arms, and fire shot from their hands into the door, incinerating it to ash as they charged into the chamber.

"Ah, Jude. I can call you Jude, Jesuit Inquisitor, can I not? I believe we're beyond mere introductions here." Archbishop O'Flaggan sneered as he moved to stand by the five priests who encircled Fin. Looking over Jude's group, he eyed Evan and Adel specifically. "And you brought your friends, the Earth Elemental and the gargoyle. How convenient. Now you can all die together."

"You're finished, O'Flaggan. Demons, torture, imprisonment of humans and paranormals… the whole ball of wax. His Holiness will have you excommunicated from the Church, and the Inquisition will execute you on the spot, without benefit of a trial." Jude's entire body burned with the flames of his anger. Some places burned hotter than others, scorching his clothing.

"The Pope? Seriously? *That's* your comeback? Surely you realize by now that this Pope you revere so much will soon be dead." O'Flaggan's laughter rang around them, shrill with his madness, echoing in the cavernous heights above.

"What are you talking about? His Holiness is in fine health in Rome. You can't reach him from here, even with your black arts," Evan snarled at the archbishop.

"The little mason speaks. I wondered if I'd have the pleasure of meeting you before you were killed, and so I have. You're shorter than I imagined."

O'Flaggan locked eyes with Evan, then turned to the priest beside him and placed a hand on his shoulder. "You know, Evan, I really should thank you. I had no idea the fae remained in this world. Their powers are legendary, although this Fin appears to be a lesser fae, being a mere Seelie sprite. Without you having been born and your power of Earth returned to this world, I probably wouldn't have found this rare specimen."

"What are you talking about?" Evan stared at Fin. He looked exhausted, and it seemed as though he were trying to speak, but he couldn't get air into his lungs. He shifted every few minutes from flesh and blood to stone, then back again, his nature as a gargoyle laid bare.

"Come now, little Earth Elemental. If you hadn't opened the gates to Earth magic, I'm sure Fin would've been crushed as a gargoyle when he was found. But he shifts during the day. He can be flesh and blood or stone, day or night, a power I'm sure you can only wish your gargoyles had. No, I will greatly enjoy delving into his power and uncovering all his secrets before I kill him for being the abomination against God that he is." O'Flaggan ranted even as Gabe, Cole, and a number of others crept into the room, spreading themselves out and taking up defensive stances for the battle to come.

The snarling and growling of demons steadily increased as more of the priests collapsed on their altars, their lifeblood having been poured out to create the evil that stood between Jude and Fin.

Jude could hardly believe what the archbishop was going on about. Surely he knew Fin wasn't really fae? If he didn't, it certainly wasn't in their best interests to enlighten him. "You'll never get away with this, O'Flaggan. You have to realize the Pope is untouchable. You'll never get close enough to hurt him," Jude yelled over the increasing din of the demons.

"Little fool! I don't have to." O'Flaggan laughed. "We're taking our leave now. Have fun playing with my demons. May we never meet again, Inquisitor."

Jude blinked as, one by one, the priests encircling Fin faded before his eyes. "No! No! Stop! Fin!" Jude yelled, running toward him as the chains holding the demons disappeared and they attacked en masse.

The earth around them trembled; roots from trees far above broke through the walls and swiped at the attacking demons. Evan's power was evident, as the gargoyles who'd followed them below rushed to their defense.

Gabe shifted and he struck with claws and beak, ripping into anything that got in the way, trying to help clear a path to reach Fin. Cole stood slightly behind him, raining bullets into the horde from his automatic weapons. Explosions rocked the cavern from the grenades tossed into the midst of the demons.

Nico sent blast after blast of fire into the horde. His wings, having sprouted from his back, glowed white-hot as he ripped into the demons, trying to get to the priests before they disappeared entirely.

Jude stood at his side, matching Nico's powerful blasts with his own until he fell to his knees, screaming. His arms shot up and out as flames scorched the ceiling of the cavern.

Nico, battle forgotten, fell behind Jude, wrapping his arms around his mate, knowing the time had come. It was now or never—Jude had to accept his fire spirit or they'd both die. "Let go, Jude. Let him come to you. You need each other. He wants to help Fin too. Let him," Nico whispered in his ear, not really sure he was being heard as Jude's body trembled in his grasp and burned so hot, Nico feared he'd be singed by the power of Jude's fire.

A screech unlike any bird he'd ever heard sounded above. Nico looked up to see an enormous phoenix, adorned in flaming feathers of red and gold, with a hint of green and blue. The bird roared with a voice like a raging forest fire and dive-bombed the demons, setting them aflame with a touch of talon, wing, or fiery breath.

"That's good, my love, but you need to get the priest," Nico whispered into Jude's ear.

The phoenix turned toward the gaping O'Flaggan; fear covered his face as he stared at the flaming bird. The phoenix dived for the priest. O'Flaggan screamed and ducked and shimmered from existence, disappearing from the room along with the last of the five priests.

Evan ran through the middle of the burning demons to Fin, but just as he reached for the bound sprite, he, too, disappeared from the room.

"No!" Jude screamed, his anguish echoed by the roar of the phoenix hovering overhead.

The heat, flames, and smoke from the burning flesh of dead demons was beginning to thicken and fill the cavern, making it rapidly unfit for anyone to remain and still live. Gabe shifted back to his human form, grabbed a bleeding Cole, and dragged him from the room, followed by the gargoyles, Evan and Adel, and the rest of the team. They'd lost. Fin was gone. Now they needed to escape with their own lives before Jude's flames choked the life from friend as well as foe.

"Jude, *mein Feuer*, you need to come back to me now," Nico coaxed, holding him against his chest, feeling the sizzle of flames too hot for even him to withstand burning against his skin, his shirt long gone to ash. "Please, baby, your phoenix is beautiful and you both deserve to live. Call him back to you so we can go home. We found them once, we will do it again, but you need to live so we can rescue Fin together. They can't have teleported far."

Jude screamed again. Tears of flame dripped from his face like molten lava as he sobbed out his failure. He'd caught Fin's determined eyes just as he'd faded from the room. The pain from the torture was getting to him, and there was nothing he could do. They'd let O'Flaggan go on his rant, and they hadn't found a way to get through his defenses to rescue Fin.

The phoenix landed in front of Jude. He stood over seven feet tall, and his song went from one of screaming rage to the grief-stricken pain of a mourning dove. The flames around the phoenix were all but gone, leaving a beautifully feathered bird. He tucked his feet under himself and wrapped his wings around both Jude and Nico, singing Jude's sadness and loss, then tucked his head under one wing and, with a last burst of flames, disappeared as Jude slumped into Nico's arms.

"Jude! No! You can't leave me!" Nico scooped Jude up in his arms and ran from the cavern, back through the prison, and up into the warehouse. "Doc! Help!" Nico ran through the prisoners and his friends who'd been injured during the battle.

Doc ran up to him. He guided Nico to a gurney and persuaded him to lay Jude down. Doc checked for vitals—Nico practically snarled at his inactivity as Doc pressed a stethoscope to Jude's chest—then looked into Jude's eyes. "He's just unconscious, Nico. He overextended himself. Give him time. He should be fine."

Nico slumped over Jude's chest. He was only unconscious… not dead. Just sleeping. Sleeping was good.

Chapter 15

NICO PACED from the fireplace to the windows, glared out the window, then stalked back to the fireplace once again. He couldn't settle down. Doc had assured him Jude was recovering from the energy loss he'd sustained when producing his fire spirit, but Nico wouldn't feel better until Jude awoke and was able to look him in the eye. They'd returned to the penthouse. The injured and beaten had been spread amongst their people, while Doc kept those most in need of medical assistance at his clinic in the building he maintained as his house.

At Doc's direction, Nico had brought Jude home, bathed him, and put him to bed, waiting for him to recover consciousness. He'd thought for sure Jude would awaken in the bath, but he'd barely stirred as Nico washed his body and shampooed the soot and smoke from his hair before settling him—clean and dried—into bed.

Nico remained restless. Dressed in sleep pants, he walked the floor, watching Jude sleep, lost in his own thoughts. He still could hardly believe the phoenix Jude had become. The amount of power Jude had unleashed was unbelievable, and the fire so hot, he'd felt a bit scorched himself. They'd survived it, though, and if Jude would just open his eyes, everything would be right…. *Regrettably, Fin is still missing. It won't be right until he comes home.*

Nico wandered back to the windows, staring out into the dawn. Fin was out there—a prisoner to a madman. But at least it seemed they had some time. The archbishop thought Fin was one of the mythical fae. As long as Fin could keep up the pretense, he'd give them some time to find him.

"Stop pacing already. You're giving me a headache," Jude complained from the bed.

Nico rushed to his side and stared down into Jude's emerald eyes. There was a red ring about the pupil that hadn't been there before, hinting at the flames controlled within. "How are you feeling, *mein Feuer*?" Nico asked as he brushed long strands of Jude's hair back from his face.

"Tired… thirsty."

Nico grabbed a glass of water from the nightstand and held it for Jude to drink through the straw. "You were so wonderful. I couldn't believe how beautiful your phoenix fire spirit is. That he's part of you…. The entire bird is so gorgeous, as red as your hair, but the wings have golden highlights and sometimes a cast of blue. He was all aflame, from beak to tail feathers. I've never seen anything like it in all my years."

"But it wasn't enough. Archbishop O'Flaggan knows who and what I am. He got away. Fin's gone, and we don't know where they took him." Jude sagged into the pillows, frustration and loss warring in his eyes. "The one thing—the most important thing—we were there to do was to get Fin and Lira back. I couldn't even get that right."

"Don't you dare take this all on yourself! Evan and Adel were there. I was there. Gabe and Cole were there. The other gargoyles and paranormals were all there. We all failed Fin, not just you." Nico climbed onto the bed and scooted under the covers. He pulled Jude's nude body against him. "At least we freed all those prisoners and we got Lira out."

"I don't know what to do now. How do we…? Where do we even begin to look?" Jude pressed his face against Nico's shoulder, wrapping his arms around his waist, clutching at Nico like his very existence depended on it.

"Since our secrets are out, you need to touch base with the Pope, let him know that O'Flaggan is one of the archbishops working against him, and tell him about your status as an Elemental. Then we all start hitting up each of our contacts and see if we can pull together any leads about where O'Flaggan might be hiding Fin." Nico massaged slow circles across Jude's back.

"Do you think we'll find him?" Jude asked, so softly Nico almost missed the question.

"I don't know, but he's alive. As long as we know he's alive, we keep looking." Nico carded his fingers through Jude's long red hair.

"How do we know he's still alive? Do we just hope…?"

"Yes. But we also trust in Lira. If Fin were dead, his mate would know. Just like if I were gone, you'd know. If Fin leaves this world for the next, Lira will mourn and probably follow him." Nico nuzzled his chin against the top of Jude's head.

"I've had enough death and demons. I don't want to think about it anymore." Jude clutched at Nico's arms, kissing his chest. "Make me forget… please, Nico."

With a finger under his chin, Nico tipped Jude's head back and kissed first his right eye, then his left. He paused before softly brushing his lips against Jude's in a caress of tenderness. He nibbled on Jude's bottom lip while his hands flowed along Jude's shoulders, across, and down along his arms, drawing them up over his head. With a sharp yank, Nico pulled the silk cord holding back the heavy brocade drapes on the canopy and used it to tie Jude's wrists to the wrought-iron bars of the headboard. The cord would never hold Jude if he didn't allow it to—the silken strands would be burned through in seconds. It was more distraction than anything, and Jude wanted it... needed it.

Nico sat up on the bed, leaned on his elbow over Jude, breaking their kiss, and glanced around the room. He grinned at Jude, then jumped from the bed to his dresser, where he pulled out a silk scarf. He returned and tied the scarf about Jude's head, covering his eyes. He loved to watch Jude's eyes—they spoke volumes to him—but this wasn't about what Nico wanted. This was about Jude's need. Nico leaned forward and kissed Jude's lips. "Be right back, lover. Don't go anywhere," Nico whispered. He stood and hurried from the room.

"Where would I go?" Jude chuckled.

Nico returned and pulled the covers down off the bed, revealing Jude in all his glory. His pale white skin appeared even more so against the dark blue bedding, his shining red hair fanned out over the pillows. The black silk scarf covering his eyes and the gold of the cord restraining him added up to Jude being a wet dream, about to become a bit wetter.

Nico put the bowl on the bed and pulled the lube from the drawer, then sat on the edge of the mattress and ran his hands over Jude's body. "You're so beautiful," Nico mumbled.

"I'm a too-pale, redheaded, freckled, skinny, short twink, Nico." Jude laughed, then gasped as Nico took an ice chip from the bowl and touched it to Jude's nose and lips.

He let the ice slide wetly down over Jude's chin, along his neck, and over his bobbing Adam's apple, and left the melting chip in the hollow of his collarbone at the base of his neck. "You have the most glorious hair. It almost appears alive in the sunlight. It shines and moves like a river of molten lava. It's aflame even when you aren't."

"Nico...." Jude gasped as Nico took another ice chip from the bowl.

Starting at Jude's wrist, he slid it down toward his elbow, following the path of the black flames etched into his skin. "Your skin is so soft, it slides under my fingertips. I'm constantly fighting with myself to keep my hands to myself." Nico drew the ice up to Jude's armpit. He watched as Jude trembled under his touch. Goose bumps rose along his skin—not from the cold, but from the anticipation of what would come next. Nico's lips caressed the tender, slightly furred skin of Jude's armpit, inhaling deeply of the essence of his scent, letting it wash over him, entrance him. He followed the ice with his hot breath and tongue, lapping at the cool water on the dimpled skin as the chip changed into droplets.

"I love you," Jude whispered as Nico reached for another chip, moved up onto the bed, and positioned himself between Jude's open thighs.

"I love you too." Nico latched on to a nipple and teased it, causing it to harden with teeth and tongue. He bathed its partner with a circling ice chip. Jude's skin pebbled to gooseflesh, drawing a moan from Jude as the ice melted and cool water ran down the side of his chest, while other droplets ran down along his sternum.

Jude began to pant and steam started to rise from his body where the water from the melting ice had accumulated.

Nico smiled as he picked up another ice chip and, using it like a pen, outlined all the muscles starting at the top of Jude's chest and moving down his abs, as Jude hissed and sucked in his stomach muscles. The chips melted quickly as Jude's desire heated up. Little flames of passion danced along his skin, warming where the ice touched. Nico picked up another chip. Starting at the base of Jude's groin, he ran it in teasing, cool, wet circles up the length of Jude's upstanding cock.

"Nico…. Ah! Ni—" Jude's head thrashed and his hips squirmed, but Nico just leaned in and locked Jude's hips to the bed as he continued the path of circles. Jude froze, giving a full-body shiver as the ice touched the glans at the head of his throbbing erection.

Nico kept the ice moving slowly under the glans. Steam rose from the contact as the small chip melted, and some of the water dripped slowly down the length of Jude's cock. Nico ran the chip around and up the slit, slipping the tiny wet chip between the spastically trembling lips. The chip slid in, and Jude's cock was engulfed in the comparably heated fires of Nico's mouth.

Jude screamed and arched his back up off the bed as Nico ever so slowly lowered his mouth, taking in more and more of Jude's length until his nose was buried in the russet curls covering Jude's groin. "God, Nico… can't last…. Oh fuck!" Jude gasped as Nico took a tight hold on Jude's balls and squeezed, pulling on them as his throat swallowed around Jude's cockhead. Jude screamed again, pulling on the ropes that tied him to the bed, trying to gain a bit of leverage so he could thrust farther into Nico's mouth. Jude shrieked, his body shivering violently as a large ice chip circled his quivering hole.

A hiss like water hitting a hot pan could be heard as Nico eased the ice past the guard muscle and into Jude, along with a finger. Water ran around his digit as the ice melted inside Jude's body. Nico stretched the puckered muscle, as he bobbed up and down, sucking Jude's cock, working his finger in and out of Jude's ass.

"Nico!" Jude squealed in warning.

"Come," Nico ordered as he sank back down Jude's shaft.

Jude wailed, losing complete control as ribbons of spunk shot down Nico's throat.

Nico rolled Jude's balls, sucking and swallowing every drop, until Jude lay completely boneless, grinning as waves of bliss washed over him. Nico added a second finger, then a third, as he lapped at Jude's semi-rigid erection, scissoring his fingers, making quick work of stretching his lover.

"Nico… oh God. More…," Jude begged as he pulled on the cord that held his hands.

"I've got you. I know what you need." Nico pulled out his fingers and reached for the lube. He sat back on his heels, then scooted up between Jude's thighs. Slick gel in hand, he popped the top, squeezed out a good amount, and covered his dick before dropping the bottle over the side of the bed.

"Please, Nico."

Positioning Jude's legs over his shoulders, Nico rubbed the head of his cock against Jude's pulsing, dripping hole. "Is this what you need, love?" Nico teased, pressing his cockhead against Jude's ass until he felt resistance, then pulling back, only to press forward again but never quite push through.

"Yesss," Jude hissed, his thighs twitching, flexing as if trying to get leverage to pull Nico toward him.

Nico growled, his control waning in response to Jude's desires. Nico pressed farther, until Jude opened for him. His cockhead passed the ring of muscles, settling just inside. Nico rolled Jude forward until he was practically folded in half, his knees resting on Nico's elbows, just under Jude's armpits. Slowly, Nico sheathed himself in Jude's body. He dropped his head and captured Jude's mouth, devouring it in a kiss. He groaned as he felt his balls kiss Jude's ass. The walls rhythmically massaged his length as Jude's body became accustomed to his invasion.

"So tight. You hold me so tight and hot…," Nico ground out as he swayed his hips from side to side. "Even after ice, your body heats up to hold me. You make me burn with need." Nico pulled the blindfold off so he could look into Jude's eyes, and yanked the cord holding his arms. Jude's hands wrapped round his neck, clutching as if for dear life. Nico drew back and pounded into Jude. Reaching between them with one hand, Nico wrapped his hand around Jude's hardened length and stroked him in counterpoint to his thrusts.

His control was lost as Jude's fingernails clawed at his shoulder and the impassioned purple flames of their mating fire lit up around their bodies. Nico jackhammered into Jude's passage, both of them beyond words, letting their bodies do the talking. There was no thinking or careful seduction, only the power and grind of sweat-covered flesh slapping against flesh. The moans and groans of men finding their ecstasy in the rhythmic dance proclaimed mutual want, desire, need, passion, but most of all, love.

Jude screamed out his passion first, filling Nico's hand with his spunk and clamping down on his cock with a viselike grip.

Nico groaned out Jude's name, coating his rectum with his semen. The aftershocks milked Nico of every drop as Jude's legs slid off his shoulders and dropped to the bed at his side. Rubbing circles on Jude's chest, Nico massaged his spunk into Jude's skin like lotion. It'd be nasty in the morning, but for now he didn't care. He eased his spent cock from Jude's body, causing both of them to moan as he dropped to the bed beside Jude, before he pulled him against his chest. Reaching down he grabbed a fistful of the covers and drew them up and over their sweat-drenched bodies as they drifted to sleep.

JUDE WOKE to cool but empty sheets. Nico must've awoken earlier. The tender burn in his ass reminded him how much he was loved. Smiling to himself, he pulled back the covers and headed for the bathroom. He hated waking up alone, but with guests in the house, it was inevitable that Nico would be up to see to them.

Once showered and dressed, Jude joined his friends in the living room. They were a rather solemn group, everyone missing the one person who'd been taken from them.

"I can't do this." Jude looked at everyone sitting around.

"Jude. How are you feeling, love?" Nico stood at the sound of his voice and wrapped his arms around him.

"I can't do this. I refuse. You all look like you've already given up. What's wrong with you people? Fin would never give up on you like this," Jude raged. His friends were all just sitting there, but Fin was out there, alive, waiting for them to find him, and yeah, he'd had his hopeless moment last night, but he was determined to find Fin. He wouldn't give up.

"What do you want us to do?" Evan frowned, looking at Jude. "Tell me what to do. I just don't know where to begin to look."

"Well, they teleported out of that warehouse. I'd assume the same rules apply, that they couldn't have gone far, right?" Jude asked, looking to Nico and Adel for confirmation.

"Yes. They pulled six priests and Fin from the room. That's not a small feat. They couldn't have left the city. But that was hours ago. They could be halfway across the country by now." Nico squeezed Jude's shoulders.

"Let's not jump to conclusions. The archbishop in charge was Father O'Flaggan. He controls the Eastern diocese under Cardinal Swift, who represents the Church of America in Rome." Jude led Nico back to his chair and sat him down. He then took up a position on the armrest, with Nico's hands on his hips.

"At least we know who the man is." Adel growled and nuzzled into Evan's neck, holding him snug against his chest on the sofa.

"Was he in charge of Father Michael? Could this interest in paranormals be linked?" Evan asked.

"Maybe… I'm not sure." Jude shook his head. "Father Michael was under a different archbishop, Kennedy. He controls the Western diocese. I don't see a direct correlation between Father Michael and Archbishop O'Flaggan yet. It may have been just the interest in paranormal beings that drew them together, or this could be a whole lot bigger than we've uncovered so far." Jude ran a hand through his hair in frustration, as Nico pulled him back down onto his lap and tucked him against his chest under his chin.

"Let's not go looking for conspiracies just yet. If this O'Flaggan is head of the Eastern diocese, then it would be safe to assume that his powerbase is here. It wouldn't make sense for him to move Fin outside his own sphere of influence. He'd want to keep him close, under his control, where nobody could take Fin from him." Gabe looked around at the others, nodding at his own logic, as he squeezed Lira's hand in support. She was still looking pale, but seemed to be getting stronger the longer she sat in the morning sun.

"Yes, logically, that makes the most sense." Adel nodded.

"Can you sense him?" Jude asked Evan, hoping he'd have a tangible link to Fin.

Evan closed his eyes, a small frown forming between his eyebrows. "All I can tell you is he's alive and I think he's currently asleep. But I can't tell you where. It's not like with Adel. I can tell you where he is at all times, but not the others." Evan sighed in frustration.

"You aren't mated to Fin. That's why you can't pinpoint him specifically. It's amazing that you have as much of a read on him as you do," Adel soothed Evan.

"Can you sense him, Lira?"

"Yes, but he is getting weaker and he doesn't know where he is." Lira slumped a bit in her seat, leaning against Gabe for support.

"Okay, so we know Fin's alive and more than likely in the area. If he's been moved, it won't have been far and probably not out of the Eastern diocese." Nico shrugged. "Not much to go on, but it's a start."

"I'll contact the Pope and let him know what we've learned. He won't be able to use me as a Jesuit Inquisitor anymore. My identity's known. He'll also have to pull in some of the agents who have worked with me in the past, to keep suspicion from them." Jude growled. "It's just so damn frustrating. I feel like my cover was blown for nothing and I still lost Fin."

"Not for nothing." Evan smiled sadly. "We saved a lot of people yesterday. Some who wouldn't have lived through another day but will now that we were able to rescue them."

"We couldn't save Fin. O'Flaggan wanted him too badly. He believes he's fae." Lira's voice sounded dry and brittle with exhaustion.

"Who knows how he'll interpret that? Maybe he expects Fin to have a pot of gold hidden under a rainbow somewhere, I don't know. The man's crazy. But that crazy buys us time to find him," Gabe said as he wrapped his arm around Lira and hugged her close, comforting her as tears fell from her eyes.

"He wouldn't want you to blame yourself. He was so happy when the two of you made up. The last thing he'd want is for you to feel you failed him. He'd be happy that you were safe and O'Flaggan didn't capture you as well," Lira whispered. "He'd be proud to give his life to save yours."

"I know. He's my guardian, and he takes his job seriously. He's also my friend, and I want him back." Jude stood and walked to the glass sliding doors and out into the cool morning air. He stood against the railing, looking out over the city. He took a couple of deep breaths, settling his nerves, clearing his mind. He could feel him now—the phoenix. He wasn't sure if the familiarity he felt with the bird was because of his recent bonding, or if he just felt more confident in himself. He'd controlled the phoenix. The fire spirit hadn't consumed him or harmed him in any way. Together they were very strong, and although he really couldn't say he saw the phoenix—because he *was* the phoenix—he still knew it was a beautiful and deadly powerful creature. He also knew the phoenix saw Fin as belonging to him, as well as all of their friends in the other room. They all belonged to him; they were part of his family, his flock. He protected what was his. Those who stole from him would burn.

Arms enveloped him, drawing him back against a warm familiar chest. "You're out here alone and on fire, my love." Nico nuzzled against the top of Jude's head, drawing the flames from his lover into himself, helping Jude to regain his dwindling control as the phoenix struggled, wanting to hunt and seek his revenge.

"Your wings were beautiful." Jude leaned back into Nico's embrace.

"Thank you. So were yours." Nico grinned and kissed his lover's temple.

There was time. They'd find O'Flaggan and get Fin back. They'd make the man pay, he promised his phoenix.

Epilogue

SAMMY AWOKE slowly. He hurt…. That was nothing new, but it wasn't the usual pain. This was a burning… but soothing… pain. Someone was applying something to his back. He was lying on… on a bed? Oh no. This was wrong. He'd never… not since he'd been taken in by Father O'Flaggan… been allowed on a bed.

"Easy, little one. Nobody will hurt you." The deep, gentle voice spoke so softly. A man sat on the mattress beside him. He was the one applying something to Sammy's back. The pain numbed as he worked, which wasn't right. Without the pain, the sins wouldn't be absolved, and he'd just have to be beaten again. "You're with friends now. O'Flaggan will never hurt you again." The voice continued as the man worked lower on Sammy's back, gently rubbing in small circles. It eased the burning sensation, pain, and tightness, taking the sting out of the inflamed tissues that'd become infected. "I'll never let him get anywhere near you."

The voice held such conviction, such strength, that Sammy wanted to believe. He wanted to wrap himself up in that strong voice and never let go. But it was not to be. The life of a Sin Eater was toil and pain; it was necessary in order to redeem himself for past-life deeds. His soul needed redemption. Archbishop O'Flaggan had told him that's why he was born malformed, born with webbed hands and feet. He was a freak and his soul was soiled beyond God's forgiveness. So he had to sacrifice himself by willingly taking on the sins of others—through beatings, starvation, and any other vile humiliation piled upon him—so he might be made clean enough to go to Heaven when he died. To survive this life was his only hope of a better afterlife.

Kind hands laid a bandage over his back and then brought the warmth of a sheet and blankets up over his body. "Can you speak?" the voice asked gently, fingers carding through his hair. "What's your name?"

"Samuel Newton." Sammy's voice croaked as if he hadn't spoken in days, which he might not have.

"My name is Gabriel Windslow. But most just call me Gabe. You're at my friend Doc's home, along with a few others who we rescued from

O'Flaggan's dungeon." Gabe continued to stroke Sammy's hair; it was so soothing. Sammy whimpered softly as Gabe shifted on the edge of the mattress.

"How is he doing?" Lira asked from the door.

"He's healing, slowly. Which Doc says is to be expected for a human," Gabe grumbled.

"He's a strong man for having survived that beating. And it looks like he's suffered many more than just that one," Lira stated before she turned to look down the hallway. "I'll leave you to him, then."

Sammy whimpered as Lira left. He was glad the pale lady was better. He didn't see Lira, but that last night together in the cell, she'd gotten so quiet. It was good to hear her voice sounding so strong.

"Sleep, Samuel. You're not alone anymore. I'll be here when you wake." Gabe stood and moved off the mattress to sit in a chair close by.

Sammy couldn't see Gabe from where he lay, but he could see just a bit of his jean-clad leg from the corner of his eye. He sighed, hoping beyond hope that perhaps God had seen the sacrifices he'd already made and heard his prayers. Maybe he'd be allowed to live for a little while without having to be a Sin Eater. Could it be possible that he might be safe and not be in pain, at least for a little while? Did he dare to try and dream… just one more time?

Glossary

ELEMENTAL LORE

To date, the Church has recognized five types of Elementals:

1. Earth, being the rarest and least-often born. Only two known in all of Church history.
2. Air, being the second rarest.
3. Spirit.
4. Water.
5. Fire, being the most prevalent, most destructive, and most volatile of all the beings.

No other information is contained in the archive as to their purpose or powers.

GARGOYLE LORE

Gargoyles

Physical Attributes:

1. Carved from a single piece of natural stone. Cannot be made of stone composite, or molded. Their original form is carved.
2. Their spirit is called to life by an Earth Elemental they call their Maker.
3. They become living stone: stone by day and living, breathing flesh and blood by night. They are protectors. Guardians. Intensely loyal and devoted to their human charges.

Hibernation:

1. Gargoyles put themselves into hibernation and sleep as stone for centuries if they feel they are unwanted or not needed and can awaken whenever they choose or when called.
2. Usually only an unmated gargoyle will hibernate.
3. Birth of an Elemental/Maker will awaken small/young gargoyles who will then seek out the Maker to guard him/her.
4. Elementals/Makers can call a larger/older gargoyle from hibernation into service to protect him/her.

Mating:

1. Gargoyles live a long, immortal life and strive to find a mate to share their immortality. Gargoyles know their fated mates often on first sight or by scent.

2. Gargoyles' devotion to the safety of their mate is overwhelming. A gargoyle who loses a mate will perish of a broken heart, often going into hibernation and never reawakening.

Hunting:

1. Gargoyles can smell evil, and when they are flesh, they will defend a territory from evil. If they discover evil, they will hunt and kill to protect their charges, consuming the evil in its entirety.
2. Gargoyles, when flesh, will hunt and eat as any living being; they need sustenance for the flesh to remain strong and vibrant.
3. A starved gargoyle will go into hibernation until it can hunt freely.
4. Gargoyles are carnivores. Although they can eat some vegetables, they do not need them as part of a healthy diet.
5. Gargoyles can consume either cooked or raw meat.

Immortal:

1. Gargoyles are immortal and will live as long as their stone body remains whole. To destroy the stone is to destroy the gargoyle.
2. Gargoyles can be killed when they are flesh and blood.
3. If mortally wounded, a gargoyle may voluntarily turn to stone to heal itself. It will awaken whole with the next sunset.
4. A gargoyle will never leave a charge unguarded and will sacrifice its life to protect its charge before it will turn to stone to protect its own life.

DAEMON LORE

Angel (daemon as known by pre-Christian history):

a.k.a.: Messenger of God

a.k.a.: Nature Spirits

a.k.a.: Spirit Guides

a.k.a.: Muse

a.k.a.: Demigod

Physical Attributes:

1. Immortal but can be killed.
2. Strength, speed, and agility significantly greater than mankind.
3. Wings, which can appear or disappear.
4. Can choose to be seen or unseen in their observation of mankind.

Mating Habits:

1. Mates are believed to be Fate assigned.
2. Mates are recognized immediately on first sight or smell, without any prior contact.

3. Mating is a permanent bond believed to last throughout eternity, beyond this world.
4. The life force of the mated individuals is said to be combined, thus a mortal mate becomes immortal when joined.
5. At the time of death of either partner, both will die.
6. Mating can be a heterosexual or homosexual partnership, as daemons are not born of procreation but created through a joining of power. A daemon comes into this world as a fully formed adult.

For a time, daemons were hunted by humanity. Their blood was believed to be the fount of youth that would give the drinker immortality. This has since been proven a fallacy, and by Papal decree, any person or persons said to have murdered a daemon will be sentenced by the Inquisition to immediate death.

Sin Eater Lore

1. A person born with a physical deformity that has marked them as being a punished reincarnate soul. In order to redeem themselves in the eyes of God and earn His divine forgiveness, they take on the punishment for sins done by others, absolving the person who has sinned. Through these deeds they earn a place in Heaven.
   a. Body must be pure, chaste, and innocent of sexual desire.
   b. Mind unsoiled by modern convenience or influence.
2. A practice followed by very few in the modern age of genetics that explain away many of the physical deformities that plagued humanity in the past.
   a. Some religious zealots remain who believe, even though genetics has explained the disfigurement, the souls of these misshapen beings are impure. They argue that the accursed individuals need cleansing for their own well-being, and therefore use them when performing the dark arts. The acts perpetrated are supposedly paid for by the self-sacrifice of the Sin Eater.
   b. Some are used in the name of sin-eating when it is an excuse to perpetrate violence on the innocent, as well as perverted sexual deviance.
3. It is the Church's belief that these beings were a means to an end in a time when fear of the unknown bred contempt. The Church does not recognize Sin Eaters as anything other than abused individuals,

and condemns those who claim to vindicate their violent actions on the blood of so-called Sin Eaters.

Shape-Shifter Lore

a.k.a.: skinwalkers

a.k.a.: hybrids—not to be confused with half-beasts such as mermaids or centaurs

a.k.a.: weres

1. Can be found across the world in many different forms of both animal and mythological beast. The most well-known being the werewolf or lycan.
2. This being has the ability to disguise himself as a man but at its core is a wild beast of unparalleled destructive deadly force.
3. These beings are completely untrustworthy and demonic in nature.
4. Most common are the single beast creatures, such as were-animals: werewolves, werecats, werehawks, amongst many others.
5. The chimera beasts, such as werebasilisk, weregryphon and werehippogriff, amongst others, are rarely seen and may be extinct. Little is known about the chimera beasts other than most of the rules regarding their lives appear to be similar to their single beast brethren.
6. Dragons, although they have the ability to transform into human shape, are not a part of this category of demon.

Stay tuned for an exclusive excerpt from

Gabe's Song

Elements of Love: Book Three

When Gabe Windslow and his friends stormed Archbishop O'Fallon's dungeon, the last thing they expected to find was a malnourished young man who'd been beaten so badly he lay at death's door. Unable to abandon someone in need, Gabe rescues the poor man and continues to care for him during the days that follow.

Branded a Sin Eater at birth by his deformities, Sammy Newton expected to die after the latest cleansing ritual he took part in. Instead he awakens to a world where nonhumans and magic are good and Sin Eaters aren't needed.

Confused by a steadily growing sense of betrayal, Sammy struggles to decide whether he should help his rescuers fight the dark forces hunting Gabe and his friends or return to his life of slavery and abuse in order to save his soul from damnation and hell.

www.dreamspinnerpress.com

PANTING, HAIR slicked with sweat and clinging to her face, a threadbare hospital gown draped across her swollen frame, the woman—barely more than a young girl—screamed her agony.

"Is there nothing we can do for her? She's been in labor for over ten hours, and her screams are making the other patients nervous," a black-dressed nun asked the doctor.

"These things take time. This is her first child. They rarely come quickly or with little effort." The doctor stood from his seat on the stool between her legs and then stepped around the bed to stand at the young girl's side. "We're getting closer. A few more hours and you should be fully crowned, and then the baby will arrive. Won't that be wonderful?"

Father Jeremiah Abraham Dragos stood in the viewing room, observing the birth. It was his last duty before he would be given a new group of pregnant girls to watch over for another six months. The hardest part of his job was watching their agony and not being able to help.

He'd become fond of Chantile Newton after he'd been charged with the care of her group of pregnant women, all of whose homes were in a rural area of upper New York. They'd gotten to know each other during their return journey from the temple, after she'd been artificially inseminated. He'd accompanied the group and saw to their needs on the journey until they were picked up from the train stations by their families. He was meant to watch over them, assisting with their care if he could. At least after the birth of this child, she'd be given a year off before she would be expected to carry again by the Church.

Watching her struggles from behind the glass wall, he remembered the past six months fondly. Abe had accompanied the young women leaving the temple to return home and counseled them until their return to the temple. It was a small, relatively anonymous part to play in society. One he was happy to fill. Chantile lived the farthest from the diocese center in New York City, making her journey the longest and her the last to leave the train.

Most of the families viewed him with respect and a certain distrust that many clergy earned in one way or another. But not Frank Newton.

The sharp whistle of the steam engine and squeal of the brakes accompanied by the lurching of the cars announced their arrival at the last station.

"Father, you'll have dinner with us? I'm sure Dad will have a meal on the table." Chantile patted his hand, a friendly gesture she'd begun to use an hour previously after the last of the girls left the train and they were the only ones on board.

"Oh, I wouldn't want to burden your family, Chantile. I'm sure the parish will have provisions stocked for me in the cabin I've been assigned to for the duration." Abe hated lying to the young woman. The diocese-owned property in the area was rough by most standards. Just a cabin by a stream with a cot and a stove. It would be his home as he made the rounds, checking on the pregnant girls.

Usually he was left to fend for himself. The mysterious *"Lord of All"* helped those who helped themselves.

"I'm sure it won't be a hardship. Dad will appreciate you accompanying me and not leaving me to my own devices at the last station, where civilization ended." She waved her hands animatedly as she spoke. She really was a lovely young woman, with a genial disposition and a kind soul.

"We'll see." He didn't want to lock her into something if her father wasn't prepared for a guest. These times were hard, and food wasn't always plentiful. Chantile might have left when times were good for her family three months ago, but the tide could have turned for her father.

He needn't have worried. Frank Newton had greeted his daughter with open arms and him with a firm handshake. Frank was a true believer in the church and its goal for a better humanity. He believed in mankind's future destiny of prosperity and kindness. He'd insisted Abe join them for a hot meal. The family—Frank, Chantile, thirteen-year-old Joshua, and twelve-year-old David—was welcoming and had made Abe feel comfortable among them.

Frank had always provided a stable home, and his sons were well adjusted. So when his wife had given birth to a girl, they'd been given the option of raising her themselves—a kindness not always granted. The following year she'd passed away while giving birth to another girl. The baby hadn't survived either.

After Chantile's eighteenth birthday she'd left home to live among the nuns at the Progenitor Temple, where she'd been inseminated and remained for the initial trimester of her pregnancy before being sent home, as church law required. The week she was due, she had returned to the temple for the birth. Chantile had looked forward to taking her place and fulfilling her duty by giving birth to the next generation. It was with pride and a little fear that she'd left home, hoping one day, if she lived long enough to fulfill her duty, she'd be allowed to rest in the arms of a man who would love her for the rest of her days.

Abe watched as Frank held his hand out to a very pregnant Chantile, helping her down from the cart she'd arrived in. Her brothers were there to see her off. She was due any day, and considering the rough train ride ahead, Abe would be lucky if none of the young women gave birth on the return to the temple.

"Frank, Chantile, boys, it's good to see you." *Abe stepped off the train and greeted them, taking Chantile's bag from one of her brothers and handing it to the young porter.*

"We will be ready to leave in ten minutes, Father. Best to get her settled quickly."

"All right, Peter. We'll be as quick as we can." *Abe gave Peter's shoulder a squeeze and a smile. He was always grateful for the boy's help. Some of these good-byes could be difficult for the families. He'd long ago told Peter to give him a time limit so the child-heavy women wouldn't have to endure a prolonged emotional good-bye on their feet.*

"Chantile, you be a good girl and come back to us. We love you, and whatever happens, it is the will of God." *Frank hugged Chantile on the platform. Her brothers each hugged her, saying their good-byes.*

"Father Abe?"

Abe turned and found Frank stood at his side. "Yes, Frank?"

"Will you be with her, through it all?" *He placed a hand on Abe's arm, his brow furrowed with worry.*

"I'm not allowed in the delivery room, but I will be observing. It is my last duty before I am assigned another group." *Abe smiled and took Frank's hand, trying to be reassuring. It was always hard on the families. Some of the women didn't come back, and they might never be told what happened to them.*

"I didn't want to tell Chantile, but I don't have a good feeling about this. My father had the gift of intuition, and occasionally I experience it as well. I-I don't believe I will see my daughter again." *Frank's fear was a common one. The medical arts weren't as good as they once were. Labor was intense, and childbirth was dangerous to the woman and the child.*

"I will watch over her and help if I can." *Abe tried to reassure the man who'd become his friend.* "But I can't make promises regarding things I have no control over."

"Thank you. Will you give me your word regarding one thing?"

"If it's within my power."

"If something happens, will you at least return with the tale? I would like to know her fate, regardless." Frank sighed, squeezing Abe's hand.

"I will do my best." Abe rested a hand on Frank's shoulder. "Now, courage, man. Don't let her see you like this. Don't mourn her where she can see your fear and before she is gone. Let her draw strength from you. I have seen self-fulfilling prophecy at work. Let her leave believing she is coming back so that she does."

"You're right, of course." Frank nodded and wiped hastily at his eyes, giving himself a shake and then visibly gathering himself and plastering a smile on his face before turning to his daughter. "Boys, give her some room to breathe." Frank approached with his arms open, giving Chantile a hug before handing her over into Abe's care.

He'd been able to give Frank little reassurance, especially since he wasn't allowed in the birthing theater until after the child was born. So here he stood, behind a two-way mirror, observing. It was where the bishops for this parish waited and watched over her, saying the blessings, praying the baby was healthy and female. Everyone else—including her family, if they'd have come for the event—had to wait outside the Blessed Center of Life, the natal hospital run by the few infertile nuns who acted as nurses and midwives. Chantile was one of the few lucky ones who actually had a doctor attending the birth of her child. She'd gone into labor in the wee hours of the morning, and as the doctor was available during daytime hours, he was in attendance. The nighttime births often were attended only by midwives, as the doctor didn't care to be disturbed.

Abe glanced at where the other man in the room lounged in a chair. His complete lack of interest in the miracle of life set Abe's teeth on edge. Monitoring births was supposed to be one of the bishop's main duties. Bishop O'Flaggan obviously cared little one way or the other about his duty.

Chantile's screams, silenced by the soundproofing built into the observation room, were growing more frequent and held an increasing sense of urgency. They tugged at his heart. He watched her struggle, but he could do nothing to aid her from behind the glass. Abe hoped for her sake that the baby would be female.

A rainbow of color washed over her straining body, a glowing aura displayed for Abe's eyes only. For all its glory and mystery, the process of birth was violent and painful. Yet in the center of her being, surrounding the child, Chantile radiated the colors of peace and tranquility. A warm glow of blues and greens enveloped her distended stomach, spreading outward to a thin line of yellow where the child's aura met hers. Chantile's pain-wracked body displayed orange and red, the colors of pain and distress, streaked with lines of black fear. Abe stared in awe at the forces of creation at work, wishing, as he often did, that they would allow him inside to assist.

"How are things going?" Abe attempted to make conversation with the bishop ignoring the miracle of birth taking place before them.

Bishop O'Flaggan glanced up from the book in his hands to the theater before him and then to Abe, as if noticing him for the first time. "It progresses as it should. She is strong and I expect she will give birth many times over, for the good of the human race and the glory of God, of course." Bishop O'Flaggan rolled his eyes. "These young women always seem to take so long to have their first few babies. They have no idea how inconvenient it is watching them for hours. This one has completely disrupted my schedule."

"I'm sorry, Your Excellency. I'd be happy to stay and act as church observer. That way you can return to your more pressing matters." It was doubtful Bishop O'Flaggan would take him up on his offer, as he was but a fledgling priest. "I've watched over her for the last six months, taken the class work for midwifery and childbirth. I've observed the birth of several of the children from her insemination group."

Something about that aura whispered to Abe. He needed to be in that room. He wanted the bishop gone. Something about Bishop O'Flaggan struck him as off, and he needed to protect Chantile and her child if he could.

The tingling that had begun as the doctor moved between Chantile's legs, signaling that the birth was imminent, was growing in intensity. This was a special birth and the child needed him. Only he wasn't in a position to help anyone. He maintained his own life by preserving his secret from everyone. Intervening on this child's behalf could destroy those secrets that protected him so well and end up with him as dead as all the others of his race.

The bishop's eyes narrowed at him, and he looked at Chantile. He seemed to be considering the option. "No. You aren't trained for this. You can't begin to understand all of the ramifications… the different possibilities that must be taken into consideration for the purity and strengthening of the human race."

"Yes, Your Excellency. Of course." Abe bowed his head, biding his time. Bishop O'Flaggan, who'd been his superior since his transfer from the Vatican, had proved himself to be a cruel taskmaster, unswerving in his pursuit of power. "I only wished to relieve you of this time-consuming task."

Controlling the birthrates in his diocese enhanced Bishop O'Flaggan's reputation among the Cardinals…. Abe initially believed jealousy of Bishop O'Flaggan's popularity had caused innuendoes to run rampant—suspicions of infanticide of the males through cruel sacrificial ceremonies, dark rites, and other unsavory behavior. After living in the parish for the past two years, Abe suspected the allegations to be true but had no proof. Bishop O'Flaggan didn't seem to care who he hurt or to respect any god. He sought only ways to increase his own power.

"Say a prayer, instead, Father. She'll get to keep a girl child. Males tend to have a higher mortality rate." Bishop O'Flaggan waved his hand toward the far corner of the room. "You may remain and watch if you stay out of the way. We'll see if you have the stomach to pursue training in this area. I wouldn't mind a second I could trust to make the right, hard decisions to do this work for me. If you prove capable of doing so, I may allow you to stand in for me in the future."

"Of course, Your Excellency." Abe walked to where the bishop had motioned. "It is my endeavor to serve in all things." Abe began rocking in place as he'd been taught to do when praying to the Church's god. He kept his eyes on his rosary beads, but glanced up through his lashes periodically to check Chantile's progress.

"You're new to our parish, are you not?" Bishop O'Flaggan was watching him; Abe could feel his gaze as if it were a branding iron, scorching his skin.

"I've been here for two years. I transferred in after completing my training in the seminary at the Vatican. I took my vows as an acolyte before His Eminence himself. The Pope believes I can learn much from observing such a respected bishop as yourself. He sent me to apprentice under the priests who have benefited from your guidance and turned this diocese into a particularly prosperous one." Abe knew he looked much younger than his actual years, a trait that had so far worked in his favor, allowing him to restart his life over and over, hiding in plain sight for centuries.

"How old are you, boy?"

"I'm eighteen, Your Excellency. I excelled in my classes and finished early. I've been a ward of the church since my birth in Rome." Abe returned to his vacillating, keeping his eyes on his beads, whispering blessings for easy birth and requesting the gods grant the birth of a girl child.

"Child prodigy." Bishop O'Flaggan snorted. "A good scholar doesn't always make a good priest. Have you at least studied the dark arts?"

"No, Your Excellency. My age prohibited such study until I reached my eighteenth birthday, which was when I graduated and was sent here. My instruction has thus far been in the true teachings of love and brotherhood for all mankind." Abe continued to rock and whisper his blessings. He had no desire to get into the dark arts. The fact that Bishop O'Flaggan was asking about them confirmed his duplicity. But it did not constitute proof of his own wrongdoing and without proof, nothing could yet be done.

"Useless, then…." O'Flaggan mumbled under his breath, then nodded dismissively.

Abe's sensitive hearing, far better than the average human's, caught the comment he'd never have heard otherwise. "His Eminence found me to be an exceptional student, issuing me a commendation in a papal bull with the explicit instructions to learn all I can and become a benefit to the community. To spread the love and peace of God our Father to all of his children. Later in life, I'm to return and instruct others in all I have learned from you so other diocese may benefit from your invaluable tutelage." The rhetoric he'd learned over the years provided the cloak he needed to live and survive in this age.

His own special brand of magic allowed him to take on a human likeness and age it appropriately over time—a power that his friends and family had lacked. The ability made him different from his own people. It had also been the one thing that saved him while they were slaughtered one by one. Only he remained to show his species ever existed. Alone. As long as he did nothing to give himself away, he could mingle indistinguishably with humanity. He'd chosen his protector carefully, hiding in plain sight among the same church that had once called for the death of all of his kind.

Chantile shrieked. Abe's self-control kept him from jumping at the sound he shouldn't be able to hear. She gripped the metal guardrails on the side of the bed. Her doctor's words of encouragement, unheard by the bishop, were as clear as if he stood at her bedside.

"…good. The head is out. One more big push and you can relax, girl." Chantile's agonized wail rang through the delivery room. A silence fell, except for her exhausted panting as they waited for the infant's first breath.

"Oh!" Abe gasped, and his breath caught in his throat. A wave of raw, invisible energy erupted from the child, blasting outward with a wild destructive force. All he could do was grab hold of it and divert the power flow into the stone floor beneath his feet before the humans noticed.

"Your Excellency, you better come in here." The doctor's voice sounded hollow and far away as he struggled with the magical backlash, grabbing for the wall to steady himself. Breathing slowly to keep from passing out, he focused on the man behind the soundproof glass, standing beside the intercom. The doctor held the bloody infant in one arm, his other hand pressed the button for the intercom. He had obviously missed a couple minutes wrestling with the power surge. Luckily, Bishop O'Flaggan must have dismissed his silence for prayer.

Bishop O'Flaggan scowled as he entered the birthing theater. Abe followed as quickly behind him as his still reeling senses allowed. "What's the problem?" He looked at the squirming, unwashed infant.

The doctor held up his finger, where a tiny fist gripped his hand. The infant's long, thin fingers were connected by delicate webbing and tipped with what appeared to be tiny gray talons.

Abe stared in disbelief. A son of Poseidon? Here? He closed his eyes and tried to think of how he could get the child out of here. The merpeople were a rare and secretive clan who prized their children and wouldn't want a babe of theirs, even a half-human babe, to be raised in this barbaric society. Since Chantile had been inseminated at the temple, exactly how this child had come to be was a bit of a mystery. Whether she'd had an encounter with one of their males before going to temple, or one of their males or a man of mixed heritage had donated seed, was impossible to say. The resulting child of immense power, if that wave of raw energy was any sign, was held in the doctor's arms.

Abe tried to come up with a plausible excuse for what they were seeing. "Maybe it's nothing… a bit of loose skin. As the child grows…."

"No, Father. This is why I didn't allow you to be here alone. This is an abomination. A Sin Eater child. Malformed at birth because of the sin he was born with." Bishop O'Flaggan glanced at the doctor. "Male or female?"

"Male, Your Grace."

"Woman, you have birthed an abomination before God." Bishop O'Flaggan's emotionless, flat tone and sneer of disgust sent a shiver of fear for Chantile and her son down Abe's back. "We can destroy the infant and your sin for having birthed this evil into the world, sending it back to hell, or you can be scourged to death. Your sacrifice would give the infant ten years' life. It would be taught its place in the world and the corrupt being it is. Upon its eleventh birthday, it would begin to take on the punishments for the sins of others so one day, upon its own death, it might receive absolution through martyrdom, and heaven. What say you, mother?"

"I don't understand?" Barely conscious, sweat dripping down her forehead, Chantile sobbed. She looked beseechingly at Bishop O'Flaggan for a long moment. Finally, her gaze fell on Abe, who stood just beyond the bishop's shoulder. "Father Abe, what is he saying? Where's my baby?"

Stepping around Bishop O'Flaggan, Abe took her hand in his. She deserved to be told, to understand why either she or her son would die today. "Chantile, the baby is malformed. He has webbed hands and feet. Bishop O'Flaggan says he is a Sin Eater, an abomination." Abe took a cloth from a nearby table and dabbed at Chantile's furrowed forehead, trying to give her a moment to grasp the horror Bishop O'Flaggan was forcing upon her. He wasn't sure if she was even clear-headed enough to understand, or if she would just refuse to accept what he was telling her.

"He's a very special child. But with such gifts there comes a great price, and only you can decide what is best. We can kill the child—" Abe glanced up, catching Bishop O'Flaggan's seething scowl. He almost stepped back in fear of the risk he was taking by speaking out at all, but instead closed his eyes and took a deep breath before continuing. "—returning his soul to suffer in hell—or, if you sacrifice yourself in his stead, your son will be given ten years of life. He'd be allowed to live with your family, to grow up and learn of your sacrifice, before taking up his duties in order to redeem his soul. He would learn what it means to be loved. Then when he is old enough, he would take on the punishment of other people's sins. His suffering would be his cleansing, so that when he dies, he'd enter the kingdom of heaven as a martyr." Abe put the towel back on the table and stroked his hand over her hair, tucking a loose strand behind her ear. "You must choose. Do you give your life for your child, Chantile?"

"I want to see him before I choose. Can I hold him? Please?" Chantile begged, reaching out and touching Abe's arm.

Abe looked up at the bishop, who nodded. He stepped over to the doctor, took the child, swaddled in threadbare towels, and brought the infant to the side of the bed. He gently placed the newborn in his mother's arms.

Chantile's gaze filled with a mother's perfect love as a lone tear slid down her cheek. She stroked the child's soft, chubby, cherub cheek with a single finger and kissed his temple. "I will die for you, my beautiful Samuel. You deserve a chance to live." She snuggled the child against her breast. "I love you, my baby boy."

"Chantile, are you sure? You are a young woman. There will be other babies...."

Focused on the newborn, Chantile no longer heard him. Her love knew no bounds, but it would be short-lived. He'd succeeded in saving the child. There was no way to save the mother.

"Father Abe, take it from her. She's named it. It is your charge now. You will see to its immediate care. I will follow up that you have put it into a good church foster family to be raised. It will know its place. She has purchased it ten years with her death, which will be carried out at once. She's to be flogged until dead. I trust I can leave the details of that punishment to you. The head of the guard is also our executioner. I will expect a report from him immediately after the deed is done, within the half hour." Bishop O'Flaggan turned toward the door. "Also, as you appear to know her, inform her family of her disgrace, that she gave her life for this abomination, and how she died. Damn waste." Having passed judgment upon her, the bishop left the room.

The doctor bowed his head until the man was gone. "Yes, Your Excellency." He clenched his fists and shook head. "Damn, I hate this job."

"Samuel is worth dying for, Father Abe." A single tear rolled down Chantile's face as she handed the baby to Abe. "You'll give him to my father, if you can?"

"I will look after him as best I am able." Abe cradled the infant gently in his arms. "I will protect him with my life." How he planned to accomplish that vow, he had no idea.

"Just rest now, child," the doctor murmured, injecting something into her IV.

Chantile closed her eyes, her arms falling to the bed.

Startled, Abe looked at the doctor askance.

"Nobody said she had to be awake for any of this. Many women pass out after birth."

Abe walked out of the room with Samuel in his arms. He needed to find the captain of the guard and order Chantile's death, then take care of the boy. At least the doctor was able to show her some mercy at the end, and with luck he'd be able to get the baby to his grandfather. Somehow he'd find a way to get them out of this mess, for her.

SUI LYNN is a born-and-raised Midwestern gal. She loves rock 'n' roll but can get a little bit country too. She has been writing for as long as she can remember and is always found with a book or pencil and paper in hand. She has two cocker spaniels who are the comic relief in her life. She loves orange soda, *Dr. Who*, and her computer, all of which she could not function without.

Sui received two M/M Goodreads Romance Group nominations: one for Best Paranormal Story of 2012 and the other for Best World Created for 2012. She has also been nominated for the Preditors & Editors Reader's Poll in the category of "all other" Novels.

Website: suilynn.com
Blog: suidlynn.blogspot.com
Facebook: www.facebook.com/sui.lynn.9
Twitter: twitter.com/#!/suidlynn
E-mail: sui.d.lynn@gmail.com

Luck and an impromptu jam session bring college student Quinn Yamamoto to the Blue Rose, a small R&B nightclub. He meets handsome club owner Enjoji Tatankata and it's love at first sight, but no one said love would ever be easy.

It's one thing after another: keeping his grades up and working to make ends meet, learning about a family he didn't know he had, reliving buried memories of horrifying abuse in his nightmares, discovering that his new lover has dangerous secrets... nothing in his life could have prepared Quinn for this.

www.dreamspinnerpress.com

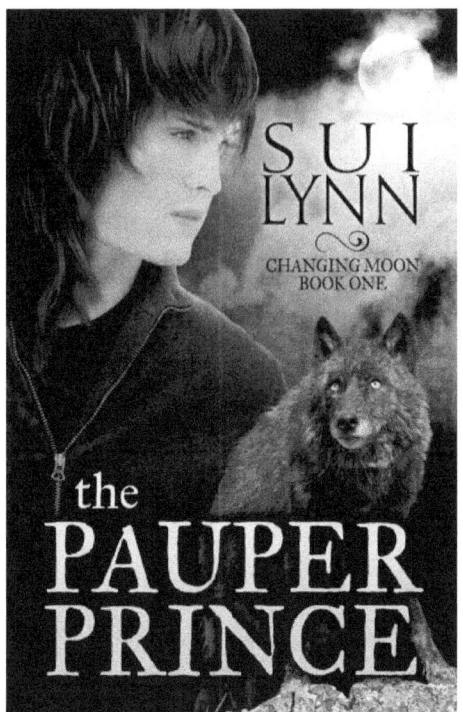

Changing Moon: Book One

Andrew Reed is smart and educated, but as long as his people are enslaved to the vampires, his options are limited. When he discovers a strange young man in his family's barn, he shifts forms and trails the thief, trying to decipher why he smells familiar with a hint of something more. Excited by what he discovers, he reveals himself to Lance, and they return to Lance's camp in the forest.

When Andrew's family takes it on themselves to "help" by investigating Lance's past, Andrew finds something neither of them could have imagined. If they band together, they have a chance to win their freedom—and a brighter future for all the races.

Changing Moon: Book Two

Lance Fitz and Andrew Reed are a blissfully mated pair, but Andrew's benefactor Stephon, a born vampire, isn't happy with the pairing, especially after he discovers Lance's pedigree. Stephon attempts to find answers using his mental connection with Andrew, and when his efforts fail, he goes after Lance's new shifter family. Enraged, Lance severs the tie to Stephon. He wants to tear apart the abusive vampire and free his mate and family for good. But before he can try, the family reminds Lance that the death of one vampire won't change the social status of shifters as an enslaved people. The fight won't end with Stephon, even if Lance succeeds.

www.dreamspinnerpress.com

Changing Moon: Book Three

When Lance is kidnapped from his adopted grandfather's home, Andrew believes there is a traitor among Lord Basil's drones, despite the fact that the born vampire supports Lance and Andrew's crusade to free shifters from vampire subjugation.

Lance awakens to finds Andrew's baby sister, Angela, and a young boy shackled to a wall next to him, and a corpse nearby. Brad, a former drone of Basil's, tortures them in an effort to drive Lance insane and prove that pureblood shifters are unstable and need to be destroyed before he gets them all killed.

Stephon comes home after a trip to an orgy disguised as an unbirthday party. His mate, Quinn, shows up uninvited and is angry at the perceived infidelity. It isn't easy to rekindle a relationship after a 270-year separation. As old arguments and insecurities resurface, Quinn decides the only way to keep Stephon safe might be to force the stubborn older vampire into hibernation, until he can defeat his father, Lord Rufus.

www.dreamspinnerpress.com

FOR

MORE

OF THE
BEST
GAY
ROMANCE

DREAMSPINNER
PRESS

dreamspinnerpress.com